I0789023

# Radiation Canary
## Greatest Hits

Geonn Cannon

Supposed Crimes LLC • Matthews, North Carolina

Published in the United States

ISBN: 978-1-944591-07-6

www.supposedcrimes.com

This book is typeset in Goudy Old Style, licensed by Ascender Corporation.

Dedicated to Brandi Carlile, Jenny Lewis, Neko Case, Ingrid Michaelson, Sara Bareilles, Tift Merritt, and all the other female musicians who inspired the Canaries and helped me make them sing.

DISC ONE

THE COAL MINE SESSIONS

## Chapter One

The party was a hazy reflection on the sliding glass door, as if ghosts from a party decades earlier were still making small-talk in the ccurtyard. Lana Kent preferred the company of the ghosts to the actual flesh and bone people who were mingling behind her. The only person she wanted to talk to was Catherine. The last time she'd seen her girlfriend she'd been surrounded near the kitchen. Lana finished her drink so she would have an excuse to go rescue her. As she turned around, a man who had been lingering in her orbit stepped forward and smiled at her.

"Lana Kent, am I right?" He extended his hand. "Jeff Hartley. It's nice to finally put a face to the voice. I love that song of yours, ah, 'Say a Prayer if You Know Any'. Really great song."

"Thanks. I'm just... refill..." She lifted her empty cup and cut an escape path through the crowd. She saw people crowded on the couch and sitting on the hearth and she felt a sting of jealousy. This was her apartment, hers and Catherine's, and the party was a housewarming. Now they had relative strangers in a place she barely felt familiar with, and they were sitting in places that she herself hadn't had a chance to sit. The crowd was a weird mix between invasion of privacy and being stuck in a place she'd never been before.

Most of the people in the apartment were friends of Catherine. Lana had work acquaintances and there were a few people she was on a first-name basis with, but she hadn't invited them. Catherine promised it would just be a small gathering and Lana took her at her word. She forced a smile as she passed someone else she didn't recognize and wondered what Catherine would consider a large group.

She finally reached the kitchen and got herself another drink. As she poured someone brushed by her, looked at her for a moment, and then continued on without saying anything. Lana called it the Celebrity Consideration. A person would take five or ten seconds to stare at her and give their brain a moment to click her together with a movie or television show. When nothing came she was considered unworthy of their time and they moved on. If a conversation couldn't double as networking then it wasn't worth having.

Lana scanned the room until she spotted Catherine. It was easy to find her; she stood head and shoulders over most people at the party due to her height and the fact she was wearing high heels. Another trick, another way to establish dominance over everyone else in attendance. Even crouching in sneakers she would have stood out. Catherine was a bright, shining person, and Lana found herself smiling despite all the thousand petty irritations all around her. But all of her goodwill vanished when she saw who was standing next to Catherine.

The Actress. Alexandra Stockton, "Sexy Lexi" to the tabloids, guest-starred on Catherine's show and the two struck up a quick friendship. The Actress was gorgeous, intelligent, and the type of woman who still called herself "Lexi" even when she was well into her forties. She began her career as an apple-cheeked ingenue before graduating to more serious adult roles. When directors started asking for actresses slightly "fresher" than her, she began splitting her time between acting and directing. She found a new life behind the camera, guiding the new crop of young starlets to follow in her footsteps. At the moment she often portrayed a mature matriarch, capable of playing CEOs, goddesses, and femme fatales in equal measure.

She was also screwing Catherine. Or, if she wasn't, the intent was certainly there. Catherine was still new to acting and she accepted Lexi's mentorship at face value. Lana wasn't convinced Lexi was entirely upfront about her intentions. As if sensing Lana's judgment of her, Lexi turned and met her gaze. She smiled ever so slightly and raised her glass in greeting. Lana offered a pinched smile. She decided she didn't want to talk to Catherine if it meant enduring Lexi's presence, so she retreated to the door. She slid it open and took her drink out into the cold courtyard.

Catherine found her there twenty minutes later. "There you are," she said softly as she shut the door behind her. Lana was sitting on one of the four concrete benches that formed brackets around the central garden. She had chosen the one that kept her out of sight from their apartment, but she could see into their neighbor's living room. They had been watching TV in the dark, and Lana was surprisingly engrossed by the soundless antics.

"Here I am," Lana confirmed.

Catherine sat next to her. The movement of the TV caught her eye. "What are we watching?"

"I'm not sure. I think this lady is some kind of cop."

"Ah." She crossed one leg over the other. "People are asking where you are."

Lana smirked. "Are they asking for me, or the lead singer of Radioactive Parakeet?"

"Oh, stop. Do you know how many people in there mangled my character's name? Half of them were probably Googling on their phone to find out the name of my show. Come on. It's fun. It's your housewarming, too."

"I don't know any of those people, Kitty."

"You're not going to learn anything about them hiding out here."

Lana said, "I'm not hiding."

"You could have fooled me." She bumped her arm against Lana's. "C'mon. I swear, if people don't start naturally leaving by nine-thirty I'll let you corral them out into the hall under false pretenses. Then we can slam the door on them together." She bent down and kissed Lana's bare shoulder. "Come on, Lala. Come back to the party. I want to show people my beautiful and talented girlfriend."

Lana sighed. "Fine. But if one more person compliments me on my cello playing, I'm going in the bedroom and I'm not coming out until they're all gone."

"Deal." She held out her hand. Lana took it and let Catherine pull her up. Catherine pushed the door open. "I found her! She was just getting some fresh air!"

Lana waved sheepishly as she reentered the fray. The rest of the party was fine, although Catherine did allow herself to be pulled back into Lexi's orbit with very little prompting. Lana found and struck up a conversation with someone who was a genuine Radiation Canary fan. He had the same questions that everyone seemed to have these days. What are you up to now? How is the rest of the band doing? Have you spoken to them lately? When are you getting back together?

The band technically wasn't broken up. Two years earlier they had decided to release a "farewell" album to let the fans know they were taking a break. Since then Karen had released a solo album while Nessa took care of her baby. Lana moved to London and did whatever work came her way. She composed the theme songs for a couple of TV shows, including Catherine's, and the rest of the time she tried getting used to London life. She still wasn't confident driving on the "wrong" side of the street.

As promised the party began to break up around nine o'clock. Lana started cleaning up the abandoned cups, which was the cue for everyone else to start saying their goodbyes. Before long only a handful of people remained. Lana was irritated to see Lexi was one of the people sticking around. She and Catherine were holding court on the chaise in the corner, talking quietly as the room emptied out around them. Lana thought about making a catty comment or forcing them to admit what they were doing, but she didn't want to seem petty. She finished cleaning up, said goodnight to some people she didn't know, and headed into the bedroom.

Catherine joined her close to half an hour later. She sighed and pushed her hands into her hair, holding it up off her shoulders as she stepped out of her shoes. Lana was sitting on the bed with her laptop open in front of her and a scratchpad on one thigh. She had exchanged her party clothes for boxer shorts and a T-shirt emblazoned with the cover of their third album.

"Well, I would call that a success," Catherine said. "Everyone loved the apartment."

"Uh-huh."

"Did you have fun?" Catherine unzipped her dress and stripped out of it.

Lana said, "It was okay. I would have preferred spending the time with you. Christening the place, you know?" She smiled and chewed suggestively on the end of her pen.

Catherine chuckled and took off her underwear before she went into the bathroom. "Keep talking like that and people will think you're a shut-in."

"Shut-ins get a bad rap," Lana said. "I'm going to play the guitar. Are you going straight to bed after your shower?"

"I am," Catherine said over the spray of water. "Sorry."

"S'okay. I'll take it out into the living room."

She closed her laptop and gathered her things. She had a file full of lyrics Karen had sent her, snippets of songs that needed music added or that were just half-formed ideas she wanted Lana to flesh out. The songs would either be earmarked for Lana's eventual solo debut, would get sent to Cartography for other acts that didn't write their own music, or it would be set aside for Radiation Canary's eventual next album.

Lana kept the lights off and set up on the chaise where Catherine and Lexi had been seated. She crossed her legs in front of her, sat the guitar on her lap, and opened the file. "I've got next Sunday's confessions all written," she sang under her breath, "and I'll have to hurry if I want to get them all in." She bit down on her pen and strummed a simple tune in the key of C. The guitar sounded fine, but in her head all she could hear was Karen's cello sweeping in behind it.

She wrote for a while, using the light of the laptop to keep track of the chords. The song would be good on guitar, but it would be phenomenal with Karen's strings. She checked the time and saw it was almost three in the morning. Of course, the middle of the night in London was dinner time in Seattle. She sent Karen a text asking her to get on Skype if she was online. She didn't have to wait long before her friend appeared on the screen from half a world away.

Despite the aggravation of the night, Lana smiled. Karen's hair was held back by a clip, she was makeup-free, and she was wearing sweats despite the fact it was only seven or eight at night. Karen grinned and waved into the camera.

"A wild Lana Kent appears!"

"Hey! I'm not interrupting mommy or baby time, am I?"

"No, no." She twisted to look behind her. "Laura is getting her snuggles in while I made dinner. It has to simmer for a while. So what's up? What time is it there?"

"It's either late or early, depending on your opinion. Do you have time to talk?"

"Sure."

Lana picked up her notepad. "I was working on some of the lyrics you sent me. 'Best Laid Plans.' It's another one of those that I think would benefit more from having your cello on it."

Karen bobbed her head understandingly. "Okay. Why don't you play me a little of what you have so far? What key is it?"

"C." Lana adjusted the guitar on her lap and strummed the opening notes. On-screen Karen had her eyes closed, one hand holding the neck of an invisible cello while the other drew the bow across its strings. "It gives it more of a voice. Do you hear?"

"I do. But it needs your voice. That's why I sent it to you. If you wanted to hire a session musician for the recording, I wouldn't be upset."

Lana shrugged. "Well, if I hire a cellist, I'd want to hire the best. The choice is between getting you to play on the song, or settling for someone subpar."

"Aw. Sweet talker."

Laura passed by behind the couch and stopped when she saw who was on-screen. "Hey, Lana!"

"Hi, Laura. How's the baby?"

"Sweet and adorable and already asleep."

Lana shook her head. "You Everett ladies are magic, I swear."

Karen twisted to look up at her wife. "Dinner is simmering. Could you check on it?"

"Sure." She kissed Karen's forehead, waved goodbye to the computer, and then disappeared out of frame again.

Lana scratched her eyebrow. "I should probably let you go eat. So I guess we put this in the file for future Radiation Canary songs."

"I guess so. How many songs are in there?"

"Not many..." Lana clicked open the file. "Only sixteen."

Karen laughed. "At least we won't have to write very much when we do record the next album."

"There is that."

"Your solo album might look a little skimpy, though."

Lana sighed. "Yeah. Not so sure about..." She was startled by movement in the hall, Catherine's pale skin and butterscotch-yellow nightie moved against the shadows. "Hey, Kitty."

Catherine stopped and leaned against the wall. "Lala. You ever comin' to bed?"

"Yeah. I was just Skyping with Karen."

Catherine smiled. "Ah. Hello, Karen!"

"Hi, Catherine. Sorry for keeping her up."

"Oh, if I know her, it wasn't entirely your fault. But it is very late, and I have to be up early tomorrow... so..."

Lana said, "Right. Karen, sorry, I..."

"No, I understand. Dinner beckons, and you need your sleep. We'll talk again tomorrow. Or, uh... damn time zones. Soon. We'll talk soon."

"Soon is good. Have a good night."

"You too."

They signed off, and Lana put aside her guitar and notepad. Catherine waited for her and then led her back into the bedroom. She pulled back the blankets and lay down as Lana went to brush her teeth.

"You know, it's funny. You have all the time in the world to chat with Karen across the globe at two in the morning, but making conversation for five minutes with people in the same room is impossible?"

"Karen and I actually have things in common."

"You have things in common with the people who were here tonight! If you'd just given them a chance... Billie likes scuba diving."

Lana said, "I don't scuba."

"Sure. You went once."

"Once."

Catherine sighed. "All I'm saying is that if you actually sat down and tried to have a conversation with these people, you might be surprised by the common ground you find."

Lana turned off the bathroom light. "I find that hard to believe. Fad diets aren't really my thing."

"See? You know nothing about these people. You just judge from your little perch. Tell me something, if this is what you think of actors, what do you think of me? Hm?"

Lana sat on the edge of the bed to take off her socks. "You're different."

"You like me because you took the time to get to know me."

"Well, I'm sorry I'm not the conversational wizard Sexy Lexi is."

Catherine growled. "Oh, God. Not this again."

"She was all over you all night."

"She's an affectionate person. She's always touching or rubbing or kissing~"

Lana said, "That's funny. I only see her do that shit with you."

"That's because you only see her when I bring her around. If you spent two seconds with her, you would see that she's like that with everyone."

"I'm not all that eager to hang out with the woman who is trying to steal my girlfriend."

Catherine muttered under her breath, then said, "You don't have to worry about that. I'm not the one who escapes relationships by cheating."

Lana felt as if she had been slapped. She sat up and looked at Catherine. "That was a low blow."

"Accurate, though. Right?" Catherine's arms were crossed over her chest. "I mean, that's what really surprises me about this jealousy streak, Lana. I've given you no reason to be jealous. But given the fact that you were in a relationship when we first slept together..."

Lana kicked away the blankets and grabbed her pillow. "I'm going to sleep on the couch."

"Should I be worried that you're going to spend the rest of the night chatting online with your ex? You left her for me, so why not go back the other way? Has a nice symmetry, really."

Lana wanted to argue, but she knew her anger would make whatever she said come out far too harshly. She settled for slamming the bedroom door and storming down the hall to the living room. She didn't know how a casual comment about the dinner party had devolved into a fight so quickly, but it wasn't completely unexpected. She and Catherine seemed to find any reason to argue lately. If they weren't stirring up a disagreement then they were going through the motions. Reminding each other when the yogurt was out. Doing chores. Arranging their schedules so they had the maximum amount of time at home together to... what? Sit and stare at each other in stony silence?

She tossed her pillow onto the couch and collapsed onto the cushions. The apartment hunt had given them a bit of excitement, the debate about each possibility gave them a welcome alternative to fighting, but now they were settled in. They still had the other apartment, so maybe unloading it would give them back the thrill.

Whatever happened, she hoped it happened quickly. She couldn't take much more of the wild swing between wall-shaking fury and quiet indifference.

## CHAPTER TWO

THE TERMINAL of the island's airport was a heptagon, and each segment housed a different part of the whole. The check-in counter for one airline was across from the main entrance at the twelve o'clock spot. The other airline was at nine o'clock across from the lunch counter. The other spaces were filled in by a bookshop, a convenience store that offered anything travelers might have forgotten when they set out on their vacations, and a door that led to the bathrooms and a flight of stairs up to the observation tower. There had been other travelers earlier, but they all went through one door to their vacation or out another door to their waiting plane.

Codie Renton was the only person in the three rows of blue plastic seats, just as she had been for the past hour. She wasn't used to waiting for a flight, wasn't used to being at the whim of airport schedules, and she didn't know how regular people managed to ever fly anywhere. Her plane was out on the runway and the preflight was done, but the storm that rolled in while she was having dinner decided to linger over the water directly in the path she had to take home. She could have gone the long way around to the south, but it seemed more prudent to just wait for it to move along. Michael, the ticket agent for Duckworth Air, was keeping an eye on the weather reports for her. She'd signed an autograph for his girlfriend and, in the silence, they had become friendly enough to share the space without forcing conversation.

She was biding her time on her phone when Michael finally said, "Looks like the storm has moved north a little more."

"Yeah?" She stood up and joined him at the counter. He turned the computer around so she could see the graphic. He had it on a loop for the next two hours showing the storm was inching closer to Canada at every half hour interval. More importantly, her flightpath home was completely clear. "Looks like I might make it home by midnight after all."

He gestured out the door. "Does that turn back into a pumpkin if you're late?"

"I'd hate to find out." She went back to gather her bags. "You keep that girlfriend happy, hear me? You're much too young for me, and the fact you're taken is the only thing keeping me from tearing my hair out in frustration."

Michael laughed and his cheeks pinkened slightly. It was good to know in this day and age that some boys were still capable of blushing.

"Have a safe flight, Miss Renton."

She waved goodbye and went outside. The tarmac was still glistening with puddles from the rainfall and the stars were obscured by a thin layer of fog that settled in after the storm moved out. The sweeping beam of the airport's beacon cut through the gloom as she crossed to her plane. She climbed aboard, latched the canopy, and settled into her seat. After a few last minute checks and a call to the tower to make sure someone kept Michael company now that she was leaving, she pushed the throttle forward and began cutting through the fog.

She only needed about six hundred feet before she reduced power and became airborne. She grinned as the floor seemed to rise underneath her. She flashed back to high school when going home wasn't an option but she had nowhere else to go. There was a tiny airport remarkably similar to the one she had just left behind near the school, and she had gone there as often as she could to watch the small planes taking off. She would lie on the ground and follow their path through the skies wondering what it was like to break free and just go... another state, another country, it didn't matter. She could be somewhere completely different in a matter of hours.

In her wildest dreams she never would have imagined the band would get her into the pilot's seat. It was just a stupid distraction to fill time in after school. And when she and Lana graduated it became an excuse to get out of the house. She loved making music, and she had loved the drums since she was a little girl, but the idea of making a career out of it never crossed her mind. But then came Karen, and with her came the band's true voice. They found themselves on track to becoming a real thing faster than Codie could comprehend. Shows around Seattle, an appearance on a television show, and then a record label showed up and offered them a home.

It hardly seemed like ten years could have passed, and it somehow seemed as if it was thirty years instead of just a decade. She was on the straight and narrow. She was a pilot who occasionally played drums for other artists. She never had to worry about money because every quarter she received a check for music that was recorded years earlier. A song was used in a TV show, an author quoted a lyric in their book, something got played on the radio somewhere in the world... she got one-fourth of the money just like everyone else. Well, everyone except Karen. She received extra because she was responsible for most of their lyrics. Still, the portion Codie received was more than enough to keep her comfortable.

The engine hiccupped.

Codie was immediately focused on the panel in front of her, looking for any indicators that would tell her what was wrong. She took off her headset so she could hear even the smallest repeat of the noise which had first grabbed her attention. With one hand on the yoke, she used the other to adjust the engine controls and circuit breakers. The hiccup came again and the leonine purr of her engines became the spluttering cough of a lifelong smoker. She had just enough time to push back her primal urge to panic before the engine cut out completely and turned her precious plane into a glider.

"Say a prayer," she whispered calmly. She angled the nose down and looked at her options. She was in a LA-270 SeaFury and, if necessary, she could have landed in the water. She was currently over one of the small islands that peppered the coast of Washington, all of which were too forested or rocky to serve as a runway. If she was going too fast when she hit the water it could be as bad as trying to land on the rocks. If she landed safely she would be stranded on the Strait with no way to get to shore.

"Come on, baby," she said. "I'll find you a place. Just hold on."

She swept her eyes across the horizon and saw nothing but hard rocks and tall trees joined together by a vast expanse of blue. She put her headset back on so she could speak into the microphone. "This is November-Four-One-One-Charlie-Whiskey, declaring an emergency. Please respond if you can hear me. This is November-Four-One-One-Charlie-Whiskey. My engines have failed and I'm seeking a location to make a safe landing. If you can hear me, I require assistance."

The image of Lana, Nessa, and Karen at her funeral suddenly flashed in front of her. She pushed it away but the afterimage remained. All for one and one for all, that was what they said. The band was the four of them. If she didn't walk away from the crash then she would be killing Radiation Canary. She clenched her jaw and aimed herself west. If she was right about which island she was over, there might be a small town on the coast. If she could make it that far...

The trees were scraping the underside of her plane. She was holding her breath when she saw the lights of the village coming into view. "Come on, please. Please." She bit her bottom lip and the scraping noises stopped. She hit the ground as gently as she could muster and still bounced in her seat, knowing she would end up with some interesting bruises from the seatbelt but not caring. The plane caromed forward through the darkness, small trees and bushes snapping on her wings as she bounced over the uneven terrain.

Codie finally stopped the crash about four hundred yards from where she touched down. The lights shone out onto a muddy field bisected by a dirt road directly ahead of her. She sank back against her seat and covered her face with shaking hands, shaking as the adrenaline evaporated and left her aware of how lucky she had just gotten. She dropped her hands back to the yoke and took a few steadying breaths, rolling her shoulders to calm herself down.

Once she stopped trembling she thought about the girls again. She had come so close to ruining everything. If she had died and they held to their vow that Radiation Canary would always be just the four of them, she would have destroyed their future careers. She couldn't do that to them. She wouldn't do that to them. She was just the drummer, easily replaced without fuss.

Through the front windshield she saw a pair of headlights rushing toward her. She unbuckled her seatbelt and stood up on unstable legs so she could be on the ground when they arrived. Once she cleared up this mess she would consider what she wanted to do next in regards to Radiation Canary. She didn't want to leave the band, not in the slightest, but she had to make sure she didn't destroy their chances of a reunion somewhere down the line. She had to let them know that she considered herself replaceable. If that ruined their "all for one" caveat then so be it, but she didn't want to be responsible for killing the Canaries.

She opened the hatch and jumped down onto the spongy grass moments before the first car reached her. She waved sheepishly as someone climbed out of the truck and shined a flashlight down the length of the plane.

"Well," he said. "I'm not usually a fan of company dropping in unannounced, but it looks to me like you didn't have much of a choice, ma'am."

Codie smiled. "Sorry if I interrupted your dinner."

"Eh, my wife's cooking. I'll take any excuse." He paused. "I'm guessing you might want to borrow a phone right about now."

"You know, I can think of a couple of calls I'd like to make, if it's not too much of an imposition."

"Hop in the truck."

She closed the plane up and went to join him in the truck. He was an older man, but thick in the shoulders and barrel-chested. A shock of white hair was falling over one eye as he turned to look at her. For a moment she thought he was going to make a comment about her skin color; a brown woman crashing her plane this close to the Canadian border, she could almost understand some wariness. But he surprised her by snapping his fingers.

"You're a singer or something, right? I think I've seen you on a magazine or on some talk show."

Codie smiled. "I'm just a drummer. We're a dime a dozen."

"Heh. Well. Okay." He backed away from the landing site and turned back toward the dirt road. Codie looked back at the plane as the man drove back to his house. She knew how important she was to the band. She knew they loved her and they wouldn't take her request lightly, but she also knew she was making the right choice. If she had been a little less lucky, it would have been a catastrophe for all four of them. It would be better if she gave them the escape hatch.

She settled back against the seat and wondered which of them would be easiest to break the news to.

It had been six weeks since the party, since the fight. Lana couldn't decide if she considered that the beginning of the end. The turmoil between them had certainly had been building before that night. Little arguments, minor boredom, and small frustrations built up and finally came to a head at the party. Once the line had been crossed it was easier and easier for them to venture into formerly out-of-bounds territory when they fought. But still Lana expected it to blow over. She knew in her heart that she and Catherine were meant to be together in the end.

So much for that idea. Catherine kept the new apartment while Lana was back at the first apartment they'd shared after moving to London. Fortunately they hadn't gotten around to putting it on the market, and some of the furniture was still in place. She lay in the bed and stared at the ceiling while she replayed the highlight reel in her mind. She hadn't showered in days. She was still wearing her pajamas, though she had taken the time to change those. She could only take so much funk.

Catherine had been the one to finally unpin the grenade. They were having dinner when Catherine brought it up as if she was commenting on something she'd seen on TV. Not only that but she had been unnecessarily cruel about it, using a tone that almost hurt more than the words she was saying. "I think at this point in our lives," she explained calmly, "we need to assess whether we're in the relationship that we'll be in forever. I'm not sure we are. Are you? Do you really think we'll be happy if we spend the next forty or fifty years together?"

"Yes," Lana had squeaked out.

"You're lying." Catherine sounded disappointed. She shook her head and hunched her shoulders. "We're not meant to be, Lana. We're already getting under each other's skin. Can you even imagine what it will be like in another five years? Or ten? God, by twenty we'll hate each other. We should make a clean break now before breaking up would be too devastating."

At that point Lana surprised herself by crying. "Right. Wouldn't want to do it after that. Because that would really fucking hurt."

"Lala... oh, shit. I'm... I'm sorry."

So Lana moved her stuff back to their old apartment. It had been too small before, but now it was cavernous. One reason she didn't want to venture beyond the bedroom was because she didn't want to be confronted by all the empty rooms. Her only companion was Daisy, a mannequin who stood in their living room. In the early days of their relationship she and Catherine took turns dressing it in random outfits. That joke had run its course early, but it still stood in the corner next to the window. When Lana arrived back with the remnants of her life, she put it in one of Catherine's shirts that she'd stolen when she packed up. Now it hurt to see it, so much that she couldn't bring herself to go take it off.

As far as she could tell, news of the breakup hadn't yet hit the gossip sites. She hadn't been online much, but she assumed her phone would be ringing off the hook if Karen or the rest of the band knew she had been dumped. She did get a few texts from Karen asking if she wanted to get back on Skype, but she ignored them all. The last one had been simple - "Everything okay? Let's talk soon." - but it had almost caused her to have a complete breakdown.

She looked at the clock. It was almost noon, so she rolled out of bed and went into the kitchen. There was food in the apartment: cereal and soups and crackers. She couldn't bring herself to actually sit down to a meal, but she knew she needed food in order to drink as much alcohol as she wanted. It was all about balance, and at the moment she was two crackers shy of affording another bottle.

As she was ripping open a box of saltines someone began pounding on the door. Lana growled quietly, crushed a handful of crackers, and threw the crumbs at the door. "Go'way," she hissed too quiet for anyone to actually hear. The unwelcome intruder knocked again as Lana pulled the sleeve of crackers out of the box. She would eat it all, and then she could have a bottle and a half for lunch. That should keep her drunk until the middle of the night.

Another knock and she pressed her fist to her forehead. She wanted them to take the hint and just leave. Obviously no one was home. What was the sense in standing there pounding on the door like an idiot? Lana flipped off the unseen knocker and started to carry her crackers back to the bedroom where she could cover her head with a pillow until the persistent asshole went away.

"Come on, Kent!"

Lana stopped.

"I still know how to pick locks. Even if you have weird British locks, I can figure them out. Criminal mastermind, remember? Open up, or so help me I'll get in anyway."

Lana let the crackers fall to the floor and walked across the living room. "Codie?"

"Ha! I knew you were in there. Lemme in." She knocked again. "I was going to wait for you to leave and then surprise you, but that might have been in poor taste considering what happened last time." She laughed. "Come on, Lana, open the damn door before your neighbors call the cops."

Lana twisted the lock and opened the door. It was Codie, in the flesh, not some drunken hallucination. Lana blinked and frowned, tears filling her eyes as she reached out to put her hand on her oldest friend's shoulder.

"I needed you."

Codie's smile faded. "What?"

"I needed you so much." The first tear fell free and rolled down her cheek, leading the way for the others.

Codie gripped Lana's arm and pulled her into a hug. "When?"

"Right now. Right this second."

"Well, here I am."

Lana laughed, crying harder as they clung to each other. Codie guided Lana into the apartment and shut the door.

## CHAPTER THREE

AFTER LANA finished crying, she peeled herself away from Codie so she could take a quick shower and change into clean clothes. She thanked Codie for not mentioning the mess and the reek as she headed out of the room. "Oh. The mannequin." Lana gestured at it without looking. "Could you take the shirt off of it? It's Catherine's, and I thought it would make things easier, but I just can't... can't look at it."

"Sure."

"Thank you. I'll be right back."

Codie stood up and undressed the mannequin. She twisted the blouse in her fists and stepped back to whip it across the plastic face. "Stupid bitch," she growled under her breath. "Hurt my friend, will you? I'll give you a hah! And a hi-yah!" She continued to flagellate the expressionless woman until she realized she was being ridiculous and tucked the shirt under a couch cushion so Lana wouldn't have to see it when she came back. She sat down on top of it and rested her elbows on her knees.

She thought about the first day of school. She was in homeroom, miraculously at school on time, already bored and dreading what was still to come. There likely wouldn't be much actual classwork being done, but teachers loved to make students "get to know each other." Codie was just fine with being unknown. She cultivated an aura of 'leave me alone' and most people honored that. Being forced to stand up to give her name and reveal something interesting about herself was like torture. She was trying to think of something to say when the princess came in.

Lana Kent, although Codie hadn't known her name yet, was the epitome of everything Codie hated. She was bright, beautiful, she was already smiling as she moved down the row of desks to her seat, and she was wearing a mauve jacket. She already had friends and she stopped to say hello to them. Codie pegged her instantly. Rich, popular, and completely without a care in the world. And, of course, the alphabetical seating chart meant that Lana sat right next to her. Lana put down her bag and looked at Codie before swinging her legs under the desk.

"Hey." Lana turned and looked at her, eyebrows raised in surprise. "You got a pencil I could borrow?"

Lana looked at the pen tucked under Codie's wristband. "Um. Yes..." She bent forward and dug through her bag until she found an old mechanical pencil. She clicked it to make sure it had lead, then handed it over. "There you go."

"Thanks." Codie sat up straighter, freed her pen, and began tapping out a simple drumbeat on the wood and metal of her desk. She closed her eyes and focused on the rhythm. The side of her boot tapped against the book rack under the desk in front of her. She couldn't afford drums of her own, but one of her friends had a friend who had an older brother who worked in a bar. They had a set-up for live music and sometimes he let her in so she could play.

"You're really good."

Codie's eyes snapped open and she looked at Lana, wondering if it was the set-up of some joke or insult. She seemed sincere, so Codie just shrugged and went back to her drumming.

"Miss Renton," the teacher said, "if you would be so kind..."

"Sorry." She looked at the pencil. She had planned to keep it, just a small screw-you to someone who seemed to have everything already, but compliments were rare. She held the pencil out. "Thanks."

"Keep it," Lana said. "Drummers gotta have sticks, right?"

"Sure." She withdrew the pencil. Her initial opinions were shattered but she didn't know enough to replace them. "I'm Codie."

Lana said, "I'm Lana. Hi." She opened her notebook, then pressed her lips together. "Hey. I play guitar. There's a rehearsal space that I get to use sometimes. It's not anything special or, you know, I mean, it's nothing, really. But they have a drum kit there. If you wanted, I could probably get you in."

Later on Codie would learn that Lana, the girl she'd assumed had no problems in the world, had just lost her mother to cancer. She was one step above homeless, and she was already working as a dance teacher to make ends meet. There were nights that she didn't get to sleep until two in the morning, and then she would wake up at five-thirty to finish her homework before she had to teach a lesson to elementary school students. Her first opinion of Lana as a carefree princess was replaced by a second opinion, and the realization that Lana Kent was probably one of the strongest people Codie had ever met.

Flash forward to the present day, when Codie was sitting in an apartment in London waiting for Lana to get out of the shower. She didn't know where she would be without Radiation Canary, but she knew that this scenario wouldn't have been on the list. Even after she met Lana and Nessa, she'd kept working at a chop shop to earn spending money. Without the band giving her another option she would probably have gotten arrested. From there the road ahead would have been bleak. She owed Lana her entire life.

Lana returned from the bathroom in a button-down shirt and jeans, barefoot and without makeup. She stopped in front of Codie. "Stand up." Codie did as she was told, and Lana hugged her again. "I thought you deserved a non-stinky hug."

Codie chuckled. "I didn't even notice. How are you? Do you feel better?"

"Marginally." They sat together on the couch. "I don't want to start blubbering and sniffling, so we're not going to talk about her. Okay? She's completely off the table for right now."

"Deal."

"Okay." She squeezed Codie's knee. "So what the hell are you doing here? Did you aim the plane east and just keep going?"

Codie laughed. "No. I flew commercial. I just... there's something I wanted to talk to you about, and we had to do it face to face."

Lana's smile wavered. "Okay. Is everything okay?"

"Yeah. Yeah, everything's fine." She looked into Lana's eyes and realized she couldn't do it. She'd flown across a continent and an ocean only to chicken out now. She had come to London so she could tell Lana to cut her out of the band. Her purpose was to save the Canaries from being up against the wall in the event of another crash, but she knew that wasn't how Lana would see it. Lana would see it as another betrayal, another breakup. There was no way Codie could be responsible for that.

Lana said, "Codie, you're freaking me out. Please, babe, whatever it is..."

"I was going to ask if you're happy."

Lana raised her eyebrows, chuckled, then leaned back and laughed. "No, Codie. No, I'm not happy. But that should be patently obvious, right? Are you happy?"

"I'm content. I wouldn't say happy." She was completely winging it now, but the words were coming easily enough. "When we put the band on hiatus, we did it so we could explore other options. Nessa wanted to have her baby, and Karen has one now, too. We're filling the time with projects. Karen has *Masquerade*, you're working on TV music, I drum for whoever Cartography asks me to. We're biding our time. For what? Something better? Maybe we were just surprised that we found our purpose in life so early that we thought we should complicate things."

Lana nodded. "Maybe so."

"I almost died."

"What?" Lana gripped Codie's arm. "When?"

"A few weeks ago. It's nothing. It... I'm embellishing. I was flying home from Squire's Isle when my plane's engine cut out. I managed to land safely, obviously, but it got me to thinking that if I died I would be taking the whole band with me. It made me realize..." Originally she had planned this moment to ask for release. She wanted to tell Lana it was okay to move on without her, that she'd done enough, and losing her shouldn't ruin everyone else's lives. "It made me realize we're all just wasting time. We're treading water for no reason. We're meant to be together, Lana. You, me, Karen, Nessa. We were meant to find each other. We took the break to see what the world held for us by ourselves. We've seen it. I know that what I have now is nothing compared to what we had. I don't know about you or the others..."

Lana scoffed. "Yeah, who would want to leave all this...?" She looked around the apartment. "I need the band more than any of you. I don't know if Karen and Nessa will want to join up, though. Karen's album is doing pretty well, and like you said she has the baby now."

Codie shrugged. "We could always just ask them. I think we've all been trying to figure out who we are, and that's great. But I also think the answer is that we are a *we*. We're Radiation Canary. If that means we have to put a nursery on the tour bus, then so be it."

Lana chuckled and put her head on Codie's shoulder.

Codie stroked Lana's hair, which was still wet from her shower. "My flight back home is tomorrow. Let me buy you a ticket. You can fly home with me and we can talk to them together."

Lana looked around the apartment. "I thought I was going to make a life here. We got this apartment as a starter, and then we moved to the other place, and I was so proud of myself. I was a grown-up. I was creating something with Catherine, and I was doing really well." She put her hand over her mouth and then brushed it across her cheek. "Best laid plans. Heh. Karen wrote a song with that title. I might have some changes to make to it now."

Codie smiled.

"Okay. I can buy my own ticket, but you have to help me pack."

"That sounds suspiciously close to work. I just got off an international flight. I planned to crash on your couch for the next twenty hours or so."

Lana grinned and bumped Codie's arm with her shoulder. "Come on. It's not too bad. I barely unpacked after I got kicked out of the new place." She tilted her head to the side. "Hey. Why did you come here instead of the other apartment?"

Codie said, "To be honest, I've been in the air for ten hours. Between layovers and jumping time zones, I'm not even sure what day it is. I just completely forgot you had moved to the other place."

Lana slipped her arm around Codie's and led her to the bedroom to start packing. "Looks like the luck of the Canaries is still working in our favor. Now stop whining and help me throw some clothes in a bag. If you do a good job I'll take you out for pizza afterward. Then we can work on tracking down the mommies of the band."

"I swear I know you from somewhere."

Vanessa Wayland shrugged with a shake of her head. "Maybe you've seen me at the Mommy & Me class. Do you go to the one on Sunnyside?"

The woman shook her head and frowned out at the field. She was Lynn Owens, the mother of twins. Nathaniel was just a bit younger, and the three were currently playing in the grass between their mothers and the soccer game being played on the open field. Lynn had a twelve-year-old daughter who was playing in the game. Scott's nephew was in the game as well, and Vanessa was there to help cheer him on. She wasn't trying to hide her identity from her new potential friend, but she also wasn't eager to broadcast the truth. She was just another mother on the sidelines.

She changed her name to Wayland after Nate was born. When they moved to the suburbs she introduced herself to all their neighbors as Vanessa. When she lost the baby weight, she kept slimming down until her cheekbones were slightly more pronounced than they had been onstage. Her hair was also longer and the combined changes made her look taller than she ever had. She still looked enough like herself that strangers sometimes stared, or she got an occasional "Did you go to such-and-such high school?" but she always shrugged and feigned confusion.

She loved her time in Radiation Canary, and her interaction with the fans was one of the top five moments of her life. Marrying Scott and having Nathaniel were two of the only things that topped it. She would treasure those long nights at the autograph table when she got to meet the people touched by their music. But if she was entirely honest she knew those fans were there for Karen and Lana. The voice and the lyrics were the main draw. She and Codie were bonus. That was fine with her, and she was grateful she didn't have to live in their spotlight, but by the same measure it made her feel disingenuous when she identified herself as a celebrity.

Scott was a few yards away with his sister. Vanessa kept alternating her attention between him and Nathaniel, her two boys. She might have been third-tier when she was on-stage, but to these two men she was the star of the show. Nathaniel looked up and smiled at her, and she waved one finger at him. He laughed and went back to whatever game he had devised with his two friends.

Lynn looked past Vanessa and sat up straighter. "Evelyn! Over here, Evie!"

Another woman made her way over, taking off her sunglasses and bending down to accept Lynn's hug without making her stand. Lynn made the introductions and vacated her lawn chair so Evelyn could take it. Evelyn settled in and dropped her voice to a conspiratorial whisper.

"You're not going to believe who I just saw. You know the lead singer of Radiation Canary?"

Vanessa's skin erupted in gooseflesh and her eyes widened.

"Lana something," Lynn said. "Sure."

"She's *here*."

"Get out!"

Vanessa was already looking around, trying to spot Lana in the crowd. Evelyn said, "I parked the car and I was coming through the lot, and there she was! There she was, just sitting in a car doing something on her phone. I swear it's her. I know because Mike put her on his freebie list." She rolled her eyes and shook her head. "At least he's not here. God knows he'd throw that in my face and try to make good on it. Never mind the fact she's gay."

Vanessa stood up. "I should, uh... Lynn, do you mind watching Nathaniel for a second?"

"Sure! Everything okay?"

"Yeah, I just need to go get something out of the car. You can take my seat." She hurried off in the direction Evelyn had come, scanning the windshields that had been turned into mirrors by the sun. Her heart was pounding as she looked for any cars that had someone sitting in it. There was every chance that Evelyn was mistaken about who she had seen. Lana lived in London, and the idea she would be at some random pre-teen soccer game was ludicrous.

Someone tapped their horn, and a hand emerged from the car window. Vanessa made her way over and, sure enough, Lana Kent was smiling at her from the driver's seat of a car.

"Good afternoon, Mrs. Wayland."

Vanessa half-leapt through the window and wrapped her arms around Lana's head. Lana accepted the assault, laughing at the ludicrous image of Vanessa's legs sticking straight out of the car. She patted Vanessa on the shoulder and then began squirming to get away.

"Okay. I could pull you on through, but you'd probably be more comfortable getting in on the passenger side."

"Right." Vanessa freed herself from the window and hurried around the car. She got in and hugged Lana from a less awkward angle. "What are you doing here?"

"Oh, you know... I wanted to see a good soccer game."

"They have soccer in England."

"What?"

"They call it football."

Lana thumped her hand against her forehead. "Now you tell me! Well, this is a wasted trip. I guess I'll head back to the airport."

Vanessa twisted in the seat to face Lana. "Is Catherine with you?"

Lana's smile faded so quickly Vanessa wanted to retract the question immediately. "No. Catherine is in England."

"Oh. Are you okay?"

"No. But I will be." The smile returned. "Look at you, though. Miss Sexy."

Vanessa scoffed. "Soccer Mom Sexy, maybe."

"It suits you."

"How did you know we were here?"

Lana showed her phone. "Scott had a Facebook update."

Vanessa rolled her eyes. "I've told him a thousand times to not announce to the world when we're not home. But this time I can't be too angry at him."

"Yeah, cut the guy a little slack." She returned the phone to her pocket. "Codie came to see me the other day. She's the reason I'm here now."

Vanessa could almost hear what was coming next, like an echo from the future. "Oh?"

"She thinks it's time to get Radiation Canary back together. But she also thinks our 'all-for-one' idea might not be fair to us as individuals. So I'm here to either invite you back into the band or get your blessing to find someone to fill in for you on the next album. We don't want a substitute. But we also don't want you to feel obligated to put aside your real life just because the rest of us want to get back into it. No pressure, no guilt, just whatever you feel is right for you."

"Okay," Vanessa said. "I appreciate that. Thank you. When do you need a decision?"

Lana shook her head. "There isn't a deadline. We haven't even talked to Karen about it yet. Codie and I are in, but we have the least to lose from spending hours in a studio or weeks on a tour bus. You and Karen have... you know, you have real lives. You have families. Codie and I will respect whatever you decide. And even if we hire someone to play piano on the next album, you will always and forever be a member of the band. You'll be welcomed back with open arms whenever you're ready. You may have a husband and a son, but you have another family, too."

Vanessa wiped at her eyes. Her previous thoughts about freedom and anonymity evaporated in the face of Lana's invitation. "Thank you. I want to. I really, really want to. But... yeah... it's a big decision. Scott and I need to sit down and work it out."

"Take all the time you need." She held out her hand. Vanessa ignored it and hugged her, and Lana laughed. "I love you, Nessa."

"I love you, too." She kissed the side of Lana's head. "Call me when you've talked to Karen."

"I will."

"And tell Codie I'm pissed she didn't come with you. Whether I play on the album or not, I want to have lunch just the four of us before you go back overseas."

Lana nodded. "It's a date."

Vanessa gave her another hug, just for good measure, and finally pulled herself away. She got out of the car and tried to get her smiling under control before she got back to her seat. Lynn and Evelyn were both watching the game, but they turned toward her as she neared as if their heads were on the same swivel. Lynn cocked her head and smiled victoriously.

"I figured out where I know you from. Va-*nessa* Wayland...?"

"Damn," Vanessa said.

Evelyn stood up and offered Vanessa her seat. "Don't worry. Your secret is safe with us. But you'll have to earn our silence."

Vanessa sat down. "Uh-oh. What do I have to do?"

Evelyn leaned in and dropped her voice to a whisper. "Do you know Justin Timberlake? He's on *my* freebie list."

Vanessa laughed. "You know what, I'll see what I can do." Her new friends focused on the game again, and Vanessa found herself rethinking her whole suburban secret identity. If Radiation Canary was getting back together for another album, she absolutely wanted to be part of it. She needed to be a part of it. She would just have to find a way to make it work with Nathaniel and Scott. Her son looked up as if he had heard her think his name, and she waved two fingers at him. One way or another, she was going to make sure she honored both of her families.

## CHAPTER FOUR

VANESSA MADE dinner after they got back from the soccer game. Scott knew something was up when he recognized the meal as chicken cacciatore, his favorite, but he said nothing as he set the table and kept Nathaniel distracted so Vanessa could cook. When they finally sat down to eat she helped Nathaniel get started on his macaroni and cheese before she broached the subject.

"So. Lana Kent was at the soccer game today."

Scott blinked in surprise. "She was? You should have called me over. I would've liked to say hi."

"She wasn't there long. She, um... she wanted to see if I would be willing to get back with the band if they went into the studio for a new album." She looked at him and tried to gauge his emotions. "If I say no, it won't be the end of the world. They'll let me choose a replacement and go forward without me. I'd be fine if they did that. I'm not sure I want to commit the time and energy to being in the band. But before I did any actual thinking, I wanted to know what you thought about it."

He looked at his food for a long moment, then pushed his chair back and walked out of the kitchen. Vanessa looked at Nathaniel, quirking her lips to one side. He stared back at her without understanding, his spoon sticking out of his mouth like a cartoon tongue. She was about to go in search of her husband when he came back with his phone.

"Sorry about just walking off like that. That 'no phones at the table' rule." He scrolled with his thumb, and then handed it to her. "There."

Vanessa looked at the note he'd opened. It was dated the day after *Radiation Canary* appeared on *Settle In, Seattle!*.

"I think it's about time you got the band back together. You've waited long enough."

She smiled at the phone for a full minute before she looked at him with tears in her eyes. "You've been saving this since then?"

"It was true then," he said. "I just didn't want you to think I was pushing you. You made your choice to have Nate, and be a mommy. And now you're ready to go back to the band." He put his hands on her shoulders and bent to kiss her forehead. "I fell in love with a musician. Even if you decide not to take them up on their offer, I know that you have a job to do. Make your choice, and we'll figure out where to go from there."

She put her arms around his waist, her head on his chest, and let him hug her. "Have I mentioned that I love you lately?"

"Not out loud."

"Then let me make up for that. I love you, Scott."

"Thanks. You're neat, too."

Vanessa laughed and knocked her head against his shoulder. "Asshole."

"I love you, Vanessa Grace Wayland. Better?"

She squeezed him tighter. "Much."

Still seated in his high chair and watching his parents through their conversation, Nathaniel rocked back and forth as he laughed at them.

Karen Everett sat with her back to the window, framed by the buildings and Puget Sound. The early afternoon light spilled across her apartment and threw her shadow against the shelves of books and LPs that took up one entire wall. The music on her stand was self-composed and currently without lyrics. There was a line of concentration between her eyebrows as she concentrated on the music and made minute adjustments. Once she reached a stopping point she would go back and make the alterations as needed.

Her cello was equal parts practice and practical. While she tried to find time to play every day, there were ulterior motives to her playing at this particular moment. She glanced up when Laura emerged from the hallway. Her wife, her beautiful and disarmingly hilarious wife. On-stage she was all rock. She growled and strutted through the spotlight with her guitar and her duster, but in real life she was sweet and goofy and always ready with a smile.

She stopped and leaned against the wall to watch Karen play, and Karen raised her eyebrows hopefully. "Is the Bug asleep?"

"He's asleep. He always goes down so much easier when you're playing. He loves your music." Karen smiled and finished the arpeggio and lowered her bow. Laura came into the living room and stepped around the stand. "What was that song?"

"Ferry Country."

"It was gorgeous. And I'm honored... you used to play for sold-out crowds who paid hundreds of dollars to hear you play music. Now I'm the only one you play for. It's a huge honor."

Karen smiled and handed Laura her cello. "Well, you and Mason."

"Right. I guess I don't mind sharing with our baby. So is that for your next solo album?"

"No. I don't know. Maybe. I keep hearing Lana's voice on it, so I'll probably stick it in the Radiation Canary file."

Karen started to get up but Laura gently pushed her back into the chair. "Again? You've almost got enough for two albums in there now."

"That's not true. Maybe a deluxe album." She smiled up at her wife. "Let me up. I want to make lunch."

"Uh-uh. Mason interrupted us this morning. I owe you."

Karen's smile widened. She relaxed into her seat and scooted her feet back against the legs of the chair as Laura knelt in front of her. "Oh, really?"

Laura shrugged. "Seems like a shame to waste this position."

She pushed Karen's skirt up and Karen lifted her hips so Laura could remove her underwear. Laura kissed Karen's knees and then traced a line up her inner thigh with the tip of her tongue. Karen settled back and hooked one hand on the seat of her chair, cupping the back of Laura's head with the other. Her eyelids fell and her head rolled back as Laura used the tip of her tongue and two fingers to tease her. Karen bit her lip and curled her toes in the carpet.

"I'm not gonna last long, babe."

"That's okay." Laura kissed Karen's mound as she pressed two fingers into her. Karen made a guttural noise and bent her knees inward. "This time it's definitely the destination... not the journey... Come for me, Karen."

Karen tightened her hand on the back of Laura's head. She lifted her hips off the chair, fingers tightening on the edge of the seat, and she came with a quiet cry of release. Laura moaned against her while she trembled, and Karen sank back to the seat before urging Laura up for a kiss. Laura settled between Karen's legs, and Karen closed her thighs in tight around her wife.

"Which do you prefer?" Laura said against Karen's mouth. "Me or your cello?"

"It's a lot more fun pulling your strings."

Laura grinned and kissed Karen again. "Good answer. Now, what did you say about making lunch?"

"Didn't you just have something to eat?"

Laura flattened her hand over Karen's face and shoved it playfully to one side. She stood up and offered Karen a hand to get her out of the chair. Karen pushed her skirt back into place and retrieved her cello so she could put it away properly. When the front door buzzer chimed, Karen answered since she was the closest. She pressed down on the response button and leaned close to the speaker.

"Yes?"

"This is your captain, requesting permission to come in for a landing."

Karen grinned. "Permission granted. Bring her in, Captain Renton. We ask that you keep noise level to a minimum as there is a sleeping baby in the cabin."

"Acknowledged."

Karen unlocked the door and snapped her fingers at Laura. "Toss me my panties."

"So rock-and-roll," Laura said as she passed her the underwear. Karen chuckled and slipped them on under her skirt. She went into the kitchen to see if they had enough leftovers to feed Codie, bent over to scan the fridge when she heard the door open and close. Laura said, "Oh! Well, hey... hi."

Karen heard someone come into the kitchen behind her. "We were just about to have lunch. Options are limited unless you're willing to eat baby food." She finally straightened up and turned around. "We have a wide assortment of..."

Lana smiled at Karen's obvious surprise. She was standing in the kitchen doorway, hands in her pockets, dressed in a red hoodie and blue jeans. She shrugged. "I'm still on London time, so I'm not really hungry anyway. Hi, Karen."

"Lana." She crossed the kitchen in one step and wrapped her in a hug. "God, why didn't you tell me you were coming?"

"And miss seeing you speechless? You must be crazy."

Codie said, "Sorry, K. She forced me to mislead you."

Karen said, "I'm still wondering why my wife, the woman I pledged to love forever, didn't give me a head's-up."

Laura showed her palms, utterly helpless. "She put her finger to her lips and shushed me! I was powerless."

Karen hugged Lana again. "I guess I can forgive it just this once. Is Vanessa here, too?"

"We invited her, but she had a Gymboree class or something. If we end up going to dinner later, she'll join us then."

"Dinner is a must." Karen led Lana into the living room where Codie and Laura were already seated. They were all keeping their voices low in deference to the slumbering infant down the hall. "So what the hell are you doing here?"

Lana looked at Codie. "We decided it was time."

"Time?"

"Radiation Canary," Codie said. "We think it's time to get the band back together to record another album."

Karen frowned at Lana. "Wait. So you and Catherine are moving back to the States?"

Lana said, "Catherine broke up with me."

"What?" The word was shrill and choked, just barely kept under control in deference to the sleeping baby. Karen grabbed Lana's hand. "When?"

Lana patted Karen's hand. "It's okay. We can talk about it later. The important thing is figuring out if we want to come back. Codie and I, the answer is an easy yes. We've basically just been biding our time with side projects. But you and Vanessa? You actually moved on. You have families, you have your solo album..."

Laura cleared her throat and started to stand. "I should leave you guys alone. This is band business..."

"You're part of the band," Lana said. "At least when it comes to this. Karen's not going to make this decision by herself, so you might as well stay."

Karen said, "She's right. Stay."

Laura sat down. "Well, you know what I'm going to say. Radiation Canary is your family. You made great music for *Masquerade*, and I love the album as much as everyone else did, but you belong with these four as much as I belong with Ella. To be honest, I'm surprised you managed to go this long without ending this hiatus." She leaned in and kissed Karen's cheek. "It's your choice, but if you need my blessing you have it in spades. I want to hear the next Canary album as badly as the rest of the world does."

Lana said, "You married a smart lady, Karen."

"She's pretty, too. Thank you, baby." She kissed Laura, then turned to Lana and Codie. "Is Vanessa in? Did she agree?"

Codie said, "Lana talked to her yesterday and she's thinking it over. I think she's been enjoying civilian life more than she expected. But that's good. It gives us a chance to go over the second point of order. We said all for one, and that's good. That means we're loyal to each other. But we need to loosen that up a little. If Vanessa says she doesn't want to do it, we have to have to option to hire a substitute. Otherwise we all have the pressure of not letting the others down."

Karen said, "I have to admit, I've thought of that myself. If I wanted to be a stay-at-home mom, if I wanted to give up performing to teach... I would have felt like I was letting you four down."

Lana said, "All for one, all four are Radiation Canary. But we can opt out."

Karen nodded. "I approve of that completely. Hundred percent."

"Me too," Codie said.

Lana smiled and looked around the room. "So whatever Vanessa says, Radiation Canary is back. Either she'll be with us or she will help us find someone to fill in for her."

Karen laughed and ran a hand over her face. Laura patted her leg and got up to go into the kitchen. "We're back. Wow. When I woke up this morning I didn't know what I was going to do with my day. Now I guess I'll be working on the songs in the Radiation Canary file."

Laura came back with some glasses and a bottle of wine. "It's nothing fancy, but I feel like this moment deserved a toast."

"Like I said," Lana chuckled, "a smart lady."

They each got a glass and Laura poured. She poured one for herself and said, "Since Vanessa isn't here, I'll toast as her proxy. To the return of Radiation Canary."

"To us," Karen said.

"Hear, hear."

They touched glasses, and they each took a drink. Karen smiled. "Wine before lunch. Is this the fast-paced world of drugs and alcohol mama warned me about?"

Lana said, "You forgot sex."

Karen grinned, glanced at Laura, and took a sip of her wine without saying anything. Lana inferred the meaning and chuckled as she took a sip of her wine.

"The one with the cello ends up being the real rock star. Who knew?"

Naomi Marrow was having a rotten day. She had left for work in the midst of an argument with her wife. She knew they would sort it out as soon as they got home, but without closure the dark cloud hung over her head the entire day. One of Cartography's newest bands was having an internal conflict before they even finished their first album, and the word from on high was that they might have to fire one of the band members just to keep things from exploding. She hated the idea of dictating a band's lineup. It was something Dash Warren would never have done, and it made her feel filthy. But if peace couldn't be brokered, then the only other option was cutting the band entirely.

She was in such a foul mood that when Karen Everett called to set up a meeting, Naomi jumped at the opportunity to see one of her favorite artists.

"I can be in Seattle by four."

"Oh. Oh, that's... not necessary. There's no hurry."

Naomi had taken off her glasses to massage the bridge of her nose. "Karen. Trust me. I need to see you, too."

Karen said, "Is everything okay?"

"I'm just... very much in need of a friendly face. Just tell me you're not dropping a bomb on my lap. It doesn't have to be good news, just tell me I won't be depressed.

"You won't be depressed."

"God bless you, Karen. Four o'clock?"

Karen said, "That would be fine."

When she hung up she called Susan. "Hey. I'm going to be home late. I have to go to Seattle for a work thing."

"Oh. Listen... about this morning."

"No," Naomi said. "No, hey, don't... I'll apologize when we're face to face."

Susan chuckled. "I was going to apologize to you."

Naomi smiled. "Maybe we both should. I was out of line, though. I knew it when I was saying it, but... look, I don't want to do this over the phone. I'll be home as soon as I can. You don't have to hold dinner for me."

"I will, though."

"Susan..."

"I love you, too."

Naomi laughed. "Always have to step on my toes. Okay. Uh, Seattle. I don't think it'll take too long. It's one of my easiest clients."

"Okay. I'll see you when you get home."

"Love you. Hah. See? Gotcha."

They hung up and Naomi told her secretary she would be out of the office for the rest of the day. She couldn't just take off from work, but going to meet Karen counted as a work outing. It was the perfect excuse, and it was exactly what she needed. She and Karen could have had a very complicated relationship. They had ever-so-briefly been lovers, and she knew she had been Karen's first-ever lover, but they'd never let their physical past get in the way of their professional relationship. They were both married now, and the water was thoroughly under the bridge. Nevertheless, she wondered if she should have told Susan who she was going to meet. She had no reason to believe it would be a point of contention but she also didn't want to upset the waters.

Almost three hours after she set out, she arrived at Karen's apartment. She was buzzed up, and the door was slightly ajar when she got upstairs. She pushed inside and sighed heavily, grateful to be done traveling for the moment. "I've had a rotten day full of crappy clients, so I hope you have some good news for me, Karen. Don't let me... down." She stopped and stared into the living room as she tried to process what she was seeing.

Lana Kent was sitting on the couch with Vanessa Wayland. Codie Renton was sitting on a stool by the kitchen counter, and Karen was in the armchair facing the door.

"What is this?" Naomi said.

Lana said, "We just wanted to know if there might be room on your schedule for a new Radiation Canary album."

Naomi took out her phone and let her purse drop to the floor as she dialed her secretary's number. She stared at the women in front of her as it rang.

"Cartography Records, Naomi Marrow's office."

"Hey, Marcy. It's me. Listen, get Chasing Eighty on the phone. Tell them that they're on hiatus until they get their shit together."

Marcy said, "Whoa. I thought you were trying to hold off on making such a drastic decision."

Naomi smiled at Lana. "I was. But I just got a line on a much better band that can take their spot."

## CHAPTER FIVE

THE MEMBERS of Radiation Canary sat around Karen's coffee table facing Naomi. Laura had taken Mason out to see Auntie Ella so they wouldn't intrude on the business meeting. After Naomi's initial shock wore off, her business side took over. "We need to decide how we're going to do this. People have been clamoring for a new album ever since your last one came out. We need to capitalize it as much as we can." She paused and held her hands up. "Without, of course, looking as if we're just digging around in their pockets."

Karen said, "Lana and I were going over some of the songs I've written in the past two years. We have more than enough for a new album, so if we wrote a few more, we could make it a deluxe release. Maybe even a double album."

Lana said, "I wanted to save this until Naomi was here so she could shoot it down immediately if she's against it. But I was thinking we could record two CDs as secretly as possible so there isn't any buzz or hype. Then we release the first one digitally for free to tease the release of the second one a few weeks or months down the road."

"A free album as publicity?" Naomi said.

Karen nodded. "And as a pronouncement that we're completely back. Any band can say they're getting back together, but marking the moment with a completed record really proves a point."

"Just don't cram it onto every iPod in the world like U2 did," Codie said.

Naomi said, "No, we'll make them go to a special website to download it, maybe. Just so we can get a feel for how many people are getting it. I like the idea. I'll fight for the free release if the management makes me."

Lana said, "And that's why recording it has to be as secret as possible. I mean, there may be some rumors since this is the internet we're talking about. If the four of us are in the same city, and we're going to a recording studio every day, then someone is bound to snap a picture with their phone. Once it's on Twitter..."

Naomi straightened and stared into space. "Rabbit's Warren."

Karen said, "Dash?"

"No. I mean, basically, yes. Dash didn't like using the studios at Cartography because all the other acts kept trying to listen in to her sessions or corner her in the hallway, stuff like that. So she had a private studio built up near Snohomish. Secluded, very private, with all the amenities. I think there are enough guest rooms that all four of you could go up there and take as much time as you need with the album without anyone spying on you."

Lana said, "I don't know if I'd feel worthy of using Dash's private space."

Naomi smirked and took out her phone. "She avoided new acts as much as possible. She sought you four out. She loaned you her plane and flew with you to Greece. I think it's safe to say she would've been fine with you crashing at her place for a few weeks. Let me make some calls. We've kept it in fine shape, but no one has used it since Dash died. We might have to do some mild renovating before it's ready to make a whole album."

She stood up and went into the kitchen to make her call. Once she was gone, Karen smiled at the others.

"It's weird. It's only been two years since we did *Fallout*, but this still feels like a reunion."

"Two years too long," Codie said.

Vanessa nodded and picked up her glass for another toast. "We took a break to make sure we were on the right path. We found out that we were. We can be mommies or wives or pilots but we will always be Canaries. We belong together, wherever the rest of our lives take us."

"Cheers," Lana said. They each took a drink, and Lana bumped Vanessa's leg with hers. "So Scott is onboard?"

Vanessa nodded. "He's being very supportive. He knows it's going to be a lot of hours rehearsing and recording and he's prepared to take over with Nathaniel when I can't."

"Sounds like a keeper," Codie said.

"Eh, he's decent enough. Too late to throw him back and start fishing for a new one." Lana forced a smile and quietly excused herself. She stood by the window with her drink in her hand, lifting it to take a sip as she looked out over the city. Vanessa watched her go and then looked at Codie. "Did I say something wrong?"

"She didn't tell you?" Karen whispered. Vanessa shook her head. "Catherine..." Karen put her forefingers together and then pulled them apart.

"Oh. Lord. She implied in the car, but I completely forgot. Lana..."

"It's okay," Lana said without turning around.

Before Vanessa could say anything else, Naomi returned and put her phone down on the table. "Okay, I talked to the caretaker. The house is fine, and you could stay there tomorrow if you wanted. The studio needs some work. I'll get in touch with Cartography and have them move some equipment in. We could trust them to keep the secret, but just to be safe I won't tell them what it's for. They figure it will take a month before it'll be ready for you to start recording."

Lana returned to the group. "A month. Plenty of time to get our ducks in a row. Right?"

Karen nodded. "Laura and I can work out a schedule, and Ness?"

Vanessa said, "More than enough time."

Naomi clapped her hands together. "Fantastic! Then it's settled." She opened an app on her phone and began making notes. "I'll keep in touch so you know how everything is going. I'll also double-check the accommodations. I think there are enough rooms that everyone can bring whoever they want. Nessa, you and Scott and the baby. Lana, if Catherine is with you~"

"Jesus Christ," Lana snapped. "Catherine dumped me, okay? Catherine fucking left my ass. Are we all caught up? Can I stop fucking updating everyone? Are we all good?"

Codie stood up and put her hand on Lana's shoulder. Lana rested her hands on the back of the couch and hung her head. "I'm sorry, Naomi. Nessa. I'm... it's just..."

"We understand." Vanessa put her hand on top of Lana's. "We're sorry."

Naomi smiled. "Hey, if that's the worst outburst we have to put up with, we'll be fine. I'm sorry, Lana."

"You guys don't have any reason to be sorry. Hey, you assumed I hadn't screwed it up yet. So you're fine. I should've..." She waved it off. "Anyway. Sorry. I'll try to keep my outbursts to a minimum."

Naomi stood up and slung the strap of her bag over one shoulder. "I should head back to Cartography and get the ball rolling. Does everyone have the same contact info?"

Lana said, "I'm staying with Codie. But email, phone, all that is the same."

"Okay. So over the next month, I want you four to get together when you can. All of you as a group, in pairs, whatever and however you can. I want you to get some songs ready so you can hit the ground running once you're up at the cabin. This is going to be fantastic. I already can't wait." She came around the couch and hugged Lana. "Let me know if you need to talk."

Lana furrowed her brow and fought back tears. "Thanks."

"I'll see you as soon as I know anything more. Karen... I don't forgive you for keeping me in the dark about why you wanted me here, but the surprise was worth it. You're on probation."

"Deservedly so."

Naomi winked at her. "Okay, ladies. Wow. You just totally salvaged my whole shitty day. My whole year. Thank you. Be in touch."

Karen escorted her to the door. When she came back Lana was sitting on the couch between Codie and Vanessa. Karen's laptop had been moved in front of them. "I thought we could go over the songs we already have, get an early start..."

"I have a better idea." She closed the computer and smiled at her band. "We're back together, the four of us, for the first time in... I can't even remember. We're all here, we're going to start working on an album again, and we have a month to prepare. I think we can spend one night celebrating."

Codie smiled. "I can get behind that plan. Where are we going?"

"Canlis? My treat."

Vanessa whistled. "We'd be fools to say no to that. I'm in."

Lana said, "We're all in. But first..." She stood up and put her hand out. "We might as well make it official."

Karen smiled and put her hand on top of Lana's. Codie's was next, and Vanessa topped them off. "We tried this before," Codie said. "I'm not sure we actually came up with a battle cry to go with it."

"Why complicate it?" Lana said. "Canaries."

The others repeated it.

Lana smiled as their hands slipped apart. She put her arm around Vanessa, still regretting her earlier outburst. "We'll get some dinner, then we'll go back to our respective corners and start making plans to spend some time hunkered down on the album."

"Can't wait," Karen said.

Codie said, "If we want to get a table at Canlis we better hurry. I'll make us a reservation online, but odds are better if we get on the road now."

"Wise," Vanessa said. "I'll call Scott from the car and have him meet us there. Karen, where did Laura disappear to?"

"She texted to say she and Ella are working on some songs of their own at Ella's place. I'll call and invite them. Make it a whole family affair." Codie and Vanessa left, but Karen grabbed Lana's hand to hold her back. When they were alone in the apartment, Karen hugged her. "Let us know if you need anything at all. Okay? If you need to walk away from the table, or the studio, or anything..."

"I will. Thanks, K."

Karen kissed Lana's cheek. "Come on. We'll let you pick the wine so you can get appropriately plastered."

After dinner, when Karen and Vanessa went home to their families, Codie drove Lana back to her apartment. In the truck Lana dug through the CDs until she found one labeled *Action After Warnings* in Sharpie. She smiled and slipped it into the player. "I can't believe you still have one of the original copies."

"Hell yeah. What, am I gonna throw it away?"

Lana closed her eyes and listened as the opening notes of 'Mutually Assured' came through the speakers. She remembered the early mornings spent driving to the studio before it opened, sneaking an hour or two before the paying acts showed up thanks to an understanding with the building's security guard. There had been mornings when Codie drove them home and Lana had fallen back to sleep hugging her guitar case. Listening to her voice now, twelve years later, she sounded so utterly young and immature. The recording was amateurish, which was to be expected, but even she had to admit there was potential in the sound.

"You could probably auction this off and make a million bucks," Lana said. "Our worst-sounding record, and you'd only have to sell one copy."

Codie parked and led Lana upstairs. She closed the door, turned on the light, and tossed her keys into a bowl. "Okay, time to cut the bullshit."

Lana stopped and stared at her. "What?"

"You can fool them, and I've given you enough time to stew, but it's time to talk. You didn't talk in England, you didn't talk on the plane, and I've given you long enough. You snapped at Vanessa and Naomi. You are not okay."

"I'm... I just got sick of repeating myself. This godawful thing happened to me, and I had to keep telling the story every time someone new came into the room."

Codie softened her voice. "I understand that. And I understand that you're still hurting. But I've known you since we were kids, Lana. I've seen you with literally every woman you've ever dated. And you've loved them all to a certain degree, and you've mourned the end of every relationship to an extent. But I never saw you fall as hard as you did for Catherine. You moved to England for her. The reason we all just assume she's with you is because we didn't see this coming."

Lana gave up the fight. "Yeah, that makes it unanimous." She sighed and went into the living room, where she dropped onto the couch. "We were fighting a lot, but everyone fights. We had a routine. Maybe she found it too dull. But what's wrong with routine?"

Codie sat down next to her. "I'm sorry."

Lana frowned at the crack in Codie's voice and looked at her. "Are you crying?"

"Yes. And if you tell anyone, I'll kill you." She wiped at her cheeks. "I was so happy you'd found someone. I thought she was the one."

"Yeah." They looked out the window, which afford a beautiful view of a brick wall. "I thought Catherine was it. She was my chance at a real grown-up relationship. We both made sacrifices. We bought an apartment together. What if I don't get another chance? What if she *was* it? What if I never fall in love with anyone ever again?"

Codie laughed. "You will. You've never had a problem with a lack of love. If Catherine didn't appreciate being boring with you, then she didn't deserve you. Come here." She guided Lana's head onto her shoulder. "You're going to be fine. You won't forget Catherine, but you'll use what went wrong to make sure the next time works out better. And maybe that will be the one that sticks."

Lana took Codie's hand, threading their fingers together. "Why couldn't you be gay?"

Codie laughed. "Because when we kissed in high school, you enjoyed it a lot more than I did." She kissed the top of Lana's head. "And I figured if I didn't enjoy kissing you, then I was definitely not even bisexual."

"Not even a little bit?"

"Sorry."

"Maybe with the wine from dinner and a couple beers out of the fridge?"

Codie said, "Keep it in your pants, Kent."

"Probably for the best." She felt a tear on the bridge of her nose and wiped it away. "You couldn't handle me."

Codie laughed.

"I can't imagine what would've happened if we said yes to the reality show. Maybe that's why Catherine wasn't interested."

"They asked you to do a reality show?"

"Last year. The rock star and the actress, plus lesbians. Lesbians sell. It would've been on one of those cable channels that celebrate the dregs of society. Duck hunters with thirty kids. Real fine company."

"Did they have a name picked out? No, let me guess. What's Your Diehl? Diehl or No Diehl. Kent Buy Me Love."

Lana groaned. "Stop. Those are all worse than the real thing. Cat and Canary."

Codie laughed. "Oh, shit. You should've done it. That title is perfect."

"Might have bought me a few more months, at any rate." She sat up and ran her fingers though her hair. "I want to go to sleep. Guest room down the hall?"

"Yeah." She reached over and brushed Lana's hair away from her face. "I wish I'd enjoyed our kiss in high school more. We could've been high school sweethearts."

Lana smiled. "I'd have destroyed you. Then where would we be?"

Codie chastely kissed Lana's lips. "I love you, Lana."

"I love you, too. Thanks for the tough love."

"Whenever you need it. Now go to bed. We have a lot of work ahead of us, and tomorrow is the first day. You should get your beauty rest."

"What about you?"

"I'm as beauty as I'm going to get. It's all about maintaining now. I only need an hour, two hours tops per night."

Codie stood up and pulled Lana off the couch. She started to leave, but Lana held onto her.

"If you had died, Radiation Canary would have been the last thing on my mind. You're not one quarter of a band, Codie, you're my best friend. You're the person I love most in this world, and losing you would have changed everything. So... fly more carefully from now on, okay?"

"I'll do my best."

"You're crying again."

Codie chuckled. "I'll kill you and anyone you tell."

"The secret is safe with me. Goodnight, Codie."

"Night, princess."

They went to their separate bedrooms, and Lana undressed down to her underwear. She moved her guitar case to the bed, opened it, and sat down with the guitar on her lap. She placed her hands, she stared at the strings, and she held a song in her head. Her thumb pressed down on one string and made it tremble with unreleased energy. She told herself she couldn't play since Codie was about to go to sleep in the next room. She told herself she didn't really want to play a song. But she had so many songs in her head ready to go. She needed to get back into practice before the band retreated to the cabin. She lifted her hand to flex her fingers, shook her wrist, and resumed the position.

Lana stuck her tongue between her lips and stared at the guitar. She had only picked up the guitar a half dozen times since Catherine left her. Of those times she'd only managed to make a sound once or twice. There was nothing even similar to a song, and her hand shook as she considered the possibility that she might be the band's weak link. What if they got up to the Warren and she failed them? Even if she backed out and they got Laura to fill in for her, would Cartography be able to call it a Radiation Canary album? Would the public accept it as the real deal or dismiss it as a shoddy replacement?

"Give me 'Emerald,'" she whispered to the guitar. "You can play that in your sleep. Just... give me 'Emerald.'" She bit her lip, her hand tensed, and she curled her hand into a fist. It took all her willpower not to swing the instrument against the wall until she was left with only pieces. Instead she reverently replaced it in the case and closed the lid.

She had a month to figure out what was wrong with her, find the thing Catherine had left broken, and then fix it. Catherine had left enough things shattered in her wake. Radiation Canary wasn't going to be her next victim.

## CHAPTER SIX

OVER THE next month they worked on the songs in Karen's file. Most were just lyrical snippets, and many were labeled Untitled 5 or "Something about the sea." They met in Karen's apartment so she could split her time between the music and being mommy. Mason and Nathaniel were instant friends and were soon inseparable, often only making a fuss when it was time for Vanessa to leave for the night. Lana insisted that it wouldn't be their 'Bitter Break-Up' album.

"Just because it's hard for me to sing a love song doesn't mean every song has to be bitter and heartbroken."

Karen murmured, "After everything you took when you walked out on me... the last thing... won't..."

Lana said, "After everything you took when you closed the door, you won't stop me from singing the way I did before."

They smiled at each other over the notebook before Karen wrote down the lyrics. They knew that a lot of them would remain unfinished, get discarded, or a few might blend to become a single song before they were done. Currently they had enough for two ten-song albums, but Karen wanted more. She pointed out the 'farewell package' they had released with *Fallout*, which had sold well but she still thought was extravagantly overpriced.

"People paid a lot for that album, for the bells and whistles, thinking it would be the last chance to support us for a while. We need to make sure the free album is substantial."

Lana agreed. When Karen suggested doing a dry run of some songs, Lana put her off. "I think we need to wait until we're actually in the space. We don't want to find something that works and then wait three weeks to record it."

"Okay. I guess." Karen thought it was more likely they would reach the studios and their lack of rehearsal would be jarring. They hadn't played together as a band for two years. There were bound to be kinks to work out. So instead of arguing she deferred to Lana's judgment and continued building their new playlist. Their sixteen snippets turned into eleven solid songs, then nine, then ballooned back up to seventeen. Lana was helping to write since she felt as if she was slacking in the music department, and she feared that her songs were too morbid or inordinately centered on her breakup.

By the time Naomi called to let them know it was time to head north, Karen had printed out twenty pages of lyrics. They drove to the Rabbit's Warren in a convoy. Laura drove Karen and Mason, Lana was in Codie's truck with the instruments and most of the luggage, while Vanessa was driving herself and Scott up with Nathaniel. The plan was there would be a single family dinner on the first night, and then the following day would be work-time. Karen and Laura had worked out a schedule that would make sure she never had to go too long without seeing Mason, and she assumed Vanessa and Scott had a similar arrangement.

The cabin was just over an hour away from Seattle, on the outskirts of Snohomish. When Naomi described it as secluded they had all pictured some rustic log cabin sitting on the side of a mountain with forest all around it. The reality was that the cabin stood on a few acres of land surrounded by a small town. When they were on the property it would be very easy to shut out the rest of the world, but just a quick trip down the winding dirt road would take them back to civilization. They would just be a ten-minute walk from a coffee shop with free wifi.

Lana nodded her approval as the small town fell away behind a wall of trees. She breathed deep and let it out slowly. No traffic noise, no obvious signs of civilization, but all the comforts of the modern world just a few steps away. The main building was almost palatial, designed to look like a two-story A-frame barn with two annexes connected on either side. There was what appeared to be a stable at the far edge of the property, short and wide and open at both ends. It was separated from the house by a rocky creek spanned by a beautiful wooden footbridge.

Lana looked at Codie and saw she seemed to be just as enamored. "I think I could get used to this really easy."

"You and me both," Codie said, lifting her hand in greeting as Karen and Vanessa pulled up behind them. Naomi brought up the rear of the procession, having joined them as they were leaving Seattle. Lana had texted to let her know they were on the way up, and they coordinated so she could fall in line along the way. Now they could see she had brought a passenger along with her. The new arrival was a black woman with her head shaved on the sides and left slightly longer on top to give the impression of a Mohawk. She was dressed in gray cargo pants and an unbuttoned shirt over a T-shirt bearing the Assassin's Creed logo.

Naomi said, "Ladies! And one boy. And the babies." She smiled. "Glad to see you could all make it. I'd like to introduce to you Sidra Bird, and I swear her last name is not why I chose her to produce this album. She's new to Cartography, but she's the best we have."

Sidra smiled. "I'm sure the name helped, though. Right? Just a little?" She stepped forward and held her hand out to Lana. "I'm a big fan. Naomi didn't tell me I was going to be working with you, just that it was a big secret project."

"Well, now you know. You're sworn to secrecy now." She shook Sidra's hand. "Looking forward to working with you. I'm Lana~"

"Kent. And that's Karen Everett, Codie Renton, and Nessa Grace. Like I said, I'm a big fan."

Vanessa said, "I'm actually going by Vanessa Wayland now."

"Oh! Okay. Sorry about that. You can call me Sid, Sydney, Sidra, Ma'am. Whatever you feel most comfortable with."

"Gordon," Lana said. "I'd be comfortable with Gordon. Can I call you Gordon?"

Sidra winked at her. "No, you may not."

Naomi said, "Now that we've settled the introductions, let's go inside. We can worry about unloading everything later. I'll give you the penny tour. The house has four bedrooms, so with Sid here you're going to have to figure out~"

Lana said, "I'll take the couch."

"We can vote," Karen said.

"You and Vanessa will have babies and spouses here half the time. Sidra is only here because she's been hired to do a job for us. So it's between me and Codie, and I've been crashing in her guest room for a month. She deserves a private space. We can vote if you want, but I'm telling you right now, I'll veto it."

"Who says you get to veto?" Vanessa said.

"Lead singer. Veto power."

Vanessa shrugged. "If you insist, I'm not going to argue with you."

"Smart lady."

Naomi unlocked the door and then passed the keys to Lana. The room was a mixture of earthy browns and orange, with stone accents on the counters separating one space from the other. The furniture in the seating area was arranged around a fireplace rather than a television.

Naomi held out her hands to indicate the open plan of the ground floor, as well as the second story landing.

"And here we are. Ground floor is the living room, kitchen, dining room area. Two bedrooms in the back. The other two bedrooms are upstairs, along with the bathroom and the rec room-slash-lounge-slash whatever you need it to be. The basement is the main studio space, but there's also a second recording suite in the backyard. There's a hot tub on the back deck."

Codie said, "Hot tub? Screw the record, let's go soak!"

Naomi grinned and ushered them toward the living room. "All right, everyone. Sit down and listen. I have something to say. It's heartfelt and sincere, and I don't want any of you trying to diffuse that by being glib or cynical. Got it?"

Lana said, "Why are you looking at me?"

"Because I know you."

"Fair enough."

Sidra, Scott, and Laura stood off to the side as Naomi addressed the Canaries. "Ladies. Dash spent so long trying to claw her way to the top of a mountain where someone would notice her. When she started Cartography she wanted to use the lessons she'd learned to make the road a little easier for bands that truly deserved to be heard. She was amazed by how many she found, including the Femme Reapers." She smiled at Laura. "I don't want you to think this praisefest is in any way diminishing how we feel about you and your sister."

Laura smiled at winked at Karen. "Hey, we know there's a hierarchy. Radiation Canary has worked hard the past ten years. They earned the praisefest."

Naomi said, "In all her time fostering new acts, she never found the one that truly spoke to her. She wanted to find a band that could fill the void left over by her if she ever chose to retire." She looked down and took a moment. "She passed away before that could happen, of course. But not before she discovered the band that she thought most exemplified everything she tried to do with Cartography. She told me that you four were the future of the label, and I wholeheartedly agree.

"Dash never told us what to do with the Rabbit's Warren. It was passed to the label by her will, but it's a bit inconvenient to act as a secondary studio. We have the schoolhouse in Port Townsend and that works well for us. So this place has been sitting unused since the last time Dash was here in 2008. Seven years it's been waiting to fulfill its purpose. And I think it's appropriate that you end your hiatus here. I've decided in honor of having the new Radiation Canary recorded in these hallowed halls, this studio will no longer be known as the Rabbit's Warren. From now on it will be the Coal Mine."

A grin spread across Lana's face. "That's a huge honor."

"Canaries in the Coal Mine," Karen said.

Vanessa nodded. "Album title, The Coal Mine Sessions."

Lana clapped her hands together. "Done. That's it. We're going with it."

Naomi laughed. "Glad to see everyone is onboard. For now, I'll leave you to it. I have a ferry to catch, so if you don't need anything else."

"Whoa," Lana said. "Where do you think you're going?"

"The... place I just said I was going. I need to get back to Port Townsend."

Lana stood up and put her hands on Naomi's shoulders. "The only reason we're here right now is because of you. I don't think you get that, or give yourself enough credit for it. You found us. You put us on Dash's radar. You made us who we are today. We're just the trained monkeys who write and play the music. There are a thousand bands in Seattle alone who could do that. The difference is that you took us under your wing and guided us. You were there every step of the way building the footpath while we were walking on it. If it wasn't for you we would have fallen flat on our faces."

Karen said, "Lana's right. We don't say it enough, Naomi, but you held this band together in those early days. A thousand things could have gone wrong and kept us from getting an album out. You made sure we got past them."

Lana nodded. "You're the fifth Canary, Naomi. And we'd be honored if you stayed and had the family dinner with us tonight."

Naomi pushed her glasses up and rubbed the bridge of her nose. "Thank you. I really do have to get back to Port Townsend. I wish I didn't. Thank you from the bottom of my heart." She kissed Lana's cheek. "I'll be back up here soon. I'll bring Susan, we'll have a whole night of it. Be sure you sing my praises where she can hear them."

Lana said, "Will do. Go on. Guide the next flock of Radiation Canaries into the studio so they can usurp our position."

"Fingers crossed." She squeezed Sidra's shoulder as she passed, then paused to give Laura a hug. "Keep me updated!"

"Will do, captain."

Lana escorted her outside. In the twilight, insects had crawled out of wherever they hid during the day to start chirping and whizzing around through the air. Lana swatted one away from her face as she checked to make sure no one had followed them. "Do you mind if I ask you a question?"

"Sure."

"Did Dash ever..." She tried to think of a way to phrase her question without panicking Naomi. "The breakup is hitting me hard. I'm worried it might affect the music. Did Dash ever go through anything like that?"

"A bad breakup?" Naomi scoffed. "The woman was practically

addicted to them. There were times when it affected her music. She would write maudlin breakup songs and entire albums were dedicated to getting back on her feet."

Lana looked back at the cabin. "That's what I'm worried about. I don't want this album to be about me. It's supposed to be our return, not my damn diary."

"Do you trust those girls in there?"

"Of course."

"Then that's all you have to do. Just trust them, Lana. They'll take care of you, just like you take care of them. The way you took the couch so everyone else could have their own room. The way all of you made sure Karen retained the rights to the lyrics she wrote. Even at the very beginning, each member of this band looked out for the other three first. That's why you're still together after all these years. That's why you'll still be together ten years from now. Trust them."

Lana nodded. "Okay."

"And trust Sid. I didn't want to say it in front of her, but she's a damn artist. She won't force anything on you. She's good at cooperating, not so good at the big picture stuff, but she really is the best."

"I'll keep that in mind."

"Good luck. Call me if you need any pep talks."

Lana stepped back and waved as Naomi backed up and disappeared on the dirt driveway back to the main road. She took a moment to look around the property. The trees were thick enough to block out the minimal noise from the nearby town. It was a safe place, and it was as close as they could get to pure wilderness without giving up some vital necessities. She looked straight up and saw a sky free of electrical wires, although she could see contrails of planes that had recently flown over. She had spent too much time in cities. Being out in the wild could be exactly what she needed to find her music again.

She heard the cabin door open and saw Codie and Simon making their way toward the cars. Codie waved her over. "Come on. First one unpacked gets to choose the temperature for the hot tub."

"I didn't bring a bathing suit."

"None of us did," Codie said. "That's what makes it so exciting."

Lana chuckled and went to join in the race. She wasn't about to get stuck freezing her ass off in a T-shirt and shorts.

In the end, they decided it would be impractical to use the hot tub until they got actual suits. They agreed they would buy some from a shop in town when they had to make a trip for groceries or other sundry supplies. Lana was grateful for the reprieve, and she was already mentally stretched out on the couch to take a quick catnap when Codie said, "I have an idea. Let's go down and inaugurate the studio. My drums and

Nessa's keyboard are already set up. We don't want to play it cold for the very first recording. It doesn't have to be anything real. Just a quick jam session. We need to let the room get used to music again."

Karen said, "That's a great idea."

Lana looked at her guitar case as if anticipating its betrayal. She picked it up by the neck and nodded. "Yeah. Let's go down and see what happens."

Sidra chuckled and rubbed her hands together. "A Radiation Canary jam session. This trip has already paid for itself. I can't wait to hear this."

They trudged downstairs with Lana bringing up the rear. The studio was a cathedral to sound, and the whole group paused for a moment to appreciate what Dash had given to them. The microphones were in the center of the room, with isolation booths in either corner if the ambient noise of the house required them to redo vocals. The production booth ran along the wall next to the stairs.

Lana walked to the main microphone and stared at it for a moment. "This was the last place Dash Warren recorded. That's really humbling."

They took a moment of silence before Lana gave them a small nod to indicate she was done paying her respects. Scott, Sidra, Laura, and the babies isolated themselves in the production booth as Lana removed her guitar from its case and draped the strap over her shoulder. Karen had asked if they preferred violin or cello for the occasion, and they left the choice up to her. She brought both down, but she put the cello aside and prepared her violin.

Lana felt the cool, smooth curve of her guitar against her abdomen. She took a deep breath and could feel it pressing back against her when she exhaled. She closed her eyes and let her hands fall into the proper position. She could hear the squeak of Codie's stool as she adjusted her position and she knew Codie was pinching her sticks between the thumb and forefinger of her left hand as she waited for her cue. She could feel Karen and Vanessa staring at her, as well as the eyes of everyone in the booth. Her thumb trembled on the string. She pressed her lips together and furrowed her brow.

"Is everything okay?" Sidra asked through the intercom.

"Yeah. Just... just need a second."

She thought of the other times in her life when she thought she would never play again. She thought of the dark days after her mother died, when everyone told her she needed to talk or cry or be around people. She couldn't talk, because her voice wasn't strong enough to say what needed to be said. She couldn't cry because she didn't have even tears. So she picked up a guitar, she strapped it on, and she played without knowing what chords she hit. She just played until her fingers were blistered and raw. When she came out of the trance she was on her knees, sobbing, and she still couldn't stop playing.

"I'm going to start us slow," she said. "Karen, I want you to come in next. Then Vanessa. We'll go back and forth, raising the tempo every... every eight beats until Codie comes in to bring us home. Then we'll go from there. Sound good?"

"Take us away, fearless leader," Codie said.

Lana smiled, held her breath, and dropped her thumb over the strings. She played an A, transitioned to C minor, then came back to A. She riffed for a moment before she turned on her heel and walked to Karen's position. She had her violin up, bow at the ready, and when Lana looked up she began playing. Lana shifted to E and Karen followed her seamlessly. Behind her, Vanessa added her voice to the mix. Lana played her way over to stand in front of the keyboard as it started to drown out the violin. Karen responded by shifting to a higher key, and Vanessa matched her with a wicked grin.

Lana felt tears on her face as she stood between them, their battle washing over her as she continued to set the rhythm. She heard Codie tapping out an extremely subtle beat but she was still surprised when she kicked it into full gear. Lana felt the music in her skin, her fingers moving over the frets without hesitation. She bent her knees and leaned forward over the guitar, her hair falling off one shoulder as she spun to aim the neck of her guitar at Karen.

The cymbals crashed, the violin sighed, and Vanessa set down a gentle bed on which everything rose and fell like riding the crest of a wave. She laughed and straightened up again to face the microphone. Through the glass of the production booth she saw Laura holding Mason, rocking her hips back and forth to the music. She took the baby's hand to point at Karen, and the baby grinned and swayed in his mother's arms. Her voice was bottled up inside of her, aching to get out, and she remembered the words to one of the songs Karen had sent her months earlier. She wet her lips and, even though she had no idea if the microphone was even plugged in, she began singing.

"And I won't take my eyes off you," she sang, "To the edge of the world, I'd follow you. Where the lighthouse can't reach, on some dark and foreign beach. In an undiscovered place. I will run to you, I will fall to you. My reward will be one glimpse of your face."

The song swept up into a natural crescendo, and Lana played them out. Codie rocked back on her stool, Vanessa linked her hands behind her neck, and Karen smiled at Lana as she lowered the violin to her side. Breathless, Lana pushed her hair out of her face and looked into the booth.

Sidra leaned toward the microphone. "I think it's safe to say Radiation Canary is not back."

Lana stared at her in disbelief. "Are you crazy?"

"Nah. To be back, you'd have to have gone somewhere. I just heard the Radiation Canary I fell in love with. No cobwebs on you."

Lana grinned and looked at the rest of her band. She was giddy to have the music back, to have proven there was hope. She played a quick riff just to prove that she could, overjoyed that there was no hesitation whatsoever when her fingers touched the strings this time. It was the first proof that while Catherine may have taken a lot away when she left, there was still one thing she hadn't gotten away with.

She looked at Karen, Codie, and Vanessa, then turned to look into the production booth.

"Well, okay then. Let's make a record."

## CHAPTER SEVEN

WITH THE musical ice broken, they decided they should finish settling in upstairs before they actually started recording. They would spend the evening relaxing and getting used to the space, then in the morning they could attack the album at full strength rather than with the dregs of their road trip adrenaline.

The bedrooms all seemed more or less identical; queen bed, twin nightstands, a TV in an entertainment system, and a great view no matter which side of the house it happened to look out on. The main difference was that the downstairs shared a bathroom while upstairs each had its own en-suite bathroom. It was decided without a vote than Karen and Vanessa, by dint of occasionally having children with them, would get those simply for convenience. Scott declared himself the pack mule for the house, carrying everyone's suitcases upstairs and depositing them in the proper rooms.

When he was gone, Laura sat by the window to give the baby his lunch while Karen unpacked. "It's not that I mind having the nicest bedroom in the house," Karen said as she hung their blouses in the closet, "it's just that I'd feel guilty if we end up being here for two months and Lana has to sleep on the couch that whole time."

"Mm-hmm."

Karen looked over her shoulder. Laura was stroking Mason's hair with one hand but looking out the window. "Honey?"

Laura looked at her and raised an eyebrow.

"What's wrong?"

"Nothing." She focused on the baby. "I'm sure you'll think of something."

"Honey," Karen said again. "What's wrong?"

Laura rocked Mason. "You guys sounded amazing today. Seriously, like you hadn't been apart for one day, let alone two years. Even after Lana's hiccup…"

"Well, she's had a rough time lately." She hung another blouse. "So why is that making you maudlin? Is it because of what Naomi said?"

Laura smiled. "No. She was on the mark there. Femme Reapers are one thing, but you four took it to a whole new level."

Karen crossed the room and knelt beside the chair. She stroked their son's arm with one hand, her wife's leg with the other. "So? Talk to me, sweetheart."

Laura looked at her. "In a couple of days, I'm taking our baby back to Seattle to work on the new album. And you'll be up here. With her."

"Oh."

"I know. I'm sorry. I thought I was done being jealous and angry about what happened. For a while, I was. But now she's single again…"

"But I'm not."

"You weren't last time, either."

Karen looked at Mason.

"I'm sorry, honey. I'm only angry at myself for feeling this way. You've proven time and again that I don't have anything to worry about. I know Lana is in your past. I know that you would slit both your wrists before you hurt me or Mason. But when I think about going home and leaving you two up here, I get queasy and upset."

"Naomi mentioned there's a recording studio out back," Karen said. "You could bring Ella up here and work on your album here."

Laura smiled. "The house is already crowded as it is. And you don't need me keeping an eye on you." She leaned forward to rest her forehead against Karen's. "I know in my heart exactly where you stand. I know in my heart where I stand. And I know that nothing will happen with Lana. I just need to get the message to my brain."

Karen kissed Laura's nose. "If you ever need a reminder, it's only an hour to Seattle. I can swing down, give you a hug, and then drive back up before anyone notices I'm gone."

"If you're making a two-hour round trip, you'd better do more than hug me when you show up."

Karen smiled. "Fine. I'll drag you into a broom closet and ravage you."

"Better."

Karen bent down and kissed Mason's forehead. He cooed and reached up to knock his fist against her jaw, squirming against Laura's chest.

"I think he needs to be burped."

"I think you're right."

Karen gave her a towel for her shoulder and stood up. "The album shouldn't take us very long to finish. We have most of the writing done. All we have to do is polish off a few lyrics, record it, and then I can come home. We've always been really fast when it comes to actually recording."

"I don't know." She looked out the window." Working here could tempt anyone to slow down a little just so they don't have to leave. This place is amazing."

"I like the view better at home," Karen said.

Laura shrugged. "Seattle is beautiful."

"I wasn't talking about Seattle."

"Sweet talker."

Karen smiled, stroked Laura's hair, and went back to unpacking. "Dinner is at six-thirty, Scott and Vanessa said they would cook for us, so we have time if you want to take a family nap."

"I think that sounds good." She looked at Mason and stroked his cheek. His eyes - large and blue, like Karen's - seemed heavy. "I think he's about tuckered, too."

"I'll go warn everyone we're about to have a sleeping baby in the house."

Laura smiled and took Mason to the crib, getting him settled in as Karen left the room. He swung his arms in the air but she could tell he was moments away from a crash. He was twelve months old, and they were well aware of his cycle. She teased his cheeks with her finger and then stroked his stomach. "Mommy's pretty silly, huh? Thinking Mama is going to be bad again. Even you know better than that, don't you?"

Mason stared up at her and she chuckled as she tucked him in.

"Yeah. But then you're the smartest baby in the whole world, so that doesn't count..."

When Karen told them the Everetts were taking a siesta, Vanessa decided to take Nathaniel for a quick walk around the grounds. She wanted him to be comfortable in the new environment and it seemed like the perfect opportunity to explore. She bundled him up in his coat and took his hand to guide him out the back door onto the deck. The hot tub was to the right of the back door in a fenced-off area that also boasted a barbeque. Scott saw the grill and she could tell he was already plotting a few meal ideas as they led the baby down the wooden stairs to the grass.

"Do you think we have to worry about any wild animals?" Vanessa asked.

"I think I saw an opossum on the road when we were driving up."

"I've never seen one of those in real life."

Scott said, "Horrible little things. They look like cats, but then they turn around and they have the stretched-face, black-eyed demon face from *Beetlejuice*."

Vanessa shuddered and squeaked. "Oh, don't remind me. That traumatized me when I was little."

He smiled and put an arm around her. They walked toward the jagged tear in the ground that cut off one corner of the clearing. When they were close enough to hear the water trickling over the rocks and black dirt in the creek bed, they stopped so Nathaniel could see the water. They were careful to stay far enough back so he wouldn't tumble in. It was only about two feet deep, but that was more than enough to have real consequences.

Scott looked at her and nudged her arm. "So. That was kind of amazing today."

"What was?"

"The music. I mean, I've seen you play before, but I guess I never realized just how much you needed it. I thought it was just a job. I never considered how much you were giving up for me and this little dude."

Vanessa said, "I didn't give anything up. I just rearranged my priorities."

"Whatever you say. Look... I know you don't need it, but I also know that being a member of the band will be a huge commitment. You're going to be spending weeks, maybe months up here away from home. That's going to be a burden, but we can deal with that. We'll make it work if it's worth it."

She smiled and finished the mantra they'd made up at the beginning of their marriage. "And this is worth it, so work it." She turned to face him, still holding Nathaniel's left hand with her right. "It'll be a lot of hours away from home. And that's just recording the album. Once it's out, we're going to have to tour. It's going to put a lot of pressure on you."

"You have talent, Ness. Crazy talent. I appreciate the rest of the band saying they'll use a substitute when they need to, but I think they would suffer for it. I think they know that, too. Don't worry about being fair to me. Hell, don't even worry about being fair to them. They'll do what they have to do, and I'll do what I need to do. And we'll all do it happily as long as you make the decision that's right for you."

Vanessa smiled and looked down at Nathaniel. "I live with two of the best boys I've ever known, and I work with three of the best girls. How'd I get so lucky?"

He put an arm around her shoulder and the three of them started walking toward the woods. "Well, a long time ago, when you were just a baby, you captured a fairy. And she said that if you let her go she would grant you three wishes. You got me, you got the band, and you got

Nathaniel. So you're all set now. Let's go see how far this creek goes."

Vanessa put her head on his shoulder. "If we see any opossums, will you protect me?"

"Hell no. I'll knock you down in the mud and save myself."

"Will you at least take Nate?"

"I'll think about it."

Vanessa cupped the back of his head and playfully twisted it as they followed the winding path of the water into the woods.

After dinner, the band adjourned to the upstairs lounge to work on songs. First, they set up the ground rules. "No social media," Lana said. "No tweeting about secret projects to tease the fans, no alluding to something big coming up. I don't want anyone to post a single picture of the studio, any of us, nothing that might start the rumor mill. Feel free to take the pictures and save them on your phone, or keep a diary. Just wait until everything is officially announced before you share them. It sounds unreasonable to say it out loud, but~"

Codie said, "You don't want to overhype it. The buildup might crash this thing before it starts."

"Exactly. I want it to be... 'Radiation Canary is back, they have a new album, and it's free, and you can go get it right now.' Patience is for chumps."

Karen chuckled. "Okay. Now that we have the gag order in place..." She revealed printouts of the lyrics from her file. Most of the snippets had only been passed back and forth between Lana and Karen, so the purpose of the meeting was to get Vanessa and Codie's input. Laura was invited to sit in as an honorary band member and Lana invited her to play on any songs that might require a bass. Laura agreed, but only if she got to borrow Karen for the next Femme Reapers album.

Lana said, "I hear her contract is strict, but I think you two can work out something that works for both of you."

"I can think of some alternative compensation," Karen said.

Sidra offered to distract Scott and the boys with her laptop, which was filled to bursting with video games. They had set up a gaming station on the other side of the room where they tried to keep their voices down so as not to distract the artists.

Karen decided they should first work on the snippet Lana had sung. "I know we were just riffing down there, but it sounded great. It was perfect for those lyrics. We should take what we had and expand it into the full song." She went through the printouts until she found the one in question. "I have it labeled as Sailmaker, but that can be fiddled with."

Lana said, "I liked the build-up. So we start slow. Not a ballad, just steady and calm. The lyrics we have are about, ah, about chasing someone down. Searching for someone who is missing. So the first few verses can introduce the narrator and explain what she's looking for..."

They went back and forth bouncing ideas off one another. Codie and Vanessa contributed musical beats to the proceedings, suggesting when they could start to build to the bridge. They were almost done when Karen was summoned for Mason's bedtime lullaby, and Vanessa excused herself to help Scott read Nathaniel a story. Codie offered to drive into town on a reconnaissance mission - "We must know what the beer and ice cream situation is before we get too settled in." - and Lana was left alone with Sidra.

The couch Lana was on formed a cube with a loveseat and two armchairs, and she was slumped down in the center with her feet up on the coffee table. Lana had the printouts from Karen's computer spread out to either side of her, pen closed in her teeth as she examined them for lyrical inspiration. About five feet away at the gaming table, Sidra was still tapping at her laptop as she played the game she'd been demonstrating for the boys.

"That was amazing for me, by the way."

"Hm?" Lana said. She'd mostly forgotten the producer was there.

Sidra kept her eyes on the screen. "Watching the four of you break down a song. It was really wild. And you don't have to worry about me giving away your secret. Mum's the word."

"Thanks." She twisted to look over the back of the couch. "Hey, what do you *want* us to call you? You said Sid, Sidra, Sydney... what do you prefer?"

She shrugged. "I answer to all of them. Sid is from when I was little and didn't want to be the kid with the weird name. Sydney came from high school."

Lana sank back onto the couch. "I'll call you Sidra. I don't like nicknaming someone just because their name is unique. Unique names are amazing."

"Thank you, Layno."

Lana chuckled.

"Listen, I really don't mind sleeping on couches. I couch-surfed for two whole years after college, so I'm completely used to it."

"Don't try to guilt me into giving you my sweet, sweet couch. You chose the bedroom and now you're stuck with it."

Sidra laughed. "Okay. But the offer stands."

"I appreciate it." She sat up and stretched. "I think I'm going downstairs now, in fact. I'll see you tomorrow. It'll be the official first day for the Coal Mine Sessions."

"Love the name."

Lana stretched her back, waved goodbye to Sidra, and took herself downstairs. The main lights were off, but the kitchen light cast a wide enough wedge of orange-yellow light for her to see. She had found blankets and pillows in the linen closet and used them to turn the couch into a makeshift bed. Normally she would have slept as close to naked as possible, but given the fact she would be sleeping in a heavily trafficked area made her rethink that practice. She chose a pair of shorts and a tank top, setting them aside to put on after she showered.

She heard someone coming downstairs and turned to see Laura descending with two bottles in her hand. "Going to bed already?"

Lana nodded toward the back of the cabin. "I'm about to go take a shower while Codie's out. Did Mason go to sleep?"

"Karen's music always knocks him right out."

Lana smiled. "What's in the bottles?"

"Ah... milk."

"Oh."

Laura put them in the fridge. "Yeah. Don't worry. I labeled them properly. Don't want an awkward bowl of Cheerios in the morning. Goodnight. Sleep well."

"You too."

Lana waited until she was gone before she took out her phone and opened Twitter. She was logged into the official Radiation Canary account, but she switched to her anonymous personal account before she went stalking. Catherine had two accounts: one verified that she used to interact with her fans, and another private account under a pseudonym. Lana went to the personal account and scrolled down to see what the former love of her life had been tweeting in the past three months.

Not long after telling Lana to pack her things, Catherine's show had been filming on location in Spain. Then a brief European tour promoting the upcoming season. There were pictures and Instagram pictures and Vines showing all the insanity. Lana left the videos on mute, but she watched them all. Six second loops of Catherine looking into the camera and smiling as she said something. Hair whipping across her face, eyes squinting against the sun.

Three weeks earlier, about to board a plane to Scotland: "Bad weather, folks! Eeep! Say a prayer, if you've got one!" And then a winking emoji.

Lana felt furious, but she wasn't entirely certain why. They hadn't gone public with their breakup, and Catherine had certainly quoted Radiation Canary lyrics before. People found it cute that she was a fan of her girlfriend's work. It was the same way they reaction when a paparazzo took a photo of Lana wearing a T-shirt with Catherine's character on it. She idly wondered if she still had that shirt and, if she did, if it would be better to use it as a nightshirt or ritualistically burn the damn thing.

She scrolled higher, to a week before. A tweet at two in the morning local time, one word: "sad."

"I hope you are," Lana whispered, fist pressed hard against her cheek. She scrolled higher, part of her looking for a continuation of the depressed tweet. An apology, a quiet request to get in touch so they could work things out, but instead she found a selfie taken in the kitchen at the new apartment. The phone was being held up over her head and angled down to reveal the food cooking on the stove, but Lana's attention was focused on the very top right corner of the frame. A sliver of floor visible next to Catherine's head, just exposed enough to reveal one bare foot and a slender leg.

Lana closed her eyes and let the phone fall, moving her arm just enough to make sure it landed softly on the couch rather than hitting the floor. She bent forward, fingers linked on the back of her neck, and fought back the tears as her mind filled with the image of Catherine having dinner with someone in their apartment. Was it Sexy Lexi? Did it matter?

Upstairs she heard Scott laugh. One of the showers upstairs was also running; Karen or Laura or Vanessa taking a shower. Happy families, happy couples, all pulled out of their real lives because she was being selfish. She had nothing, so of course she would want to turn back the clock to a time when she was on top of the world.

Sidra came downstairs. "Night, Lana." She paused. "Lana? Everything okay?"

"Yeah. Just... headache."

"Aw. I have some aspirin if you need it. I'll leave the bottle in the downstairs bathroom."

"Thanks." She lifted her head and pressed the heel of her hand to one eye. "I appreciate it."

"Sure thing. Sweet dreams."

Lana reached into her bag and dug around until she found a notepad. She flipped to a blank page, sniffled, and rested her pen on the page. "Everyone is finding their own," she wrote, "I thought I'd found mine but I was wrong. I knew I found my soul mate and she was certain she hadn't. I'm tired at the thought of starting over, not sure that I can." She closed her eyes and moved her thumb into her mouth, nibbling on the tip of it. "I'm lying all alone when the day is done. I'm terrified of ending up as no one's Someone."

She touched the tip of her tongue to her top lip and flipped the notebook to one of the back pages. It was far enough to the back she doubted anyone would have found it by accident, but the book fell open to the proper page due to how often she worked on it. The page was filled with black ink, scratched-out phrases, notes to herself, and a single paragraph in the center.

"I didn't think I'd be good at this, so I actually wrote the whole thing down." She skimmed. "...our ups and downs... no one else I'd rather... followed you to England, follow you anywhere... Catherine Diehl, will you marry me?"

She stared at the speech she'd never had a chance to give. She carefully tore it out, leaving the little pieces in the binding. She tossed the notebook onto the coffee table and held the paper in both hands. She tore it in half, in half again, and then shredded the remaining pieces. She had been building up to giving the speech for close to a year. She'd agonized over every word and phrase, more than any song she'd ever written. Now she was choking on the words she hadn't gotten a chance to say. Even now that she knew the answer would be no, there was something tragic in the anticlimax.

Lana cleared off the couch and curled on her side, forgetting about the shower or changing into her pajamas. She pretended to be asleep when Codie came back, and she remained where she was as the rest of the cabin put itself to bed around her. Soon the house was dark and silent, and Lana pulled the blanket up over her head so no one who came downstairs would see if she cried during the night.

## CHAPTER EIGHT

THE DREAM was a memory, but even knowing that didn't help her stop it. She and Catherine were returning from an awards show where they had acted as glorified seat fillers. Catherine wasn't up for any awards but she was there to look good for the camera. They'd had an argument at the ceremony but they couldn't really get into it until the ride home. The reason for the fight was lost to Lana's subconscious, so she only remembered angry words as Catherine slapped on the light and spun to face her in the entryway. Lana had responded, and Catherine had grabbed the front of Lana's jacket to press her against the wall.

Then they were kissing, Lana's face still contorted in anger even as she unbuttoned the leather pant she'd worn to the party. Catherine broke the kiss and got down on her knees to work the pants down Lana's thighs, and Lana had pushed Catherine's head against her crotch. Catherine took the hint, and Lana writhed against the wall as her underwear was pulled away to give Catherine's mouth room to attack.

The dream faded to another instance, another fight, and the silent treatment that ended when Lana gave Catherine a backrub that soon strayed below the waist. That time they had sex on the couch, but there were very few surfaces in their apartment that they hadn't made use of. When they moved Lana joked that Catherine was just looking for new locations to have sex. The bed, of course, and the shower, the strip of tile between the kitchen island and the stove, once in the laundry room, once in Catherine's car parked in the back parking lot of the building.

However else they might have failed in the relationship department, they were fantastic at the sex.

A sound from the kitchen woke her, pulling her up out of the dream to realize that she had moved a pillow between her legs at some point during the dream. She hoped the blanket had disguised any thrusting she might have been doing as she moved the pillow back up to the arm of the couch and slowly sat up. It was ridiculously early, the light coming in through the curtains still blue and gray. Her feet were freezing so she bent down and pulled on her socks even before she stretched and turned to see who was in the kitchen.

Vanessa smiled sheepishly. "Sorry. Nate had me up early, so I thought I'd get started on breakfast."

"It's okay." She ran her fingers through her hair and grimaced at the tangles she found.

It was their fifth day at the cabin, so she was getting used to people in search of food acting as her alarm clock. They had spent the past four days in a blur of writing and recording for the new album. They already had two songs pretty much completed and Lana was already prepared to join Naomi in singing the praises of Sidra to anyone who would listen. The woman was a goddess among producers. She didn't intrude on the songs, didn't pretty them up any more than necessary. She showed her talent with a light but generous hand. Lana was prepared to ask for Sidra on any future albums they did based on what she'd done with those first songs.

She stood up and stretched. "I'm going to take a shower."

Vanessa said, "Okay. Last night Karen and Codie said something about going for a jog this morning. Were you going to join them?"

"No. You?"

Vanessa shook her head. "I do tai chi."

"You do? Since when?"

"Since Nathaniel. You're welcome to join me."

Lana shrugged. "If you don't mind doing them with someone who looks like she just learned how to stand up."

Vanessa smiled and glanced at her, then did an honest to goodness double-take. "Wow. You're gorgeous without makeup."

Lana smiled. "You're still half-asleep. You're hallucinating." She squeezed Vanessa's arm as she went past and went into the bathroom. Codie and Sidra had each colonized the space on either side of the sink with toiletries and sundries. Lana stood in front of the mirror and looked at her reflection to see what had prompted Vanessa's compliment. She made an O with her mouth and dropped her jaw, widened her eyes, and turned her head one way and then the other. No makeup, hair completely destroyed, bags under her eyes. This was the kind of look tabloids paid big bucks for. She wondered how much they would pay for a picture of how she looked at that very moment.

"Gives new meaning to the term 'face value'..."

When she got out of the shower she dressed and went into the living room. Karen, Laura, and Scott were sitting around the table with the children seated in high chairs within easy reach of their mothers. Lana offered them a hurried 'good morning' as she went back to her nest. She dug out her notebook and quickly scribbled what she had been singing in the shower. "Paint up my face, I'm your work of art. Spend an hour on my hair before we're ready to start. If I take off my mask and show myself true, would you still appreciate my face value?"

When she finished, she took the pad to the dinner table and put it down next to Karen's plate. She served herself from the plates Vanessa had left on the counter, then sat down next to Scott. Karen was still looking at the lyrics. The fingers of her left hand were subconsciously moving as if she was playing a melody.

Karen said, "Naomi would probably want us to do the video without makeup."

Lana shrugged. "I'm fine with that. And you guys don't have anything to worry about, but if you'd prefer not to..."

"No, I like the message," Karen said. "I want to work on it later today. Were you happy with where we left 'Imaginary Cities'?"

Lana nodded. "I think it's as complete as it'll get. It sounded fantastic to me."

"I agree." She flipped through a few pages of Lana's notebook and scanned the other lyrics she had written. She read one and covered the page with her hand. "Oh. Sorry, these are personal."

"No," Lana said. "I mean, yeah. But if you like something there..."

"Are you sure?"

Lana shrugged. "I said I didn't want this to be a bitter breakup record, but I'm willing to share. Which one are you looking at?"

Karen pointed and passed it to her over the table instead of reading it out loud.

*"Your elbow in my softest places*
*The pillows left creases on our faces*
*Your breath was bad, but mine was worse*
*We thought we found a steady course*
*Buried together in the sheets*
*Blankets covering all but our feet*
*That was the place we'd have killed to stay*
*But we had to rise and face the breaking of the day."*

Lana nodded. "We can use this if you want." Codie came out of her bedroom then wearing a pair of briefs and a tank top. Lana whistled before she reached the end of the hallway. "There's a boy in the room, Miss Renton."

Codie stopped and balanced on the balls of her feet, waved a thank-you, and turned back to dress more appropriately for mixed company.

"Spoil-sport," Scott said. Vanessa elbowed him in the side, and he smiled at her.

Codie returned a few minutes later in sweatpants and a T-shirt. It was the last day for the boys to be there. Scott and Laura were packed up to head back to Seattle after lunch, and they would be taking the babies with them. Scott would come back up as often as he could, but Laura needed to get back to work on the Femme Reapers' new album. Lana assumed that was the reason Karen and Vanessa were being so touchy-feely with the babies at the moment.

"Are we still on for the jog?" Codie asked as she sat down with her food.

Karen nodded. "After breakfast or before lunch?"

"We'll see how I feel once I get these eggs in me."

Laura said, "How long do you guys figure you'll be up here?"

Lana shrugged. "We finished two songs in the first five days. How many did we end up with?"

Karen said, "We're up to twenty-three. We need to figure out how many will go on each album, but we definitely have enough for one. We may have time to work on the second one even after the freebie is released."

"I'm thinking twenty-six total, thirteen on each album."

Vanessa said, "Any particular reason?"

Lana shrugged. "Thirteen songs is a good size for an album. Ten seems too short, fifteen is too many. Thirteen is right in the sweet spot."

Vanessa agreed, so thirteen was established as their goal for *The Coal Mine Sessions*. That meant the second as-yet-untitled album still needed three songs, but those could be put on the back burner for the time being. They still hadn't figured out what the release schedule would be. Cartography might dictate that for them, but they didn't want to wait too long after the initial release. They would strike while the iron was hot to fully capitalize on the comeback buzz.

After breakfast Karen and Codie headed out for their jog. Lana, Scott, and the recently-awake Sidra went out on the deck so Vanessa could lead them in some rudimentary tai chi exercises. Lana surrendered quickly and watched until Karen and Codie got back from their runs. Karen lurched up onto the deck and collapsed with her head on Laura's lap.

"Next time I suggest going for a run, you can be sure someone is chasing me."

Codie smiled and slapped Karen's leg. "You did fine."

Karen sat up. "Tell her."

"I'll tell her later."

"We were talking about songs over breakfast. Tell her."

Lana said, "Am I her?"

"You are."

"Then tell her."

Codie used her sleeve to blot the sweat from her forehead. "I... wrote a song."

"You did?" Lana said.

Codie shrugged and sighed. "Sort of."

Vanessa said, "If it's anything like 'Walla Walla Sweetheart,' I want to hear it right now."

Codie shifted uncomfortably. "It's not a joke song. It's a... look, I don't even know what it is. But it means a lot to me. I'm not sure I'm ready to share it yet. I just mentioned it to Karen because you guys were saying we needed three more songs."

"Whenever you're ready, we'll treat it with the proper respect. We may joke about 'Sweetheart,' but it's a great song. I'm sure this one will be worthy, too."

"Thanks. And if I do eventually decide I want someone to sing it, you would be the only one I trust, Lana."

Lana nodded. "I'll wait until you think it's ready. For now... all you health freaks probably want to shower, so get on that. Then we'll reconvene downstairs in the studio so we can get to work. Sound good?"

"Sounds great." Karen patted Laura on the arm. "Carry me upstairs."

Laura got up and offered Karen her arm. While everyone else went to shower and change out of their workout clothes, Lana went downstairs to the studio. She strapped on her guitar and stood in the empty space, lightly strumming a random tune. She could hear water in the pipes from the downstairs shower and was inspired by the steady rhythm of it. She played her fingers across the strings as gently as she could, her eyes closed and head bowed as she tried to match the liquid gurgling. All of her anxiety was gone. The reluctance to play, the inability to begin a song, it was all an ancient memory.

She looked up when she caught movement in the corner of her eye and saw Sidra in the booth. She nodded at Lana as she sat down and started recording. Lana focused on the music until the water shut off. The red light went off right after she stopped playing, and Sidra whistled at her through the intercom.

"That was amazing. I don't know what we're going to do with it, but I thought you might want it saved for future reference."

"Thanks, Sid. I appreciate it."

The rest of the band joined them soon after, fresh from their showers. Karen had written another line to Lana's song - "Dawn breaks so hard you cut yourself on the pieces" - and Lana immediately added it to the chorus.

Laura brought Mason into the booth so he could hear his mother play one more time before they went home. Lana took a drink from her water bottle and turned to address the band.

"Let's try 'Cathedrals' once straight through just to hear how it sounds. We can go back and fiddle with it as needed."

Karen plucked a string. "No pun intended."

Lana smiled and stepped up to the microphone. They played the intro - piano and cello - and then Lana joined in as she sang the first vocals.

*"Earth's tallest cathedral is five hundred feet high*
*A monument of faith casts its shadow on those who worship*
*Throwing around echoes of the sermon*
*Ever-present in the corner of your eye*
*Elegant Gothic spires stretch their arms into the sky.*

*Another church shines red when the neon brightens*
*Standing all but empty on a corner by the liquor store*
*The preacher raises his voice above sirens*
*His congregation would rather listen to the barman*
*But he's there every Sunday and he won't be beaten*

*Everyone has their own private religion*
*Everyone prays to some kind of god*
*And there's some sort of heaven we hope to get in*
*So I've got next Sunday's confessions all written*
*And I'll have to hurry if I want to get everything in.*

*My faith is written by drunks and preached by a junkie*
*Our hymns come through the static on late-night radio*
*And our holy books gather dust in dark libraries*
*Let's read from Scripture, just you and me*
*The Book of Cervantes and the Gospel of Bowie."*

She stepped back from the microphone for the interlude, turning to face Vanessa. She moved to a lower key as Karen went higher, the cello overtaking the guitar to sweep them into the chorus. The song had been inspired by a particularly long red light when she found herself staring at the church described in the second verse. It made her think about the Vatican and Notre Dame, the stately and historic churches that towered over their landscapes, and she wondered what, if anything, made one church better than another.

Lana fully faced her band and smiled as she watched them play. Her friends, her family, her personal holy women. Years ago she had sworn she would never believe in anything or anyone again. Radiation Canary proved her wrong. Karen Everett, Codie Renton, Vanessa Grace Wayland. They were her rocks. They were who she could run to when she was hurting or frightened, and they were the three people in the world she knew she could always count on no matter what. They had given her back the music, and her voice, and for that she would forever be grateful to them.

At the end of the interlude she returned to the microphone. Through the glass she saw Laura dancing with Mason, and Sidra was bobbing her head to the beat. She couldn't believe she had nearly allowed Catherine to take this from her. She turned away from the microphone again, prolonging the interlude so she could look at Codie. Codie raised her eyebrows questioningly but didn't hesitate on the beat. Lana smiled at her, and Codie winked back.

Lana returned to the microphone to sing the rest of the song. With her guitar in front of her and her girls at her back, she knew there was nothing she couldn't overcome.

## Chapter Nine

SARAH WILEY was shooting a video that included motorcycles, muscle cars, and a drag race. Cartography had found an abandoned racetrack where the majority of the video could be done, and Naomi was on-set to watch the first day. Sarah was imminently talented but she could be a bit of a diva when she was shooting a video. It was really Naomi's fault. She had catered to Sarah when she was first starting out just to make sure the girl was comfortable. Now Sarah expected everyone working on the video to bend over backwards whenever she snapped her fingers. She was a good kid at heart. Naomi would just have to sit her down and have a conversation about proper behavior.

She was debating how best to approach the topic when her phone rang. "Naomi Marrow."

"Hey, Nay. What's going on?"

Naomi grimaced and stood up. She had been sitting in the stands to watch the crew set up, but she needed to be moving to deal with this conversation. "Martin. What rag are you working for now? Or have you devolved down to posting your ramblings on a personal blog?"

Martin Phillips was a gossip reporter and part-time paparazzo. He was the kind of guy who would follow a celebrity around on a scooter for three days just to get a picture of them taking out the trash in their sweats. When he laughed into the phone she pulled it away from her ear as if he could transmit something through the speakers.

"I get by, Nay, I get by. Listen, I'm hearing some rumors about your girls. I just wanted to know if you'd be willing to confirm it."

She bared her teeth. A rumor was nothing at this point, but she was livid that someone might have leaked. The girls had only been at the cabin for three weeks. She didn't know how much longer they needed, but if the rumor mill was already swirling... "I can't even pretend I know what you're talking about. What rumors? What are you making up this time?"

"Oh, the innocent game. Okay, I'll play along. Kitty Diehl."

Naomi stopped walking and frowned. She was so thrown by the change in topic that she didn't have to feign the confusion in her voice. "What about her?"

"She's been seen in London with Sexy Lexi, getting cozy, going to dinner together. Meanwhile Lana Kent is AWOL. I talked to some of my fellow shutterbugs and they say she hasn't been seen at their apartment in something like two months. The Cat and the Canary are on the outs, it seems."

Naomi shuffled through several responses at once. Lana and Catherine's breakup was bound to come out, and if it was a big enough story it could distract people from looking for the real headline. Before she could get too excited, Martin spoke again.

"And then there's the other thing."

"Oh, you're giving me a two-fer? How sweet, Martin."

He chuckled again. "Someone else has gone off the grid, it seems. Lots of people have seen Laura Everett around Seattle with the baby. But you know who is never with her?"

Naomi's heart rattled against her chest. She took off her glasses and pinched the bridge of her nose.

"So Lana Kent and Karen Everett... how did it happen this time? Kitty Diehl dumped Lana, so she went running back to her ex? Karen left Laura for Lana once before."

All pretense of professionalism faded from Naomi's voice. "If you print a word of this, it will be the end of your career. Do you understand me? Karen and Laura are fine. They're together and happy. Don't drag their names through the mud just so you can get a few clicks to whatever internet hellhole you're providing content for this month."

Martin snorted. "So you're telling me it's just a coincidence that Kitty Diehl has a new flame? At the same time Laura Everett is playing a single mom? And Karen and Lana are nowhere to be found? They disappeared together, Naomi. I don't even have to speculate. I can just print the facts and let the readers do the work for me."

"Don't, Martin. Okay? I can swear to you on a stack of Bibles that there is nothing going on between Karen Everett and Lana Kent. The Everett marriage is as strong as it's ever been."

"Then where is she? Why is her wife living alone and taking care of the baby by herself?"

Naomi leaned against the wall. "Is that what you do? Sit outside people's houses and track their comings and goings? What possible good can it do to fabricate an affair?"

"Hey, if people stopped clicking and tweeting and gobbling this shit up, I'd have to stop writing it. Until then, I'm posting the story. You want me to put you down as a no-comment?"

Naomi was breathing hard, angry at herself for getting into an argument with this weasel and angry at him for having such a shitty job. "No. I have a comment for you. Karen Everett is a proud supporter of Codie Renton's 'Westward Sky' program to help disadvantaged girls discover a love of flying. If you would like to donate or learn more about the charity, please visit their website."

Martin said, "That's your quote?"

"Might as well get some mileage out of whatever click-bait title you end up using. I'm not going to waste the opportunity by talking about some fantasy you concocted. Have a good afternoon, Martin. I hear the unemployment line is lovely this time of year. You should consider getting in it."

She cut off the call before he could respond and tapped the phone against her forehead. She did some mental shuffling of her schedule and tried to figure out when she had the time to go up and warn the girls about what was about to happen. She would have to drive up after the video shoot, and then she would have to drive back to catch a ferry home. The travel time alone would be at least four hours, not to mention however long she would have to spend at the cabin brainstorming ways to nip Martin's story in the bud. There was every chance she wouldn't get home until midnight.

Susan was going to kill her.


Tensions were running high in the Coal Mine. It was inevitable that five women living together in a house, even one that had three bathrooms, would eventually start getting on each other's nerves. It had been a week since Laura and the boys left. Karen spent most of the first day moping about how much she missed Mason, while Vanessa always had her phone nearby in case Scott texted her. Codie, Sidra, and Lana had just about had enough of sharing the downstairs bathroom. Lana was still sleeping on the couch despite a handful of attempts by Karen and Codie to switch with her.

"I'm fine where I am."

"Don't be a martyr," Codie said.

"I'm not being a martyr, I just don't feel the need to kick anyone out of their room."

"By suffering. Yeah. Definitely not a martyr. I don't know what I was thinking."

"Oh, go screw yourself."

They managed to keep their bickering out of the studio. As soon as they were in place, instruments in hand, all the petty disagreements faded away. Even then an innocent comment had the potential to balloon up into something worse.

"You know what they say," Vanessa said as they marched single-file up the stairs after a successful session. "Music has charms to soothe the savage breast."

"Beast," Karen said.

"No, I think it's breast."

"Why would it be breast?" Lana said. "That doesn't even make sense. Savage beast."

Codie said, "Karen's right."

"Oh, what do you know?" Vanessa said.

"I read."

Lana dropped herself onto the couch. "Yeah. Cereal boxes."

"Fuck you, princess."

Lana held her hand up and flipped Codie the bird. Vanessa had taken out her phone when they got upstairs and held the phone in Karen's face. "William Congreve, the savage breast."

Karen pushed Vanessa's hand away. "Congratulations. You're a genius."

Codie wandered into the kitchen and groaned when she saw a spoon had been left behind after breakfast. She held it aloft like a smoking gun. "How hard is it to wash a damn dish?"

"Are you sincerely asking?" Karen asked. "Because you haven't done a single load since we got up here."

When Naomi arrived a half hour later, Karen was stewing in her room, Vanessa was making dinner, while Codie and Sidra had put aside their war over the bathroom to play a game together on her computer. Lana was reading on the couch, so she was the only one who saw the headlights of Naomi's car as it came up the drive.

Naomi stood in the door and took in the stony silence. "Everything okay, ladies?"

"Roommates," Lana said. "We each have four of them. It's been two weeks." She shrugged. "We're not letting it affect the music."

"Okay." Naomi looked skeptical, but she was willing to let it slide. "Where's Karen? We need to have a band meeting."

Lana lifted her head toward the stairs. "Karen! Get your ass down here."

Naomi sighed. "Sure. Everything's fine here..."

Karen came downstairs already in her pajamas. "Hey. What's going on?"

"We have a small problem. It involves you. Well, you and Lana."

They looked at each other as Karen sat down in the armchair. Codie and Vanessa came in from the kitchen and sat in the living room, while Sidra lingered at the threshold between the two spaces. Naomi stood in front of them and explained what she'd learned from Martin. Lana tensed when she heard Catherine was already dating someone else, but she got angry when she found out where the gossip hounds had followed the trail.

"That's bullshit," Lana said.

Naomi nodded. "I agree. But like he said, he just has to print the facts. People are going to jump to conclusions without any help from him." She looked at Karen. "We have two options. The one I like least is simply announcing the album. It would ruin what you're trying to do, but it would also dispel any rumors that you two are shacking up together. I don't want to do that after everything we've done to keep it under wraps. So the best option, I think, is to take Karen back to Seattle. Just for a day or two. She can spend the weekend shopping with Laura and Mason, make sure she gets seen..."

"Use my family as a prop," Karen said.

Naomi sighed. "As disgusting as that sounds, yes. But it's not selling a false story. You love Laura and Mason. You would be with them if you could. Basically all I'm asking you to do is take a vacation. From the looks of things around here, you could definitely use a break from each other. Two days in town."

Lana looked at Karen, who had covered her face with both hands. When Mason was born, Karen and Laura kept a tight leash on any and all press about him. They referred to him as "Bug" in interviews because they didn't even feel comfortable having his name in print. They were fiercely protective of the boy, and rightly so. Now she was being asked to violate that privacy just to shut up a few bloggers?

"I'll do it," Lana said.

Everyone looked at her, but Naomi was the one who spoke. "You'll... do what?"

"I'll go back to Seattle and hang out with Laura. It would serve the same purpose, right? If Karen and I were having some illicit affair, I wouldn't be having lunch with her wife. At the very least it will confuse the matter enough that people won't jump to the easiest conclusion."

Naomi considered that angle and nodded slowly. "That could work. Actually, I think it would work better than sending Karen back. It doesn't have to be anything elaborate. Lunch, window-shopping, taking a stroll through the mall. It will defuse the situation and hopefully get people to move on to another story. I'll call Laura and set it up."

Karen said, "Does she already know what's going on?"

"No. I wanted to talk to you guys before I worried her about it."

"Let me talk to her first," Karen said. "If there's even a threat of gossip about me and Lana getting back together, I want her to hear it from me."

Naomi said, "That's fair."

Karen went to Lana and bent down to hug her. "Thank you."

"No sweat. I like Laura. It's no big deal to hang out with her for an afternoon."

Karen smiled and went upstairs to get her phone.

The conversation seemed to have dissipated the tension in the room, as presenting them with a common enemy had forced them to put aside whatever grievances they had to stand together. Vanessa rubbed her hands on her thighs and scooted to the edge of the couch. "I should go back and check on dinner. Naomi, you're welcome to join us."

"Thank you, but no." She checked her watch and exhaled sharply. "I have two ferries to catch. I'm not going to get home until tomorrow morning as it is. How is the album going?"

Lana said, "Really well. This past week has been really productive. Even if I have to take the weekend off to go back to Seattle for the press, I imagine we'll only need a few more weeks before we're ready to start putting it together."

Naomi grinned. "Fantastic. Nice to have some good news for a change." Karen came downstairs. "How did she take it?"

"Fine. Lana, she's free on Sunday if you want to do it then."

Lana nodded. "Works for me."

Naomi said, "Thanks, you guys. And I'm sorry for dumping this in your laps. I know you have enough to worry about and this is just an unnecessary distraction."

"We needed an unnecessary distraction," Codie said. "Otherwise we might have ripped each other's heads off."

"Do you need a mediator?" Naomi asked.

Lana shook her head. "No. You go home. You may only get to spend five minutes in your own bed, but I'm sure your wife is going to want those five minutes. We can take care of ourselves. We'll work something out."

Naomi used the restroom and took a thermos of orange juice for the road. When she was gone, Lana took her position to address the group.

"Now that we've broken the ice, we do need to address the fact we've been at each other's throats lately. We've kept it out of the studio so far, but we need to figure out how to address it before it gets any worse. I'm open to suggestions."

Sidra said, "Well... I may be out of line, since I'm not really a member of the band..."

"No, but you've been as annoying as anyone here," Codie said.

Sidra smiled. "Okay. There was a band I worked with a while back who had the same situation. They loved each other to pieces, but then they were forced to spend all day every day together and the friction just started to wear them all down. Arguments and little offenses, it started to add up. So the lead singer decided they needed a way to work out their frustrations in a safe manner that would also reinforce their bonds."

Codie threw her arms up. "Orgy!"

Lana grinned. "Sure. But no boys allowed."

"Cancel the orgy!"

Lana gestured at Sidra. "What's your idea?"

"I don't know how I feel about this," Karen said.

"What are you worried about?"

"Property damage. Grievous injuries."

"That's what the protective gear is for." She lifted her gun and checked the payload. "Besides, the paint is water-soluble. Even if it gets on our clothes or something, it'll get washed away."

Vanessa ran her finger over the trigger guard. "What if a deer comes wandering out while we're doing this? I don't want to paintball a deer."

"We'll be making enough noise that no wild animal is going to come anywhere near us."

They were standing on the front porch, each of them armed with a paintball gun. There was a store in town that rented the guns and protective gear, and Sidra offered to pay the rental fee so they could get out some of their aggression and frustration with one another without causing any real damage.

They had scattered coins of various amounts in the front yard. Codie and Sidra had volunteered to be the first runners. Codie because she wanted to set the bar high, and Sidra because she felt it was only fair since the game was her idea. They would run out into the yard with flashlights and gather as much money as they could in five minutes while the three gunners on the porch shot at them. Then Lana and Karen would put on the rest of their protective gear and take a turn as runners. Vanessa would go last, along with anyone who wanted a chance to raise their score. When the game was over they would count up each person's take. Whoever had the most money at the end of the game was the winner.

"Do paintballs hurt?" Karen asked.

"We're about to find out," Codie said as she came outside. She had donned all the gear, her voice muffled through the facemask. She slapped one glove on top of her helmet, rocked her head side to side, and then bounced a few times to get limber. Sidra was equally armored, and she bumped her wrist against Codie's arm guard.

"Are we doing teams?" Sidra asked. "Is it going to be me and Codie combined...?"

"Every woman for herself."

Codie and Sidra took a starting position on either side of Karen. Lana and Vanessa were on the outside corners of the porch.

Vanessa had the stopwatch. "On your marks... get set... go!"

They shot off the porch, leaping over the steps and racing out into the grass. Codie had strapped the flashlights to her wrists so she could sweep the ground in front of her more easily. Lana brought her gun up and aimed at her best friend's back.

"Twenty-five damn minutes in the shower," she growled, her lips curled into a grin as she pulled the trigger. "Let's see how long it takes you to wash that off!"

Codie yelped, and Lana whooped victoriously as she lined up her second shot.

## CHAPTER TEN

PAINTBALLS, AS it turned out, did hurt. Even through the padding they were still aching when they finally ended the game and went back inside. Vanessa ended up winning with a grand total of two dollars and five cents. Her reward was that she got to keep everyone's money, which she gratefully accepted and then dumped in a jar on the kitchen table. "Beer money," she explained. "Just one step closer to clearing the air around here."

"Beer always makes things better," Lana said. "But how about next time we just talk things out? I don't want to shoot you guys again. And I really don't want you guys shooting at me. I think Codie was aiming for my face."

"I was aiming for your tits. Bigger target."

Lana smiled and put an arm around Codie's shoulders. "For what it's worth, for anything I've done to you guys, I'm sorry. I'll try to be more considerate."

"Same goes for me," Karen said. "I know I've been horrible to be around, but I need to suck it up and focus on my work."

Vanessa said, "You miss your baby. That's understandable."

"We'll all be better." She kissed the side of Codie's head. "Now, let's wash the paint from our hair, change into our jammies, and get a good night's sleep before we attack the rest of the album tomorrow."

"Sounds like a good idea to me," Karen said.

They said their goodnights and then split up, Karen and Vanessa upstairs and Codie and Sidra to the back of the ground floor. Lana confirmed her skin and hair were paint-free thanks to the ski mask she'd worn during her round. She had welts on her arms, and she was sure there were more on her back, but she didn't want to bother with them at the moment. Instead she picked up the flashlights and went back out to the yard.

She was still scanning when the door opened and Sidra came out. She had changed into a yellow T-shirt and gray sweats after her shower. "Hey. Saw you out here walking the grid. What are you doing?"

"I just wanted to be sure we got all the coins. I don't remember how much we started with, and I don't want a stray penny getting caught when the next time the caretaker comes out to mow."

"Considerate. Pass me a light, I'll help."

Lana handed her the flashlight and they slowly panned across the grass together. Every few feet there were smears of orange, yellow, green, blue, and red; paintballs that hadn't hit their target.

Sidra moved toward the tree line. "You know, this is a lot easier without anyone shooting at us."

"This was a good idea. It gave us an outlet for all the frustrations we've been feeling and it made us work together as a team at the same time. You saved us a lot of grief."

Sidra shrugged. "Sometimes you have to know how to handle the talent. I'm supposed to make you sound good. It doesn't all happen with the mixing board."

"Yeah. Well, you're great with that, too. I don't think we've ever sounded better."

"Well, thank you." She stopped at the driveway and looked up. "Wow. Turn off your flashlight for a second."

Lana did as she said. They were immediately thrown into full darkness, but the sky above them was a deep velvet full of stars.

"Oh, wow. I guess I haven't been out of the city enough. Is it always like this?"

"What, the sky?" Sidra chuckled. "Yeah, it's pretty much unchanged for the past century or so."

"Century?" Lana said.

"Yeah. That's when they finally locked it in."

Lana chuckled. "I'm going to get a crick in my neck from staring up." She sat down on the grass and stretched out. "Oh, yeah. Come down here. It's much better."

Sidra stretched out at an angle to Lana, their feet almost touching but their heads far apart. Lights were still on in the house, but they were far enough away that they didn't interfere with the view.

"It's the perfect time machine," Sidra said. "All these stars have burnt out. Thousands of years ago, when we were still crawling out of the muck, these stars were already dead. By the time the light of our sun reaches where they used to be, we'll be gone. Up there, that's the distance past. Down here is the far future. And we're stuck in between."

"Wow." Lana grinned. "I like that."

"Me too."

They stared up in silence for a long while. Lana's mind continued to race until finally she said, "What if no one cares?"

"About the stars?"

"No. What if no one cares about Radiation Canary? The album? We're going through all this to keep it a secret so we can have a grand unveiling. We're giving it away assuming anyone would be willing to pay for it." She turned her head to look at Sidra's profile. "What if the fans walked away when we did, and they're not willing to come back?"

Sidra thought for a moment. "Do you know how long the album is going to take to record?"

"A couple more weeks, maybe."

"But when you started, you had no idea how long you would be working out here."

Lana shook her head. "No."

"Neither did Naomi. She came to me and she asked if I would drop all my current projects, leave my apartment, and come up to a cabin in the middle of nowhere for an undetermined amount of time. I asked her why. She said Radiation Canary. I asked when she needed me to be ready. People care about this band, Lana. They care about you, and the music. They never stopped."

Lana reached up and wiped at her eyes. "Thank you."

"Sure." She grunted as she got back onto her feet and wiped off her backside. She turned and looked down at Lana. "I know you're dealing with a lot right now. The album, the breakup, the stress of having five people under one roof. I can't help you with all of the stress, but if you need a rebound fuck, I just wanted to let you know I'm available."

Lana looked up at her. "Oh."

Sidra grinned. "Just putting it out there. I mean, that way everyone in the house could have a bed. I know you're not ready for a relationship. That's not what I'm offering. I'm just offering... I don't know... a warm place to sleep and a friendly face to wake up to in the morning. The offer is there if you want to take it. Goodnight, Lana."

She started to walk away, but Lana said, "Hey, Sidra. Help me up. I'll walk back to the house with you." Sidra walked back and offered Lana her hand. They stood together in the dark, and Lana sighed. "I'm going to be honest with you. I'm not sure I'll be able to do... what I really want to do. Part of me still feels like it would be cheating on Catherine. Even though God knows what she's been doing, and it's been two months, so it stands to reason..."

"Hey." Sidra put her hands on Lana's shoulders. Whatever happens will be fine with me. Even if we just go in there and go to sleep, I'll be glad that you get to sleep in a real bed. You won't swap, so maybe you'll be okay with sharing."

Lana stepped closer. "Let me just try something." Sidra nodded, and Lana kissed her. Sidra slid her hands down Lana's arms and then moved them to her waist. The kiss only lasted for a few seconds before Lana pulled back. She put one hand on the back of Sidra's head and nodded. "Okay. As far as rebound mistakes go, I think I'm really going to enjoy this one."

Sidra smiled and took Lana's hand to lead her back into the house.

Codie showered off the remnants of the paint from her arms and out of her hair and retired to her room with her notepad. She had been working on her song ever since revealing its existence to Karen, but she still wasn't sure it was worthy of the band. She tried to hear Lana singing it and couldn't help feel it was subpar. She'd written it in her head while flying over Puget Sound during a summer storm. The water below and the thick rainclouds above had made her feel like the ocean had curled up and around her.

She started with the title: "In the Wind Between Two Oceans." She even attempted to figure out how Lana would play the opening. A minor, to C, to G, then repeated. She would accent it with a subtle drumbeat while Karen came in at the start of the first verse with the violin. In her head it sounded the first droplets of rain building up into a full storm. A few cymbal crashes here and there would indicate the growing thunder.

"It's been hours since I last saw dry land," she murmured under her breath, "but I know these waters like the back of my hand. The stars are blinded by clouds rolling down like curtains... cast aside with a magician's sleight of hand." She tapped her pen against her front tooth. She knew Karen and Lana liked to pepper their lyrics with literary references, but she couldn't think of anything related to water. Poseidon might count...

She heard the sound of Sidra's bedroom door closing, then the thump of a body dropping onto the mattress. The night before, or any of the nights leading up to it, she would have growled or muttered under her breath about inconsiderate assholes who couldn't be quiet when their neighbors might be sleeping. Now she took it in stride. The paintball game had been the perfect outlet for her frustrations about being cooped up in the cabin. She loved Lana, Karen, and Vanessa, but they could be monsters sometimes. She was sure they thought the same about her. Now she felt capable of coexisting with them as long as it took to finish the album.

Sidra laughed, and then she heard a quiet "shh." She lifted her head and looked at the wall as if she could see through it, wondering if maybe she had just heard an artifact of the wind or...

Another laugh. This time it wasn't Sidra.

Codie slipped off the bed and moved stealthily across the room. She pressed her ear to the wall and listened intently. Hushed voices, the sound of a bed protesting under shifting weight, and the sound of shoes hitting the floor. Two shoes... then a third... and a fourth. Karen was married and Vanessa was straight and married, so there was only one possibility. Codie smiled and listened for a moment more - that moan was definitely Lana - before she went back to her bed and retrieved her earbuds.

"Good girl," she said as she drowned out the sounds coming from next door with Brandi Carlile. She ignored the music and went back to working on her lyrics, hoping that Lana and Sidra finished before she decided to turn in for the night.

Naomi parked in front of her bungalow at twelve minutes past one in the morning. She rested her head on the steering wheel for a moment, almost too tired to even make the walk up to the house. The ferry to Whidbey Island had been late, and then she'd had to race to catch the second one to Port Townsend. Stupid Seattle and stupid Washington and all its stupid water. But by sheer luck she had made it and now her day was finally over.

After close to a minute she realized she was in danger of falling asleep in her current position. She summoned whatever reserves she had left and grabbed her bag before she gave up and just slept in the backseat. Susan had left a lamp on for her in the living room. When she opened the front door, Henry the Dog came trotting in from the kitchen to greet her. She crouched down so he could give her kisses, his nose nearly knocking the glasses off her face, and she gave him a thorough scratching on the neck and back before she sent him off to do whatever doggie errands he had to do.

She went into the living room to turn off the lamp and was surprised to see Susan sitting beside it with a book in her hand. She looked up and her silver-brown hair fell across one lens of her glasses. She swept it aside with the back of her hand as she smiled.

"Hi."

"Hi. You didn't have to wait up for me."

Susan patted the couch beside her. "When you called and said you would be home late, I took a nap. I only woke up about an hour ago. Sit."

Naomi bent down to kiss Susan's lips. She laid her head on her wife's shoulder and let gravity pull her the rest of the way down to the sofa. She pulled her legs up and curled herself on the couch with her head against Susan's chest. She could hear her heartbeat through her blouse. Susan put her hand on the back of Naomi's head and teased the short strands of hair.

"Long day?"

"So long. Mostly just driving. Five hours in the car. I'm sleepy, I have a headache, I'm irritated even though everything went well…"

Susan shushed her and guided her head down to her lap. She took off Naomi's glasses and massaged her temples. The tension behind her eyes faded almost immediately; she felt her entire body relaxing with just a few short strokes.

"You spent all day taking care of people. Let me take care of you."

Naomi smiled, but her expression was tortured. "I spent my whole day running around taking care of Radiation Canary and Sarah fucking Wiley. When is it your turn? When do I spent a whole day making sure you're taken care of?"

Susan smiled down at her. "Your clients are like children. They need to be babysat, you need to hold their hands. I understand that. I'm a grown-up. I need you here when I'm sad, or when I'm lonely I need to know I can reach out and you'll be there. I know that if I ever need you, I'll come first. I don't need you devoting all your free time to me. I don't need you putting off important things just so you can sit beside me at a restaurant or in a car. Your body was running around Seattle all day, but your heart was right here. It's all tangled up in mine."

Naomi sat up and kissed Susan, running her fingers through the long, lustrous hair. "Will you take me to bed?"

Susan nodded and pressed her lips to the tip of Naomi's nose. She put her book aside and helped Naomi up before taking her hand to lead her to their room.

## CHAPTER ELEVEN

LANA WOKE with someone holding her. She remained as still as possible so the spell wouldn't be broken, her eyes still closed and her breathing steady. She remembered who it was and why they were in bed together and she smiled, moving her hand under the blanket to stroke Sidra's forearm. Sidra pulled her arm back and twisted her hand. Their fingers laced together as Sidra brushed the hair away from Lana's neck to kiss the warm skin.

"I know you're awake."

"I don't care."

"I can make you care." Sidra's free hand moved over Lana's body, finding her curves and exploring them thoroughly before moving on. When she reached her thigh, Lana bent her knee and parted her legs to let Sidra's hand move between them. Sidra chuckled and moved her lips to Lana's ear as her fingers explored. Lana writhed and stroked Sidra's arm. "Well, look who is awake."

"I didn't know you played dirty."

Sidra winked at her. "I have all kinds of ways to make my talent do what I want them to do. So hi. Good morning."

"Good morning."

Sidra let go of Lana's hand to brush the hair out of her face. "Last night was amazing."

Lana rolled over. She moved her free hand to Sidra's chest. "It was. Even better than paintball."

"Glad to hear it. Also glad I haven't lost my touch. It's been a while since I was with a woman."

"Well, you know what they say. It's like riding a bicycle. A very satisfied and very good-sore bicycle."

Sidra kissed her. "I'm just happy I could help. How are you feeling, conscience-wise?"

"I'm fine. It's fine. There were a few moments when I thought..." She shook her head. "But I know I didn't do anything wrong. Trust me, as much as I hate to admit it, I know what it feels like to cheat. This was different. So maybe this helped me admit Catherine and I are really over." Lana slid her hand over Sidra's breast, tracing the curve until she reached the nipple. "This is just casual, rebound sex. But how long does a rebound relationship generally last?"

Sidra shrugged. "I don't know. It seems reasonable that as long as we're in the same house and we're short a bed, you and I might as well keep on sharing this one. And if one of us crosses the center line in the middle of the night..."

"It's only reasonable," Lana agreed. Sidra kissed her. The kiss lingered, both of them ignoring their morning breath to enjoy the moment. "As long as we don't let it interfere with the work."

"Right. Absolutely."

"And we don't run off every five minutes to tear each other's clothes off." She kissed Sidra's neck, and Sidra stretched one leg across Lana's body. She moved her hand up between Lana's breasts.

"We can be professional. A hundred percent. And speaking of, uh..." She looked at the clock. "Even if we had slept apart, we would still have over two hours before anyone would expect us to start recording. We could have an early breakfast. Or go for a walk. Or..."

Lana put her finger against Sidra's lips. When she stopped talking, she put the finger into Sidra's mouth and let her suck on it.

"Or... two hours... we could be very casual in two hours."

Sidra grinned, pulled Lana's hand away from her mouth, and guided the wet finger down between their bodies. Lana smiled mischievously.

Karen glanced at the couch as she passed, then looked into the kitchen. "Is Lana in the shower?"

Codie smirked at her cereal. "No. Still in bed."

Karen frowned and looked at the couch as if she might have missed her. "Still... oh. Did she and Sidra finally swap?"

"Nope. Sidra's still in bed, too."

Karen stopped with her hand on the cereal box. "Wait."

"Yep."

"Really?"

Codie said, "Really. Well into the night from what I could tell. I finally managed to fall asleep with a couple of pillows over my head."

Karen smiled and brought her cereal to the table. "Good for her. I've been really worried about her. She took this whole Catherine thing really hard. Some of the songs she wrote for the album..."

"Yeah," Codie said, lowering her voice to a whisper. "I didn't want to say anything, but you're right. There were a couple of them I..."

Karen tilted her head. "What?"

Codie looked over her shoulder to make sure Lana wasn't sneaking up on her. "Like 'Enough for You.' Heartbreaking shit. Putting all the pain of the breakup on herself, apologizing to Catherine for not being enough? And then 'I'm Breakable'..."

Karen said, "'I'm Breakable' scared me."

Codie nodded. "When I heard it, I was glad we were all staying together in the same house so we could all keep an eye on her."

Karen frowned. "You don't think... I mean, it's bleak, but you don't think Lana would have hurt herself, do you?"

"I don't know. 'I never thought I could feel so fragile, didn't know I'd be played for such a fool. Shattered me into pieces and all I can think is, I never knew I was this breakable.' I wanted to hide all the damn knives in the house after I heard her sing that."

"But you think she's okay now?"

Codie shrugged. "I think she's closer to okay. In the past, I think the main reason Lana's cheated on so many of her girlfriends is because she uses sex to close the book on what came before. She knows it burns a bridge and there won't be any going back. When your relationship was finished, she found Catherine. Before that, there was Alia and those two girls she found in Vegas. This time she got the rug pulled out from under her. I think sleeping with someone new is just a ritual she needs to move on to the next thing."

"I just hope Sidra understands that's what the stakes are."

Vanessa came in from outside. "Morning."

"Where are you coming from?" Codie said.

"I was out for a walk."

"I've been up for an hour."

"And I've been up for two. Karen, tell her."

Karen smiled. "Baby schedule. I woke up at five this morning and wrote for a while before I could go back to sleep. It feels weird sleeping through the night. My body doesn't want to do it anymore."

Codie shuddered. "The horror..."

Lana came into the room. "What horror?"

"These two maniacs have been up since five."

Karen said, "Ah, I went back to sleep. Vanessa is the one who exercised."

Vanessa stuck her tongue out. "You worked on a song. I may be a maniac, but you're a dork."

Codie chuckled. The same conversation a day earlier would have led to stony silence and irritated sighs. Now that the tensions had been thoroughly dissipated they could joke and kid with one another again. It felt like their entire getaway had been reset. She watched Lana in the living room as she retrieved her clothes and a towel from her suitcase and then headed back toward the bathroom.

"Going to conserve water, Miss Kent?"

Lana smiled and winked as she went past them. "Enjoy your breakfast, girls. I want to be in the studio by eight-thirty."

"Strict!" Codie said. "Be sure your shower buddy knows the schedule. Maybe bring it up while she's doing your back."

Vanessa furrowed her brow. "Shower buddy?"

"Sidra."

Vanessa said, "Sidra? Wow. Girl's got taste."

"Which one?"

She thought about it for a moment. "Both of them, as a matter of fact."

Karen smiled and nodded her head in agreement.

During one of their breaks, Sidra took some recording equipment upstairs. Karen found her in the backyard near the footbridge, microphone held straight up over her head as she listened to the feed through a pair of large headphones. The headphones were so large that they made her nearly-bald head look small by comparison. She turned in a slow circle and smiled when she saw Karen watching her. She lifted one finger on the hand holding the microphone. The recording device was slung over her shoulder and hanging against one hip like a purse. When she was finished she reached down and stopped the tape.

"Sorry about that," she said. "I wanted to get some ambient sounds to fill up some quiet moments between songs. I'm going to run it by Lana before I do anything to the actual recordings, and they won't go on the masters, but I thought since we're up here in this gorgeous place, we might as well use it."

"Sounds like a good idea. Do you have a second? I wanted to talk to you about what happened last night."

Sidra nodded. "I think I know what you're going to say. It's not a one-time thing, but it's also not a relationship. Lana seemed like she needed someone. I was available. I know the lifespan of whatever it is ends when we leave here, and I'm okay with that."

Karen said, "Good. But me and the others, we just wanted to be sure that you understood that we'll do anything to protect Lana. She puts on a good game, but when she gets hurt she tends to stay hurt. She runs and hides until the hurt is gone. It's great that you're here for her, and I agree that she needed someone to be with her. But even though you're both on the same page, you have to be careful."

"We will. Or I will. And if I feel like I don't know what to do, I'll definitely be relying on you and the other girls to give me some advice. Lana is a special person. She's strong and vulnerable and talented and... she's just special. And I don't think we'd be happy-ever-after together, I'm grateful to have a chance to spend a little time with her. And if spending time with her has the added effect of helping her get through a rough time? That's just a bonus. Don't worry. I'll tread carefully."

Karen said, "Good. We just wanted to be sure. We all love Lana."

Sidra smiled. "Yeah. It's kind of like the big sister coming to make sure the new girl's intentions are good. Trust me, I know that I'm the fifth wheel in a really unique situation."

"You're fitting in just fine. And hey, now the number of people in the cabin who have slept with Lana is even with the number that hasn't. You have brought balance to the room."

Sidra laughed and held out her hand. After a moment Karen slapped it. "An elite club, I'm sure."

Karen wasn't too sure about 'elite,' but she didn't say anything. "I'll let you get back to your recording. You should also try it after dark. Last night during the game I kept hearing frogs back here. I love frogs."

"Me too. I'll see if I can find any. How long until we go back downstairs?"

"About twenty minutes."

"I'll be ready."

Karen nodded and went back to the cabin. When she reached the back porch she turned back to see Sidra was already crouched down by the creek so she could record the sound of running water. From day one she had worked hard to make sure their new album sounded as pristine as possible. She supposed if she could be trusted with that, then trusting her with Lana's heart wasn't too much of a stretch.

When they returned to the studio, Lana shuffled together the songs they already had finished. She set up camp with Sidra in the production booth and listened to a mix to hear how they would sound together, mixing and matching them into a temporary order. She moved "Wheels Up" to the beginning due to the title, followed by "Soothing Sea Sounds" and "Echoing Mirrors." Sidra said, "I think we need to redo the vocals for 'Landfill of Beautiful Strangers.' You and Karen picked up a great harmony about halfway through. I think if we get you in the iso booth you can recreate it, really make it pop."

Lana nodded. "Okay. We can do that while you're editing it, right?"

Sidra said, "Yeah. That way we can make sure we have all the best parts in one place."

"Excellent." She looked through the glass and leaned toward the intercom. "Karen. Do you have your Don Quixote song ready to go?"

Karen nodded. "I'm ready whenever you are."

"Okay. We'll do that one first. If we stick to sixteen, how many songs do we need before the first album is done?"

Sidra counted. "Wow, only three. Is that right?"

Lana shrugged. "We've been working hard." She hit the intercom again. "Codie. Your song. How close is it to being done?"

Codie's eyes widened. "It's, ah... a work in progress."

"Could we give it a run-through? I want to put it on the first album if it's at all possible."

"Uh. Sure. Yeah. Let me go grab my notebook."

Lana nodded and Codie stood to go back upstairs. "Okay, Codie's song, Karen's song, and then we need one more. We'll work that out, and then while you're doing your mixing and mastering magic, the rest of us can work on figuring out the album art and liner notes. It's hard to believe we almost have a whole album finished. A few weeks ago we hadn't even been in the same room together for over a year and now..."

"Hard work pays off." Sidra looked through the glass. "So the hiatus is officially over, right? This isn't a one-and-done, official farewell?"

Lana said, "No, we have the second album to do. The one we're actually going to charge people for."

"Right. But after that... I'm not angling for more work here. I'm asking as a fan. I want to know there's more than two Radiation Canary albums to look forward to."

Lana looked at her friends in the studio. Karen was sitting on Vanessa's stool behind the piano, while Vanessa was using her laptop to video chat with Scott and Nathaniel before they started working. Codie was in position, drumsticks resting on one thigh, and she threw her head back to laugh at something Karen had said.

"I made a mistake," Lana said softly. "We all did. We thought Radiation Canary was our step to something bigger. We thought... I don't know what we thought, but we were wrong. Our purpose was right here. We should have stayed right where we were. So if I have anything to say about it, yeah. We're going to stay together for a long time."

Sidra nodded. "Good. And even though I wasn't angling for work, I do hope you'll think of me when the time comes."

"Oh, absolutely. I'd have you even if you were strictly professional. But if having you around means we can continue our extracurricular activities..."

"That would definitely be a job perk."

Lana stood up and kissed the top of Sidra's head to go back into the studio. "We're going to do the Don Quixote song first, then we'll see what work Codie's song needs to have done on it."

Codie had come back in time to hear the end of what Lana was saying. "It still needs a lot. Karen, I hope you can clean up some of the horrible parts."

Karen smiled and took the notebook pages from her. "I'll see what I can salvage."

They took their positions, and Sidra said, "Okay, this is 'Words of Wisdom and Woe (from a Self-Proclaimed Madman)', take one."

Lana nodded that she was ready and began the intro. Karen had gone through the original *Don Quixote* and extracted over a dozen phrases and idioms that were still being used four hundred years later. It was hard to tell if the play invented the phrases or merely popularized them, but either way there were enough to fill a notebook page. She strung them together into a song, and Lana had written the music to finish it off. It was a happy song, peppy, and she discovered that just playing the opening chords was enough to put a smile on her face. She rocked her shoulders and worked her hips as she played into the first verse.

*"Can you ever have too much of a good thing?*
*Is it madness if you only see what's worth seeing?*
*It gets so bad you'll split your sides from laughing*
*The old man said familiarity will breed contempt*
*But I have a feeling you haven't seen anything yet.*

*Forewarned is forearmed, you better look before you leap*
*You live and learn and turn over a new leaf*
*Forgive and forget all your old injuries*
*Make sure the armies you're facing aren't just flocks of sheep*
*You'll find you have the devil to pay, without a wink of sleep.*

The song didn't make a lot of sense, but she knew it would be a favorite at live shows. It was so much fun to sing, and it would be so much fun to listen to, that the words hardly mattered. Lana moved back from the microphone during the interlude and switched to a lower key to let Karen and Vanessa overtake her.

The music had a vaguely flamenco feel to it, thanks to the Spanish source material. It wasn't something they'd ever done before but it worked extremely well. Lana felt her instincts as a dancer coming through, her arms stiff from the effort of keeping them still so she could play the guitar. Instead she moved and swayed, extending her leg and bending the knee before twisting her body around on the straight leg, rolling her head in time with the music. She imagined at a live show they could have a guest guitarist play the interlude so she could do a proper flamenco dance, which she would also have to practice. But if the people paid for a show, they should get a show.

When she finished swaying and twisting around, she saw Karen was holding back laughter. Lana winked at her and moved back into position for the final verse. As she sang she step-stomped and swayed her hips to the beat.

*"The old man said it's needs must when the devil drives*
*Thanks for nothing; I have other fish to fry*
*A bird in the hand is worth the two you let fly*
*So I'll have my cake, I'll make hay in the shining of the sun*
*I may have lived my life like a madman but I'll die like a wise one."*

When the song ended, Karen lowered her violin and laughed. "Nice little improv dance there."

"I'll see if I can remember it for the video, if we do one." Lana smiled and repositioned her fingers. "Okay, let's take it through one more time just so we can give Sid a track without the stomping noises in it."

"That would be swell of you."

Lana winked at her and counted them in.

## CHAPTER TWELVE

IT WAS decided that on Sunday, the whole band would drive down to Seattle with Lana so they could have a day off. Vanessa was going to spend the entire day at home suffering through whatever football games Scott decided to watch. Codie was going to take out her plane for a few hours. Karen wanted to spend time with Laura and Mason, but knew that doing so would defeat the purpose of the whole trip. Instead they made plans to have a quiet dinner at home and Karen would visit her Dads at the hardware store.

Lana and Laura went to lunch and made sure they got a table outside despite the chill in the air. Lana held Mason and did her best to look completely relaxed and casual. She saw a few people snapping pictures but couldn't tell if they were professional paparazzi or just fans who would put the pictures up on Facebook or their blogs. Either way the pictures would help defuse the gossip sites claiming Lana and Karen were having an affair.

In the meantime, the two were forced to find things to say to each other so they weren't simply sitting in silence.

"How's your album going?" Lana asked. She was wearing a hat, and Mason pushed it up so he could grab a handful of her hair.

"It's going really well. Sorry... he loves long hair."

Lana chuckled and removed her hat. "It's fine." Mason wrapped her hair around his hand.

"Ella and I are doing a theme sort of album. It's called *Reasons for*

*Admission* and all the song titles are reasons a woman cou_d get admitted to a mental institution back in the eighteen-hundreds."

"Existing While Female?"

Laura grinned. "Basically, yeah. Imaginary Female Trouble, Novel Reading, Kicked in the Head by a Horse..."

Lana laughed. "It's good that they cracked down on that. Can't have a bunch of crazy women running around putting their heads behind horses."

"I think my favorite is Tobacco & Masturbation."

"Now *there's* a song title. I would listen to that." She locked at Mason, stuck her tongue out, and he pulled her hair harder. "How are you and Karen not bald yet?"

Laura laughed and reached across the table to help her out. She lowered her voice. "I wanted to say thank you for doing this. I know the rest of the band is getting a day off to do whatever they want and you're stuck here playacting to shut up internet idiots."

"It's my fault those idiots are giving your family a hard time. This is the least I can do. And if you want me to take Mason tonight so you two can enjoy your time off properly, I'd be willing."

Laura raised an eyebrow. "Seriously? You know that's a baby, right?"

"What's so hard? I just cover its cage and make it think it's time for bed, right?"

Laura laughed. "You cannot watch my baby. But I appreciate the thought. I think Karen's dads want to take care of him tonight."

"Oh, I'm not getting between the Dads and babytime."

"How is your album? Karen hinted that she might get to come home soon. That's good news."

Lana nodded. "We're working on the final songs right now. We should have the first album ready to go in about three weeks."

"Have you given any thought to how you're going to break the news?"

"Some. Not enough. Part of me has been so certain the secret will get out that I didn't really want to get too excited about it. But now it looks like we'll get away with it, so..." She shrugged and saw someone with a large, expensive camera hanging around his neck. He crouched next to a potted plant outside the restaurant and brought the camera up to take a picture. Lana pretended not to notice him. "Should I wave?"

Laura shrugged. "If you do people might assume this is staged. Which... you know... they'd be right. Just do what you would normally do and ignore him."

Lana picked up her water and took a drink, using the glass to block her face as much as possible.

"If Karen is free in a couple of weeks, would Ella and I be able to borrow her? We have a song called 'Vicious Vices' and I think it needs a violin to give it sort of a baroque feel."

"I think you could convince her."

Laura wiggled her eyebrows. "Okay. I think we've posed long enough. Not that I don't love your company. But the Bug needs to have his lunch, too. I'm not about to let the paparazzi get a shot of that."

"Fair enough. I'll get the check."

"Yeah, right." Laura signaled for the waiter.

After she dropped Laura and Mason off at their apartment, Lana called Sidra to see how she was spending her day off. She was sitting at home alone and eagerly invited Lana to come over and hang out with her. She was surprised when she realized the address was in Denny-Blaine, the land of gated private residences and meticulously cared-for lawns. She was vaguely aware that Kurt Cobain had killed himself somewhere nearby but she had no idea where the house was. Thanks to the steep slope of the land, it seemed impossible to find property that wouldn't have a view of Lake Washington.

Sidra's house was on the left side of a quiet cul-de-sac. Her neighbor across the street had dolphin and star balloons tethered to their mailbox along with a sign over the garage that declared someone named Margot was eight years old. Lana parked and took a moment to look around at the tall fences draped with greenery before she walked up Sidra's driveway.

When Sidra answered the door, Lana said, "Exactly how much are we paying you?"

Sidra grinned. "Not a penny more than I'm worth."

"I can go with that," Lana said.

"Come on in." She kissed Lana hello and shut the door behind her. She was wearing a pair of shorts and a T-shirt with the Batman logo on the chest. "I was just hanging out playing games. Don't mind the mess. My roommate kind of went animalistic while I was gone. Primal urges, washing dishes as needed, stacking pizza boxes sky high. So..."

Lana said, "Aha, roommate. That makes more sense."

Sidra offered her a drink and went to the kitchen to retrieve a couple of beers. Lana stood in the foyer and took stock of the house. To her right was a dining room, littered with the aforementioned takeout, and to her left was the living room. A massive flat screen television occupied the center space in an entertainment center decked out with games and books. Lana whistled as she went into the room. "Wow. So I guess if you didn't have a roommate you would be living..."

"In whatever loft apartment had enough outlets to support this bad boy, yep. You know, we've been hanging out together for weeks and I've actually been inside of you, but now it's like, it's, oh my God. Lana Kent is in my house."

Lana smiled. "I'll try to keep the diva demands to a minimum."

"Appreciated. So, ah... did you come over to hang out or did you come over to hump up on me a little? I'm open to either, by the way. My roommate is out of town until tomorrow, so we don't have to worry about being interrupted."

Lana chuckled and gestured at the game paused on the screen. "Why not both? I could go down on you while you finish your game."

Sidra went still and affected a very serious expression. "That's the dream."

"Then get your pants off."

Sidra took off her shorts and underwear and sat down, placing one foot on the coffee table as Lana knelt in front of her. She used a throw pillow for her knees and told Sidra that she wouldn't be upset if the back of her head was used as a cushion for the controller. Despite almost ten minutes of trying their best, they discovered that neither task was suited very well for multitasking. Sidra eventually turned off the game and let Lana finish, then pulled her up onto the couch to get her out of her clothes.

"The couch is fine with me," Sidra said, "but if you'd rather, I do have a bed at the back of the house. And the bed comes with all kinds of toys."

"Toys?" Lana raised an eyebrow. "Take me to the toys."

It was nearly dark before Lana lifted herself off Sidra and collapsed to one side of her. Sidra laughed breathlessly and reached out to pat Lana on the hip. They panted in stereo toward the ceiling briefly, the sweat drying on their skin, until Lana became aware of a slight dizziness despite the fact she was lying down.

"I need fluids," Lana said. "I'm seriously about to faint."

"Orange juice?"

Lana nodded, and Sidra got to her feet and hurried out of the room. Lana pushed herself up against the headboard with the pillow behind her back. She took the opportunity to finally look around Sidra's room. The dusky sunset light coming through the window was still bright enough for her to recognize the art deco "Rainmakers for Wizards" poster from one of their tours was framed behind the closet door. When Sidra came back, Lana gestured at it.

"I guess you really are a fan."

"Oh, yeah. That concert was amazing. It was what made me want to work with Cartography. If they were dealing with your kind of talent, I wanted in." She handed Lana a bottle of orange juice. She also had one for herself, and two bottles of water. She put the backups on the bookshelf before she crawled back into bed. "You four blew me away."

"And you said, 'one day I'll have the lead singer in my bed.'"

Sidra smiled. "Full disclosure, I had a crush on Codie first. Still do, in fact. Bad girl with a pilot's license. But her straightness presents an insurmountable goal." She shrugged and patted Lana's hip. "You're a pretty good consolation prize, though."

Lana laughed and moved Sidra's hand to her inner thigh. "Do you have your phone? I want to check the internet."

Sidra looked and retrieved it from the nightstand. "If you find any porn, it was already there when I bought the phone."

"Sure, sure. I'll let you show me the best stuff when I'm done." She opened Google and entered her name. "I just want to see if my little game with Laura worked."

The first hit was a news story posted forty-five minutes earlier by a British entertainment site. The thumbnail showed Catherine, so Lana braced herself before reading the summary. "Chic and sexy Kitty Diehl arrived at the premiere of the new Olivia Childress thriller with actress Alexandra Stockton. Kitty and Sexy Lexi were very touchy-feely for the gathered press. This seems to put the final nail in the coffin of Kitty's relationship with singer Lana Kent, who is still flying under the radar."

"It's nice to know she's moved on," Lana said.

Sidra said, "You do realize you're in bed with a naked woman whose hand is between your legs, right?"

Lana smirked. "You have a point."

"No, I don't. I was just being snarky. You and I are having fun, but she's going out on dates, getting her picture taking. I'm sorry."

Lana sighed and scrolled back to the search results. "I don't care anymore. As long as they're not still claiming I'm off having some sordid affair with Karen."

"Try searching for your name plus Laura Everett."

"Right." Lana typed in both names and received several results. Halfway down the page she saw a blog post titled 'Put the Rumors to Bed!' "Here we go."

The post started with a cellphone picture of Lana and Laura walking through the parking lot at the mall. Mason was riding on Laura's hip, and Lana had her head bent down so she would be looking into the boy's eyes. The author of the post identified them, identified when it was taken, and then continued: "Can we please stop speculating about Lana and Karen's relationship now? They broke up six YEARS ago and Karen is MARRIED now. She and Laura have a baby (and the Bug looks adorable here!) Can we PLEASE just leave them alone? They've moved on. It's kind of sick that we HAVEN'T."

"Wow, good for her," Sidra said.

Lana nodded. "Hopefully more people will say the same thing. Karen and I weren't meant to be in a relationship. We loved each other so we assumed that meant we were *in* love with each other. We're smarter now. She has Laura and I have..." Her voice trailed off.

"You have me," Sidra said as she moved her hand higher between Lana's legs. "For right now, at least. And right now is all that matters."

Lana kissed Sidra's nose, then her lips. "I'm grateful for that."

"How grateful?"

Lana smiled. "Let me rehydrate and then I'll give you a full demonstration."

Karen spent the day with her Dads, who put her to work on the cash register at their hardware store. Only a handful of people recognized her. Of those only a few said anything about a famous musician working at a small hardware store. Karen said, "Well, you know how the music business is these days. Gotta pay the bills somehow." The experience was surreal. In less than half an hour checking out hammers, nails, and rolls of duct tape, she was transported back to her teenage years. Part of her expected to go back to the old house and spend a few hours in her room practicing.

She wondered how many hours she had spent sitting on that little folding chair, staring at sheet music until it all blurred together. Her mother bought the violin to make up for all the fights Karen had to endure. The lessons got her out of the house a few hours every week, but the tension was still in the air when she got home. The violin led to the cello, and Karen was proficient in both by the time she got to high school. Eventually her parents succumbed to the inevitable and filed for divorce. They finally realized their problems stemmed from the fact Karen's father was pretending to be someone he wasn't. He met Ted, they fell in love, and peace fell in the Everett household. She would never be grateful for the pain and hurt her parents had inflicted on each other during those tumultuous years, but the music they gave her was silver lining.

When she clocked out, she told her father that she expected to see a check for her six hours of work. He promised it would be in the mail first thing next week and told her how much he and Ted were looking forward to playing grandpa that night. She stopped by the supermarket on her way home and picked up the ingredients for cider-glazed pork chops. It was Laura's favorite meal, and Karen decided she needed to be pampered for everything she'd suffered in the past few weeks.

She cooked while Laura took a nap with Mason. She woke them both for the family dinner, they ate, and Karen gave Mason a bath before her father and Ted came to pick him up. It was a chance for Karen and Laura to enjoy a night to themselves. After she kissed them goodbye, Karen went into the living room and curled up to watch TV with Laura on the couch. The flashbacks to her teen years faded as Laura stroked her arm. This was her family now.

"It's weird to watch TV," she said during a commercial. "There's one in every room up at the cabin, but I don't think any of us have actually turned them on."

"Do you want me to turn it off so it'll be easier to go back?"

"No, I want to see how this ends. I'm just surprised how unusual it feels to sit here and watch TV." She stroked Laura's leg. "It feels weird to be here with you, too. But a very good weird."

Laura bent down and kissed Karen's temple. "It's been very odd to not have you here, Cricket. The house gets so insanely quiet. And of course Mason is going crazy without your music. I took out some of your old demos just to have something playing when I put him to bed." She stroked Karen's hair. "And he's not alone. I've missed you like crazy, you know."

"I know. I hate not having you up there with me. But I know you have your own album to work on." She rolled onto her back so she was facing up. "Sleeping alone sucks. When I was growing up I couldn't imagine sharing a bed with someone. But now I keep reaching for you." She put her hand out and Laura found it, squeezing the fingers before bringing them to her lips for a kiss. "It definitely helps me sing some of Lana's breakup songs, though. It really puts me in that place of... what would happen if I lost you and Mason."

Laura whispered, "Oh, hon. You know you don't have to worry about that. I'm nuts about you. The kid is pretty fond of you, too."

Karen smiled. "Yeah, until dinnertime. Then I'm just that lady who isn't mama."

Laura laughed. "So. Lana has a lot of breakup songs?"

"Some. They're fairly generic in terms of... you know, not specifying anything. But once people hear the album, the rumors of her and Catherine breaking up will be confirmed."

"I didn't say anything today, but she seems so sad. I almost wanted to invite her to dinner just so she could keep playing with Mason. She loves that little boy."

Karen grinned. "Yeah. Dinner with a happy couple might be a little much for her right now. Besides, I bet she tracked down Sidra."

"The producer? Why?"

"They started sleeping together." Laura's eyes widened. "It's a casual thing. Neither of them is pretending it's anything other than what it is. They're both available and Lana really needed an outlet for her frustrations."

Laura said, "Huh. I didn't think Sidra was her type. I only saw her that first week, but she seemed a little immature for Lana's tastes. Those video games?"

"Video games don't make someone immature."

"I guess." She moved her hand to the collar of Karen's blouse. "Do you have any raunchy songs on the album? Knock-down, drag-out, censored on the radio songs about gettin' some?"

"Not that I know of."

Laura bent down and licked Karen's lip. "Want to be inspired to write one?"

Karen grinned and sat up, pulling Laura to her. Suddenly she didn't much care about the end of the show they were watching.

## CHAPTER THIRTEEN

Rested and rejuvenated after a day at home, the Canaries once again returned to the Coal Mine for the final push on their album. Laura insisted on taking the time to drive Karen up, surrendering two hours of her day so they could spend one of them together. Codie flew in to a nearby airport and Vanessa picked her up on the way. Sidra and Lana carpooled together as Lana ended up spending the night at Sidra's house.

When Lana saw Codie, she pulled out a roll of printed paper and used it to swat her friend on the shoulder and upper arm. Codie defended herself by twisting her arm around Lana's and pinning it to her side. "What's the big idea, Kent?"

"I'm pissed at you. I read 'Wind Between Two Oceans.'"

"Oh." Codie let Lana go and tensed for a brutal review. "What did you think?"

"I think you're a jerk, and I'm angry that I didn't write it. I love it, Codie. It's amazing. The title is beautiful, and the music notations you put in..." They were in the living room by that time, and Karen was lying on the couch looking out the window. Lana released Codie and went to hand her the printout. "Karen. Read the song Codie wrote, then help me kill her so we can take credit."

Karen took the rolled-up paper but didn't continue the assault. "Okay."

Lana dropped onto the floor. "Hey. What's with the mope?"

Karen shook her head, but her eyes were filling with tears. "Nothing.

Laura just left."

"Ah." Lana put her hand on the back of Karen's head and leaned in to kiss her forehead. "Sometimes a one-day reunion can be worse than none at all, huh?"

"Yeah." She wiped at her eyes and sat up. "I'll look at Codie's song."

"No rush. Take some time for yourself."

Karen nodded, but she was already unrolling the paper. "Oh, I already love the title."

"Right?" She patted Karen's shoulder. "Take your time, okay?"

"I will."

Lana stood and saw Vanessa had stopped to pick up groceries. An army of brown paper soldiers stood on the counter, and Lana picked one up to help put things away. "Smart of you to stop for this."

Vanessa said, "I thought we might be at risk of having no food whatsoever if I didn't. But it's okay. I don't mind being the den mother of the group."

"You keep us fed, Karen gets us to bed at a reasonable hour. Between the two of you, Codie and I might actually get in the habit of being adults."

"We're not miracle workers. Here, that needs to be refrigerated..." She took the food from Lana and glanced at Sidra as she headed downstairs. "So, ah, you two showed up together. I assume you spent the night together, too?"

Lana nodded. "After the little publicity stunt with Laura, I was feeling kind of lonely. It's not a problem, is it? We're keeping it professional."

"No, not at all. When you and Karen were together, and then after you were together, you proved that you can keep your head in the game no matter what is going on in your personal life. I'm just glad you found a way to get Catherine off your mind. Scott saw something online about her this weekend and we were afraid you might have seen it as well."

"Oh. Yeah, I saw that."

Vanessa wrinkled her nose. "I'm sure it was taken out of context."

Lana paused with a box of Hamburger Helper halfway to the shelf. "Wait. Are you talking about the pictures at the Olivia Childress premiere?"

Vanessa stared at her. "Yes."

"How can a picture be taken out of context?"

"It's..."

Lana sighed and put the box down on the counter. "Tell me."

Vanessa tried for a moment to think of a way out of it before she finally pulled her phone out of her pocket. "I'm not going to say it. I'll let you see it for yourself." She tapped the screen a few times and then handed the phone over. The article was an informal interview that occurred at a reception after the premiere. The reporter giving the interview casually mentioned that Sexy Lexi was present when Catherine was answering the questions. Vanessa had helpfully scrolled down to the pertinent section.

BEN ROSENBERG: Admittedly, people are a bit surprised to find you here with Miss Stockton rather than your long-time partner Lana Kent.

KITTY DIEHL: Relationships end. It's a fact of grown-up life. Lana and I were together for six years, and we had a good run, but neither of us thought it would be... you know... forever. We were having fun. We had a lot of fun. But it ran its course. And now she can go write some sappy breakup songs and see what else is out there. It'll be good. It'll be good for both of us.

Lana turned the phone face-down on the counter. "I guess we were just having fun that whole time," she whispered. "News to me."

"Lana..."

"No, I'm glad I know." She handed the phone back to her. "Uh, sorry. I... I think I'm going for a walk. I can put the rest of these away when I get back."

Vanessa said, "Don't worry about that. Do you want someone to walk with you?"

"No. Thank you."

She walked out past Karen, who had finally pulled herself up off the couch. She had Codie's song in her hands, and she frowned at Vanessa as Lana stormed outside.

"What happened?"

Vanessa sighed and slumped against the fridge. "I'm thinking we should have gone to a cabin in the mountains that didn't have wifi."

Naomi considered calling the gossip rag to gloat, but there was more pride in being silently superior. Any whispers about a tryst between Lana and Karen had been effectively quashed by the photos of Lana having lunch with Laura. As an added bonus, people seemed more focused on Lana's adorable antics with "baby Bug" than the fact she was spending the day with the wife of her supposed mistress. Naomi's favorite picture showed Lana staring straight ahead with an almost completely horizontal Mason lying across her lap, his right hand tangled in her hair. Lana's expression was one of complete surrender and helplessness, while Mason seemed to be laughing uproariously.

The pictures were absolutely perfect. People liked cute, and there were enough shots floating around on gossip sites and personal blogs that soon the affair rumor would be completely dead. She'd spent the entire weekend at home with her phone turned off, doing work around the house and spending time with Susan. She did her best to refresh Susan's memory about why they started dating, long before the wedding vows and the long absences spent catering to the whims of childish musicians.

They'd met fifteen months earlier, and they'd been married two months later. Everyone was shocked by how quickly they moved, but Naomi and Susan both knew there was no point in waiting. They fit together so well that Naomi thought they could have gotten married on the second date. She'd never believed in soulmates, but Susan complemented her in ways she didn't even know was possible. She knew in her heart that Susan was the one she'd been waiting for, so why put off making it official?

The last word she'd gotten from the Coal Mine was that the first album was near completion and the band would soon be ready for the grand unveiling. She would have to be ready for the maelstrom that followed: personal appearances, interviews, concerts, maybe a tour... Radiation Canary was coming back and they were going to create huge waves when they landed. It was her job to make sure nothing got wiped out by the ensuing tidal wave.

For once she was feeling absolutely at peace with her professional and personal lives, so it made sense that a note from Cartography's CEO was waiting on her desk. All it said was "I need to see you first thing this morning, please."

She sighed and put her things down before she headed to his office. "Well, at least I had a nice weekend."

The CEO was Oscar Burke, the man who had taken over after Dash Warren's untimely death. He was hand-picked and, from day one, his only goal had been to see Dash's vision through to the end. Naomi loved him and he seemed to love her. She was one of the only people who had been with the label since its first days. She hoped her seniority didn't mean she would be one of the first people sacrificed in the name of budget cuts. She didn't even know if they were in danger of budget cuts.

The building started its life as an elementary school, and the CEO's office was originally the principal's. It was centrally located rather than hidden up on the third floor. That was one of the things Dash loved most about it. She wasn't above or removed from her talent; she was right in the middle of everything at all times. The woman who bought a cabin so she wouldn't have to interact with other artists on her label wanted to make sure she was available if anyone ever really needed something. Naomi felt a twinge of loss and pain as she often did when she thought too often about Dash, but she pushed it aside as she went into the office.

Burke's secretary, a young woman named Julie, smiled when Naomi came in. "He said you would be stopping by. He's on a call, but you can go on in."

"Thanks, Julie."

She gave a perfunctory knock and then stepped inside. Burke looked up, waved her in with two fingers, and hastily finished his call. Naomi took a moment to scan the wall across from his desk. Photos of Dash with all of the label's original lineup, the bands she plucked from obscurity and turned into worldwide celebrities. On the adjoining wall was a display of the gold and platinum albums the label had produced, several of which carried the name Radiation Canary.

"Naomi," Burke said. "Thanks for stopping by. I know you've been busy lately."

"I always have time for you, Oz. What's going on?"

He gestured at the seat across from her. "Cancer."

She stopped halfway into the seat. "What?"

"Diagnosed last week. You know my trip to New York so I could see a few bands I'd heard about on the internet? My wife saw the bands, I went into the hospital. I didn't want anyone to know until I had a solid confirmation. It's cancer."

Naomi sank into the chair. "God. I'm sorry. How serious is it?"

"It's bad. You know, as opposed to one of the good cancers." He smiled and rubbed his upper lip with his finger. "This company survived losing one CEO, but it was by the skin of its teeth. I don't want to put it through that kind of turmoil again just because I don't want to give up the seat. I soon won't be able to do the job and it'll be better if there's a gentle transition. To be frank, I thought Dash should have given you the position. I don't know why she didn't."

Naomi blinked behind her glasses. "She knew I was happy with my current job. Getting promoted would have been a burden."

He nodded. "How about now?"

"Oz?"

"You started Cartography with Dash. This is your baby. I wanted to make the offer to you first."

Naomi thought about her promises to Susan, the late nights and the hundreds of miles she put on her car just driving from one musician to the next to put out fires. The CEO wouldn't have to deal with the talent on a day-to-day basis. On the other hand, the CEO didn't get to go out and see the talent on a day-to-day basis. Radiation Canary was finally back, and she was just going to abandon them?

"Do I have time to think about it?" She closed her eyes and shook her head. "No, I mean... God, you're obviously working on a tight schedule."

"I can stick around for a few months," he said. "I'd like to have your answer as soon as possible, of course. If you decide to stay where you are I'll have to put together a list of second choices."

Naomi said, "You don't even have a list yet?"

"You've always been my first choice, Naomi. You deserve the job, and you can do it better than I ever did. Go ahead and take the rest of today off, talk it over with Susan, and let me know."

"Thank you." She stood up. "Radiation Canary... they're still working on their album. I would like to at least see that through."

Burke nodded. "Of course." She started for the door and he stopped her by saying her name. "The CEO can do whatever she wants. That includes checking in on their favorite acts from time to time. You'll be shackled to this desk a lot, but you won't necessarily be restricted from doing the parts of your job that you love now. I'm just saying."

She smiled. "Thank you, Oz. I'll keep that in mind. And if you need anything during your treatment, I hope you know Susan and I are just a phone call away."

"I appreciate that. Give her my love."

"I will."

She left the office, smiled at Julie, and walked out into the corridor. She walked to the opposite wall and sagged against it. Decades ago this hall had been swarming with kids, none older than ten years old, and she could almost smell the rubber of their sneakers, the pencil shavings, the bubble gum reek. She took off her glasses and pressed the heels of her hands against her eyes. Her breath was coming in short and rapid gasps. She could be the head of Cartography Records. She looked to the heavens and exhaled shakily.

"Dashiell, if you set this up somehow... I know you. Up there conspiring with the angels..." She chuckled and wiped at her eyes, then took out her phone. She dialed Susan's number and paced toward the area where a bank of lockers had once stood.

"This is Susan Marrow."

She smiled and pressed her fist against the middle of her chest. "Sue."

"Naomi? Are you okay? You sound odd."

"I'm fine. I'm... I, uh, I got a day off."

Susan said, "And you're taking it? That's not like you."

Naomi laughed. "Can you meet me for lunch? Either at home or somewhere nice. There's something I want to talk to you about."

"Good or bad?"

"Good. I think either way it'll be good."

Susan said, "Then I'll make the time. Can I call you in twenty minutes after I've moved some things around?"

"Sure. Susan... I love you."

"I love you, too. I can't wait to hear what this is all about."

Naomi smiled. "I think you'll be happy. I'll talk to you soon."


It took them an hour to get a version of Codie's song they were happy with. Codie's idea of using music to mimic a thunderstorm was a hard nut to crack. They experimented with different sounds before they got something they were all happy with. Vanessa and Lana weaved their instruments together for rain. Karen stood in for the wind, while Codie simulated distant thunder that rolled ominously closer. When they were finally finished Lana declared they should take a fifteen minute break before they came back to add the vocal track.

Sidra said, "Karen, your phone has been ringing off and on for the past twenty minutes. I checked to see if it was Laura, but it said it wasn't a saved number, so…"

Karen frowned and set down her violin, grateful that Sidra eliminated her worst fear immediately. She excused herself and went into the booth. "Did they leave a voicemail?"

"No." Sidra turned in her chair to watch Karen dig through her bag to retrieve her phone. "I just heard it ringing every four or five minutes. Someone definitely wants to get in touch with you."

"It would seem so." She checked the call log. "This is a London number." She called it back and leaned against the wall as it rang.

After a few seconds the call was answered. "Hello, Karen."

She tensed. "Catherine. Uh. Hi." Sidra pursed her lips and turned to face the glass again, giving the illusion of privacy. "I… you were trying to call me."

"Actually, I was trying to get in touch with Lana. I figured either you or Codie would be my best chance of finding her. Is she there?"

Karen looked through the glass. "I'm not sure she'll want to talk to you."

"Well, that's too fucking bad, isn't it?" Catherine snapped.

"Hey." Karen wanted to respond with anger, but she managed to tamp it down. "I don't know what you're so pissed off about. She's the one who had to see you and Sexy Lexi parading around London while she was here heartbroken and sick."

Catherine laughed. "Right. Because I'm the big bad ex who dumped her, I should be punished, right? I broke her heart so I deserve whatever I get."

"Well…"

"Then she'll be happy to know that my life has been hell these past few weeks. Alexandra is my friend, and she forced me to get dressed and go out to have a good time because I could barely get out of bed. I was sick with worry, Karen. Literally, physically sick. I went over to our old apartment so we could maybe clear the air, part on good terms, and she was gone. No note, nothing. She had fucking vanished. I couldn't find her on the phone, she wasn't using email or social media, she had completely evaporated off the face of the Earth. I thought…" She took a deep breath, and Karen thought she was either crying or trying very hard not to. "She was so hurt when we broke up. I thought maybe she had hurt herself."

Karen looked through the glass at Lana, who was standing behind

Codie's drum to go over the lyrics. When Catherine spoke again, her voice was marginally softer.

"Part of me knew she hadn't. I knew she wouldn't kill herself over me. I'm not quite that narcissistic. But the longer she went without popping her head up, the more I thought... maybe in a moment of weakness...?" She exhaled a shaky breath. "Then Alexandra dragged me out to a movie premiere, and in the lobby of the theater, someone shows me a picture of Lana and your wife having a casual brunch in Seattle. That's why I said those hateful things in the interview. I was fucking livid that she seemed to have no idea what her disappearance had done to me. And the reason I'm calling is because even those pictures aren't enough. I need to hear her voice. I need to know for sure that she's really okay."

Karen said, "Can I call you back?"

"Yes. Just please, even if she doesn't want to talk to me... I don't know, have her send a photo holding today's newspaper? Something. Anything."

"I'll see what I can do. I'll call you right back." She hung up and tapped the phone against her forehead.

Sidra looked over her shoulder. "That sounded intense."

"Yeah." She sighed and went into the studio. "Lana. Can I talk to you for a second?"

Lana said, "Is everything okay?"

Karen gestured toward one of the soundproof isolation booths. Lana joined her inside and Karen closed the door. "Did you tell anyone where you were going when you left England?"

"No."

"Why not?"

Lana shrugged. "There was no one to tell. Apartment was paid up, our mail had already been forwarded to the new apartment, we weren't really close with our neighbors."

"Did you tell Catherine?"

Lana frowned. "No. Why would I?"

Karen slumped against the wall. "She thought you had killed yourself, Lana."

Lana's eyes widened. "She what?"

"You go into this downward spiral after she breaks up with you, then suddenly you leave the country and go completely silent because we're working on this secret project. From her point of view, you had just vanished. She was devastated."

"Oh, sure. She looked really devastated in those pictures."

"Sexy Lexi was just trying to help lift her out of her funk. Then she saw the pictures of you and Laura hanging out and she got a little vindictive. I think under the circumstances it's... maybe a little understandable."

Lana said, "Are you taking her side?"

"I'm on your side," Karen said. "Always, a hundred percent. Never forget that. But I also believe what you did hurt Catherine. You owe her an explanation, if not an apology."

Lana glared at her. "She just decided we were done, Karen. She just cut things off, walked out the door, and the next thing I know she's on the internet running around town with someone else."

"Kind of like when you left me."

Lana flinched. "That was…"

"The same thing. Imagine what would have happened if you came back and I was just gone. Imagine how you would have felt."

Lana sighed and took Karen's phone. "Is it the last number called?"

"Yeah." She rubbed Lana's shoulder. "We'll be here if you need the moral support."

"Thanks. And… thanks for playing devil's advocate, even if it was against me."

"Any time."

She stepped out of the booth and closed the door so Lana could have privacy for the call. Codie and Vanessa acted as if they hadn't been watching through the glass.

"Everything okay?" Codie said.

"Yeah. Lana just had to tie up some loose ends."

## Chapter Fourteen

NAOMI PICKED Susan up from work and took her out for ice cream. They put the dog in the car and drove down to the ferry lanes. They parked at the bank where they could look out over the wide harbor with the cliff rising up to their right. It was where Susan had proposed to her. She remembered the day vividly, how Susan had been so nervous that she had to read her proposal off a sheet of paper. Naomi had responded by taking from her wallet a folded sheet of paper that had the first draft of her own proposal written on it. They'd only been dating for three months, but waiting any longer seemed ridiculous.

Naomi explained Oz's offer. "I would be home every day at the same time. No long trips to Snohomish, no babysitting in Seattle, no phone calls about album art at four in the morning."

"Are those pros or cons you're listing?"

Naomi said, "I love my work. But it's not fair to you. I'm away so much..."

Susan put her arm around Naomi's shoulders, an awkward position in the car but manageable. "You were here the day we rode the ferry to the mainland together and struck up a conversation that turned into dinner. You were here the day we got Henry." The dog lifted his head off the backseat at the mention of his name. "You were here the day we got married, and I know that if I ever need you, you'll come running no matter where you are. The truth is, I would love to have you by my side twenty-four seven. But that would involve a cage and shackles, and I'm not that kind of girl."

Naomi chuckled.

"We took so long to find each other. So many years looking and not finding each other. Five minutes or five hours, I count every second we're together as a blessing and a gift. I don't feel I'm owed more. I'm not jealous of your commitments. If you take the job and we become the couple who is sitting at the dinner table every evening at six-thirty, great. If you keep the job you have now and we're the couple who has dinner at midnight, fine. But I don't want you to sacrifice a job you truly love for one you're not passionate about just because you think you owe me a schedule."

Out in the harbor she could see sailboats bobbing up and down on the tide. A ferry was scheduled soon, but at the moment the dock was clear.

"I think I know what I'm going to do."

Susan said, "Oh?"

"Yeah. I think... I'm going to take you home and make love to you."

"Now that is an idea I can get behind one hundred percent."

Naomi finished her ice cream and started the car, stopping at the exit so they could throw their trash into a conveniently-placed bin. She still didn't know if she was going to take Oz's offer. She would miss all her clients like crazy, especially Radiation Canary, but if the choice was between managing them and spending more time with her wife, there was no contest. Now that she knew Susan's opinion on the matter she could take the time to decide what would be right for her.

The days that followed were filled with a renewed sense of urgency. Music was hashed out in the studio and then instantly committed to a digital recorder. Lana and Codie worked together on "Wind Between Two Oceans," which Lana was already considering one of the strongest songs on the album. She offered to move it to the second album so they could use it as the title track, but Codie refused. "I don't want my title to be responsible for the whole album. I don't think I could handle that." Lana acquiesced and kept it on the first album, but she moved it to the bottom of the track list so the other songs could build to it.

They would wake up in the morning, have a communal breakfast, and then traipse downstairs to sing or play music or argue over a particular turn of phrase. Their arguments were rarely filled with true ire; even the morning Lana punctuated the statement "You. Don't. Even. Know. How. To. Speak. Properly!" by bouncing pieces of wadded-up paper off Codie's head ended with all smiles.

Laura brought Mason up for a weekend, and Lana convinced her to play bass for two songs. She also provided background vocals for Karen on "Best Laid Plans." When Laura went home she reminded Karen of their tit-for-tat agreement; she had worked on the Canary album so she wanted

Karen in the studio for the Femme Reapers.

The final song they worked on was actually one of the first they had written. "The Sailmaker's Daughter" had originally been Karen's vocal, but Lana asked if she could be the one to sing it. Karen agreed and pointed out that she considered herself the understudy, taking over only when Lana didn't want to take the lead.

Lana said, "Show of hands, who here has a solo album?" She stared at Karen until she finally, reluctantly raised her hand. "There it is. Now, shut up and let me sing your song."

The song began with piano and guitar, so she nodded at Vanessa that she was ready. She began to play and stepped closer to the microphone.

*"I thank my lucky stars every day that this car still starts*
*When I turn the key to warm the engine as the dawn fades*
*And I shudder and I'm reminded of the promises we made*
*When we fogged up the windows to cover the glass with hearts*

*The coffee is only there to thaw my fingers*
*And I hate how much that pot smell lingers*
*Now I hope it doesn't stick to my clothes*
*How I got to this point only God knows*

*Even in the summer the sun doesn't shine on this city*
*And I'd turn my face away even if he appeared*
*These heavy grey rainclouds suit me perfectly*
*They rolled over my head the day you disappeared*

*I watched my mother make sails when I was a girl*
*She'd take me down to watch the ships in the harbor*
*Her sails carried ships and their people to the seven wonders*
*Snaring the wind to pull them all over the world*

*Someday I'm going to build a boat from plywood and glue*
*I'm going to steal my mother's sail, head off into the storms*
*I'll bear any rough seas I find and I'm going to break through*
*I swear I'm not going to stop until I'm back in your arms*

*And I won't take my eyes off you*
*To the edge of the world I'd follow you*
*Where the lighthouse can't reach*
*On some dark and foreign beach*
*Or an undiscovered place*
*I will run to you, I will fall to you*
*My reward will be one glimpse of your face."*

After the bridge was a lengthy interlude that led into the final verses. Lana watched her friends as they played, smiling at Codie before she turned back to finish the song.

Silence fell after the music faded. "'As the harbor is welcome to the sailor'," Lana said into the mic, "'so is the last line to the scribe.' And so is the last note to the singer." She stepped back and strummed a chord as she turned to face the band. "Thirteen songs, fifty minutes and seven seconds of music, and Radiation Canary's ninth album is a wrap. Beautiful work, ladies."

Karen and Codie whooped while Vanessa applauded them. Lana took off her guitar and placed it on the stand, then waved her bandmates in for a group hug. They had actually recorded twenty songs, with six left to do for the second album. But as of that moment they had the thirteen they wanted for the free album. Codie's song wound up being the climax of the album, followed by a small and intimate song with Karen's vocals called "Twist Ending."

Codie joined the hug, her arms around Karen and Vanessa. "I'm doing this under duress."

"As long as you're doing it, punk," Lana said.

Sidra came out of the booth and stood to one side until the hug broke up. She crossed her arms over her stomach, hands clasping the opposite elbow, and she smiled when Lana looked at her.

"Hands down, best album I've ever worked on. We still have to do a lot of work getting it mastered, but I know Cartography is going to be very happy with it. Oh, and Lana, that quote about harbors and sailors... I left that in, but I'm going to fade it and add a few seconds of silence between the end of the song and the quote. Sound good?"

"Sounds perfect. Thanks, Sidra."

"No problem. Right now, you four ought to celebrate."

Lana pulled Sidra into the hug. "The five of us. We couldn't have done it without you. And we're not celebrating yet. We still have a lot of work to do before the album is ready. And I want to go ahead and do the last six songs for the second album while we're here. Actually, the outdoor studio... Sidra, do you think we'd be able to get in there for the last songs?"

"I don't see why not. The hardest thing would be moving Codie's drums out."

"Okay. We can work on that, and then we can figure out the actual track listing. I think *Coal Mine Sessions* is pretty well set. For right now we can focus on the fun things. Album art, liner notes, that sort of thing. We've been working almost non-stop on recording since we got here. Dash Warren made this place as a refuge, so let's use it as one. Karen, I know you've been dying to go back to Seattle. Go. We'll call you if we need something, but you need to spend some time with that wife of yours. We can relax just fine without you.”

Karen smiled. “Are you sure?”

“Look at you. You’re already halfway out the door. Yes, go, have fun. Vanessa, you can go, too.”

Codie said, “So it’s just you, me, and the woman you’re sleeping with hanging out in a cabin for a few days. That won’t be awkward at all.”

Sidra said, “You’re welcome to join us, Codie.”

Codie raised an eyebrow and tilted her head to one side as she pretended to contemplate it. “I think I’ll pass. My own baby has been calling to me. I think I need to take her out for a real flight.”

“So it’ll just be the two of us at the cabin, ‘working’ on the ‘album’?” Sidra said, making air quotes with her fingers.

Lana put an arm around her waist and said, “Yeah, but... all work and no play...”

The next morning, everyone but Lana and Sidra headed out. Karen returned home in time to save Laura from one of Mason’s temper tantrums, and she soothed him back to calm by playing her cello for him. Vanessa told Scott the album was all but finished and he rewarded her by forbidding any and all forms of household chores. She was to simply sit on the sofa - or lie in bed if she preferred - and play with Nathaniel while Scott took care of whatever needed to be done around the house.

Codie went directly to her hangar to inspect her plane and then take it out for a symbolic trip back to Squire’s Isle. She hadn’t flown the route since her engine failed her, and she felt like doing so after finishing the album would be a nice bookend to the project. She needed to successfully complete the flight home to give closure to the incident. She was confident that the emergency landing wouldn’t be repeated. The cause had been found and corrected, and she had all the confidence in her plane. Still, she gave it a thorough inspection and rested her hand on the fuselage and closed her eyes for a moment. She didn’t call it a prayer or a blessing, but she nevertheless felt better when she went to file her flight plan.

At the Coal Mine, Lana assisted Sidra with mixing the album. She had her phone with her so she could occasionally call or text someone for their opinion on a choice that had to be made. Karen agreed on moving “Cathedrals” to the second album, and Vanessa agreed to redo her part on “Echoing Mirrors” so it would be more prominent. Sidra played the nature sounds she had recorded earlier and gave Lana an example of how they would sound in the silence between songs. “Enough for You” faded almost to silence before the subtle sound of a babbling brook faded in, building a bridge to the opening notes of “The Sound of Your Voice.”

“The way I figure it,” Sidra said, “it won’t deter people from listening to the songs individually, but it would reward the people who listen to the album straight through as intended."

Lana grinned. "You have enough to do this for every song?"

"I think so. If not I can always just go out and grab more. I keep hearing a horned owl outside at night, but by the time I get my recording stuff ready they've all gone quiet. I'm determined to get them on the album."

Lana rubbed her leg. "Maybe we could camp out in the stable tonight."

Sidra pursed her lips. "Ooh, I like that idea. Get all nice and cozy in the sleeping bags..." She turned back to the board. "So. This might not be any of my business and feel free to tell me if I should just shut up. But I got the feeling a couple days ago you had something of a knock-down, drag-out with your ex. That was her on Karen's phone, right?"

"Yeah, that was Catherine. I found out I might not have been the innocent victim in the breakup."

"Ouch. That always sucks."

Lana laughed. "Yeah, doesn't it?" She pushed her hair out of her face. "We fought for the first time without all the anger getting in the way. I discovered that I don't want her back, but... god, all that time we wasted."

Sidra shook her head. "Don't say that. Not wasted. The tragedy isn't the time you spent in the relationship. The tragedy isn't even that it had to end. You grew and loved and got to see what it was like to be in a relationship. Your time with her showed you that you were ready for that kind of commitment. Catherine didn't take away your happy ending, she just changed a few of the details around. Her part is just going to be recast."

Lana rested her elbow on the mixing board and smiled at Sidra. "That's a beautiful sentiment."

"Feel free to steal it for a song."

"I just might." She leaned forward and kissed Sidra. "Thank you for putting me back in one piece. And for fiddling with the album in your spare time."

Sidra bumped her forehead against Lana's. "Happy to do it. Like I said, it's easy with a group as talented as you four. I was heartbroken when you said you were going on hiatus. And getting the chance to be part of your triumphant return? Oh, yeah. That's... that's made my career." She kissed the corner of Lana's mouth. "And I like that I get to have sex with you a lot."

Lana laughed. "Yeah, that's not a normal perk. But it's worked out well for us so far."

"Indeed it has." She leaned back in her chair. "So have you given any thought to what the album cover will be?"

"Lots of thought, but no decisions. I think Cartography will want our pictures on it again, but I'm sick of that."

Sidra stood up and motioned for her to follow. "I was outside in the stable and I wanted to show you something. I had an idea."

They went up and outside, crossing the lawn to the stable. As far as Lana could tell, it had never been home to any actual horses. She remembered reading a story somewhere about Dash getting very interested in becoming an equestrian but nothing had ever come of it. There were stalls along one side of the building but the rest was an open space filled with discarded instruments. An old piano stood prominently in the center of all the junk, and Sidra had presumably dug out an old cello and rested it against the side.

"There are some guitars buried back there, too," Sidra said. "I thought maybe we could pull these out and set them up like they're an abandoned set. You know, like the music was just waiting for you to come back. Then we can shoot it so you're looking past the instruments out the back door at the trees..."

Lana crouched and framed the shot with her hands. The top of the evergreens that encircled the cabin created an inverted dome of blue sky. She thought about it under a blue filter to create a deeper feeling of abandonment and gloom, with "Radiation Canary - The Coal Mine Sessions" written across the top in simple white font.

"I like it. It's classy and elegant. It sets the right tone." She stood up and kissed Sidra. "Let me guess. Photography student?"

"Dated one for a few semesters. Sometimes it rubs off."

Lana grinned and looked at the clutter. "Help me dig out a guitar. I don't see any drums, but I definitely want Codie represented somehow."

"Well, you're doing two albums. If Codie can't be represented on this one, maybe the second could be a plane."

Lana stopped and looked out the back door. "We could name it after her charity. Westward Sky."

Sidra smiled. "Sounds like an album to me, boss."

Lana winked at her and went back to moving around the trashed instruments.

## CHAPTER FIFTEEN

EVERYONE WAS invited to the Coal Mine to hear the album for the first time. They made it into an event, black-tie and champagne. Lana insisted on calling it a "fancy-dress" party and blamed the past few years spent living in England. They had finalized the artwork and liner notes, and signed copies of the disc would be given out to everyone in attendance. Karen's dads, Laura's sister, a couple of Codie's friends from the airport, and a few of the neighborhood women who had discovered Vanessa's 'secret identity' were filling the large ground-floor space to capacity. Karen's mother attended with her new husband through Facetime on Karen's phone, and people took turns carrying it around so she didn't miss out just because she was three thousand miles away.

Though the party was to celebrate the album's completion, the band wasn't technically the guest of honor. Lana had approached Naomi about turning the celebration into something of a surprise party, and Naomi agreed to the inclusion of a special guest to the invite list.

Nick Young, the host of *Settle In, Seattle!*, was a big reason for the band's early success. They appeared on his show as part of the "Friday Night Auditions" segment and he quickly became the band's first, biggest, and most powerful fan. They'd gone back to his show a number of times throughout their career, and Lana couldn't think of a better place to announce their new album. He was kept completely in the dark as to the purpose of the event, told only that it was a surprise.

Naomi and Susan picked up Nick and his date in Seattle and drove them up. His date was a producer named Madeline, and Naomi swore them both to secrecy before they even left city limits.

"I hope you've given some thought to the fifteenth anniversary show," Nick said. "We'd love to have some of the acts you represent."

Naomi said, "Oh? Anyone in particular? Who would you want if you could have anybody?"

Nick laughed. "Well, anybody? Radiation Canary. But if Karen Everett isn't busy, she could promote *Masquerade*. It's a hell of an album."

"It is. I think Karen is busy that day, but I could ask Regan Duffy if she's doing anything."

"Oh, hey. Regan Duffy is nobody's second choice. That would be amazing."

Susan smirked at her wife, expressing how evil she was being without saying a word. Naomi winked at her and drove on in silence.

When they got off the highway and started toward the cabin, Nick watched the small town roll past and chuckled. "You know, I heard Dash Warren had a cabin up here. Some kind of private studio. Did the record company keep that after she passed?"

"Uh, yeah. I think we still have the title."

It wasn't until they were parking in front of the house that Nick realized they were actually at Dash's private studio. Naomi was shocked at how glorious the place looked; every light was on, and rows of paper lanterns had been hung on the porch so people could make their way inside without tripping. Nick got out of the car and offered his elbow to Madeline as Naomi and Susan led them to the front door. They were almost there when Karen stepped out to greet them.

"Karen!" Nick gave her a one-armed hug so he didn't have to let go of his date. "We were just talking about you on the drive up. What are you doing here?"

"I'm actually hosting the party. Well, me and Laura. And some of our friends."

"Well, thank you for the invite. I..." He blinked in surprise at who had just passed by the door behind her. "Codie?"

Codie came back and smiled. "Hiya, Nick. How you doing?"

"I'm doing fine. It's great seeing you." He hugged her as well. They stepped inside and Karen took their coats. "Karen, Codie, this is Madeline Andrews. She's a producer on *Settle In, Seattle!* Madeline, this is Karen Everett and Codie Renton. They're one-half of Radiation Canary."

Madeline smiled. "Nice to meet you. I love your band."

"Thank you," Karen said. "I'll be sure to tell Vanessa when I see her." She twisted. "Vanessa?"

Vanessa came down the stairs. "Yeah?"

"This is a producer on Nick's show. She likes the band."

"Oh. Thank you. Hello."

Nick was smiling widely enough that it nearly split his slender face in half. "Wow, this is almost perfect. It's too bad that Lana Kent is in London."

"Don't you read the papers?" Lana asked as she came into the room. "I was in Seattle just a few weeks ago. I had dinner with Karen's wife."

Nick stared at her, then slowly looked at the others. "What's... going on?"

"This is why you were sworn to secrecy, Nick," Naomi said. "Hi, ladies."

"So... what's going on? You're thinking about a reunion? Please tell me you're thinking about a reunion."

Lana said, "No. We're not thinking about a reunion."

His shoulders sagged. "Get my hopes up. Drive me all the way out here. But a party with my four favorite celebrities is definitely not a disappointment. Did Naomi tell you about our fifteen anniversary show? We'd love to have you make an appearance, maybe perform one of your hits..."

Naomi smiled. "Why don't you come with us, Nick? We need to have a talk."

He excused himself from his date, who went to mingle with Scott and Laura. The band followed Naomi and Nick upstairs to the lounge.

Naomi closed the door. "We need you absolute secrecy, Nick. We need to know if the band agrees to be on your show, it will be a surprise appearance. We don't want anything leaking before we're ready. Is that possible?"

He frowned at her. "Why would it have to be a secret?"

"You didn't listen to Lana, Nick." Karen opened her purse and took out a CD. "We're not thinking about a reunion. We already thought about it. We're not only back together, we're already finished with the new album. We've been recording it up here under the radar."

Nick could only stare at the album she was holding out. "You have a new album ready to go?"

"Not only that," Lana said. "We're giving it away for free."

"Free? You're going to come on my show, announce you're back together with a finished album, and then you're giving it away for free?" He laughed and wiped a hand over his face. "I don't need the ratings. The video would go viral almost instantly. The only problem would be the studio audience. We could bribe them to keep quiet, but the odds are someone will tweet or Facebook about what happened. Rumors would get out. It might only be a few hours before the show airs, but..." He bit his bottom lip. "We could go live."

"Really?"

"I'll ask the network. It's the fifteenth anniversary and we've been good for them, so they might be amenable to it. It would really be the only way to keep the secret." He finally took the CD Karen was holding out to him. "*The Coal Mine Sessions*. This artwork is beautiful." He turned it over and looked at the track listing. "Is there a CD player around here?"

Lana said, "The point of this party is to let everyone hear it. We're going to have dinner, have a few drinks, and then we'll play it for the first time."

"Huge honor," Nick said. "Thank you for..." He looked at Naomi. "Thank you for tricking me. If I'd known we were coming up here for this, I'd have been like a damn two-year-old bouncing in the backseat."

"You're very welcome." She rubbed her hands together. "Now, let's get downstairs. The sooner we eat, the sooner I can find out what you ladies have been doing all this time."

They went back downstairs where Sidra and Scott had finished setting out the food. They ate, drank, and were generally merry until they adjourned to the living room. Sidra set up the sound system while Lana stepped up on the hearth to address the group.

"Hi, everybody. Thank you for coming up here to share this with us. Laura, Scott, thank you for loaning your wives to us. I know it wasn't easy being separated from them all this time, but hopefully it will be worth it. For those of you who don't know, we've been cloistered up here putting together a new album. Two albums, actually. We're releasing one for free next month, and the other one will follow in a few months for... you know... money. Because we're generous, not stupid."

The crowd chuckled.

"Okay. Uh, the liner notes?" Karen handed her a copy. "Okay. I just wanted to take a moment to read the liner notes of the album. 'The band wishes to thank Cartography Records, for their unending support. Naomi Marrow for her guidance: she truly mapped the way and kept us on course, and we can never forget how much she has meant to us. Lana wants to thank the band, who has always been there to catch her when she fell, and who helped her get back on her feet when she needed it the most.'" She sniffled slightly, but powered through. "'Karen wishes to thank the love of her life, Laura, and their son, the Astounding Bug.'" Laura made Mason clap his hands at his mention. "'Vanessa Wayland would like to thank her husband and son, Scott and Nathaniel, for their endless support and love. Codie Renton would like to thank...'" She looked to her right, where Codie was smirking at her. "I thought I told you not to edit this before it went to print."

"Oops. Read it."

Lana sneered at her, sighed, and looked at the notes. "'Codie Renton would like to thank Lana Kent, for literally everything in her life, for seeing her as something more than a hooligan and a punk, and for...'" She pulled her lips back against her teeth. "'And for being my sister and my best friend.' I'm going to kill you for that, Codie."

The assembly applauded, and Lana took the opportunity to wipe her eyes. "Those are the thank-yous. And now, Karen has handed out the discs, so you'll all have lyrics to follow along if you'd like. Sidra, are we ready? We are ready. Feel free to talk or mingle while the songs are playing. We're not going to hold you hostage and force you to listen to every note. Just enjoy yourselves and hopefully enjoy the music. Thanks."

She stepped off the stage and knocked her knuckles off Codie's chin. "Bitch."

Codie hugged her. "Serves you right for not reading them before you got up there. I do love you, Lana. I don't throw those words around lightly."

"I know. I love you, too." She kissed Codie's cheek and then stepped back to smile at her. "We did it. The free album is done."

"Yeah. All that's left now is waiting for the live show and seeing how people react."

Autographs were requested and received while the music played. Laura asked everyone but Karen to sign her album and, when Nick pointed out her omission, she said, "Well, Vanessa is my favorite..." The band welcomed the opportunity to focus on signing the album so they weren't staring at their friends and relatives to see how they felt about the songs.

When the last note of "Twist Ending" faded into the nature sounds Sidra had recorded outside, the party broke into applause. Lana waved them off and shouted, "Oh, you're all biased!"

Naomi herded all four girls into the kitchen and shook her head at them. "You're seriously giving that away for free? That's the best album you've ever done. If you give it away, you might not be eligible for the Grammys. And this could win you a Grammy."

Lana said, "That would be great. But I want to focus more on rewarding the fans who stuck by us. The ones who shelled out fifty bucks for our 'farewell' album package. They've stuck by us for over ten years. I want to give them that." She looked at the others. "If I'm outvoted—"

"Absolutely not," Codie said. "*Coal Mine* will be free, and *Westward Sky* will be back to commercialism. That sucks for the label. I know having a Grammy award on the wall would be a big deal..."

"No. No, it's a bigger deal to be the label that rewards its fans. And hey, if the second album is anything like this one, we won't have to wait long for the Grammy anyway."

Vanessa held up one of the CDs they'd spent the night signing. "You know... we made these for the party, but we could always have a physical release as well. You would at least have to charge for shipping. So why not make the actual CD cost... five dollars, or something."

Naomi brightened and looked at Lana for confirmation. Lana nodded. "I wasn't even thinking about the physical release. Even I haven't bought an actual CD in years. Forget the Grammy, charge five bucks just so the label won't go broke on this."

"Excellent. Thank you." She clasped Lana's hands. "You four are the best thing I've ever done for this company. I'm honored that I was able to pull you in."

Karen, Codie, and Vanessa embraced her. Not long after that the party started to break up. People had to make the long drive back to Seattle or its suburbs, and they each promised they would be listening to the album again as soon as they got into the car. Lana pointed out that the length of the album should cover the whole drive home.

Vanessa and Karen decided with their significant others that they would also be going home to sleep in their own beds rather than staying at the cabin. Karen left right after her Dads so they could caravan together. Naomi and her wife also left and, since they were Nick's ride, he also bid them a goodnight. He kissed Lana on the cheek and thanked her again for giving him the opportunity to be a part of their career.

Sidra was going to stay behind, but one of her friends called and invited her to an after-midnight party in Seattle. Eventually everyone had left but Lana and Codie. They spent a half hour cleaning up the debris from the gathering before Lana collapsed on the couch. Codie finished loading the dishwasher before she came back and threw herself into an armchair. She flung her leg over one side and let her arm dangle to the floor.

"Being social is exhausting."

"Amen. Did everyone else go home?"

"Just you and me, princess."

Lana chuckled. "Wow. Who would've thought, all these years after homeroom?" She rubbed her forehead. "You know you're my longest-lasting relationship?"

"And you're mine."

"I'm glad you're not gay, though. If we'd had sex, we would have just screwed everything up."

"You don't know that. Gay Codie might put up with a lot of your crap."

Lana smiled. "No, I know myself. I'd have cheated on you or pushed you away or... we would have broken up at some point. I don't have any doubt about that. I'd much rather have you as my straight best friend than a bitter ex."

"Even if the sex would have been phenomenal."

Lana scoffed. "Oh, it would have brought the house down. Are you kidding me? No one would ever have screwed your brains out like I would have."

Codie smiled. "Have you ever thought about it?"

Lana looked at her in the dimly-lit living room. "What? You and me? Nah..."

"Come on, Lana. Honestly."

Lana laughed. "Once or twice. Maybe. Over the course of the decade-plus we've known one another, yeah, you maybe slipped into a fantasy or two. I refuse to accept blame. You're hot, you're a badass, you're a pilot. You're sexy. I am but a woman."

Codie grinned. "I'll have to be careful not to get drunk around you."

Lana stuck her arms out and made grabby-hands. "Can't... resist... sexy... drummer..."

Codie rolled off the chair and bent down to kiss Lana's hands. "If I was ever going to have a threesome, I'd want it to be with you."

"Deal. But leave the guy at home."

"Are you camping out in Karen's room?"

"Yeah."

"Then I'll take Vanessa's. I'll see you in the morning."

Lana said, "Okay. Goodnight, Codie. And thank you for everything."

Codie went upstairs and left Lana alone in the dark downstairs. From her position on the couch she could see out the window, the grayish purple of the sky above the trees. When the album was finished they would tour and promote the hell out of it. They would go out on the road and spend countless nights in hotels, visit towns without learning their names, and move on. Then when it inevitably quieted down, Codie would go back to her plane. Karen and Vanessa would have their families. And she would be the odd one out. She was homeless, sleeping on Codie's couch, and alone. Karen, Vanessa, and Codie all credited her with putting the band together and making their lives possible. She wondered when she would get around to making her own life come together.

## CHAPTER SIXTEEN

WHEN THE euphoria of actually playing a new album for their friends and family wore off, the band reunited at the cabin to record the final songs for the second album. Naomi pointed out that if they could release it by the award cutoff date they might still be eligible for a Grammy. "Not that I want you to rush or anything. But if there's a chance it could be ready by that time..." They promised to see what they could do and focused on the work.

Lana and Karen collaborated on a few songs, and Codie helped Sidra set up the drums in the upstairs studio. Lana suggested leaving the doors open to let the nature sounds seep in. "Last time you brought the nature sounds to us. This time, why don't we go to nature?" Sidra said that she could rig up a way to make it work.

Almost half the songs they still had to record for the second album - "The Tragedy of Time Wasted," "Learning How to Sleep," and "Where You End the Story" - were directly related to Lana's breakup with Catherine. They were setting up for "Where You End the Story" when Lana walked up to Karen and took her aside.

"I can't sing this. I could probably pull through it today, but I'm picturing concerts. I'm picturing a room full of people singing it back to me... I can't. I can't sing this."

Karen put her hand on the back of Lana's head and shushed her. "It's okay. I'll take over. I'll do this one, okay?"

"Thank you."

Karen moved to take the central position while Lana moved off to the right. Karen said, "Sidra? We're swapping out lead vocals on this one. Probably a couple others. We can go back and pick up my cello later, yeah?"

"Yeah, we can. I thought *Coal Mine* was a little uneven vocally, so this should balance it out. Just keep me updated."

Karen nodded and wet her lips in preparation to sing. She looked over her shoulder at Lana, who mouthed 'thank you' again. Karen smiled and faced forward to watch for Sidra's cue.

The half-dozen songs dubbed "the outdoor tracks" were shuffled around the album so they wouldn't all show up in one block. Lana could hardly believe it, but their nonstop work had paid off. Their tenth album might be ready to go by the time the ninth was released. Their celebration for *Westward Sky* was more intimate than *Coal Mine*; the five of them listened to the album alone, with champagne and smoked salmon that Codie prepared using a recipe she'd gotten from an old boyfriend. While they listened, they discussed potential album art.

"Given the title," Vanessa said, "and the incident that prompted Codie to get us all back together, I think it would be great to have her plane on the cover. Or a plane, if she doesn't want it to be hers."

Lana said, "A plane is good. But just a head-on shot of the plane? An aerial view looking down at a plane on the runway?"

Codie said, "Oh, I vote for that."

"Well, it's *Westward Sky*," Karen said. "I would love it if we could get some aerial shots. Over the wing, or from the tail..."

Codie said, "There are some beautiful vistas around Squire's Isle, up in the San Juans."

"Vistas?" Lana said.

"Shut up, I know words."

In the end they decided to mount a camera on the tail of the plane while Codie flew a circuit of the islands just to see how the shots turned out. Before they parted once again, Lana picked up her glass and stepped up onto the table.

"Before we go, I just want to give one more toast to all of you. All of us. But as of right now, we're completely spent. We have two albums ready to go, but we have absolutely nothing for the next one. When we came here, I said it was so we could do those two albums. We never talked about what was coming next. I assumed, and I hoped..."

"We're in," Codie said.

Karen smiled. "Of course we're in."

Lana looked at Vanessa. "You put this whole life aside for your family. If you want us to respect that, we will. We can find a replacement for you if that's what you decide."

Vanessa stood up and tapped her glass against Lana's. "I can be a working mama. I'm not going to let you three have all the fun without me. Scott and I are going to work something out. You bet I'm in."

Lana jumped down and hugged Vanessa. "Good. I was bluffing about the replacement." She turned to face the group. "So now... we plan for the big public reveal. The anniversary episode of *Settle In, Seattle!* is in two weeks. We need to get ready. We need to figure out what song we're going to do to announce our return."

Sidra said, "My vote is for 'The Sailmaker's Daughter.' That song gives me chills."

"I think Naomi would agree with you. It's not exactly a radio-friendly length, but we can make it work. For now..." She looked around. "I think we need to say goodbye to this place. As great as it would be for us to all move in here permanently, I don't think that's what Cartography had in mind."

Codie said, "I don't know. We could make it into a reality show. *The Real World* meets *The Monkees.*"

"*The Real Monkeys,*" Karen said. "Damn, is it too late to change the band name?"

After the meeting, Lana asked Sidra to walk outside with her. They went to the footbridge and looked out at the point where the creek disappeared into the woods. Lana rested her elbows on the handrail and Sidra leaned next to her.

"I don't know if we're officially together," Sidra said, "but this is still technically the breakup conversation, right?"

Lana smiled sadly. "The way I see it, we have two options. We could walk away now grateful for the time we've had together, or we could try to force what we've been doing into a full relationship. I'm all for giving it a try. But I don't think we would mesh well together in the long run."

Sidra nodded. "I play way too many video games."

"I'm up all night with the guitar."

"At least this way we can walk away, no hard feelings, and then if we get horny in a few months we can hook up without any awkwardness."

Lana whistled. "I like that plan. I like that plan a lot."

"You know... 'No One's Someone'? That's not true. That's never going to be you. You're a wonderful person, Lana. You're funny and smart and kind. You care about your friends' happiness more than your own. Do you know why we worked out? Because you knew the end was coming. We were only going to be together while we were working on the album, so we had a vague end date somewhere in the future. You got close with Catherine, but then she pulled the rug out from under you. You said you always cheated to end a relationship."

"Not always..." Lana muttered.

"Well, close enough. Who did you lose?"

Lana tensed. "What?"

"I'm a fan, but I'm not the kind who reads extensive biographies on celebrities. If I know too much about their pasts, it just makes things awkward when I have to work with them. But I get the feeling you lost someone close to you when you were young."

"My mother," Lana said. "She died of cancer."

Sidra nodded. "Part of you is afraid of that happening again. Think of it like rock-climbing. You're always looking for the next grip so you won't be left dangling. Just have faith that what you're holding onto won't give way, and you'll be fine." She leaned close and kissed Lana's cheek, then her lips. "I've really enjoyed our time together. And you're going to make someone really happy someday. You just have to give them the chance to make you happy, too."

Lana wiped away a tear. "Well, now I'm thinking maybe we should date after all. You seem to know what's good for me."

Sidra laughed. "No. No, I'm someone else's someone. I'll find him or her, just like you'll find yours. And in the meantime, if we're both still single when you're working on your next album, I'll be glad to start things up again."

"That sounds like a fantastic plan." She moved her hand to link their fingers. "You're a fantastic producer. Even if we hadn't gone to bed together, I would sing your praises to anyone who would listen. Even if you're seeing someone when the next album comes along, I want you back behind the board. I want your talent behind the board for every Canary album from here on out, sex or no."

Sidra looked down at the water. "That means a lot, Lana. Thank you."

"Come on. Let's head back before Codie drinks all the champagne."

Naomi was on-hand to officially lock up the Coal Mine when the band left. She handed the keys to Lana and said, "This is your set. If you ever need to come up here to hash something out, or just to get away, the door will always be open. Even if we have another band in here, you'll be welcome. It's called the Coal Mine because it belongs to the Canaries for as long as they need it. Understood?"

"We understand," Lana said. "And thank you."

Naomi nodded and helped Lana carry her bag to the car. She was going to move back in with Codie, at least until she could find a place of her own. She'd decided that even thinking about going back to London was a waste of time. She and Catherine were completely finished and Catherine was the only reason she wanted to live in London in the first place. Seattle was her home and it would be again.

*Settle In, Seattle!* began advertising their anniversary show when it was still a week away. Lana and Codie were watching the night Nick made the announcement. They had spent the day looking for Lana's new home, and they were both exhausted from the effort of changing into their pajamas to watch TV. There was a bag of chips between them and they took turns reaching inside for a handful.

"We've been advertising this for a while," he told his audience, "and now all of a sudden we're telling you it's going to be live. Why would we do that? Well, because we can." He grinned and waved off the laughter. "No, no, we have reasons. We're doing it live because we know this show is Seattle's baby, but it's broadcast across the nation. We want to give all of our fans the feeling of being right here in the studio audience. We're going to have some big surprises on the anniversary show, and if we recorded it earlier in the day, it would leak. You know it would leak. We don't want anything to get spoiled. So we talked to the network, and they said 'whatever you want, Mr. Colbert.'" He sighed and shook his head. "They're still not entirely sure who I am. But I digress. Be sure you tune in live to our anniversary show, or you will regret it."

Lana said, "No pressure, though."

Codie chuckled. "At least he's not making the audience vote on us again."

"That's true." She sucked the crumbs from her fingers and then pointed at the screen. "Did you really sleep with him?"

Codie's smile was all the answer she needed. "Who told you?"

"Nessa."

"Ah. Should've sworn her to secrecy."

Lana laughed and then tilted her head to the side. "Is it still considered star-fucking if you're both celebrities?"

"I'm counting it."

"Me too." She held up her fist and Codie tapped her knuckles. "Nice get."

"Thank you. And speaking of getting, I am getting myself to bed." She stood up and bent down to kiss the top of Lana's head. "I know you're eager to find a place, but don't be hurrying on my account. I get lonely too, you know. I like having a roommate."

"Thanks, Codie."

"Sleep tight."

"Hey, Codie..."

Codie came back to the end of the hall. "Yeah?"

Lana stared at the TV. "How do you do it? Being alone."

"I'm not alone." She walked back to the couch and rested her arms on the back. "I have you and Karen and Vanessa. I have my plane. I have everything I need."

Lana looked at her over the top of her head. "That's not what I meant."

"I know." She stroked Lana's hair. "I don't know. I wish I did so I could teach you, make it easier on you. I have lovers who come and go, like Nick." She gestured at the screen. "I love them and I appreciate them while they're here, but when it's time for them to go... they go. Kind of like you and Sidra. You two had a pretty decent arrangement."

Lana nodded. "But I can't do that with every woman I meet. I can't just walk into every relationship knowing it's going to be temporary."

"You want to be in love."

"Yeah. Fuck me, right?"

Codie squeezed Lana's shoulder. "You're going to fall in love again. And not with someone like Catherine Diehl. Someone who will appreciate you. You're going to find a person who will move to a whole different country for you. Know why?"

"Because I'm not going to fucking uproot my life a second time?"

Codie laughed and straightened up. "Because you're worth it, Lana. Get some sleep. We have some big days coming up."

"Yeah. Okay."

Lana turned off the TV after Codie was gone and went into the guest bedroom. She left the lights off and stretched out on top of the blankets, her hands on her stomach. The apartment was the same one Codie was living in when the band first hit big. Instead of moving to a nicer place she simply fixed up the one she already had for a fraction of the price. She kept her old van but she added a second car just for convenience. And then, of course, there was the immense purchase of her plane. But other than those relatively minor things, Codie was still the exact same person she'd been when they were still playing dive bars under the name Little Cat Feet.

Back then they'd had nothing but cover songs and half-assed instrumentals. She was a stripper and a dance teacher who sometimes played music on the weekends. She remembered the nights dancing on stage, specifically the nights when there had been a rare woman in the audience. Sometimes they were there with a boyfriend or husband, but sometimes they would show up by themselves. Drawn by their curiosity, eager for a taste of what it would really be like without actually crossing the line.

Lana moved her hand to the front of her pajama pants. She remembered one woman, Sarah, who seemed as if she'd gone through Lana's entire routine without blinking. After her set Lana went out to make conversation and offer a private dance. Sarah explained that she often thought about being with another woman but she couldn't bring herself to cross the line. Lana told her the dance was just a dance, and if she wanted to see what it was like to touch something or kiss something, she would bend the rules "just this once."

She remembered being in the small, curtained-off area, with the plush seats and the dim lighting, and how awestruck Sarah had seemed by her movements. When people found out Lana was a stripper they treated her differently. If they were charitable they would ask what she was saving up to do, or what she was in school for. The plain truth of the matter was that she *liked* stripping. She got paid extremely well to dance, which was her first passion before music took over her life. And then there were moments like these. She loved these moments even when they were with men. Sex was a religion, and at that moment she was... not a god, but a prophet. She was selling sex and fantasy to these people and they were paying very well for it.

Lana bent her knees out and put her hand between her legs. Sarah had nervously touched Lana's thigh, and Lana had smiled at her with a wave of hair falling into her face. She tucked it behind her ear and covered Sarah's hand with hers. "It's okay. Touch me."

In her memory, Sarah drew in a shaky breath and slid her hand up over Lana's hip. In the present, Lana used her thumb to lift the elastic of her pajama pants and moved her hand inside, brushing the back of her fingers over her skin the way Sarah had. She remembered the trembling, the warmth of the other woman's hand, and she felt the thrill of knowing she was the first woman Sarah had ever touched this way.

As Lana touched herself she thought about the sex-as-religion analogy, remembered how powerful it had been on the stage. She knew there was no way she would be able to get up and dance, not as famous as she'd gotten, but with a good enough disguise... she could go to her old club where she could count on people being discreet. She bit her bottom lip as she pushed one finger inside herself, curling her toes as she rocked her hips back and forth. Maybe she needed to be on the other side of the worship, to be the recipient of sexual energy instead of the provider...

She brought herself to orgasm as she remembered how Sarah's lips had felt on her stomach. They parted with a simple and almost chaste kiss on the lips. Sarah thanked Lana for all her help, but Lana never knew if she had satisfied her urges or gone on to actually be with another woman. Whatever the outcome had been, Lana felt proud to be a part of her journey.

In the afterglow, she made a promise to herself that she would find the time to visit a strip club before they did *Settle In, Seattle!* She needed to partake of a little worship before putting herself out there again.

## CHAPTER SEVENTEEN

THE BLITZ leading up to the show was absolute insanity. Lana imagined it would be worse for the other acts on the show. On the day it was going to air, the band was driven to the studio in a van with tinted windows. There were other surprise guests slated to appear on the show - big name movie stars, favorite characters, and a special appearance by the mayor of Seattle. Nick Young had acquired quite a fan base over the years, and Radiation Canary was just one of the many acts the show had introduced to the world.

They showed up at the show's usual filming time to rehearse, and it seemed like everyone on set was a fan. As soon as they stopped playing they were swarmed by people who had been waiting in the wings. "Are you actually getting back together? Is this a special performance, or...? I can't believe you're actually performing. People are going to go insane."

Karen was backstage with her foot up on a crate, her skirt draped over her knee to leave her lower leg exposed as she adjusted the lace on her boot. She was aware of someone approaching her, but she didn't look up from picking at the stubborn lace with her fingernails.

"Mrs. Robinson, I think you're trying to seduce me."

Karen grinned. "A classic." She looked up and her face went slack. "Oh. Wow. Olivia Childress."

The actress held her hands out to either side and bowed her head forward. She was taller in person, and her normally blonde hair had been dyed brown. The color suited her olive skin tone, and Karen hoped it was a change that was there to stay. She was also wearing her show outfit; black leggings and a sleeveless white T-shirt with a ruffled front. "In the flesh. I heard you were in the building and I wanted to say hello. Is it true the whole band is here?"

"Yeah. We're performing. You listen to Radiation Canary?"

Olivia nodded. "Oh, yeah. I actually asked for your music to play in one of my movies."

"Over the sex scene," Karen said before she could stop herself. She blushed and then tried to conceal it by laughing. "I mean, uh, yeah. I vaguely remember."

Olivia laughed as well. "I've been a big fan of yours for a while. I know we're not supposed to post anything online until after the show, but... would you mind?"

"Absolutely not. I'd like one to send my wife."

They stood next to one another and took two photos, one with each phone, and Karen tried not to give away how flustered she was to have her arm around Olivia Childress.

"I've been a fan of yours for years, too," Karen admitted. "Ever since you were on *The Dead Men*. And, ah, my wife and I saw the movie that used our music."

"Oh? Did you enjoy it?"

Karen tried not to smile and felt as if she was about to break her face. "It was... good."

Olivia laughed. "I'm glad. It was really great meeting you. I wish I had a CD with me that you could autograph or something."

They were under strict orders not to reveal the album's existence until the show, but Karen nearly cracked. "Stick around and find me after the show," she said. "We can sign things for each other."

"Sounds great. And a little naughty." Her grin widened. "Aha, I made you blush again."

"God, you're dangerous."

Olivia stuck her tongue between her teeth and winked before turning to go back to the green room. Karen pushed her hair out of her face once the actress was gone, fanning herself as she texted the picture to Laura. She got a reply within a few seconds. "Please tell me you took the opportunity to grab her ass."

Karen stuck her tongue out. "You'll have to dust it for prints."

"I'm game if she is."

Actually Laura had taken Mason over to stay with the Dads. They didn't want him exposed to the lights and crowds and loud music. They would watch the bouncing baby and put him to bed while Laura was at the show to support Karen.

In the hours before the show began, they went through the set list a half dozen times. Since the show was live they couldn't afford to miss any cues or take the time to set up instruments. Codie's drums and Vanessa's piano would be set up immediately after the monologue, and the band was set to perform at the forty-five minute mark. Karen had a ball of putty that she used to keep her fingers stretched and warmed-up before a performance, shaping and reshaping it to keep her fingers and wrist moving. Codie saw her pinching and squeezing it and smirked.

"What?"

"Nothing." She looked at her magazine again. "Does Laura ever help you with your finger exercises?"

"She does whatever is necessary." Someone passed through her line of vision, and her eye naturally followed him out of the room. "Holy crap. Was that..."

"It was."

She sank down on the couch next to Codie. "We're hanging out with celebrities. Like really big celebrities. Huge stars."

Codie patted her knee. "You notice how many of those huge stars asked for our autograph?"

Karen shrugged and looked around. "Doesn't make it any easier to comprehend."

Nick came through on his way out, dressed to the nines in a tuxedo complete with cummerbund and a flower in the lapel. He paused to thank everyone for being there, then stopped in front of Karen and Codie. He smiled and clasped his hands in front of his chest.

"Thank you so much for being here. You four are going to blow the roof off this place. Where are Lana and Vanessa?"

Codie said, "They went home. About an hour ago. Huh. They should've been back by now."

Nick's eyes widened and the color drained from his face. Before Codie could take pity on him, Lana approached with a bottle of water. Nick exhaled sharply and his shoulders sagged with relief. He pointed at Codie and said, "Don't you ever do anything like that again."

"I make no promises, chief." She winked at him, and he smiled knowingly at her.

"The show is starting soon, so I better get into position. I can't wait to hear you four sing again. It's going to be fantastic."

Once he was gone, Lana bent down to kiss Karen and Codie on their cheeks. She wished them luck and went to watch the show from a monitor. She hadn't been able to stop moving, bouncing from one corner of backstage to another. Every now and then someone would stop her to say hello, and she could stand still long enough to have a conversation, but as soon as they said goodbye she would be off again. She had too much nervous energy, but she didn't want to expend all her resources before they performed. She would hate to look tired and worn-out for their big return.

She finally found a place to sit and planted herself there. She thought back to their first appearance on the show, back when absolutely no one had known or cared who they were. Now she couldn't sit for five minutes without a production assistant gravitating toward her to see if she needed something to drink or eat. That was another benefit of staying on the move: no one could corner her.

Finally the show began. Nick came out to great fanfare and took his bows. When the applause finally died down, he clapped his hands together and smiled.

"Thank you, ladies and gentlemen, thank you so much. You have no idea what that means to me. Fifteen years ago I was told that I was finished in the entertainment industry. I was told there was no way I could ever host another show. This network not only stood behind me, they built me up. And they gave me a chance to introduce you to some absolutely marvelously talented people, some of whom have agreed to come back tonight to honor the show's anniversary. And we wouldn't be here without all you wonderful viewers tuning in every night. So to thank you, and to thank them, I am bringing you together once more right here on the *Settle In, Seattle!* stage.

"Now when we switched to doing this live, there was a lot of speculation on the internets about what we had up our sleeves. Did we have surprise guests? Did we have giveaways? Did we have a bunch of shit we wanted to say without the censors getting all up in our asses? The answer to all three is yes. And we wanted to make sure all of our fans, no matter where they lived, got a chance to see it live along with the fine Seattleites who came to see us in person. Any show can do a giveaway to the studio audience, but how many shows give away something to every single person watching?"

The audience cheered.

"That's right, we have a free gift tonight that will be available to every fan we've got. What is it? I'll give you a hint... TCMS. That's all you get. TCMS. Now while everyone is speculating about that, we have a lot of ground to cover and we can't go back and edit for time. So let's get this show on the road, shall we? Settle in, Seattle, because it's going to be a surprising one."

During Olivia Childress' interview, Lana and Karen were escorted through the wings by a woman wearing a headset. They all hunched over and ran as if they were expecting gunmen to open fire on them at any moment, weaving through the maze of narrow corridors cluttered with carts of equipment and tools. Karen was surprised by how much it felt like they were sneaking into a warehouse, except for the rare spaces where they could see the blue curtains of the set through breaks in the wall. Nick's band was playing through the commercial break, the music echoing through speakers that made it seem like they were everywhere at once.

The stage manager stopped at the entrance to the stairs used to get the audience to their seats. She turned and moved the headset mic out of her way. "You girls ready?"

"As ready as we'll ever be," Lana said.

She nodded. "Bird One and Bird Two are almost in place. Three and Four?"

"Three and Four are ready," came the muffled reply.

The manager gave them the thumbs up before scurrying off to deal with the next fire. Lana and Karen hugged, then headed upstairs and around the bend. There were two doors, one for each aisle of the studio's stadium seating. Lana took the one at stage right, and Karen took stage left. They were both wearing earpieces and had small, almost invisible microphones hooked over their ears and protruding out in front of their lips.

The house band ended with a flourish as the show came back from commercial, and Lana and Karen could both hear him in their earpieces. Codie and Nessa were onstage and concealed by a large projection screen. Lana took a deep breath and hooked her thumbs together. She made the flying gesture with her fingers and Karen copied it back to her.

"Welcome back, folks!" Nick said. "Welcome back to the show. We've had a lot of great guests tonight, mostly because when we called people up they were all willing to come and say hi if just for a minute or two. But the problem with doing a live show, the trick, is getting all these people here at the right time. It's not always possible, unfortunately. But we do have contingency plans. Our next guests really wanted to be here, but just in case something came up, they put together a little video for us."

Lana smiled. The video had been filmed earlier that week at the Coal Mine.

"So please, enjoy a brand-new music video and a brand-new song... from Radiation Canary."

The crowd erupted. Karen sagged back against the wall as if she'd been hit by a physical wave, while Lana laughed and put her hands over her ears. She knew the video had started because she could hear the music, and the audience fervor began dying down so everyone could hear the music. Lana closed her eyes and envisioned what they were seeing.

The video opened on a slow, mournful piano solo as the camera panned across the derelict instruments from Dash's stable. Photographs were stacked on top of the piano and stapled to the wall. Everything was tinged with a shade of blue-purple as the camera swept past and faded into a shot of Lana standing on the footbridge. As the instruments faded out, Karen's cello kicked in.

In the video, Lana wore a long black coat with the collar up, and the audience cheered again before she could even sing anything. She smiled and tears rolled down her cheeks. She was wearing the same coat that was in the video, just as Karen and the others were dressed the same. As the camera moved in closer, Lana looked up from the water and began to sing.

*"I never thought I'd have to get over you*
*I never thought you'd be anything but forever mine*
*Maybe if I sit here long enough I'll make it true*
*Maybe if I see your empty side of the bed one more time*
*Then maybe I'll know why I wasn't enough for you."*

At the end of the verse, video-Lana picked up a loose photograph that had blown out of the stables and looked at it. She stuck it in the pocket of her coat and walked along the footbridge as the shot faded to the gentle hill behind the stable. Karen was standing next to a tree, head down, and the audience cheered again. Hidden in the shadows, Karen looked up through her lashes at Lana, who mimicked a beating heart with her hands.

In the video Karen began singing the second verse. The main reason they'd chosen "Enough for You" was because it had them both on vocals. Lana wanted to remind people that they were a dual-lead band, and she believed Karen had as much right to sing on their grand return as she did. Karen bit her bottom lip as the second verse began.

*"I never thought this was anything less than forever*
*I thought we could see our way through any stormy weather*
*When the rough seas rose up I promised I'd anchor you*
*We always said we could stand against the winds together*
*But I don't know when I became less than enough for you."*

When she went into the chorus, Vanessa and Codie began singing harmony. In the video, Karen turned to see them walking through the woods to join her. Karen smiled and turned to face them. Codie turned away first, letting Karen and Vanessa follow her. As they sang the chorus they walked toward the stable.

Karen wiped her hands on her skirt and looked at Lana. Lana winked at her.

Video-Codie and Video-Vanessa walked into the stable and out of sight. Video-Karen stopped at the door and turned to see Video-Lana running toward her. She smiled and waited through the musical interlude, and they faced each other in front of the stable door.

In real life, Lana took a break and pushed open the access door. The door swung closed behind her, and she was standing at the top of a steep flight of stairs leading down to the stage. On either side of the stairs she saw hundreds of audience members, their heads lit by a blue aura as they watched the video. The next moment had been meticulously timed. Video-Lana stepped into the stable and the video image went to black. At the same moment a spotlight snapped on to illuminate the real Lana Kent standing in their midst.

She picked up the chorus as she began to descend the steps. Her voice was almost completely obliterated by the audience's cheering, and she couldn't help smiling as she held her hands out to brush the fingers of people she passed. Seconds after she began singing, Karen came through the opposite door and sang her part of the round. The cheers amplified to almost deafening levels. Karen replied to the lines Lana sang a moment later, turning the chorus into a call-and-answer.

*"Do I let you go or do I stand to fight? (I don't know how I get up each day)*

*Will it make a difference if we yell all night? (And it gets harder the longer I stay)*

*I don't know how I'm going to get out of this mess (Tell me how to fix it, what to do)*

*The moon's gone dark, I'm stuck in the wilderness (When did I stop being enough for you?)*

*Did you become more or did I become less? (How much more until I'm enough for you?)"*

By the time they reached the stage, the screen had lifted to reveal Codie and Vanessa. Lana put on her guitar and Karen lifted her violin. They began playing as the pre-recorded track faded out, blending as perfectly as they could. Lana heard a misstep, a second or two where the tape ended and they still weren't quite on the mark, but she doubted anyone else heard it over the audience.

Lana stepped forward to sing her part of the chorus one last time, tears in her eyes as she looked out over the crowd. They were on their feet now, some of them making the canary gesture with both hands as they cheered. When the song ended their voices somehow became even louder, and Lana flicked her guitar pick into the crowd.

Nick made his way over and stepped in front of Lana, swinging his arms wide in an attempt to make everyone be quiet. He tapped an imaginary watch on his wrist, made a 'wrap-it-up' motion, but the crowd couldn't be calmed. Lana stepped forward and put her arm around Nick's shoulders. He looked at her and she shrugged helplessly. Finally Nick began to shout so he could be heard.

"Okay! Okay, okay, okay. We don't have a lot of time. I'd love to let you give these ladies all the love they deserve, but we're on the clock here. If you keep cheering they won't have time to sing another song, which is what we had scheduled." The audience began to settle, and he grinned and looked at Lana. "Hi, Lana."

"Hi, Nick."

"That was a fantastic song."

"Well, thank you. It's available on our new album, *The Coal Mine Sessions*."

The audience cheered again, and Nick waved his arms to stifle them. "Don't get them going again! But that's great news. It's great to hear you're working on a new album. When can these folks go out and buy a copy?"

"They can't," Lana said. "But if they go to the Radiation Canary website, the album is going live right now. It's finished, it's fantastic, and it's free."

The crowd erupted again. Nick pushed his hands through his hair in aggravation. "I told you not to do that to them!" He shushed them once more. "Now... now, we don't want people to get the wrong idea. You said the album was free on your website... tonight only, right? In honor of the show?"

"The album is a gift to all of our fans, everyone here who gave us that amazing welcome, and everyone at home watching. The digital album is completely free. It will always be free. And it's available to anyone who wants to go pick it up. The physical copies will cost a little just because they cost money to produce, but you will always be able to get all thirteen songs from the new album for free."

Nick started the applause that time and shouted into the camera. "You heard it here first, ladies and gentlemen! So go to their website, you already know the address, and get your copy of *The Coal Mine Sessions* for absolutely... completely... not-one-penny! Go! Now! What are you waiting for? We'll be right back and they're going to do another song from their new album. You don't want to miss it!" He got up close to the camera and grinned.

"Radiation Canary is officially back, ladies and gentlemen!"

Disc Two

Westward Sky

## CHAPTER EIGHTEEN

KAREN HARDLY remembered anything about the actual show. They performed "The Sailmaker's Daughter" and ended the show with "Say a Prayer (If You've Got One)," both of which received riotous applause. Nick thanked everyone for coming out to see the show, as well as his guests, and motioned for the band to keep playing through the credits. The show finally went off the air, the audience was released, and Nick invited everyone to stick around for an on-stage after-party. Karen was sitting at the guest couch when Olivia Childress weaved through the crowd and came directly toward her.

"That was amazing!" she said, holding up her phone. "I've already downloaded the album. I can't wait to hear it."

"Thank you so much!" Karen said. "And what you said earlier about the autograph... we have some copies of the new album in the green room. I'll grab you one if you want."

Olivia beamed. "That would be fantastic. Thank you so much."

"No problem. Come with me." She led Olivia backstage to the box Cartography had dropped off earlier. Earlier in the week they set up a table at the Cartography offices and spent almost six hours signing each one. Now the box was half empty after Nick's crew and the rest of the guests had taken their pick. Karen plucked one out and presented it to Olivia. "There you go. Signed and everything."

Olivia flipped it over to look at the track listing. "This really is a great way to reintroduce yourselves to your fans. A free album? That's nuts. Amazing, but nuts. I respect you for doing it."

Karen shrugged. "We wanted to thank them for everything they've done for us."

"I'm sure they feel appreciated. So..." She looked up again, and Karen was almost startled by how blue her eyes were in real life. They always popped on-screen but that could have just been special effects. Now she knew the truth. "You're going to make more music videos, right? I mean, of course you are."

"Yeah, we're thinking about a few pitches right now."

"Whatever you end up with, if you need an actress, let me know."

Karen laughed. "Thanks, but I'm not sure we could afford you."

"You can afford me," Olivia said. "If you can give away an album, I can give away a random weekend to shoot some scenes for you. Just let me know where you need me and when. I'll show up."

"Wow. That's amazing. Thank you."

They exchanged numbers, took another photo, and Olivia added it to her Instagram and Facebook. Once it was sent out, she winked at Karen.

"I can't wait to listen to the whole album. I'll be sure to let you know what I think of it."

As Olivia left the green room, Vanessa was coming in. "Hey. I couldn't find Codie. Would you let her know I'm heading out?"

"You're going home already?"

"It's almost one in the morning, K."

Karen checked her phone in disbelief. "Wow. I guess I forgot the show was live this time. I'm all filled with adrenaline."

"You earned it." She kissed Karen's cheek. "You and Lana coming down the stairs like that? It was magical. We were watching the audience on the monitors, and they were stunned. You should've seen the looks on their faces. Codie and I are lucky to have you."

Karen hugged her. "I think we're all lucky. Thank you for being here, Nessa. If we'd gotten a substitute, we wouldn't have been Radiation Canary. You can talk all you want about how lucky you are to have us, but we're lucky to have you."

Vanessa sniffled. "Every now and then you make me remember I didn't even want you in the band, and it makes me feel like shit."

Karen laughed and kissed Vanessa's forehead. "Emotional sabotage. It's my niche. Say hi to Scott for me."

"I will. And you, to Laura and Mason."

"Will do. Goodnight, Vanessa."

Later on, closer to two o'clock in the morning when even the hardest partiers were beginning to flag, Laura made her way to where Karen was leaning against a piece of the set. Karen was so startled to see her wife - and exhaustion was partially to blame - that she teared up when they kissed hello.

"I knew I'd find you hiding out somewhere. That's not how it works, beautiful. You don't get to be the big rock star and then play the wallflower."

"I was pretending the rock star part. The wallflower is a hundred percent authentic."

Laura put her arms around Karen's waist and swayed with her. "I want this flower printed on actual wallpaper. I'd plaster my whole house with it."

Karen kissed her and pulled her closer. "Hopefully I'll be around enough now that you won't need it. I know we both have tours coming up, but we should have some time. I won't have to be holed up at the Coal Mine anymore. We should have a few days together, at least."

"Mm. I'd like that. And the grandpas said they were keeping Mason all night... so... you think you can stay up a while longer for our own party?"

Karen kissed the tip of Laura's nose. "Yeah. But we should get out of here now."

"Right."

On their way out, they spotted Lana and Codie sitting together in the nosebleed section of the audience. Karen pointed to the door and waved goodbye, and Lana blew them both a kiss. Codie raised her glass, and Karen used Laura's left hand to make the canary signal. Codie and Lana copied it back to her as she and Laura headed out the side exit.

"We should probably think about heading home, too." Lana wiped her hands over her face and looked at the time. "My phone is about to die, and that's the universal signal that you've been out too long. How did people know before cellphones were invented?"

"Their carrier pigeons would die. Hey." She nudged Lana's foot with hers. "You have your apartment key, right?"

"Yeah. Why, you abandoning me?"

"A certain late-night host might have asked me to hang out with him after the party."

Lana whistled and patted Codie on the thigh. "If you want to bring him back to you place, I can crash somewhere else. It's no big deal."

"Nah. Guys like to spend the night in their own bed. Plus it gives me a chance to snoop around a TV star's apartment."

"Okay. Well, have fun. Don't do anything I wouldn't do." Codie raised an eyebrow. "Well, except the obvious."

Codie chuckled. "You did an amazing job tonight, Lana."

"Only because you all covered my mistakes." She held out her fist and Codie rapped her knuckles against it. "Be good, Codie."

"I'll do my best. Goodnight."

Codie got up and descended the stairs to go in search of her date. By that point all but the stragglers had made their way home. Building security was doing their best to usher everyone else out, so Lana decided it was time to make her way home as well. She retrieved her things from the green room, posed for a picture with someone from a TV show she vaguely remembered seeing once, and wandered outside into the parking lot. Inside it was easy to forget there was a real world waiting beyond the curtains and brightly-lit set pieces. Celebrities became regular people searching a parking lot for their cars, like a half-dozen Cinderellas slipping into a pumpkin for the long ride home.

Lana decided to walk until she found a bus stop. The studio was tucked away in an otherwise residential part of Queen Anne, close enough to see the water but far enough away that businesses hadn't filled up every corner. She walked uphill toward Key Arena and saw the Space Needle shining above it in the distance. She could smell salt water on the air and breathed deep, holding her arms out to either side as she strolled down the quiet streets.

The moment was quintessential Seattle. This was the town that built her, for better or for worse, and she couldn't imagine calling any other city home. London was fine, London had history and class. London was beautiful in a way most people couldn't understand, and she loved it for what it was. But it wasn't home. She had tried to force it to be for Catherine's sake and that had probably been part of their problem. She still loved Catherine and had a feeling she would for a long time, but now she was certain they didn't belong together.

She found herself wishing for something to drink, although she didn't feel like going into any of the bars that peppered the neighborhoods around the arena. Dick's Drive-In was nearby, and she could stop in for one of their massive ice-cream cones. She didn't know what she wanted to do. Altering her route toward any specific thing seemed like too much of a commitment, so instead she danced herself down the sidewalk singing under her breath.

"New York's an apple that quickly gets rotten... Philly's Brotherly Love is too often forgotten..." She hummed the rest of the chorus and chuckled to herself as she reached the cross-street in front of Key Arena. She thought there might be a bus stop to the south, but Dick's and the bars were north of her. Codie's apartment was also south.

As she stood on the corner debating the choice, a car slowed down at the curb behind her. Lana looked toward it just as a spotlight mounted on its side snapped on, and she held up a hand to shield her eyes as she heard a car door open and close.

"Evening, ma'am," a woman said. "Could I see some ID?"

Lana reached for her wallet and fished out her license. She handed it over to the silhouette. The cop held it up so she could see the information. "Everything okay tonight?"

"Everything's fine, Officer..." She looked at the name tag. "Officer Hollenbeck."

"Kind of late to be wandering around."

Lana smiled. "Please don't arrest me. I'll do any breathalyzer you have, any tests you want to give me. I'm not drunk. I'm just over-tired and running on adrenaline."

"Uh-huh. What do you have going tonight?"

"I was on TV. Earlier. I was a guest on *Settle In, Seattle!*'s live show."

Feigned interest as she filled in the information from Lana's license. "Oh? What do you do?"

"Lana Kent?"

"Yep. That's the name I see here," the cop said without looking up.

Lana realized that the officer didn't recognize her. Maybe she wasn't a fan, maybe she wasn't the sort who kept up with music, but it was an opportunity to just be a normal person for a moment. "I'm... a stripper. I dance at Club Nightside. I'm also a dance instructor. I teach kids. Elementary school, mostly."

"They have strippers on *Settle In, Seattle!* now?"

"It was a special episode."

"I'll bet it was." She handed the license back. "Okay, Miss Kent. I'm bored and you're willing, so why don't we go through a few of those sobriety checkpoints? Just for my own peace of mind."

Lana smiled. "Sounds like fun, Officer. Where should we begin?"


The next morning Vanessa reached to shut off her alarm only to realize the sound was a text alert. She reached for her glasses instead of fiddling with her contacts, squinting as the screen brightened and the blurry shapes solidified into real words. As she read it, Scott snorted and cleared his throat before rolling over to rub the small of her back. "It's too early," he said in his grizzly-bear grumble. They had only gotten to sleep a few hours ago, and Nathaniel would most likely be waking them up no matter how late his mommy and daddy had been out the night before.

"It's from Naomi," Vanessa said. "They're tracking downloads from the site. It's already broken a thousand in a couple hours."

"Is that good?"

She chuckled and put the phone back on the nightstand. She rolled over and cuddled up with her husband. "It's pretty impressive, especially for being the middle of the night."

"Good." He kissed the top of her head before he moved his hand down to the waistband of her pajamas. "Can I get an autograph?"

"Is an autograph really what you're after, Mr. Wayland?" She brushed her lips across his as she shifted her weight to straddle him under the blankets. "It must be. I see you brought a pen with you."

"You might want to double-check that."

She moved her hand down. "Oh! Why, you're right. Goodness, I'm so sorry. That's not a pen at all. That's a damn marker..."

He laughed and began pulling at her clothes.

"Your phone... is buzzing..."

Karen reached for it, but Laura snagged her wrist and moved it back to the headboard. "Hey!" Karen laughed breathlessly. "You said..."

"I just didn't want you to hear the noise and get the wrong idea. That buzzing is your phone. This buzzing..." She used her thumb to flick a switch. She stopped thrusting her hips for a moment, her toy still inside her wife, and pressed the egg against her. "This buzzing is something different."

Karen cried out, and the phone stopped trying to get her attention.

The face of Codie's phone was so bright that it cast the entire room in its pale white glow. She opened her eyes, searched for the source, and lifted her head off Nick's chest to look at the screen. Nick was still softly snoring and she didn't disturb him as she read the text from Naomi. She smiled and put the phone back, then rested her chin on Nick's chest to watch him sleep. They were both naked under the ribbon of sheet tangled around their waists. She could smell his sweat and was surprisingly okay with the muskiness of it. She bent her leg and drew her foot up his thigh.

Their first time had been a casual fling over Thanksgiving years earlier. She didn't have anywhere to go, and she offered to fly him to his family's get-together. It was the first time she had seen him as a real live person and he'd impressed her enough that she was willing to go to bed with him. She told Vanessa because, even though Vanessa was married, she felt the need to honor her friend's crush. Vanessa was happy enough to live vicariously.

They'd only gotten together a handful of times since then. It was always quick, always casual. Once she called to ask him over and he said he was currently seeing someone. She hadn't been jealous, only mildly annoyed that her first choice wasn't available. So why was she now staring at him while he slept? That was some relationship bullshit, and it had no place in their arrangement.

She put her head down and kissed his chest. Of course she had feelings for him. Anyone who could fuck her the way he did... he seemed to have a fetish for food, but she had to admit there were worse feelings than having honey licked off of her naked skin.

She didn't know if she was ready to settle down, and she really had no idea what Nick's feelings on the matter were. He didn't seem like the type to lock down with a ring and a marriage certif– she found herself choking just thinking the words. But maybe, just maybe, if she did end up seeing Nick Young more often than not, and if they did enter into some kind of exclusivity... once again, there were worse things in the world than that.

Petey's was an all-night restaurant with three rows of outdoor bench seating. Lana was sitting in the middle of the center row. She had a hot dog and soda in front of her, with a second one across from her. The night was still enough that she could hear the buzzing of the fluorescent bulbs above her. She had almost finished her fries when the cruiser pulled into the parking lot. Officer Avery Hollenbeck got out of the passenger side and walked up to Lana as her partner went to the window to order his own meal.

Officer Hollenbeck was on the smallish side, olive-skinned, dark-haired, and the polar opposite of Catherine Diehl in every single respect. Lana hadn't gotten a good look at her during the traffic stop, but now under the bright lights of Petey's, she found she liked what she saw. She'd taken a risk asking when she would be on break and arranging this impromptu dead-of-night date, but she knew if she hadn't tried she would have regretted it. She had enough regrets for the time being.

When she reached the table she took off her hat, placed it next to Lana's cup, and straddled the seat before lowering herself down onto it.

"I didn't think you would show up."

"I probably shouldn't have. My partner laughed at me the whole way here."

Lana looked toward the ordering window to see the other officer was trying very hard to look like he wasn't watching them. "Why?"

"He couldn't believe I didn't recognize the lead singer of Radiation Canary."

Lana smiled and pushed the unopened hot dog across the table. "I got you a peace offering."

"Thanks." She unwrapped the foil. "Stripper and dance instructor, huh?"

"That wasn't a lie. I did both of those things before the band got big."

"Huh." Hollenbeck took a bite of her hot dog and chewed thoroughly before she spoke again. "So Radiation Canary. Grunge? Punk?"

Lana smiled. "No. More, ah... folk rock. We try not to label it."

"How many guitars do you have?"

"Just the one. Plus a cello and violin."

Hollenbeck nodded thoughtfully and took another bite of her hot dog. "That's certainly interesting."

"Yeah. So what do you do for a living?"

Hollenbeck stared at her, then laughed and shook her head. "Victor said your band was on hiatus or broken up or... something. He didn't really know the specifics. He got all excited when I said you were on the show." She looked over. "He's probably on the internet right now looking up why you were there."

"We're back. We spent the last few months recording an album and we just released it for free."

"Free?"

"A gift to the fans."

Hollenbeck nodded slowly. "Okay."

They ate in silence. Lana finished her hot dog and wiped her fingers on a napkin before she picked up her phone. She typed a few words, then turned the phone around so Hollenbeck could see the video she had chosen. The video was for a song called "Falling Up," and it featured a very tasteful nearly-nude shot of Lana flying through the air. The night was quiet enough that the music was even audible at a low volume. Hollenbeck raised an eyebrow as she watched the naked part of the video, but she didn't comment.

When the video ended, she leaned back and nodded. "So that was you. Are you naked in all your videos?"

"No. I chose that one special."

"Because you assume all female cops are gay?"

"No, because I hope the attractive ones who let me buy them hot dogs at three in the morning are at least bi-curious."

Hollenbeck couldn't help but smile, scanning her eyes over the street behind Lana. "You said your new album was free. Where?"

Lana told her the URL. "You can download it whenever you want."

"Okay. I'll download the album, give it a listen. How can I get in touch to let you know what I think of it?"

Lana wrote down her phone number.

"I could hate it."

"I can take an honest opinion."

Hollenbeck smiled slightly and nodded. "Okay, then. Thanks for the hot dog. I have to get back on patrol."

"Thanks for not taking me downtown. Oh... what's your partner's name?"

"Victor Keane."

Lana said, "Officer Keane!" She waved him over and signed her name on the back of a napkin. "Your partner tells me you're a fan. Would you like to take a picture?"

He grinned. "Absolutely. My wife won't believe it."

She stood up and posed with him while Hollenbeck took the picture on Keane's phone. Lana shook his hand, thanked him for listening, and then began gathering her trash while the officers walked back to their car.

"Miss Kent," Hollenbeck called. Lana looked up. "Try to stay out of trouble."

Lana saluted, winked, and smiled as she went to dump her trash in the receptacle.

Her phone buzzed on her way back to the bench, and she looked to see that their album had already gotten downloaded a thousand times. She laughed and slipped the phone back into her pocket.

Who said nothing good ever happened after midnight?

## CHAPTER NINETEEN

BY MORNING, the band was all over the internet. The headlines were all variations of "Radiation Canary makes surprise appearance on Nick Young's show" and "Band marks return by releasing surprise free album," with an assortment of pictures showing Lana's surprise appearance in the audience, the band accepting their applause after the song ended, and shots of them performing from every angle. A good amount of websites also featured the *Coal Mine Sessions* cover art with a download link. By the time Lana woke up at noon, the album had been downloaded nearly two hundred thousand times. She called Naomi to make sure it wasn't a glitch and was gleefully told the numbers might be even higher.

Naomi chuckled when she explained. "We have pre-orders for the CD from Amazon that we're hurrying to fill. We're not sure of the exact numbers yet, but they seem to be moving pretty quickly. Apparently even when you want to give it away for free, you still have fans willing to buy it."

They had also taken over the morning talk shows. Clips of Lana and Karen's entrance were trending on YouTube with eighty-two thousand hits and counting. Naomi said they had been bombarded by requests to appear on other talk shows. "Now that the secret is out, you four are going to be busy as hell. We need to work out a schedule and start thinking about a tour."

By the end of the first week, *The Coal Mine Sessions* was the number one album in the country. "Face Value" was the first single, and they were scheduled to shoot a music video for it sometime later in the month. Karen told them about Olivia Childress offering to appear in one of their videos for free, and Naomi promised to call her bluff on it.

Two weeks after their first meeting on the street, Officer Hollenbeck called Lana and asked her out to dinner. Lana had just finished moving out of Codie's apartment to a condo in Ballard and suggested having dinner there instead of going out somewhere. "By now I'm sure you've confirmed I'm famous," she said. "I've had people following me with cameras twenty-four seven since the night we met. You don't need them hassling you, too."

Hollenbeck agreed and they set the date. That morning Karen and Vanessa had appeared on a talk show to discuss how they split the time between their children and their career while Lana and Codie had met with Naomi to hash out a tentative concert schedule. She was still working on it when the doorbell buzzed. Lana checked her hair in the mirror, smoothed down the front of her blouse, and opened the door to see Avery looked very, very different out of uniform.

"Wow." She cleared her throat. "I was going to call you 'Officer' all night as a joke, but that outfit is dead serious."

Avery's hair, out of its braid, tumbled down over her shoulders in a thick, dark wave. She had bangs that brushed her eyebrows. She wore a blue sheath dress that showed curves that had been hidden by her vest, and her high heels added a few inches so that she appeared to be Lana's height. She reached up and touched her curls.

"I actually got this done today. I'm going to have a hell of a time gathering this all up at work tomorrow. You better be worth it, Miss Kent."

"I'll try. Come on in."

Avery said, "Something smells fantastic."

"I'm not taking any credit. I had Ray's whip up some kasu black cod for us."

"I didn't know Ray's delivered."

Lana shrugged awkwardly. "Well... I asked nicely. And they knew my name. Not that I throw around my name at the drop of a hat just to get special treatment. I figured just because we couldn't go out didn't mean you had to settle for a microwave dinner."

"How sweet. I appreciate you pulling the strings. And I've heard great things about the kasu. I can't wait to taste it for myself."

Lana served the fish onto plates, and Avery helped her take them into the kitchen. "So you've had a couple of weeks," Lana said as she sat down. "What did you find out about me online?"

"Nothing."

"Nothing? Wow. You must be a lousy cop."

Avery smiled. "I'm a great cop. But after confirming you were who you claimed to be, and listening to a few of your songs, I decided to stop digging. You introduced yourself to me as a stripper. I thought that might be a hint that you wanted someone to see beyond your fame. So I didn't read any gossip or internet chatter. I didn't check for you on Facebook or Twitter. I'm probably Seattle's least-educated person on the subject of Lana Kent."

"Wow. That's impressive. Thank you. So as a reward, is there anything you want to know? Ask me anything."

"We'll start simple. How did you get started in the band?"

Lana explained the slow coming-together of the band - meeting Codie in school, then sharing Vanessa's rehearsal space, and the miraculous arrival of the girl on the wall - and their life-changing appearance on *Settle In, Seattle!* In return, Avery revealed that she became a cop because of television shows. "No family tradition, no big moment when a cop saved my life. I saw cops on TV, and I realized I wanted to help people."

"That's admirable. In a way, I think I respect that more than tradition or being personally saved. You chose to help others without any outside influence."

Avery shrugged. "I'll take admirable over butch any day. Everyone assumes that because of my job I'll be into sports or extreme workouts or nonsense like that. I once had a woman take me rock climbing on our first date. What kind of lesbian spends her night getting her fingertips torn up by rocks?"

Lana laughed.

"So a romantic dinner in a beautiful condo is exactly my speed. Thank you for that."

"You want femme? I can do femme." She took a sip from her wineglass before pushing back her chair. She turned on her iPod, found something slow and instrumental, and held out her hand. "Would you care to dance, Officer? I'll lead."

Avery placed her hand in Lana's and they moved to the empty space between the table and the kitchen. They danced slowly, moving together easily, and Avery rested her head on Lana's shoulder after only a few seconds. Lana smiled and turned her head to kiss Avery's hair. It was so full that it was hard to avoid, but at she didn't mind.

"How about some hard questions?" Avery said. "The questions that are tough but always eventually have to get answered."

"Sounds good. Who goes first?"

"I will. Yes, I have shot someone. I don't regret it. I have nightmares about it sometimes. But I know that if I was faced with the same situation, I would do it again in a heartbeat."

Lana said, "Okay. The scars on my arm. I don't know if you noticed them."

"I did."

"I was stabbed. A fan broke into my apartment. I tried to get away. She stabbed me in the arm and the back, and I managed to use my guitar as a bludgeon. I-I killed her." She said it quickly, rushing through the bullet-points of the most terrifying moment of her life.

Avery stepped back. "I remember that. There was a vigil at the Space Needle. That was you?"

"Yeah."

"Wow. I was on duty that night. I'm glad everything turned out okay for you."

"Me too."

They danced for a bit longer, until the track ended. When the room was silent Avery stepped back and looked at Lana. "Thank you for a fantastic night. It's the best one I've had in a while."

"Me too," Lana said. "But I just got out of a long relationship. I had my rebound fling, but I'm still trying to get over everything that happened."

"Some of the songs on your new album kind of... prepared me for that. Sounds like she really hurt you. I'm fine with going as slow as you need. I like you. You're funny, and smart. And really hot." Lana laughed. "So we had a really good first date. Hopefully we can repeat it on a second date. And we'll go from there." She found Lana's hand and brought it to her lips. "Thank you for tonight. I'll try to think of something to top it for our next night out."

Lana said, "Good luck. I freakin' brought it tonight."

Avery laughed. "Is it still taking it slow if I kiss you goodnight?"

"Let's try it."

They kissed. Lana moved her hand to Avery's hair and threaded it through her fingers. She brushed Avery's top lip with her tongue and then pulled back. Avery kept her eyes closed, her lips slightly parted.

"There's something you should know about me," Avery said. "I know I was kind of cold the night we met, but I was on duty. And tonight I was a little guarded. But if this keeps going, I'm going to lighten up. I save that for the people I truly care about."

"I'd be lucky to count myself among that number." She kissed the tip of Avery's nose. "I like the idea of knowing a side of you most people don't get to see."

Avery smiled. "Ditto. I've never known a celebrity in real life."

Lana said, "Be prepared to be very bored. It means a lot of studio time and lying around scribbling in notebooks. Occasionally talk shows."

"Sounds interesting. I can't wait."

Lana escorted her to the door. "So I'll call you to set up our next date."

"Okay. You know, I really did like the music. You're an incredibly...

appealing performer."

"Oh?"

"Yeah. You have a sexy voice."

Lana leaned in and kissed Avery's cheek, then whispered in her ear, "You haven't heard my sexy voice yet, Officer."

Avery shuddered. "Oh...kay. Okay. Wow." She tucked her hair behind her ears. "I should go if I'm going to go. I'll call you. Or you call me."

"Or something," Lana said. "If I take too long, you can always put out a warrant on me."

"See if I don't. Goodnight."

Lana waved goodnight and watched until she reached her car. She waved again and closed the door, then went about cleaning up the remnants of their dinner. She hadn't told Codie or the others about her date, but she wasn't sure why until that moment. She didn't want to put too much pressure on one meal and a hot dog in the middle of the night. Telling them would have made her feel obliged to report in and tell them if there was a chance of turning it into something more. At the moment it could exist on its own without the pressure.

She didn't know if there was a long-term future with Avery, but she felt very good about it. The first date left her aching for the second. From there, it was anyone's guess where it would go. But she'd spent too long mourning the end with Catherine. She'd used her pain for the album and it was time to move on.

A few days later the band gathered at Cartography's offices to shoot their first video for the new album. Lana was the one who brought up the idea of doing the video sans makeup, but Naomi jumped onboard as they expected she would. When they arrived they wore whatever they put on that morning. The shoulder of Karen's shirt was oddly stained by some spit-up that came from the last time she'd fed Mason. Lana's hair resembled a rat's nest that was only tamed by a pair of pencils stuck through it. Vanessa wore her glasses and workout clothes.

Lana glared at Codie as they went into the studio space. "This is bullshit. You're more beautiful without makeup."

"Blame God," Codie said.

The video was being directed by Brooke Anderson, an actress famous for her role on a critically-acclaimed sitcom who wanted to branch out behind the camera. She was still a newbie, and she wanted to cut her teeth on something relatively easy. She didn't want to take on a full half hour of television or a movie, so music videos were a way to get her foot in the door.

The plot of the video was simple. It would begin with Brooke and Naomi would be fretting about the band arriving too late for hair and makeup. When the band finally does appear, they would walk right past the "beautification station" and pick up their instruments exactly the way they looked when they got out of the car. Lana wasn't wearing a drop of makeup, and both Karen and Vanessa were dressed like any mother at any daycare in the Pacific Northwest. Karen was wearing leggings with a run in them, while Vanessa was in one of Scott's old dress shirts. Codie, as Lana complained, looked almost exactly the same as always save for the fact her hair was pulled back in a bun.

When they showed up, Naomi looked at Lana and hissed. "Oh, my God, you're hideous. YouTube will have to censor this monstrosity."

Lana grinned. "You're just happy people will finally know you're the prettiest one out of the four of us and we've been keeping you off-camera all this time."

Naomi rolled her eyes. The crew was set up and, since the band really didn't need hair and makeup, filming got underway almost immediately. The band got into a car that drove them around the building. The driver had an earpiece that would give him the cue to pull up in front of the building. Naomi and Brooke fretted and followed their scripted lines, and the car arrived without delay. The band tromped inside with Naomi and Brooke trailing behind them, snapping about how late they were and how they might not have time for makeup.

"Where are they going?" Brooke asked when they bypassed the beauticians.

"I don't know," Naomi said.

They walked out into an open area with a plain white backdrop. Lana put on her guitar, Karen took a seat and lifted the cello from its case, and Codie and Vanessa took position at their instruments. The pre-recorded music began playing, and they all mimed playing their instruments. Lana hated the fakery, but she knew it was necessary for the video to work. As the intro ended, Lana stepped back and for the first time their faces were revealed to the camera, blemishes and all.

Lana winked into the camera as she began to fake playing her guitar.

*"You think you know me*
*But you've never seen me before*
*You've seen me on TV*
*On the magazines or at the store*
*These cameras always follow me around,*
*Cover my face and keep my head down*
*But you've only ever seen the mask*
*You call me beautiful, you never asked if*
*This illusion is real or merely plastic*

*Paint up my face, I'm your work of art*
*Spend an hour on my hair before we're ready to start*

*If I take off my mask and show myself true,*
*Would you still appreciate my face value?*

*You've always got to be on,*
*Dress up just to grab the mail*
*Never have a bad day, don't frown*
*Wave, grin, please stay out of jail*
*If you want a private moment you're just out of luck*
*Keep the curtains drawn if you're getting… intimate*
*You've got your own life, so be careful of mine*
*Walking down the street with me in the sunshine*
*And you'll end up on every website online*

*Paint up my face, I'm your work of art*
*Spend an hour on my hair before we're ready to start*
*If I take off my mask and show myself true,*
*Would you still appreciate my face value?"*

Lana stopped lip-syncing for the musical interlude and took a step back from the mic, turning to face Karen. Vanessa was chewing bubble gum and, as Brooke moved in for a close-up, she blew a bubble and let it pop over her lips. Lana laughed and looked down to watch her fingers move over the fret. She had written the song while she was sleeping with Sidra, but the lyrics seemed perfect for her current whatever-it-was with Avery. She nodded her head in time to the music and stepped back in front of the microphone for the next verse.

*"Everyone's comparing themselves to the prom queen*
*I'm bright and shiny and always squeaky clean*
*But I wake up half-dead just like everyone*
*Shave my legs and pluck off all my hair*
*The spotlight shines and I look just like heaven*
*You wouldn't even recognize me if I was laid bare.*

*Look at me and see just an ordinary pretty face*
*The same you'll see every day in a dozen places*
*We're tall and short and fat and thin*
*Makeup, heels, Spanx, just to fit in*
*We spend thousands of dollars trying to look better*
*One day we'll learn we're more beautiful without the armor*

*Paint up my face, I'm your work of art*
*Spend an hour on my hair before we're ready to start*
*If I take off my mask and show myself true,*

*Would you still appreciate my face value?*
*Will you ever even know my face value?"*

The music ended and Brooke clapped her hands over her head. "Absolutely amazing, girls. I really love this song, too. I almost feel bad wearing makeup for my part."

Lana shrugged. "There's nothing wrong with wearing makeup. We're just saying..."

"No, I get it. You're saying the emphasis put on being perfect is wrong. I totally understand." She put her hands on her hips. "Okay, we've got the performance bit down. Now I want to get a few pick-up shots individually. Karen, would you mind being first?"

"Nope. Just point me where you need me."

"I like that attitude," Brooke said. "Hopefully we can get you all out of here at a reasonable time." She snapped her fingers. "Let's get to it! We've got a video to finish."

## CHAPTER TWENTY

THE COVER of NotesBook Magazine featured a larger-than-life picture of Lana Kent, Karen Everett, Vanessa Wayland, and Codie Renton standing behind Mount Baker. A banner reading "How to Stage a Comeback" ran across their waistlines. The article inside discussed the stunt of releasing an album for free download rather than fully capitalizing on their fans' goodwill. By the time the article ran, sales of the physical CD had done well enough to prove the album would have broken sales records if it was offered as a more traditional release. They broke one million downloads in just under a week. The CD sales were surprisingly high, given the general slowdown in album sales.

NotesBook interviewed Lana Kent, while Rolling Stone had an in-depth interview with all four band members. Entertainment Weekly gave the album an A-, which other critics seemed to agree with. Vanessa estimated the average rating was somewhere around a high B, low A. The "Face Value" video was generating a lot of buzz for their decision to go completely makeup-free.

Lana was interviewed about the video on a podcast and laughed when the host said it was a brave move for any band, let alone a girl band. When she finally stopped laughing, she explained. "No, I just think it's ridiculous. We're all in our thirties. Two of us are married with children. And you still call us a girl band? Would you call U2 a boy band? We're a band. Gender doesn't enter into it, whether we do a video without makeup or not."

Avery Hollenbeck found herself following entertainment news for the very first time, skimming the internet for articles until someone showed her how to set up an email alert for specific names. She didn't want to hear any gossip - "Catherine Diehl spotted in Seattle. Reunion with Lana Kent in the works?" - but she was intrigued to see experience it from both sides of the equation. So far she and Lana had evaded the photographers, but Lana had prepared her for the possibility that their fans would eventually discover she existed and speculate about who she was.

It took a few weeks, but her true fear finally did come to pass. She arrived for the morning briefing to find the NotesBook cover on the table where she usually sat. She smirked as she tucked it inside her folder and took a seat. Al Spencer came in a few minutes later and thumped her on the arm. "Hey, Holler-back. A bunch of us are going to Whistler's after shift. Give me a chance to win back my dart championship from you."

"The grudge match will have to be postponed. I have a date."

Her partner Victor had just arrived. "Yeah, she does. Do you know who she's seeing?"

Spencer shook his head. "I'm surprised she's dating anyone. I thought she took a vow of celibacy or something."

"No," Victor leaned back and tapped his pen against his chin. He met Avery's glare with a self-satisfied grin. "You know Radiation Canary?"

"The band? Yeah. My wife loves them."

"Not as much as Avery does. She's dating the lead singer."

Spencer whistled. "No way. She's way too hot for you, Holler-back. Tell you what, when she realizes she's slumming it, why don't you send her my way?"

"Sorry, Spencer." She waggled her pinkie finger at his crotch. "It might be small, but it still counts to a lesbian."

She was used to the banter, but it made her realize that everyone in the world knew who she was dating. All she had to do was say her name and whoever she was talking to would get a flash of information from the deep pockets of their brains. "Oh, yeah, I heard she got stabbed a few years back," or "Wow, she's incredibly sexy." The most disturbing one she'd heard was "Oh, she had those pictures online a few years ago. Her and two blonde ladies, but not a lot of clothes." The idea that the woman she was dating had a sex tape that people she knew might have seen was a completely foreign experience to her. It was going to take a lot of adjustment for her to be comfortable with that level of exposure.

That night, she and Lana were going on their first in-public date. Lana warned about the paparazzi and the possibility Avery would be the topic of speculation online in the morning, but all the warnings were waved off. She told Lana there were worse things in the world than being connected to a talented musician. They tempted fate after dinner by going for a walk, but no one seemed to notice them.

"I need to know something before this goes further," Avery said. "I know the whole sex, drugs, and rock and roll mythology. I can't be connected with anyone who uses illicit drugs."

Lana smiled. "We're clean. We occasionally smoke some pot, but Karen and Vanessa have their babies around too much for us to do it often. Do you want me to quit?"

"No reason to. Pot's legal. But would you, if I asked?"

"If the choice was between having a joint from time to time and not being with you, it would be a lot easier to give up the weed."

Avery smiled. "Good to know."

"You smell a lot better. Usually."

Avery laughed and threw her weight against Lana's side. "Flirt." They walked on, stopping at a corner to let traffic pass. "So no hard drugs, no alcohol... I don't have to worry about being the cop who is dating someone in rehab?"

"I'm clean."

"Good to know." She squeezed Lana's hand. "We should turn back."

"Are you getting tired?"

Avery shook her head. "No. But if we keep walking, it would be faster to just go all the way to my apartment than turning back to get your car."

Lana turned to face her. "So what if we kept walking?"

"And you would get a cab?"

"Maybe. In the morning."

Avery stepped closer. "Why, Lana Kent. If I didn't know better, I would think you were angling to stay over at my apartment."

"It's a very nice apartment from what I've seen. The bed looks very comfortable."

"Oh, it is. Big enough for two. We could put a row of pillows down the middle to make sure no one strays in the night."

Lana kissed her. Avery put one hand in the small of Lana's back and pushed it forward as she angled her hips to meet her halfway. Lana rolled her hips and Avery turned her head to break the kiss. She scanned the street around them and saw that they were thankfully still alone.

"Okay... no drug charges, but maybe public indecency..."

Lana laughed huskily against her cheek. "Sorry. Maybe we put this off too long."

"How about we make up for it now?"

"Yeah." Lana kissed her again, then took her hand to continue their walk.

When they got to Avery's apartment, she took the time to turn on the kitchen light and dump her things on the counter before Lana pressed her against the counter. She kissed Avery's neck and reached around to hook her fingers on the edges of Avery's jacket. Avery let her peel it off and tossed it toward one of the chairs. Lana brushed Avery's hair out of her way and continued the assault on her neck.

"I'm glad we waited," Avery said. "I wanted to know you were ready."

"I'm ready," Lana said, placing her hands on Avery's hips to spin her around. "I'm ready for you." They kissed as Lana slid one hand down and under the waistband of Avery's pants. Avery was well aware how many people would have killed to hear Lana Kent whisper those words, but she pushed the thought away as quickly as it had formed. She wasn't screwing a celebrity, she was making love to a woman she had grown to admire more than she would have thought possible. She wasn't quite ready to say they were in love, but the threshold was definitely there.

"What do you want?" Lana whispered breathlessly, one hand in Avery's hair as the other moved along her waist. "I want to do everything to you, so you'll have to narrow it down for me."

Avery whimpered and put her hands in Lana's hair. Five weeks earlier she had seen a woman wandering down the street outside Key Arena and assumed she was a drunk or a prostitute. Instead she found this remarkable, magical woman who seemed endlessly fascinated by an ordinary beat cop. And now she was asking for direction? She kissed the corners of Lana's mouth and then kissed down her cheek to her ear.

"Take my pants off. Get on your knees."

Lana moaned and complied. She pushed up Avery's shirt to kiss her stomach before moving lower to the lacy edge of her panties. Avery shivered when Lana's breath washed over the thin material.

"Did you wear these for me?"

"I..." She pushed her hair back and looked down. "I've worn nice underwear on all our dates. Just in case."

Lana kissed her mound through the underwear and Avery gripped the counter behind her with both hands. "Jesus. Sorry..."

"Don't be. Let your knees go weak. I'll catch you if I have to."

Avery shuddered again. Lana moved the underwear out of the way and let it fall. Avery stepped out of it, still wearing her shoes as Lana kissed her skin. Avery curled her fingers around the edge of the counter, eyes closed and lips parted, rocking her hips forward to meet Lana's lips and tongue. She clenched her teeth and growled, irritated at how close she already was.

Lana, aware she was holding back, looked up at her. "Let yourself go. I want to taste you. This is just the first time. The first time can be fast." She kissed Avery's pubic hair and then dragged her tongue over the sensitive flesh. Avery moaned and put her hand on the back of Lana's head.

"Make me come, songbird."

Lana once again followed her orders and used her fingers and tongue to push Avery over the edge. Avery very nearly lost her balance, but Lana pressed her back against the counter and prevented her from falling.

Avery sucked her top lip under the bottom, her jaw thrust forward, and rocked her head from side to side until Lana stopped kissing her thighs and stood up to kiss her lips. Avery pushed her tongue into Lana's mouth and let Lana push it out again, spreading her legs so Lana could stand between them and press against her.

"Undress me," Lana said.

"Eventually." Avery gripped the collar of Lana's blouse and smiled at her. "You said the first time can be quick, but the other times can be slow. Well... I'm going slow."

Lana smiled. "Don't torture me, officer. I can complain to your CO."

Avery kissed Lana's lips, took her hand, and led her out of the kitchen to the bedroom.

Afterward they rolled away from each other, occupying the furthest reaches of the mattress on either side with the sheets between them. They were both exhausted and overly sensitive to even the slightest touch so they mutually decided it would be best not to tempt fate. Lana was lying properly with her head near the pillows while Avery was inverted. When she felt safe enough to touch and be touched without causing an explosive reaction, she reached over and drew one of Avery's feet to her. She put the foot between her breasts and began massaging it.

"Oh, God. That's amazing."

"I figure they call you flatfoot for a reason."

"That's detectives," Avery purred. Even her voice was markedly different than it was during the day. All the swagger and bravado was gone, replaced by a liquid and lethargic murmur. "You have a thing for feet, do you?"

"I do." Lana kissed the big toe. "It's not that weird, as fetishes go."

Avery propped herself up on her elbows, and Lana admired what the new position did to her breasts. "I have some of my own."

"Tell me."

"If I wanted to tie you up... blindfold you..."

Lana smiled. "That could be fun. How S&M are we talking?"

"Very minor." Avery rubbed her other foot over Lana's breast. "I don't get off on dominating someone. I just like keeping your hands still and doing whatever I want to you. Maybe I could tickle your feet until you scream."

Lana bit her bottom lip and sucked Avery's second toe. "I'm glad we waited."

"Me too. It doesn't seem like that long, looking back. I mean, at the time it was torture. But now, I'm really glad we waited."

Lana put down Avery's feet and crawled over to her. She stretched out next to her at the foot of the bed and brushed the hair out of Avery's face. Avery smiled at her and kissed the inside of her wrist.

"It's so strange thinking I might see something about this on Facebook tomorrow, you know? 'Lana Kent escorted home by frumpy cop.'"

"Frumpy? Must be one of those fake reports. 'Lana Kent escorted home by raven-haired beauty,' that would be the real headline."

Avery moved her hand to Lana's stomach. "Are you staying the night?"

"Yeah. I kind of expect to make a habit of it."

"Good. This bed has been empty too long."

Lana kissed her between the eyebrows and then drew Avery's head down to her chest. Avery snuggled closer and soon fell asleep to the sound of Lana's breathing. Lana stayed awake for a bit longer but, for the first time in a while, her sleeplessness was caused by a reluctance to let go of the day rather than fear of what tomorrow would bring.

Mason was standing on legs that bowed out to either side, his arms extended with the palms facing the floor as if he was trying to push himself up onto an invisible surface. He moved his body up and down in time to the music, smiling when he saw Laura and Ella smiling at him. Karen laughed from the couch and remembered the first time he'd been confronted with the fact Laura was a twin. He was used to seeing two mommies, but now there was a second woman who looked exactly like one of the mommies. Sometimes Karen wondered if he thought there was a lookalike of her somewhere out there. Maybe in his world everyone had a double.

The Cowan sisters, the Femme Reapers, were on the other side of the glass recording a song for their new album. Karen had the day free, so she was playing "babysitter" for Mason since Laura had taken care of him while Radiation Canary worked. It was also an excuse to hear her wife play. The Reapers were loud, Gothic, sometimes raucous, but she loved it. Sometimes she just needed a good growl with her music, and the Cowans provided it in spades.

Since Karen was there, they wanted her to fulfill her promise to play violin on one of their songs. She already knew their whole album by heart already since she'd heard Laura rehearse it two dozen times, so she would be ready whenever they called her in. For the time being she was simply enjoying the company of their son and the music of her wife.

The door to the booth swung open and Naomi entered. She glanced at Karen and did an honest-to-goodness double take. "Karen! You're here."

"I am."

"Good. Great. That's perfect." She looked through the glass. "Are they almost done?"

Naomi was breathless, almost frantic. "Naomi? Is everything okay?"

"Hm?" She looked at Karen and then waved off the question. "Fine, fine, fine. It's... fine. I'll tell you all together." She looked at her phone and then gave in. "No, I have to tell you now. What comes to mind when

I say the name Morrison Barrie Becker?"

"M.B. Becker?" Karen said. "Uh, 'Eight Oceans,' 'Carry You With Me,' 'Variations on a Scream,' 'Written on Skin.' He's a legend."

Naomi's smile threatened to break her face. "He's here. He was vacationing in Alaska when he was inspired to work on a song. He doesn't want to fly all the way to his studio in Toronto, so his people were calling studios here to see who was available. We were free so we told him to come by here. M.B. Becker is going to record a song for his next album right here."

Karen said, "That's amazing!"

"It gets better. You know his voice has been... failing lately. He's getting older, and he can't hit all the notes. He usually has his Darlings sing harmony for him."

"Right."

"They're in Toronto. He asked if we had any female singers on site."

Karen said, "He wants Ella and Laura to sing backup for him?"

"And you! I mean, since you're here."

Karen laughed. "Wow! That's amazing. When is he going to get here?"

"He's on his way from the airport now." The music ended and Naomi beat the producer to the mic. "Girls, we're going to need to borrow the studio for a few minutes."

Naomi explained the situation to Laura and Ella, both of whom agreed instantly to give up some of their time to the legendary crooner.

Fifteen minutes later a pair of black sedans pulled up in front of the building. Laura gripped Karen's hand with hers as they watched a pair of insanely gorgeous woman who couldn't have been more than twenty as they opened the back door to the lead car. They each offered a hand to the man inside, and he eased himself up out of the seat.

Morrison Barrie Becker was somewhere over ninety, though he never admitted to the exact number. He was stooped and bent, but somehow still managed to look as if he was in command as he was eased into a wheelchair and rolled up the ramp to the doors. He wore a white suit over a black T-shirt, his eyes hidden behind a pair of wraparound sunglasses. His fedora was tilted low over his forehead to shade his beaked nose.

The teenager pushing his chair stopped him in front Naomi. "Mr. Becker. It's an honor to have you here today. I'm Naomi Marrow. This is Laura and Karen Everett, and Ella Cowan. They're from Radiation Canary and the Femme Reapers."

"Say a prayer, if you've got one," he warbled, "I've got demons I can't outrun..."

Karen felt a warm buzz hearing such an icon singing words she'd written. "That's us all right."

He nodded and then aimed a finger at the twins. "Femme Reapers, I don't know."

"We're probably less your style," Ella said. "But we're willing to change it up for your track."

He lifted a hand to the other young girl. "My daughters will give you the sheet music and the lyrics." He suddenly looked forward again. "None of you are the one who twerks, right? You wear all your clothes when you sing?"

"Yes, sir," Laura said.

He made a noncommittal sound. "Good. What those people are doing is spectacle, not music. Cartography is Dash Warren, Cartography is... music. I trust you. Let's go record a song, hum?"

His daughter wheeled him inside, and Naomi turned to rub Karen's arm before she and Ella followed him inside. Laura smiled wryly at Karen.

"Never heard of us, huh?"

"So? This is your chance to make him a fan."

"His daughters. And here I had him pegged as a dirty old man."

Karen put her arm around Laura, kissed her cheek, and led her inside.

## CHAPTER TWENTY-ONE

VANESSA SETTLED Nathaniel in the shopping cart and pinched his shoe between two fingers so she could give his foot a shake. He laughed and gripped the cart handle in front of him as she wheeled him into the store. She was still anxious about it tipping over or him tumbling out, so she continually touched him or put a hand on his shoulder to keep him steady. Her first stop was the paper towel aisle - they needed some anyway - and she placed a package on either side of him for extra padding.

As she was packing him in, she became aware of someone in her peripheral vision lingering at the head of the aisle. She looked up, but the person slipped away before she could get a good look at them. She assumed it was just another shopper trying to find something specific and continued down her list. Scott filled out the grocery list because he was an assassin when it came to making them. Step one, go through the each room to ascertain what was needed. Step two, rearrange the list according to their placement in the store. She went straight to the back and worked her way across, then forward. She never had to backtrack or walk from one side of the store to the other, and his thoughtfulness shaved valuable minutes off her shopping time.

In the dairy section, someone took a jug of milk from the freezer and stopped mid-motion as she was putting it in her cart. When she was waiting in the deli, she heard whispers. "No. Looks like her, though." And "I think she plays the keyboards." Her face flushed as she took her order and continued on Scott's list. She was fine with people staring. She knew some people would recognize her and whisper. But she didn't know why they should infringe on her day unless they actually came up to talk to her or ask for an autograph.

She was getting bread when she saw someone with a cellphone raised to take a picture, and that was when she realized she was going to have to take a stand. She held up her hand to block the lens. "Sorry, could you not? I'll gladly take a picture with you, but I would prefer if you don't take a picture of my son."

"Oh, I'm so sorry."

"It's okay." She posed for the picture with the girl, thanked her for listening, and then went on with her list. When she'd gotten everything Scott had written down she went to the clothing section and searched around until she found a suitably wide-brimmed hat. She put it on her head and struck a pose, making Nathaniel laugh before she placed it on his head. She always understood Karen and Laura's reasons for calling Mason "Bug" in interviews, but she'd never had the problem herself. She was never as prominently famous as Karen or Laura. But now that Radiation Canary seemed to be on every magazine cover she saw, it was harder to be inconspicuous.

When she got to the checkout counter, the teenager behind the register looked at her and then cut his eye toward the NotesBook Magazine still on display by the candy bars.

"Did... you find anyth-- everything all right?"

Vanessa smiled. "I did, thank you."

She began loading her items onto the conveyer belt and wondered how Lana managed to get through a single day without being swarmed by fans and photographers and cellphone photographers. Karen would have it even worse. Incredibly famous and with a baby? She couldn't even imagine the hassle. She made a mental note to ask if she could do anything to lighten their loads the next time she saw them. Even if it was something like picking up their dry-cleaning so they didn't go out, it would have to be a great relief.

She looked behind her and saw a woman in line had been sneakily trying to get a picture with her phone. She resisted the urge to sigh and smiled as she angled her body so Nathaniel wouldn't be caught in the frame. Celebrity life must have been so much easier before everyone had a damn camera in their pocket.

Their first concert was at a tavern in the University District, promising lots of rowdy college students. Karen and Lana were still fiddling with the set-list an hour before they went on, huddled up backstage in the green room. It was going to be their first time performing their new songs in front of people, and they wanted to be sure it was just right. Lana got a text and vanished only to return five minutes later with a beautiful brunette in tow. She was dressed in jeans and a purple T-shirt that showed off surprisingly well-muscled arms. She looked nervous as Lana put an arm around her.

"Ladies, this is Avery Hollenbeck. Ave, this is Karen, Vanessa, and back there is Codie."

Avery smiled shyly. "Hi."

"The famous Officer Avery," Codie said. "Nice to finally put a face to that goofy grin Lana's been wearing for the past few weeks."

Karen shook Avery's hand. "Backstage passes to a concert. That's a pretty nice date."

Lana said, "I knew a guy who knew a guy. She's going to be sitting in the audience, but I wanted to give her a chance to meet you before the show. I thought it might make it harder for her to heckle us if she didn't like the music."

Avery grinned. "It was great meeting you all. Lana gushes about you all enough and I've listened to your music enough that I almost feel like I know you. It's... a little bizarre to be standing here right now. I'm used to Lana, but now I'm standing in a room with three celebrities acting like they're just normal people."

"We are normal people," Codie said. "At least right now. We don't bring out the cocaine and hookers until after the show."

Avery laughed and said, "Codie. Lana told me you've been friends since you were teenagers. I wanted to let you know I plan to treat her right."

Codie's smile wavered and she nodded solemnly. "That's good to know. She deserves it."

Avery looked at Lana. "Well, I certainly think so." She kissed the corner of Lana's mouth and rubbed her back. "I'm going to go grab my seat before the young hooligans show up."

"I'll walk you out."

Codie's smile returned as soon as they were gone. "So that's Lana's sexy cop. Smaller than I expected, but not bad."

"Did you see those arms?" Vanessa said. "Yow. When Lana said she got picked up by a cop, I didn't think she meant literally."

Karen laughed. "She seemed sweet. And she makes Lana happy. That's all I need to know."

When Lana came back she stopped at the door and held her arms out as if inviting an attack. "Okay. Let me have it. Mock me, tease me..."

Codie smiled. "I like her. She seems to know that if she hurts you, I'll kick her ass. I like that in your girlfriends."

Vanessa said, "Again I call attention to the arms. You're tough, Codie, but I think even you would have a hard time going up against her."

Lana said, "But I'd pay money to watch that fight. Who wants to pitch in for enough Jell-O to fill a kiddie pool?"

"Fantasize later," Karen said. "We've got a show to do. First live show in a long time, if you don't count *Settle In, Seattle!* Are we all ready?"

"Ready-ready."

They gathered in the middle of the room for a quick embrace, and Lana kissed Karen and Vanessa on the cheeks. "Break legs." She grabbed Codie's hand and stepped closer to whisper in her ear. "I really like her, Codie. Be honest."

"She's amazing. She's funny. She's sweet." She kissed Lana's cheek. "I like her."

"Good. Let's go kick some musical butt."

Backstage, Lana turned on her phone to test the camera to make sure it was working. She nodded at the stage tech and he took a laptop out on stage. He placed it on a stool behind Lana's microphone, crouched to turn on Skype, and Lana's face filled the screen.

"Hey, everyone! Thanks for coming out tonight. Before we begin, we wanted to take a moment for a public service announcement. It's been a while since we did a live show, and something we noticed the last time seems to have become an even bigger trend. We just wanted to get out in front of it right away and try to make our point clear.

"You would be pretty annoyed if we did the whole show like this. You didn't pay money for a ticket, clear your schedule for a night, ignore whatever work or classes you should be focusing on, and drive out to the theater just to watch a concert on your phone. We get that you want to document the experience, we get that you want this moment preserved, but if you're filming the entire time, you're not preserving anything. You're taking yourself so far out of the moment that there's nothing to look back fondly on."

"We're not going to be strict monsters about recording at our concerts. You might record your favorite song, there might be a moment or two that you want to remember later, but the whole show? Come on. No one wants to watch an entire concert on a laptop screen. Not when the real thing is right in front of you."

She walked out with the phone held out in front of her, smiling as she walked out on stage. "So please, for your own sake, put away the phone and just enjoy the show." She turned off the camera and dropped the phone onto the laptop. The stage tech came out to remove them, and Lana began to strum her guitar as the rest of the band joined her onstage. She looked over her shoulder to make sure everyone was in position before she played the intro to "The Next Ferry."

Avery was seated on the aisle at what she estimated to be the midpoint between the stage and the exit. She had joked to Lana that she would be the oldest person in the room due to the fact the venue was only a few blocks from the University of Washington, but the amount of utter children in the audience was horrifying. To be surrounded by so-called adults whose earliest memories were of the early-aughts was almost enough to ruin the buzz of excitement she had about seeing her girlfriend performing for the first time. She soothed herself by constantly recalling that she could arrest anyone she wanted for public intoxication and, with that power came enough calm for her to enjoy herself.

Lana came out strong with her monologue about filming, and Avery actually saw people putting away their phones as the band took the stage. The band met that initial strength and carried it through their first and second songs. The crowd occasionally sang along and responded enthusiastically after each one faded out, and Lana would step back from the microphone with a smile as she waited for the next one to begin.

Occasionally Karen needed to swap out her cello for a violin, a process that only took a few seconds with the help of a stage manager. The gap was covered by Lana bantering with the audience. She picked out a couple in the front row and grilled them about their relationship. "Is this a date? It's not your first date, is it? I'd be worried about someone who wants to spend the first date in a dark room facing away from each other, that's all I'm saying. But I guess that's what a movie is, huh? Man, dating is weird. Where did you meet?"

When Karen put aside both instruments to sing lead on a song called "The Question," Lana moved back to perch on Karen's stool. Avery was lucky enough to have experienced what it was like to have Lana Kent quietly playing guitar in a corner of the bedroom, and her pose was so casual and inviting that it felt almost as intimate despite the crowd of people in the room with them. She smiled as she watched her, very aware of just how it was possible for the whole world to fall in love with her. And while Lana played, she watched the rest of her band, perfectly willing to sit in the corner so they could have the spotlight for a change.

They played for almost ninety minutes. By the end, Lana was sweaty and breathless during the banter but still giving her all for every song. Someone brought out a bottle of vitamin water for her and she drank it while Karen took lead again. Finally, Lana took center stage once more and adjusted the microphone as Karen retrieved her violin.

"Thank you everyone. Thank you for coming out tonight, and downloading the album. If you were one of the people who bought the CD... thank you so much. We love all of you and we're so grateful we came back to find you waiting for us. We're going to be in the lobby after the show signing autographs, and we'll be here until everyone has been through the line. I know I yelled at you about the cameras during the show, but by all means have them out for that. Pictures are free."

She started playing the introduction to "Say a Prayer," and the crowd erupted. Their applause and whistles died down before Lana began singing, and the room filled with reverent silence. When she reached the end, she changed the lyrics. "If anyone is there, if anybody cares. If you hear my plea, I need you to save me. I need you to save the girl on the wall." She held one arm out to indicate Karen, and the crowd cheers for her. "I need you to pray for Nathaniel's mom." The other arm held out toward Vanessa, and more cheers. "Say a prayer for my oldest friend," Lana sang, her voice cracking on the last word. Avery saw Codie smile as Lana composed herself. "And for the scarred guitar. Say a prayer. Please, say a prayer for us."

The music faded and the crowd went insane. Avery put two fingers in her mouth and whistled as loudly as any of the kids, watching as Lana followed the others off-stage. She knew that Lana would let her go backstage to wait while they signed autographs, but she didn't want to just sit around doing nothing. Instead she got in line with everyone else and slowly advanced through the lobby. The wait was close to a half hour before they rounded a corner to see a long table covered by a white sheet.

The nearest side of the table was occupied by theater staff who was selling merchandise: CDs, posters, T-shirts, stickers, and other things she couldn't make out from far away. Every now and then, at the seemingly-distant opposite end of the corridor, she saw one of the band members stand up and lean across the table to have their picture taken. She bought a CD she didn't already have - *Action After Warnings* - and a sticker with the band's logo on it. If her fellow officers were going to put Radiation Canary things in and on her locker, she might as well beat them to the punch.

Codie was the first one in the row, and she smiled when she recognized Avery. "Who should I make it out to?" she asked. "Allie, right?"

"To eBay," Avery said. "Beloved highest bidder."

Codie smiled and signed her name, then passed the CD to Vanessa. When the CD got to Lana, she looked up with a professional smile that softened when she saw who it was for.

"You didn't leave halfway through? I'm shocked."

"I had to wait for my favorite song. It's not my fault you played it last."

Lana stood up and leaned across the table to kiss her. The crowd behind them whooped and hollered, and Avery's laughter broke the kiss. She buried her face on Lana's shoulder.

"How much extra is that?" a woman from farther down the line called.

"Calm down, perverts. She's my girlfriend."

The crowd awed, and Lana sat down to sign the CD for her. "Are you heading home or do you want to stick around?"

"If I stick around, will you drive me home?"

"Yes, ma'am."

"Then I shall."

Lana ushered her around the table, offering her hand for balance as she stepped over the barricade between the table and the wall. One of the theater workers offered her a chair, and she sat in the corner to watch the rest of the autograph session. Everyone who came by was awestruck just being in the presence of their favorite band. Avery watched their interactions, how tightly the fans closed their eyes and how wide their smiles were when Karen or Vanessa or Lana stood up to hug them, and realized she'd never truly appreciated how famous the band was. Seeing them on magazine covers or television was one thing, but actually seeing the people who bought the merchandise really brought it home.

Finally the last group of fans was at the table. Lana congratulated them. "You may have waited the longest, but it's going to be easy as hell for you to get out of the parking lot."

They signed the final album, rolled up the last poster, and posed for the last picture. Worker bees that Avery assumed were hired by Cartography began boxing up the leftover merchandise, what little there was of it, and Lana went backstage to retrieve her guitar. She also grabbed Karen's cello and violin cases and came back looking like a roadie instead of the lead singer of the band.

"We'll meet up tomorrow at the rehearsal space?" Vanessa confirmed.

Lana said, "Yeah. See you then."

They headed out, and Lana looped her arm around Avery's waist to draw her close. Lana smelled like sweat, but it was a good odor. It was the smell of hard work and giving her all.

"And now... what, you just go home? Shower and go to sleep?"

"What else would I do? I'm exhausted."

Avery said, "I know, but... you just held that entire crowd in thrall. It seems weird to just go home now."

"I could go home with you, but you have an early shift. And I have to be at the rehearsal studio by nine." She sighed. "Ah, screw it. Let's quit our jobs so we can go home and fuck all night."

Avery laughed. "Tempting. But we probably shouldn't."

"Damn it." Lana kissed Avery's cheek. "I do have to let the adrenaline dissipate or I can't get to sleep. Sometimes I work out. Sometimes I just walk around for a while."

"Get laid?"

"That works, too. Tease." She angled her head to kiss the spot behind Avery's ear that had always proven to be a hit in the past. "I'll still drop you off at home. But I won't stay. We need to be strict with ourselves."

Avery nodded. "Right." She moved her hand down to Lana's ass and squeezed hard.

When they got into the car, Avery put her now-autographed CD in the player. "Which one is your favorite?"

Lana advanced the disc to "The Importance of Your Radio" and told Avery how they had recorded the album in the pre-dawn hours using free studio time donated by a friend of a friend. They listened to the song in comfortable silence. When it ended Avery reached over and swept her hand under Lana's hair to stroke the back of her neck. Lana pulled up in front of Avery's building and walked her upstairs. Avery chuckled and leaned over to kiss Lana's cheek.

"I don't know many people who can claim they saw a concert and then got escorted home by the star."

"Well, some people are just special, I guess."

"I guess."

They stopped outside Avery's apartment and spent a while kissing goodnight. Lana stroked Avery's hair and combined a moan with a whimper when she finally pulled back. "I should go if I'm going to leave." She kissed the tip of Avery's nose. "I'm going under protest, however."

"I'll note that in your file."

"Thank you, officer." They kissed again, a bit longer this time. Lana growled and nipped Avery's bottom lip. "Really going now."

Avery nodded and smiled knowingly. "Okay."

"We're leaving on tour in a couple of days. There's a chance you won't see me much over the next few weeks. Months, really."

"Okay."

She touched Avery's cheek. "Just know that I'll want to see you. Every day."

"Me too."

Lana held her gaze for a minute before she said, "I love you."

Avery stared at her and then blinked. "Wow. I know how hard that must have been for you to say after... a-after everything. Thank you. And I love you, too."

Lana smiled. "Phew. You made me sweat a little for that."

"Sorry."

"It's okay. It ended well. I just wanted to be sure I said it before I left."

Avery said, "I'm glad you did. And if I get a couple of days off, I may fly out to wherever you are to spend some time with you."

"Let me know. I'll buy your ticket."

Avery tightened their hug. "I like having a rich girlfriend."

Lana laughed and kissed her again. "Okay. I'm really going this time."

"Get out of here. Goodnight. Thank you for the concert." Avery waited by the door and watched as Lana walked back to her car. Avery smiled to herself as she unlocked the apartment and went inside. She looked at the CD and the four names scrawled over the artwork. Definitely one of the best concerts she had ever been to. She chuckled and took off her jacket, heading down the hall to get ready for bed.

## CHAPTER TWENTY-TWO

KAREN HELD the phone in front of her as she walked from the living room to the bedroom. They had woken up while the sun was still down, fumbling around in the dark while trying not to wake Mason. Eventually he did wake, and Karen took him to have breakfast while Laura offered to pack her bags. "We're heading to this little island town to do a podcast, then we're coming back here tonight to do the show before leaving on tour. So we're kind of running around like chickens with their heads cut off." Laura was packing the bag on Karen's bed, and she looked up as Karen came in. "Laura offered to pack for me."

"Oh, that was sweet of her. Hi, Laura!"

Laura said, "Who is that?"

"Olivia Childress." She turned the phone around so Olivia could wave. Laura waved and went back to packing. "We're trying to work out a schedule where we can meet up to discuss video ideas. We're on tour and she's filming, so it's kind of hectic."

"Uh-huh," Laura said.

"We don't even know what song the video will be for." She kept the phone up as she opened a drawer and began digging for something.

Olivia said, "Well, I love 'The Sailmaker's Daughter.' But I would imagine you or Lana want that for yourselves."

"You could always be the one she's pining for," Karen said.

Laura said, "Karen..."

"Found it." Karen pushed the drawer shut and put the notebook down on the bed. "A few months back I had an idea for a video~"

"Karen," Laura said, louder this time.

"Yeah, sweetie."

"Where's Mason?"

"He went right to sleep. He's in his crib."

Laura started to say something, but she looked pointedly at Karen's phone before she went back to folding. Karen watched her for a moment before she went back to the notebook. "Uh. Anyway, the video I was talking about... it might be done to death, but I still think we could do something interesting with it." She trailed off as Laura walked out of the room. "Uh. Actually, why don't I email you the information? It'll be easier for you to dissect it that way."

"Okay. I should probably get going, too. I'm going to be on-set all day, but if you have any other ideas feel free to shoot them along."

"I will. Talk to you soon." She disconnected and left the phone on the bed as she went in search of her wife. "Lo?" She checked Mason's room and then went into the living room where Laura was just sitting down to the table with a cup of coffee. "Everything okay?"

"Everything's fine."

"Lying."

Laura looked at her. "No, it's fine. I was packing for you so you'd have time to spend with Mason before you left for your tour. If he went back to sleep and you had time for a phone call, then you have enough time to pack your own fucking bag."

Karen flinched. She rounded the couch and sat down next to Laura. Laura kept her eyes straight ahead, looking out the window at the early morning. Karen reached over and stroked the back of Laura's head.

"Tell me what's wrong."

Laura started to say something and then just shook her head and looked into her coffee. "I feel like you just got back from the cabin. And while you were there, I felt like a single mother whose partner had visitation rights. I know this is the big push, and that you have to get your faces out there, but I miss you. I guess I just got spoiled the past two years having you all to myself. And I'm grumpy because I didn't get much sleep last night."

Karen kissed her cheek. Laura turned her head so their lips met. "The best part about technology is that we don't have to be completely separated. I won't be in a cabin this time. I'll be in hotels with internet fast enough that we can Skype whenever we want. Naked."

Laura chuckled and rested her forehead against Karen's. "I love you."

"I love you, too." She moved her lips up to kiss Laura's forehead. "Are you sure that's all that's bothering you?"

"Yeah. I'm just hormonal."

"Ah, should've realized. I had a three-day head start, so I should've been prepared." She pecked the corner of Laura's mouth. "I'll finish packing. Stay here, listen to the monitor, and I'll bring you chocolate in a few minutes."

Laura smiled. "Thank you."

"Sure." She got up and walked away, but she stopped at the end of the hallway to look back. Laura was still staring out the window, coffee cup cradled in both hands, lost in her thoughts. She knew Laura's time of the month wasn't the real reason behind her anger, or at least not the whole reason, but she didn't want to force it. Whatever was bothering her would come out when it was time. She would be there to take care of it whenever that might be.

The town where they were recording the podcast was on an island a hundred miles north of Seattle. Codie offered to fly them up to cut out some of the travel time, with an added bonus of saving them time on the ferry. Lana originally planned to invite Avery along, but she realized there wouldn't be any time for sightseeing or shopping, so she promised to pick up a postcard at the airport if she had the time.

The island was called Squire's Isle, and the town was December Harbor. Codie was familiar with the town; she had spent quite a few weekends flying around the area and they had the best airport in the archipelago. On the flight up, she casually mentioned that she knew this time would be different from her last visit to the island.

"What happened last time?" Karen asked.

"Last time was when I had to make the emergency landing."

"You were leaving this island? Okay, pull over. I want to get out."

The podcast studio was on the ground floor of the island's radio station. They were greeted by the host, Nadine Powell, who escorted them into the surprisingly spacious soundproofed room where they could set up. There was already a drum set and keyboard, as promised, but Karen and Vanessa had brought their own instruments.

Nadine was older than they expected given her "Pixie" moniker. Lana had expected someone closer to twenty than forty. She definitely earned the name from enthusiasm alone. "Sorry if I'm a bit hyper," she said as they were finally sitting down to record. "We normally just have local celebrities on the show. The mayor, a reporter for the town paper. I even had my parents on once. This is just a really big deal for me. I'll try to tone it down a little for the show."

"Hyper is good," Lana said. "We're all nervous and awkward when we have to talk about ourselves on the radio, so it should balance it out."

Nadine settled in on her side of the table and checked her schedule. "Okay, the way I have it is the intro, which is boring promotional and advertising stuff. Then we talk for a bit. I was thinking I would start with Lana or Karen..." She looked over the rim of her glasses and Karen pointed at Lana. "We'll start with Lana. Then Karen, and Vanessa... I really want to hear about balancing motherhood with being a rock star."

Vanessa said, "Hah, okay. Sure. I'll try to come up with something."

"Then, Codie, we'll move on to your charity. After that we'll have you play something live in studio. Two songs?"

"As many as you want," Lana said.

Nadine said, "No, that's not true. The podcast is only an hour long, so there has to be a limit. But we'll see how much time is left after we finish talking." She ran the tip of her pen down the checklist. "Oh, and my wife wants to meet you. She's the station manager and a big fan. That doesn't have anything to do with the podcast, but I wanted to warn you before she burst in here as you were getting ready to go."

"Consider us warned," Karen said.

"Okay!" She gave the signal to her producer that she was ready. "Let's get started."

She played the intro, a quick musical rift that introduced her and the podcast, then leaned in closer to the microphone. "Hello, and welcome back to the Pixie's Podcast. Whether you're here on the island or somewhere else out there in the internet wilds, welcome. And this month there's a very good chance you're listening for the very first time because I have some extremely special guests here in the studio with me right now." She smiled. "Welcome to Lana Kent, Karen Everett, Vanessa Wayland, and Codie Renton. Collectively known as Radiation Canary. Now you all say hello at the same time so no one can possibly tell who is saying what."

All four said their greeting.

"Fantastic! We have a lot to talk about. We're going to cover that sneaky, sneaky trick they pulled by putting together a whole album in secret and then just giving it away for free. We're going to talk about their next album which we *will* have to pay for, and we'll also talk to Karen and Vanessa about what it's like to be mommies with such demanding careers and schedules. We've got a lot to go over, so you're going to want to stick around after these quick commercial breaks to pay the bills. We'll be right back."


They ended up talking for close to ninety minutes, and Nadine said they would trim it down to as close to an hour as possible. Lana suggested singing a few extra songs to pad it out to two hours so she could just cut the interview in half to make two different episodes. They had the time before they needed to be back in Seattle and Nadine was more than willing to keep talking. They played a handful of songs from *Coal Mine* and, at Nadine's request, Lana and Karen did an acoustic version of "Land Among the Stars." Karen was afraid it would be awkward sitting in a room singing for an audience of one, but it was no different than singing in the studio with only the producer watching.

Nadine thanked them for coming in and, as promised, they took a moment to say hi to Nadine's wife, Miranda. When they finally got out of the studio and back to the airport, they still had three hours before they had to be in Seattle for the concert. Lana decided to spend the flight napping - "Wake me up if we start to crash. I don't want to wake up dead." - while Karen texted with Laura from the front seat. Codie glanced over as Karen shut off the phone and stuffed it into the chest pocket of her coat.

"Everything okay?"

"Laura's not answering."

Codie shrugged. "Maybe she's busy."

"Maybe. She was acting weird this morning."

"Weird how?"

Karen shook her head. "Grumpy, irritable... I don't know. Maybe she's just on her period, but she's not usually..." She sighed and looked out the window. "I've been spending a lot of time away from home. The cabin, talk shows, shooting videos, and now the tour. I guess I have been turning her into a single mother. And she has her own album to promote."

"Well, if anyone can work it out, it's you two."

"Yeah. I just don't like it when she freezes me out. She knows how much I hate it, so that makes it the perfect punishment."

From the back, Vanessa said, "Yeah, no one likes to be ignored."

Karen grinned and unbuckled her seatbelt. "Sorry. I'll come back there and talk to you. I probably shouldn't be bugging the pilot anyway."

Naomi arranged to meet the Canaries at the venue where they would be playing the first stop of their tour. She had their itinerary with her and went over it while she was waiting for them to arrive. They had a grueling twenty-five city schedule taking them all over the country and crossing back home through Canada. They would be on the road for almost four months, not counting the dates where they would have to catch a plane to make it to the next stop in time. Two shows in Washington, including one at the Gorge Amphitheatre, one in Oregon, two in California. Then Arizona, Colorado, Oklahoma...

She leaned back and pushed her fingers under her glasses to rub her eyes. The tour was important not just because it was their return to the public performances, not because they had to bridge the gap between the release of their free album and the one that would cost full price, but because it would be the last one she spearheaded. Just thinking of it made her sad, so she focused on her work.

The band arrived for rehearsals and Naomi greeted them in the green room. "We have everything finalized for all the legs of your tour. I need to know if you want anything added to the normal riders we send out. And you'll even have a couple days every month where you can fly home and unwind for a few days before you head back out."

"Always looking out for us," Lana said.

Naomi hadn't planned to break the news then, but she couldn't wait for a better opening. "Actually that's something I need to talk with you about. This is going to be my last tour with you."

Everyone stopped. Karen put down the bottle of water she had just picked up and stepped closer to her. "Is everything all right?"

"Everything's fine. It's bad news, but with good consequences. The CEO of Cartography was diagnosed with cancer a while back. He's been sticking with the day-to-day but he doesn't want to leave us rudderless the way we were when Dash passed away. He wants a bit of overlap with control, so the new CEO is going to be advancing while he's still healthy enough to lend a hand. The new CEO, uh, is... is going to be me."

Lana smiled. "You'll be the head honcho of the whole place?"

"It would seem so." Karen hugged her. A moment later the other three also closed around her, and Naomi laughed. "Well, geez. If I'd known you would be so glad to get rid of me..."

Karen said, "Not that. You deserve this. You've been carrying this label on your back since before we ever showed up. I know you said you weren't ready to take over for Dash, but if you think you're ready now, then you must be."

"We're so happy for you, Naomi," Lana said.

Vanessa said, "We can't promise to love the next person as much as we love you, but we'll give her a chance. It'll be a her, right?"

Naomi said, "I honestly don't know. We have a couple of people who would be great, but I haven't even talked to any of them about it. I'll still be with you for this whole tour, and I'll ride out the next release with you, but then I'll be chained to a desk."

Karen said, "Your wife must be thrilled."

"Yeah," Naomi chuckled. "She said she would be happy either way, but I noticed she seems to be counting down the days until I'm tied down in Port Townsend from nine-to-five. I'm kind of eager for it myself. It'll be nice to have dinner with her on a regular basis."

Karen smiled in an oddly sad way and nodded.

"I'm going to miss the hell out of you four, though."

Lana frowned. "We're not going anywhere."

"Right. You hardly ever saw Dash Warren. You probably don't even know Oz's name. I'm not saying that's a bad thing. It's just that the talent never really interacts with the business side unless they absolutely have to. It's two different worlds. That's fine, but it's sad nonetheless."

Karen said, "Dash was our hero and our boss. Oz was the guy whose name was on our checks. You're our friend. We're going to make time for you, Naomi. Even if it's just to have dinner at your house with your wife, we're going to see each other as much as we can."

Naomi smiled. "Yeah?"

"Of course," Lana said. "And if you and Susan ever need a place to stay in Seattle, my guest room is the only hotel you'll ever need."

"Thank you. All of you." She wiped at her eyes and grunted at herself. "I swear, I had an easier time breaking the news to Susan. But I know why. You four are the best thing I've ever done in my career. I have no doubt you would have found your way eventually, but if I did anything to make it even one step easier—"

Lana said, "Anything? Naomi, we never worried about anything. Tour dates, accommodations, studio time, nothing was ever a problem. It took us months before we realized you were paving the way. You never said a word about it. And I know whatever you were doing behind the scenes saved our bacon more than once during the shit I used to pull. You made us bulletproof."

Naomi was crying unabashedly by that point, and she kissed Lana on the cheek. "Thank you, Lana. Thank all of you. I'm just glad the timing worked out so well. I'm glad I'm able to be here to reintroduce you to the world." She sniffled and wiped her face again. "And on that note, we should go over the tour dates so you can confirm them with your significant others. We made sure that you all have dual-occupancy hotel rooms just in case anyone decides to join you at any point during the tour."

"Thank you," Lana said.

Naomi smiled broadly. "Anything for my birds."

## CHAPTER TWENTY-THREE

THE BETWEEN Two Oceans tour officially kicked off with a raucous concert in their hometown. Avery, Laura, Scott, and Karen's parents were all backstage to officially see them off. Karen was initially very careful with Laura but she had apparently put aside whatever was bothering her for the night. Lana invited her out onstage to play during a few of their songs, and Laura agreed without hesitation. She tended to gravitate toward Karen's little section of the stage. They locked eyes as they played, and Karen found herself falling in love with her all over again. The shine of sweat on her forehead and upper lip, the way she would wrinkle her nose when she focused on hitting the right chord, and the loose strands of hair that would stick to her cheek and neck when she moved with the music.

After the show and the encore, it was time to take Mason home to bed. Karen asked to delay the autograph session just long enough for her to walk Laura out and say goodbye properly, and she helped load the car seat. Once he was secure she turned and put her hands on Laura's shoulders.

"I'll let you know for sure when you can expect me to come home. And you can come visit us. We have three whole days in New York, and I know Mom wants to see her grandson and daughter-in-law." She stroked Laura's hair. "But I want to see you before that. I can't go months without you."

Laura kissed her. "I'll find out when I'm free. I'll chase you across the country if I have to."

Karen smiled. She wanted to ask if they were okay, if whatever had caused the spat that morning was solved, but she knew bringing it up would only foul the air. So she stroked the smooth material of her wife's coat, kissed her again, and promised that she would keep in touch through wonderful, wonderful technology. Laura clutched Karen's hand before she pulled out of the embrace. For a moment Karen thought she was going to address their problem, but the tension faded from her grip before she spoke.

"Have a good time."

Karen took Laura's hands in both of hers and kissed the knuckles. "If you need anything while we're gone, I'm only a text away. We're hiring local musicians at most stops, so there will be backup violin and cello players in case I have to come home."

"You won't. I'll be fine." She stroked Karen's cheek. "I have an album to work on myself, you know. And when this tour is over, you'll be back home for a good long stretch. Right?"

"Of course." She kissed Laura one more time. "I should go. The others are waiting for me."

"Yeah. Have fun. Take a lot of pictures of where you're playing."

"I will. See you soon."

Karen reluctantly let go of Laura's hands and went back inside to sign autographs. When she got to the door she looked back to see Laura was watching her. She smiled and waved, and Laura lifted her hand in response. There was something about her smile that seemed off, but Karen couldn't read much into it at such a distance.

**Second Show**
**The Gorge Amphitheatre, George, WA**

Lana's hair was tamed under a newsboy cap, but the wind still picked up the few loose strands to whip them around her face as she leaned in toward the microphone. "How's everyone doing today?" The crowd spread out on the ground before the stage responded in cheers and applause that echoed off the natural outcroppings around them. They were performing at The Gorge, an outdoor stage perched on the edge of a cliff overlooking the Columbia River. The sun was beginning to set behind the stage; the distant sky was a deep purple while overhead it was a blend of blues, purples, and pinks.

Lana smiled at the response and looked to her left. "I don't know if we have any songs worthy of this view, but we'll try to keep you entertained while you're appreciating how awesome this place is." Lana stepped back and turned to face Karen, playing the intro to "Echoing Mirrors." They were dedicated to showing fans that they were the exact same band they'd always been, but Lana had made one major change to her concert persona: sleeves. Her first few years performing on-stage had proven how hot she could get under the spotlight, so she tended to perform sleeveless. After the attack, when her arms bore the scars of the stabbing, she remained sleeveless as an act of defiance.

Now though, she saw no reason to keep up the tradition, especially given the cold winds blowing up out of the gorge and sweeping over the stage. For this concert she was wearing a thick blouse under a gray vest and skinny jeans. She was barefoot, and Karen couldn't figure out if she was dancing because she was swept up in the music or because she was trying to keep her toes from freezing. They played through "Mirrors" and moved on to "Words of Wisdom and Woe." They could sing the new songs a thousand times in the studio, could hear them on the radio or iPods, but they didn't really feel alive until they were performed in front of a screaming crowd.

Part of her had forgotten the thrill she got from performing. She didn't want to be one of those obnoxious performers who claimed being on stage was her drug, but it really was intoxicating. In between songs Lana stopped and chatted with the audience. It was hard to be intimate in such a sprawling setting, but she made it work. She moved to the very edge of the stage and the people she called on were more than willing to raise their voices to be heard.

"We're going to do this next one a cappella... Codie, Nessa, get down here. Karen..."

They moved to stand with her near the front of the stage and harmonized while Lana sang "Save Yourself." She raised her voice to be heard but, after the first verse, the wind miraculously died down and the world became still. Karen glanced at Vanessa and rubbed her arm as it erupted in goosebumps. Karen reached out and bumped the back of her hand against Vanessa's as they continued backing Lana up.

The sun was down by the time the show ended. They had a bus for the trip between the Gorge and Portland, a trip that would get them there in the middle of the night. Lana had taken a few dozen pictures on her phone while it was still up, and they sat down together to choose which ones would go on the official Twitter feed. All four of them had access, but the feed was mainly updated by an employee of Cartography. They had been on the road for an hour before Vanessa called it a night so she could call Scott from her bunk. Karen followed her a few minutes later, leaving Codie and Lana sitting in the communal kitchen.

Lana settled in the corner of the table, head turned to watch the road lights go by out the window. She looked exhausted but thrilled, and Codie knew that combination would lead to a crash. When Lana eventually passed out Codie got up to retrieve a blanket from the sleeping area. She tucked her in, and then picked up Lana's phone. She thought about the idea that had occurred to her, wondered if it was crossing a line, but she figured no one would be offended.

She opened the camera and snapped a picture of her sleeping friend, then sent it to Avery. "I'm sure she would have said goodnight if she'd had the power - Codie." She smiled and tucked the phone into Lana's vest pocket. Lana murmured in her sleep and opened her eyes just enough to see who was touching her.

"Want me to carry you to bed?"

Lana smiled. "No. Thanks."

Codie bent down and kissed Lana's cheek. "Goodnight, princess."

"Night-night."

**Third Show**
**Crystal Ballroom, Portland, OR**

Lana knelt on the stage with her back to the audience, one arm out in front of her to snap a picture of the audience behind her. She sat up and got off her knees to look at the picture, smiling as she tried to quickly transfer it onto Instagram. She added the caption "Live on stage RIGHT NOW! Love you, Portland!" and sent it off. She stepped back to the microphone as she slipped the phone into her pocket. "I would've tagged you all, but I think it would take a while to get the proper spelling of everyone's names. So be sure to go find yourself on the picture when you get home."

After their performance at the Gorge, even the immaculate cotillion of the Crystal Ballroom felt small and confined. That was a good thing, though; what it lacked in spectacle it more than made up for in acoustics and a connection to the audience. An hour into the show, Codie did a surprise cover of Cyndi Lauper's "Girls Just Wanna Have Fun" that had the crowd screaming. It had always been her karaoke go-to, and Lana had been trying for years to get her to sing it in concert. Something about the grandiosity of the building made her decide the moment had finally come. She came down from the drums and danced with Lana as she sang, while Karen and Vanessa did their best to mimic the synthesizers of the original. Thanks to Laura, Karen had heard the Emilie Autumn version and was able to manage what Lana called a "kick-ass impromptu violin solo" in the middle of the song.

They finished the show, signed autographs, and were back on the road by midnight. It was nine hours to their next stop: San Francisco. They would drive through the night and arrive early in the morning. There was plenty of time for sightseeing and playing tourist before the show. Karen emailed Olivia Childress and found out she was near San Francisco. They arranged to meet for lunch so they could continue talking about the video.

She was sitting at the dinner table with Vanessa having a midnight snack. Lana and Codie were both asleep, but the mommies were on a schedule that meant they often woke up at strange hours and had nothing to do with their time. They had smiled knowingly at each other when Vanessa slid out of her bunk and tiptoed into the kitchen. They were sitting across from each other with a yogurt each, both of them on their phones.

"This is crazy," Karen said as she sent off the email.

"What is?"

"I'm trading emails with Olivia Childress in the middle of the night. I'm kind of blown away by the fact she even knows my name."

Vanessa grinned and spooned another mouthful of yogurt. "I know how you feel. I'm at the store and someone asked me for an autograph. I'm just a mother. I'm just like a dozen other women shopping here, you know? I know I don't have it as hard as you or Lana. But it's still a shock every time someone strange calls out my name in public." She cleaned her spoon. "How do you and Laura deal with it when it comes to Mason? I know you call him Bug in public, and I really do like that, but I didn't think of that when I had Nate. Everyone knows his name. I just hate people taking pictures of him. I'm not even sure why. It just seems inexcusably creepy."

Karen said, "Yeah. We just try to be aware when we're out with him. We know we can't protect him from everything, but giving him a name just for the press kind of puts up a wall. And it tells people in no uncertain terms that we're not willing to have him exposed to all that kind of nonsense. For the most part they respect that. The ideal thing would be to cover him from head to toe in a sheet or let him wear a mask whenever we take him out, but Michael Jackson made that weird for everybody."

Vanessa laughed. "He made a lot of things weird for everybody." She finished her yogurt and disposed of the spoon and container. "I'm going to go lie down and hope it confuses my body into falling asleep." She kissed the top of Karen's head. "Thanks for sitting up with me."

"The mommies have to stick together. Sweet dreams."

When she was alone, Karen's phone buzzed and she looked to see a text from Olivia. "Answering emails in the middle of the night? People are going to think you're some kind of party animal."

Emails from a celebrity were one thing. Personal texts was a whole different strangeness. "How about you? Can't sleep?"

"Reading scripts. Where are you?"

"Almost out of Oregon."

"Making progress, at least. I should get back to highlighting lines. Fun, fun. I have my tickets to see you tomorrow night!"

Karen chuckled. "You're seeing me for lunch. Isn't that enough?"

"Not for me. Sleep well."

"You too."

She leaned back and held the phone for a moment, then opened a new text to Laura. "You awake?" She waited five minutes, then ten just in case she was feeding Mason, then sent another text. "Long, long, long highway, long, long way from home. Missing you. Missing our boy. Missing our bed." She sniffled and touched her knuckle to the corner of her eye. "I hope you're having sweet dreams. I love you high and I love you, Lo."

She turned off her phone to save the charge and looked out the window. They were surrounded by forest and tall rocky cliff faces, and she thought of the stories Laura sometimes told Mason when they were trying to get him to bed. Karen would play and Laura would come up with a story on the spot about princesses and dragons, and just thinking about missing one made her tear up. She knew she had missed a lot of them when she was at the cabin, but she'd been in a fixed position then. One hour on the road and she would be home. In a few minutes she would be in California with a whole state between them. She knew it would get easier in time. She just wasn't sure she wanted it to.

She closed her eyes only for a moment, lulled by the sound of wheels on pavement, and soon became aware of the fact she was about to fall asleep with her forehead on the glass. She thought about getting up and getting into her bunk, but that would take more energy than she was willing to expend. Instead she folded one arm on the table and put her head down just before sleep finally took her.

## CHAPTER TWENTY-FOUR

**Fourth Show**
**The Fillmore, San Francisco, CA**

THE RESTAURANT Olivia wanted to meet at was some sort of organic sandwich and salad place in the Financial District. She ended up deciding on a sandwich and hoping there was a chance to get some real sustenance food before the show. Olivia Childress arrived a few minutes after she ordered wearing a pale yellow sundress under a black sweater. She was carrying a purse large enough to pack for an overnight trip, and her face was shaded by both a large hat and large sunglasses. She smiled as she sat down and peeled off the elements of her disguise, running a hand through her hair as she sank into her chair with a sigh of exhaustion.

"Sorry I'm late. Traffic. And of course as I'm trying to leave my hotel is the perfect time for my agent to call." She grunted and waved her hands in front of her face. "God, I sound like a jackass. I'll just apologize for being late and stop there. Hi."

"Hi," Karen laughed. "It's fine. I was emailing my wife."

Olivia said, "Oh, isn't the future amazing? Sending letters to each other from wherever? We take it for granted, but even ten years ago, who would have thought?"

The waiter arrived and they ordered. When he was gone, Karen said, "I've been thinking about what the video could be about..."

"There's plenty of time for that. I don't want you to think this is just a business meeting. I'm a fan of yours, Karen. You seem to think of me as some big-time celebrity, but we're equals. I'd like to be friends. That means no video talk. This is just a getting-to-know-you meal. How does that sound?"

"That sounds great. I'm a big fan of yours, too."

"A fan of a fan. That works out beautifully, I think. Mutual-admiration society." She winked and took a sip of her drink. "So tell me about yourself. Were you born in Seattle?"

Halfway through the meal, Codie and Vanessa came into the restaurant. Karen waved them over, but Vanessa demurred. They sat near the window and Karen refocused on her conversation with Olivia. She learned about where Olivia had grown up, and Karen shared about her parents, all information that was readily available on countless websites. There was something deeper in sharing it personally, however. Hearing the stories directly from Olivia made them more than just anecdotes on a talk show. By the time they were done eating she felt like something had changed. She was no longer eating with a celebrity, she was spending time with a friend who just happened to be in a few movies.

They had a good-natured argument over who would pay the check before Olivia ended up with it. She paid and they agreed they would meet up after the concert to hash out details of the video. "And if we don't work it out tonight," Olivia said, "we'll have plenty of time later."

After she left, Karen made her way over to Codie and Vanessa's table. It became obvious there was some kind of weird energy over their table. Vanessa was doing her best to keep her gaze averted, while Codie was drumming two fingers on the table next to her plate. Karen couldn't imagine what they might be fighting about, but she still approached cautiously.

"Hey, Karen," Vanessa said with a hint of care.

Codie stood up and faced Karen. "We need to talk."

"I... what?"

Codie grabbed Karen's arm hard enough to hurt and hauled her through the restaurant to the women's room. Karen looked back at Vanessa who now seemed apologetic. When they got to the bathroom Codie let her go and stooped over to check the stalls. Karen watched her, completely confounded, until she deemed the room was empty. She turned and leveled a finger at Karen.

"What in the hell do you think you're doing?"

Karen was so startled by the fury that she felt tears springing up in her eyes. "I-I don't... I don't know. What did I do? Codie, I'm sorry..."

"I watched you fuck it up once and I didn't say anything. I'm not going to give you a second chance and I'm damned sure she's not, either."

"What? Who? Who did I fuck over?"

Codie flicked Karen's ear. "Laura!"

"Ow!" Karen cringed away from Codie in case of another attack.

"Laura? What..."

"You don't know what she's mad at you about? That!" She nearly shouted the last word. The door started to swing open and Codie turned on whoever was about to come in. "Does this *sound* like a room you want to be in right now?" The door closed and they were left alone. She looked at Karen again. "You cheated on her with Lana. Somehow you got her to take you back, and I'm glad for you, because you two are so good together. But if you think I'm going to let that happen again..."

"I'm not cheating on her! You think I'm sleeping with Olivia?"

"I think that was more than just an innocent lunch."

"We're friends. We were just talking."

Codie said, "Yeah? How much have you been talking lately? Skype, email, texts. Vanessa said you were texting her last night at one o'clock in the morning. You keep all your clothes on for that?"

"How dare you? You don't know my marriage, so why don't you just mind your own business?"

Codie said, "I don't know your marriage, but I know what I saw. And I know that if Laura has been seeing it, I... she's..." She stepped back and looked at her feet. "That poor woman has been through this before. She had to see you with Lana after you cheated with her, Karen. She has to see you with Lana *now* that the band is back together. You really don't know why she's mad, why she's distant, why she's sad? Because she's been here before. She lost you once and she's waiting to lose you again."

The fight ebbed out of Karen. "I... I'm not going to sleep with her."

"Isn't that what you said before you ended up naked with Lana and Dash in Greece?"

Karen's face was burning red, and the tears that sprung up when Codie started yelling now spilled over her cheeks. Codie went to the sink, folded a paper towel, and brought it to her.

"Here."

Karen dabbed at her eyes. "I'm a cheater."

Codie sighed. "You made a mistake. You're... maybe you're just the kind of person who makes that sort of mistake easier than someone else would. That just means you have to be more careful. Maybe Olivia's not the kind of person to respect a marriage. Maybe she'll make a move and you won't know how to stop it. I know how much you love your family. I know you would never consciously do anything to endanger that. But maybe you needed someone to come in and slap some sense into you."

Karen put her arms around Codie and hugged her. "Thank you. Did you actually have to flick my ear, though? That hurt."

Codie chuckled. "I thought it might be kinder than the slap."

"Debatable. But still, thank you. And Laura thanks you." She used the paper towel to dab her eyes. She thought about all the mornings she'd spent talking to Olivia... "Oh, God."

"What?"

"The morning we left for the tour, Laura was packing for me so I could spend time with Mason. I was chatting with Olivia instead."

Codie said, "Oh, Karen..."

"Mason went to sleep and Olivia called! I didn't... I didn't think about how it would look. But Laura became so cold. Angry. I didn't understand why." She wrinkled her forehead. "God, I blamed it on her period. I'm as bad as a guy."

"Never that bad."

"I'm shocked she hasn't divorced me already."

Codie said, "I'm sure she's not there yet. But she's... probably waiting for the other shoe to drop. If I were you, I wouldn't waste any time throwing myself at her feet for forgiveness."

"I won't." She kissed Codie's cheek. "Thank you."

"What are sisters for?"

Karen smiled and made sure she looked presentable before she left the bathroom. Vanessa looked up as they came back to the table, her face neutral as she looked between Karen and Codie for evidence of what had happened in the bathroom. Karen reached the table first, smiled, and bent down to hug Vanessa.

She kissed Vanessa's ear. "You let her do the rough stuff, huh?"

"I thought she was better suited for it. Did you cry?"

"A little."

"I would have caved if you cried."

Karen laughed. "Better for all of us that Codie was here, then." She straightened up and squeezed Codie's hand. "I'm going to go call my wife."

"Be sure you're at the theatre for rehearsal."

"Yeah." She looked at the food on the tables around them and leaned in closer. "Are you really going to eat here?"

"When in Rome, have romaine," Codie said without much enthusiasm.

"There's a place around the corner that is literally called Super Duper Burger."

Codie slapped the menu shut. "Sold."

Karen said, "Come on. I'm buying."

"Didn't you already eat here?" Vanessa said.

"Yeah, if you can call that eating. I need some French fries or something. Something greasy."

Codie said, "A woman after my own heart. Lead the way."

"Should we call Lana?"

"No, she's at the theatre already. I think she had a date."

Lana bought a cup of frozen yogurt from a shop near the theatre and brought it back in time to make her date with Avery. She was on a swing shift, so the middle of the afternoon was her bedtime, and Lana had promised to be available to have dinner with her. Their computers linked up and Lana smiled at the buffering image of her girlfriend before it snapped into life. Avery had drawn all the shades and left the lights off so it looked like night on her side of the screen. Her makeup was off and she'd already traded her work clothes for a T-shirt.

"Hey, there. You look exhausted."

Avery laughed. "Thanks, sweetie. I hope you don't mind, but I'm just going to have a sandwich. This is going to be a quick date."

"That's fine." Lana brought up her yogurt and licked off the pointed tip.

Avery sat up a little straighter. "What'cha got there?"

"This? Oh. Frozen yogurt. I wasn't really hungry for lunch because I had a big breakfast, but I didn't want to just watch you eat. So I got a snack." She licked it again, dragging her tongue slowly across the side before curling it into her mouth. She smacked her lips. "It's good."

"Yeah. Looks good." Avery tucked her hair behind her ears and shifted in her seat. "So h-how's the tour going? Making good time on the road?"

"Mm-hmm." She licked again and turned the cup for another angle of attack.

Avery moaned. "Damn it, Lana."

"What?" Lana asked, the picture of innocence. She made sure to draw out the lick as long as possible, curling her tongue and then touching it to the corner of her mouth in case there was any dripping that had to be caught. "I'm just enjoying my snack."

Avery glared at her, smiling hungrily. "Well, what if I don't want lunch anymore?"

"What do you want?"

"Are you alone?"

Lana nodded. "I always lock the door when I have my snacks." She closed her lips over the peak of the yogurt, cleaning her lips with a quick swipe of her tongue. "Why?"

Avery leaned back in her chair and put a hand between her legs, one shoulder hunched as she touched herself. "You're a very bad influence, Lana Kent."

"I'm just having some fro-yo." She winked, smiling as she curled the tip of her tongue over the snack. "I can't help it if you have a filthy mind."

"God, I've missed you." Avery's eyes closed as the muscles of her arms began working. "Keep talking to me."

Lana put her yogurt aside. "I wish I was there with you."

"I'd still only let you watch."

"Watching is okay." She rested her chin on her hand and bit the fingernail of her pinkie. "I always knew there was porn on the internet, but I had no idea it was so hot."

Avery chuckled breathlessly.

"Have you been touching yourself while I've been gone?"

"Yeah..."

She clucked her tongue. "It's only been a couple of days. You're going to have to pace yourself."

Avery moaned. "Can't help it."

"Do you use porn? Or do you just lie back and think pretty thoughts?"

"Sometimes I watch your videos."

Lana laughed. "Sure you do."

"Uh-huh," she said. "'Falling Up.' So much skin." She grunted and arched her back.

"Maybe I'll make you a special video. Sing you a lullaby."

Avery said, "I like your voice."

Lana nibbled on her fingertip as a substitute for what she really wanted. "I want you to come for me, Ave. Right there in your dining room." She had moved her own hand between her legs, knuckles in the padding of the seat so she could rub herself against her wrist. "I want to see you come. Right here, right now, for me. You look so beautiful when you come. I love your voice, too, when you're whispering my name..."

"God, Lana..."

"Come for me, Avery."

Avery grunted, her free hand gripping the edge of the table as she bucked against her fingers. She bared her teeth and held her position for a moment before she released a sigh, sank back, and blinked unfocused eyes at the screen. She chuckled and pushed her hair out of her face as a blush rose in her cheeks. She cleared her throat and straightened up in her chair.

"Well, that was... something."

"It was. Sorry I distracted you from you lunch."

Avery blew air past her lips. "I needed you more than that sandwich. How's your yogurt?"

Lana looked at the glistening heap. "Melted. After that performance, I'm not surprised."

Avery laughed. "I love you, Lana. I can't wait to see you."

"Me neither." She kissed her fingers and held them up to the camera. Avery did the same. "I love you. Get some rest."

"I'll try. Have a good show."

"Fingers crossed."

She shut off the computer after they'd said their goodbyes. She was cleaning up the mess she'd made with the yogurt when Karen came into the room. "Hey..."

"Hey. Wasn't that locked?"

Karen stopped. "I guess not. Should it have been?"

"No, it's fine now." Her ears burned red a little. "Could've been a little embarrassing a minute ago."

"Oh. I just wanted to know if I could use your computer. Mine is on the bus, and I need to talk to Laura. It's kind of important."

"Missing the lady?" Lana said. She'd meant it as a joke, but Karen's expression made her shift moods. "What's wrong?"

"Nothing. We just have to talk." She smiled. "Everything's okay. Or it will be."

"Okay. Yeah, my computer's ready to go." She stood up and offered Karen the chair. "I'll give you some privacy. Do you want the door locked?"

Karen nodded. "Yes, please."

Lana knew Karen would tell her if it was something that needed to be said, so she just squeezed Karen's shoulder and left the room.

Karen had texted when she was in the studio with Ella and asked if she had time for a quick private video chat. Laura didn't know how private it needed to be, but she asked for a fifteen minute break and found an office where she could lock the door if necessary. When the screen came to life she smiled and waved. "Hey, from high up on the coast! How are things down there in the sunshine?"

Karen smiled and waved back. "It's nice. Do you know what kale is?"

"Yes. Fake California food. Don't eat any of it. It'll stay in your system for months."

"Noted." She smiled tightly. "How's Mason?"

Laura smiled as she tended to whenever their son was brought up. "He's with the nanny right now. He got tired of listening to mommy and Aunt Ella play their music, so now he's playing with his toys in Naomi's office."

"Good. Give him kisses from me."

"Always."

Karen looked down, her hair falling across her face. "I called because I wanted to say you don't have to worry anymore."

Laura's heart thudded hard against her chest and then missed the next beat. "Worry?"

"About me and Olivia. About how I've been with her lately." She looked up into the camera. "I didn't know what I was doing. Codie had to point it out. Given my track record, you had every right to think the worst. I can't believe how dense I was being. But from now on, no more middle of the night emails or texts, no Skyping with her during family time, nothing beyond what is necessary for the video shoot. And even the majority of that should go through Lana now. I'll bring it up with them later. But I wanted you to know that... you don't have to worry about anything happening between me and her."

Laura had leaned forward to rest her head on her clasped hands. When Karen finished talking, she sat up and wiped her eyes. "I should apologize to you. What happened with Lana was... was years ago. You and I hadn't even been dating very long at the time. At the very least you should have had the benefit of the doubt from me. It's just that I saw you with her, and I remembered how you used to be with Lana, and I saw it all happening again. If I'd just taken a second to think it through, I would know there wasn't a chance. If nothing else, you've earned my trust."

Karen smiled and touched the computer screen. "I wish I could hold you right now."

"Me too." She touched her screen as well, both of them looking into the screens instead of their cameras. "You shouldn't sacrifice your friendship with Olivia because of this. I know you like her, and she seems like a good person."

"But if it makes you uncomfortable..."

"If it makes me uncomfortable, I'll tell you. And you can adjust accordingly. I'm not going to forbid you from hanging out with people hotter than me. You'd never get to leave the house."

"Hey."

Laura smiled. "Sorry. I know you hate when I get down on myself."

"It's not so bad. It means I get to spend a little time building you back up. I love you, beautiful lady."

"I love you, too. Thank you for calling and putting my mind at ease. I've just been so crazy, with you being gone so much and then spending all this time with such a beautiful, talented woman..."

Karen said, "If you remember, I bought my first Femme Reapers album before I ever knew who you were. I've been drawn to you since the very beginning, Laura. And no one, no Lana Kents or Olivia Childresses could possibly compare to you in my eyes. You're the woman I always dreamed of ending up with, and the best partner I could ever hope to raise a child with. I would never risk what we have for something inferior in every way. I'll never sacrifice you, or Mason, or our family for anything."

Laura said, "When do we get to see each other in person again? Chicago?"

Karen nodded. "Chicago. Five shows between here and there."

"Much too long. Maybe Ella and I can work hard to get ahead so I can get a vacation. I can travel around middle America with you on the bus."

"That would be amazing," Karen said. "But don't rush anything. Your album is going to be amazing, and you need to give it your full attention."

"I'll be able to focus now. I'll be counting the days until Chicago."

"Talk to you soon."

"Okay. Bye, Cricket."

"Bye, Lo."

She shut off the computer and sat back, feeling a weight lifting off her shoulders. She would have to do a lot more to fully make up for what she'd nearly done, but the foundation had been set. For the moment there was nothing else that could be done, and she had a concert to get ready for.

## CHAPTER TWENTY-FIVE

ANOTHER SHOW and another round of autographs, all four members of the band struggling against the urge to turn the meet-and-greet into a robotic routine. They interacted and posed for pictures when requested while fighting exhaustion. When they finally left it was back on the bus, into their bunks, and four hundred miles to Anaheim. As soon as they arrived they did a call-in radio show to give away tickets to the show. They had four days in Anaheim and they took advantage of their free time to visit Disney California Adventure.

Lana looped her arm around Codie's as they walked through the park. "Long way from homeroom, huh?"

Codie said, "Light years."

The following night they were back onstage, then they had a night to rest in the hotel before they went back out on the road. This time they left during the day, and Codie sat up front with the driver so she could get to know these anonymous people who were driving through the night just to get them to the shows on time.

Lana began complaining about the heat as soon as they crossed the border from California to Arizona. She changed clothes three times before lunch and ended up in a thin-strapped top, no bra, and a pair of cut-off shorts. She sat by the window in the hopes the wind blowing in would cool her down, but it was just a blast of super-heated air with the added bonus of grit getting caught in her mouth.

Codie saw her outfit and pointed out that she would be more covered-up if she wore a bikini.

"Don't tempt me," Lana said, pinning her hair up to get some air on her neck. Out the window she saw vast stretches of sand and scrub brush. "People actually live in places like this? On purpose?"

"Look at the bright side," Codie said as she snapped a picture of Lana, "at least you can work on your tan. And your girlfriend will like the sexy pics. Half-naked and dripping sweat. It's hot in two different ways!"

Lana snatched her phone back. "Stop sending my girlfriend porn! It's weird."

They convinced Lana to keep most of her clothes on during the show, though she stripped down to a sweaty T-shirt during the last half hour. That night was the first major break in their tour's routine. The bus took them to the airport, where they caught a flight that would take them to Denver. The altitude was jarring to all four of them, and they were forced to accept the flight crew's offer of oxygen masks to prevent altitude sickness.

On-stage Lana referenced the tips they had been given from people who worked at the theatre. "We have to be careful of what we drink, we have to eat lots of carbohydrates, sucking on that oxygen like we're on a foreign planet... Anyone who lives here can probably visit anywhere else in the country and feel like Superman."

They had a few days in Denver, but most of it was spent in their hotel. They requested first floor rooms just so they would be that much closer to the ground, but it didn't help much. They were advised to get as much sleep as possible and they took it to heart. Vanessa was almost convinced it would be worth it to fly home, spend a day with Scott and Nathaniel, then fly to their next stop. Karen convinced her that doing so would only lead to jet lag worse than their altitude sickness, and Vanessa reluctantly agreed she had a point.

Around the time they were getting acclimated to the altitude they were on a new bus to their next stop. Two days in Wichita which included an appearance on a radio show and an interview with the local news. Karen and Lana were both feeling a bit dizzy from being shuttled from one stage to the next, singing for anonymous crowds or to a small phalanx of cameras and microphones, then moving on to the next one. From Wichita they went to Oklahoma City, where they spent the night before catching a morning flight to Chicago.

Chicago was the sort-of midpoint of their tour, so they had a whole week there to prepare for a single show. It also felt a bit like a family reunion: Laura and Scott flew in with the babies, Avery showed up on the second day, and Naomi arrived on the same flight to hash out any issues that may have come up during the first half of the tour. The couples headed to their hotel rooms while the hellos were still being exchanged, Vanessa and Karen at least taking the time to make sure Codie didn't mind being saddled with two children before they took their spouses to the elevator.

Naomi sat with her in the hotel lobby and chuckled once the dust clouds had evaporated. "Well. I guess we'll have the band meeting after everyone is, ah, sufficiently rested."

Codie said, "Lots of napping going on this week."

"It would seem. How about you? I'm surprised you're free to babysit. In between relationships?"

"Sort of," Codie said. Mason was on her lap, while Nathaniel had flopped over on his back and was looking up at the ceiling. "There was someone. I kind of thought we were getting serious, but..."

"Really?" Naomi said. "I'm surprised I haven't heard about it before now."

Codie smiled sadly. "There really wasn't anything to tell. We hooked up now and again. It was fun. No strings attached." She sighed and lifted an eyebrow. "Then I started to get feelings, like I wanted to stay over at his place even if we didn't do anything. I wanted to take him to dinner." She chuckled. "I wanted to take him flying. That's a sign I'm really losing it for someone, if I want to take them up in the plane. It's like meeting the parents for me."

Naomi smiled but didn't interrupt. Mason reached up and grabbed a handful of Codie's hair, and she let him twist it around his hand.

"I didn't tell him any of this. I don't even know if I was going to, or if I was going to let it fade away on its own. One night I called him up to see if he wanted to get together, and he... he's seeing someone. It was pretty serious. So I was benched."

"Ouch."

"No, no. Not ouch. He wasn't breaking any rules. When we got together the first time, it was strictly casual. Every time after that, just for fun. I was the one trying to make it more." Mason let go of Codie's hair and crawled off her lap to see what Nathaniel was up to. Codie watched him go. "Serves me right, I guess."

Naomi said, "Not at all. He might not have been wrong, but neither were you. You're allowed to have feelings for someone, Codie."

Codie shrugged. "Oh... I know you like to be kept apprised of any conflict, even if it's been worked out. This whole thing sort of led to me... uh, I kind of attacked Karen in the bathroom back in San Francisco."

Naomi's eyes widened. "Attacked how?"

"I thought she was getting ready to cheat on Laura. I blew up. Apparently I wasn't just seeing things, because Karen thanked me for giving her the tough love. But I learned my lesson. No more yelling at people just because they managed to fall in love and... be happy."

"Oh, honey." Naomi got up and sat next to Codie.

"No," Codie said. "Don't put my head on your shoulder and pet my hair and tell me to let it out, okay? I'm not heartbroken or distraught. I'm sad. I can handle sad."

Naomi said, "Okay. I won't tell you that I was nearly fifty when I met the love of my life. Or that I had my heart broken a thousand damn times before it finally happened. And I won't say that if I'd known all that pain was just currency to get me to Susan, or that if I had to do it all again I would."

Codie said, "Good."

"I'll just sit here. In case you need someone to help you with the babies."

"As long as that's settled."

Naomi smiled and patted Codie's hand.

Codie said, "I'm not going to say how much it's going to suck when you're gone. You were the best guardian angel we could have ever hoped for, and at least seventy-five percent of our success is because of the sweat you put into it. Just so you know I'm not saying stuff, too."

"Noted. So we'll just sit here with the children not saying anything."

"Great," Codie said.

Naomi laughed and picked up one of Nathaniel's toys to see if she could entice him over.

As soon as they were in their room, Karen pressed Laura against the wall and stepped back. She undressed herself with Laura helping on occasion, kneeling to pull down Karen's pants or to help her out of her shoes and socks. She stroked Karen's legs, kissed her hands and her lean, muscular arms, and let her lips glide across Karen's breasts before finding her lips. Laura kept her clothes on for the most part, though her panties were discarded and her blouse was unbuttoned. She whispered for Karen to take off her bra, and Karen complied as long as Laura put her blouse back on once it was removed.

"What's the point of this?"

"Supplication. Letting you have the power." She cupped Laura's breasts under her shirt. "Is that okay?"

"As long as I get to be naked eventually."

"Oh, that is for certain."

Laura smiled and cupped Karen's head in her hands, kissing her as they moved to the bed.

Karen started at Laura's toes and slowly moved up her body, making her tremble by the time she reached her navel. She kissed the skin on either side of her belly button before moving higher, pushing aside the unbuttoned halves of her blouse and stroking the curve of Laura's breast with her fingertips. She hovered over Laura, knees on either side of her thighs, and turned her hand around to drag her nails over the exposed skin of her chest. Laura shuddered and opened her eyes, reaching up to take a handful of Karen's hair. She pulled slightly and Karen obediently moved up to kiss her.

Karen hadn't said she was sorry for her unintentional indiscretion, and Laura hadn't asked her for one. They both considered the whole Olivia Childress landmine to be a closed book. This reunion was simply an affirmation of their love for each other. The sex was an apology for all the time Karen had spent away from her, all the time spent on the album or touring or working on a video. She slipped her tongue into Laura's mouth, and Laura held it for a moment between her lips. Karen moaned and went still until Laura decided to let her go, giving back her voice.

Karen offered Laura her hand. Laura took two fingers into her mouth and kept eye contact with Karen as she wet them with her tongue. Karen pulled her hand free and then moved it between their bodies. She kissed Laura as she put her hand between Laura's legs and began to stroke her. She pulled back and bit Laura's lip.

"Do you want to finish this fast or slow?" she asked in a husky whisper.

"Make me scream," Laura said.

Karen nipped at her bottom lip again and used her hips to guide her hand. She slipped her other hand around Laura to the small of her back.

Laura moved her lips to Karen's ear. "You're holding me like I'm your cello."

Karen smiled and kissed Laura's neck. "Then let's see what kind of music you make."

"Tell me what I want to know."

"I'm not going to tell you anything. I asked for a lawyer."

Avery put her weight on one elbow, twisting to kick her pants off and over the edge of the bed. "This isn't Good Cop, Bad Cop, Kent. Some kindly detective isn't going to come through that door and tell you I'm a hothead. You're dealing with me. So you're going to tell me what I want to know or things are going to get very bad for you."

Lana flexed her arms and pulled her wrists forward. The knot in the sheet slipped and her right hand sagged down. She and Avery both looked at it and Avery rearranged her weight to fix it. She pulled it tight and looked down at Lana.

"Comfy?"

"Yeah."

Avery resumed her sneer. "Tell me what I want to know!"

Lana smirked. "Is this really fun for you?"

"Well. Yeah. It was my idea. If you don't want to be tied up..."

Lana said, "No, that's fine. I get that a hundred percent. But... being a cop is your job. It's not too close to reality for you?"

Avery shook her head and brushed her hand over Lana's cheek. "We all have fantasies that cross over with reality, right? I mean, if you wanted to play Rock Star and the Adoring Fan..."

Lana's eyes widened. "Ooh. Can we play that next?"

"We'll see how tired we are. But yes, it's fantasy. It doesn't cross over. I mean, I question people, but I don't do interrogations. Even if I did, I doubt I would do them like this."

"You might consider it. I'm feeling very forthcoming right now."

Avery grinned. "Do you like this?"

"I love it." She lifted her head for a kiss, but Avery pulled back just before she made contact. Lana whimpered and Avery relented. She had missed kissing Lana, missed feeling her move underneath her. The thrill came from the fact it was Lana, the woman she loved, but now that she was a full-fledged fan of the band she had to admit there was a certain thrill to hearing a celebrity moaning her name. She wondered how many people fantasized about being in her position, how many role-playing games involved a whispered request to "Call me Lana..."

She opened her eyes and watched Lana's face. They didn't know. They knew the person who stood on stage, smiling and singing, stomping her feet with the music. If they only knew who she was in real life, they'd know that no fantasy could live up to the real thing. Lana finally opened her eyes, having closed them during the kiss, and searched Avery's face.

"Everything okay?" she whispered.

"Everything's perfect," Avery replied. She brought her voice up as she flattened her palms against the mattress on either side of Lana's head. She shook the bed and jostled Lana. "Talk, Kent! Tell me what I want to know, or things are going to get very bad for you, very fast."

Lana said, "Fine! You want to know?"

"I want to know," Avery said, rocking back and forth so that her breasts lightly brushed over Lana's. "I want to know real bad."

"Talk to the man in the boat. He knows everything. But you'll never find him."

Avery looked confused for a moment, but then a smile spread over her face. "Oh. The man in the boat. I think I've heard of him." She slid down Lana's body, kissing her breasts as she passed. "I've heard he can be tricky." She parted her lips and let the tip of her tongue roll across the flat expanse of Lana's stomach. The skin was warm, and she turned her head to rest her cheek against it for a moment. Lana reached down and stroked her hair.

Finally Avery settled between Lana's thighs, lifting one leg to rest on her shoulder. She slid her hands down the outside as her lips brushed the soft inner skin. Lana curled her fingers around her thumb, biting her lip as she looked down. Avery smiled up at her.

"I think I found where the little man in the boat is hiding." She dragged her bottom lip over Lana's folds, and Lana squirmed.

"Better hang on, sweetie. I'm going to treat him like a hostile witness."

Lana groaned, then cried out as Avery's tongue began moving against her.

## CHAPTER TWENTY-SIX

**Tenth Show**
**Mandel Hall, University of Chicago**

AMBER DAWSON checked the clock as she left her dorm, confirming that she had plenty of time to get to the hall. She guided her bicycle out of the building with one hand as she tried untangling her earbud cords with the other. She finally gave up and stopped at the door, securing the iPod in her pocket and pressing the buds into her ears. She had a special playlist that shuffled through all of her favorite Radiation Canary songs, and the first one up was from the new album. She didn't have those memorized yet and felt there was something almost magical about an unfamiliar song from a band she knew so well.

She already recognized this song as "The Sailmaker's Daughter." The song's intro was a quiet piano melody from Nessa Gr~ no, Vanessa Wayland. Amber remembered she had changed her name when the band went on hiatus. She was a wife and mother first, and she respected that choice. She pedaled out of the courtyard and to the main road as the music filled her ears. There was something almost holy about Vanessa's piano, something that reminded her of going to church with her parents. Karen came in with the cello, and Amber felt herself smiling.

The first time she heard Radiation Canary was three years earlier when she was a junior in high school. She'd been aware of the band for a while but never sought them out or really paid attention to their music. But one night she was curled up in her bed, having locked herself away there to avoid seeing other people. Earlier that day, the Supreme Court had declared same-sex marriage equal throughout the country. It was the perfect opportunity to ask the girl she had a crush on what she thought. It was a casual question, meant to test the waters for the "I think I like you more than I should" conversation, but Amber's palms were sweating so much she had to blot them on her sweater. And then her heart had nearly shattered when Hailey said, "I wish those people would just back off. Like, who cares what gross stuff you're doing in the bedroom? Don't make us look at it, please."

So there she was, on her bed fighting the urge to cry over the fact that the only person she had any feelings for was a homophobe, and she'd turned on the radio just so her parents wouldn't overhear any sniffling or sobbing. There were a few banal rock songs, but then there was a gentle and inviting piano tune backed up by a guitar. The cello came in a few minutes later, and then a woman began singing. She sat up on her bed and stared at a spot on the wall as she was drawn in by the music, swaying along and trying to move her lips to the lyrics even though she didn't know them yet.

*"You thought you were ready, then the moment arrives*
*No matter how hard you fight you seem to be always losing*
*Don't forget that even if you're standing in the ruins*
*The fact you're standing at all means you've already survived*

*Surviving is easy, just don't let it knock you down*
*The hard part is treading water so you won't drown*
*It feels like you're getting knocked down time after time*
*When your head is underwater, you'll still have your hand in mine*

*Hold onto this moment, don't let it go,*
*Nothing is certain, what's next I don't know.*
*Don't look back at the disaster*
*Try to see what happens the day after."*

By the end of the chorus she had been online trying to find the song. She bought the entire album and listened to "The Day After" on repeat for the rest of the night. She found interviews on YouTube, including one where the interviewer asked Lana Kent about coming out. For the whole interview Lana had been squirmy, uncomfortable, bashfully laughing or deferring questions to her bandmates, but for that question she sat up straighter in her seat.

"People think it's this big moment, coming out. And it is. It absolutely is. But it's dozens of big moments. You come out to your family and your friends, and then when you get new friends, or someone in your family gets married, or you get a new job. It's a constant act, and it never gets easier. But you get a little better at it as time goes by."

The next morning she went downstairs and told her father she thought maybe she was more attracted to girls than boys. He thought for a minute and then said, "I was kinda looking forward to harassing whoever took you to the prom. I guess I can put the fear of God into a girl as easy as a boy." Then he put his hand on her shoulder, squeezed, and told her that her pancakes were getting cold.

She didn't end up going to prom, but a girl named Melissa took her to the movies. It wasn't the first time she'd gone out with someone but it was the first time it felt like a romantic date.

It started to rain during her ride, just a light drizzle, and she pulled her hood up over her head. When she arrived at Mandel Hall, she chained her bike to the rack outside. She loved the hall, with the ivy clinging to its gray stone tower. It felt as if she was entering a castle until she was actually inside, when the medieval trappings gave way to classic Victorian architecture. She was given the choice between standing in front of the stage or taking one of the seats in the balcony; she chose sitting and was directed upstairs. If she was going to see Radiation Canary live, she wanted to be comfortable.

Sitting in the balcony was like having box seats at the opera. She made her way to a seat that would have a clear view of the stage and sat down next to an older couple. Once she was settled they introduced themselves as Joe and Claire Mackenzie. She made polite chitchat with them for a bit, but all her attention was on the empty stage. The drums were there, as were the keyboards, and Karen's cello was standing up next to her chair. She was eagerly drumming her hands on her thigh as the room filled with the susurrus of voices and rustling of cloth as people found their seats. Through the Gothic windows she could see the rain had settled in but it hadn't quite graduated to a thunderstorm yet.

Finally the lights dimmed, leaving only a few spotlights aimed at the stage aglow. The people who had chosen to stand started the applause and, in the shadows, she could see someone move through the shadows across the stage. She picked up the cello and began to play, low and slow, then built up into a livelier tune as the lights came up. Lana Kent led out Codie Renton and Vanessa Wayland, and Amber thought she would lose her voice from cheering.

Lana's guitar was slung so that it rested on her hip, held in place with one hand like it was a holstered gun waiting to be drawn. Vanessa might have been her favorite, but Amber had to admit that Lana Kent was a sexy-ass woman. She was wearing skinny jeans, black-and-white checkered shoes, and a white V-neck under a black vest. Her hair was down and she reached up with her free hand to hold it out of her face as Codie and Vanessa got into position. She walked to Karen, said something that made her smile, and then swung the guitar around in front of her as she approached the microphone.

"How's everyone doing?" she asked, receiving a cheer from the assembled group. "I hope everyone managed to stay dry coming in tonight. We appreciate that you braved the weather. Hopefully we can make it worth your while. Some of the songs we play tonight will be new songs, some of the songs we play tonight will be old songs, but they'll all have one thing in common... they will all be Neil Diamond songs."

The crowd didn't seem onboard with that idea.

"Okay. Okay, fine. We'll play our own stuff. But let me tell ya, 'Forever in Blue Jeans' killed in Phoenix." She backed away from the microphone and turned to face Karen to play in the first song. They started with "Simply Messing About in Boats," then moved on to "Icarus" and "Wet Coast." The first new song they played was "The Sailmaker's Daughter," which seemed important to her somehow. The fact it was the first *Coal Mine* song played, as well as the first song on her iPod when she biked to the show, had to have some kind of importance, though she couldn't figure out what.

After "Daughter," Lana walked to the edge of the stage. The people who had chosen that area were now close enough to touch her, and Amber cursed herself for choosing comfort over the opportunity to be that close to the band. In the end she didn't accost herself too badly. There was no way she would have been brave enough to close the distance between audience and performers. It was much better to have good seats where she could enjoy the music.

Lana was bantering with one of the audience members. "You chose to not have seats? It's the same price as up there, right? Man, you guys got screwed. But at least you can see up my nose. That's gotta be something you can't find on YouTube. I hope. What's your name? Enid? That's a cool name..." She continued on like that for a bit until she walked back to her position at the mic. "Sit down, if you can, please sit down. It's bad enough we have to stand up for the whole time. Except for Karen. And Codie. And... Vanessa, do you have a stool back there? Goddamn it, who the hell came up with this arrangement?"

Karen offered to trade spots with her, and Lana sat down while Karen took lead vocals for a few songs. Amber didn't know which singer's voice she preferred; they were fairly balanced on every album, but Lana took the lead a bit more frequently. But there was no doubt that Karen could carry her own when it came to singing. Her solo album, *Masquerade*, had proven she didn't have to rely on Lana. Amber liked the album well enough but it was in no way a substitute for the real thing.

During the next break, the twinkling tone of a cellphone came from the standing-room crowd. Lana immediately tried to find the source and hurried to the edge of the stage. "Don't answer, don't hang up." She went down the three steps and the crowd parted for her as she reached for the offender's phone. The girl handed it over, then used both hands to cover her face as Lana answered the call.

"Hello? Who is this?" She listened. "Oh, okay. Who were you trying to call? Brittany's busy. Did she tell you she was going to a concert tonight...? Over? No, it just started. Listen." She held the phone up and the audience cheered. "You hear that? Yeah, we're right in the middle of it... Who am I? I'm Lana Kent. No, I'm really her. Can Brittany call you back? Okay. Thank you very much." She hung up and, as the audience laughed and applauded the move, she found the camera and took a selfie with the very red-faced Brittany before returning the phone and hurrying back to the stage.

Karen said, "And now everyone is going to have their friends call them in the middle of our shows."

"Not once I start memorizing the numbers and writing them on bathroom walls." She smiled and winked at Karen. "We've been hanging out in the back catalogue a lot tonight, so how about a new song? How about a *really* new song, like one you haven't heard?" The crowd cheered. "Okay, this one is from our upcoming album. Sad to say, it won't be free. But hopefully you'll love it as much as you loved *Coal Mine*. This one is called 'Cathedrals.'"

As they sang, Amber watched Vanessa. She thought it was odd for her to gravitate toward one of the two straight women in the band, but she'd always had a strong affection for the piano. She took lessons when she was little, but it started to get in the way of her schoolwork and eventually fell completely by the wayside. There was also the added connection that Vanessa's music was the sound that made her pay attention to the band in the first place.

The crowd's reaction when the song ended was enough for Lana to say, "Thank you. Wow, thank you so much." She let the applause die down. "We're kind of running out the clock here, and we're not going to waste time doing a fake encore just to get more applause. So we're just going to keep playing until they run us out of here. What do you think about that?" The crowd roared. "Well, all right. We're going to do another new one, since 'Cathedrals' went so well. This one is called 'Cold Shoulder'..."

All too soon the show was over. They ended with "Say a Prayer (If You've Got One)" that had Amber in tears. When they waved goodnight she stood with the rest of the crowd to give them the ovation they'd earned. Lana took Karen's hand with her right and Vanessa's with her left. Codie took Vanessa's left hand, and the four of them stood at the edge of the stage to take a bow. Lana blew kisses, and Karen waved over her head with both hands as they headed backstage again.

When they were gone, the sound system began playing prerecorded versions of their songs as the crowd filed out. There was a merchandise table set up outside, and a printout taped to the wall pointed everyone toward the autograph line. She stopped by the merchandise and bought a T-shirt with the tour's logo on it, then went to join the line for autographs. There were already quite a few people lined up by the time Amber arrived, but she didn't care if she had to wait until two in the morning. She staked her flag behind a woman wearing a Rainmakers for Wizards T-shirt and settled in for the long haul.

They inched forward slowly, so slowly, but she had my iPod to keep her company. She didn't have class in the morning, and she knew her roommate would appreciate the solitude to study. The last time Radiation Canary came to Chicago, she hadn't been a big enough fan to shell out for the ticket. As it turned out that had been their last visit before taking a hiatus. Not only were they back, they were performing at her university. She wasn't going to let something like a long line get in the way of getting the full experience.

Slowly they inched forward, and finally she could actually see the band. They were at a round table in the corner, and someone who worked for the university was letting people come forward one at a time to let all four sign at once. Amber rubbed her palms on her coat and tried to think of what she would do or say when she was standing in front of them. It was different from meeting the President, of course, but to her perspective it carried the same weight.

After waiting what seemed like hours, the last few people seemed to speed by. The man in the black dress shirt waved her forward, and she approached a table where Lana Kent, Karen Everett, Vanessa Wayland, and Codie Renton were focused on her and her alone. She managed a smile. "Hi."

"Hey there," Lana said. "Did you like the show?"

"I did. I love your music." She sarcastically cheered herself for such an original thought as she put down the CD she'd brought with her, a well-used copy of *The Middle Distance*. "Sorry it's all beat up."

"I love the beat-up ones," Lana said as she took it and uncapped her Sharpie. "It means it lived and it was listened to. It was in book bags, cars, coat pockets... this didn't just sit on a shelf gathering dust. Battered is better. Who should we make it out to?"

"Amber." She smiled wider and ran her eyes down the row, settling finally on Vanessa. "Nessa... uh, Vanessa. Hi."

"Hi," Vanessa said. She looked up and Amber almost chickened out. She found her reserves of strength and said, "I'm really glad you came back with the band. I heard in an interview that you were thinking about sitting it out, but I'm so glad you didn't. You play the piano so beautifully. It was the first thing I heard in a Canary song, and it made me love it. The band wouldn't have been the same without you."

Vanessa looked like she was on the verge of tears. "Thank you so much, sweetheart. Thank you." She stood up and came around the table, and then Amber was being hugged by her idol. She laughed, but it came out as a sob, and Vanessa patted her shoulder. "You made my night. Thank you so much."

"I... yeah, you're... welcome." She laughed nervously and wiped her eyes with her knuckle. Vanessa saw that the others had signed the CD, so she bent over the table and added her name. She turned and placed it in Amber's hands.

"Thank you again. You have no idea what that means to me."

Amber wanted to tell them how much their music meant to her, how much it had changed in her life, but she knew the crowd was getting restless behind her. So instead she thanked them all again - noting how absolutely gorgeous Lana Kent was up close and in person - and followed the staffer's directions to leave without passing the entire line again. She found herself outside under an overhang. The rain had lessened slightly, but she made sure to safely wrap the CD with the shirt she had just bought before tucking it into an inside pocket of her coat. She wasn't taking any chances with it getting ruined.

She unlocked her bicycle and pushed off, pedaling across the street before turning back to look at Mandel Hall. It looked even more like a castle (or a cathedral, her mind provided) in the dark, with golden spotlights planted along its foundation and shining up at the stone. She smiled and figured it was appropriate, since the whole night had been like a fairytale. It would be hard to get up and go about the day tomorrow, but she would make it work. At the moment all she could think about was Radiation Canary, Vanessa Wayland, and how music could be magic. Hell, they were practically the same word, save for a few letter substitutions.

Amber chuckled at herself and pushed off again, weaving the bike over the rain-slickened sidewalk on her way back home. She hadn't bothered to put in her earbuds, but her head was filled with songs nonetheless. As the rain alternated between a downpour and a light drizzle, she rode back to the dorms singing "Face Value" under her breath.

## Chapter Twenty-Seven

AVERY VAGUELY remembered Lana coming in during the night, sitting on the edge of the bed, and telling her to go back to sleep when she began to stir. A few hours later she woke for real and rolled over to see Lana passed out beside her. She smiled and pulled the blanket higher on Lana's shoulder before she eased off the bed and went to the bathroom. She took her phone and searched for any mention of Radiation Canary and Mandel Hall. A girl named Amber Dawson tweeted a picture of a signed CD cover. "Met the band tonight at Mandel Hall. Got a hug from Vanessa! Amazing concert!" The hashtags were "Radiation Canary" and "Chicago."

There were other photos as well, taken from multiple vantage points. Avery had been seated in the balcony, and she'd gotten a thrill being among the true fans. Hearing an entire room sing along with words her girlfriend helped write was awe-inspiring. Lana had power over every person in the room. When she spoke, eight or nine hundred people listened. When she told a joke, they laughed. And then after spending close to two hours at the concert, those same people stood in line for hours just to spend a few seconds with the band. She tried to stick it out with them, but eventually she had to beg off and go back to the hotel.

She heard movement in the bedroom. "Ave?"

Avery came out of the bathroom with her toothbrush. "Right here."

Lana dropped her head back onto her pillow. "I was afraid you'd already left for the airport."

"I have two more hours here." She put the brush back on the counter and returned to bed, crawling up Lana's body to cuddle her, the blankets between them. "I would have woken you up, but you got in so late I thought you needed the sleep. What time did you finally get finished?"

"I'm not even sure." Lana covered her mouth to hide a yawn. "It's easier than knowing exactly how long we were sitting at that table. It goes by so quickly anyway."

Avery said, "Everyone appreciated it. I found a couple of people on social media who said it was the best night ever. You did that for them. I'm so proud of you."

Lana smiled. "I had a lot of help."

Avery kissed her. "The band is amazing. I can't believe I never listened to you guys before."

"But you're a convert now?"

"Absolutely."

Lana sighed. "Finally! Now I can move on to the next one. It's so exhausting getting fans this way." She started to get up, but Avery wrestled her back down. "Let me go. There's someone in Dubuque who hasn't heard 'The Importance of Your Radio' yet."

"You're not going anywhere."

They wrestled for a bit, with Lana finally getting the upper hand. Lana straddled Avery and pinned her arms over her head. "I was heartbroken when I met you, you know. I'd been seeing a woman who got me through the rebound phase, but I was still... I was just pieced together with glue and duct tape. I spent days sitting in my apartment getting drunk before Codie showed up. I was a fucking mess, and I was on the first leg of a really dark journey. Codie woke me up, Sidra Bird started the ball rolling. Then I met you."

"I made it better?" Avery said.

"No. You made me realize I'd go through it all again if it meant I still get to meet you at the end of it. You made it all worthwhile."

"Lana," Avery whispered. "I love you."

"I love you, too."

They made love slowly, tenderly, and Lana held Avery afterward. "Are you sure you have to go home today? I could smuggle you onto the bus."

"Unfortunately," Avery said. "If I want to keep my job, I probably should get back."

"Job? You don't need a job. I'm a super-rich celebrity."

Avery said, "You'd be richer if you didn't give away your albums."

Lana shrugged. "Just the one."

Avery kissed Lana's shoulder. "Where to next? Kansas City?"

"Yeah. And after that..." She reached for her phone and checked the itinerary, ignoring the emails and texts she'd received in the night. "Memphis, Atlanta, et cetera. When's the next time you can get off long

"We've made a huge mistake. Couldn't this city at least have the right name? Kansas City in Missouri? At least Oklahoma and Indiana got it right..."

Codie said, "You're not going to shit all over the city's name during the show, are you?"

Lana said, "Probably not. But just to be on the safe side, let's go find things for me to talk about besides the fact they named their city wrong."

They played Kansas City without causing an incident by insulting the city's name, then moved on to Memphis. Lana knew Memphis very well, and she nearly caused a riot - the good kind - with a cover of John Lee Hooker's "One Bourbon, One Scotch, One Beer." That was enough to get the crowd on their side, but Lana took it one step further by adding a blues riff to "Fist-Shaped Windows." By the end of the night she was drenched with sweat, breathless, and chugging water from one of the bottles that had cropped up around the microphone stand.

In the autograph line after the show, they met a woman who had gotten the Canary logo tattooed on her arm. The band signed it, then Karen took a picture of Lana framing the tattoo with her hands. The woman informed them she was going to the artist in the morning to get their autographs tattooed using the Sharpie lines as guide.

"Oh! I can't tell if that's cool or creepy." Lana said. "I'm going with cool."

They stayed in Memphis three more days - Lana claimed it was just so they could have as many barbequed ribs as possible - before they set out once more. Their next show was in Atlanta, and it was there they would meet with Staff Sergeant Jamie Keogh to set up her daughter's surprise. Naomi had worked out all the details, and Lana was nervous about making the moment as perfect as possible.

Keogh arrived stateside twelve hours before the concert and met the band backstage. She thanked them for being so generous with their time, and Lana said, "It's a very small effort on our part compared to what you've done. We're honored to do it. We've got most of it figured out, but we thought you might be more capable of working out a battle plan."

Keogh smiled. "I'll see what I can do."

**Thirteenth Show**
**Buckhead Theatre, Atlanta, GA**
Lana took a sip of water and swished it around in her mouth as she walked back toward the drum set. She wiggled her hips a bit, which caused whoops and whistles from the audience, and she smiled as she swallowed her mouthful. They were halfway through the show, and her adrenaline was making her buzz. She took a deep breath and let it out through pursed lips as she walked back to the microphone. "You guys are awesome. Thank you so much for having us here. We set these tours up

so far in advance, we're never sure when exactly we're going to end up in a certain place. Is anyone out there having a birthday?"

They had anticipated the possibility they would have dozens of people either lying or actually having a birthday, and a few hands went up. Lana pointed at a man. "It's your birthday? Was it your idea to come here or your girlfriend's? Yours? We have a male fan!" The crowd cheered. "We're happy to have you here. We didn't get you a gift. Sorry. Actually, no, show your ID to the merch table and you can have a T-shirt. Happy birthday."

She moved on to the next person. "Is it your birthday? Five days? Geez, five days? That's kind of borderline. This is your birthday present, though? Should we count that?" The crowd concurred that it was close enough. "You got lucky this time. Same thing as the other guy. Free T-shirt. Come on, who else? We've got a lot of birthdays in this crowd, I know it."

Staff Sergeant Keogh's daughter was named Alyssa. She'd come to the concert with her father, who knew exactly what was happening and was instructed to make her raise her hand if she didn't. But she did raise her hand, and Lana recognized her from the photos Jamie had provided.

"Is it your birthday today, or soon?"

Alyssa said, "Two days."

"Two days is a little better. Who is that, your dad? Hi, dad. It could be worse. She could have asked you to take her to a OneDirection concert." The audience laughed. "Did he get you the tickets for your birthday?"

"My mom sent them. She's stationed in Afghanistan."

Lana said, "Wow, let's have a round of applause for her mother. That's amazing. Although now I feel bad. I always feel bad when our armed forces spend money on things like... like concerts, you know? We get to sit here and have a concert because she's over there fighting, and we're taking her money? She deserves something special for her money, don't you think?" The audience agreed, and Lana waved her up. "Come on up here."

Alyssa remained planted in her seat, but her father urged her to go up. She was visibly shaking when she got to the stairs, and Lana came down to help her up. "It's okay," she said away from the microphone. "What's your name?"

"A-Alyssa."

"Hi, Alyssa. What's your mother's name?"

"Staff Sergeant Jamie Keogh."

Lana nodded and guided her to a stool Karen had moved to center stage. "Okay, Alyssa Keogh. I know we gave the whole deal about not using cameras. But Dad, if you want to record this for Mom, it would be fine with us. Have a seat, Alyssa." Alyssa sat on the stool and laughed nervously as Lana put a hand on her shoulder. "We want to make sure your mother gets the biggest bang for her buck. Do you have a favorite song? Any song you want to hear, we'll do it right now. Even if we've already played it tonight."

Alyssa laughed harder. "Oh, my God, my mind's gone blank!"

Lana laughed. "It's okay, just relax. If you want we can just sing something randomly and dedicate it to your mother and everyone with her over there."

"No, no, uh... uh, it's... 'Away from Shore.' Mom loves that one, and I wrote the lyrics in the care packages I sent her."

Lana said, "Okay, Karen? That's yours. Ha, ha, you have to try not to cry when you sing it after hearing that story. Good luck."

Karen stuck her tongue out and moved to take the front mic. Lana remained where she was next to Alyssa. "You can help sing along if you want. If you don't, that's cool, too."

"I can't believe this is really happening."

Lana winked at her and began to play. Karen wet her lips and began singing.

*"Fog clears to reveal this morning's shoreline,*
*After last night's rain washed another day away*
*I don't know why I'm here out on this windswept pier*
*Feels like it's been days since I watched you disappear*
*But I know you're coming back someday*
*I know when you do, you'll be here to stay*
*And when you love something you have to let it go*
*I'll stay standing right here because in my heart I know*

*Though the night is black, I know you'll be back*
*I know that you'll come running back to me once more*
*And you will now that I waited, our reunion is fated*
*And we'll never count the time that was wasted*
*I'll be here, no matter how far the waves carry you away from shore."*

Lana turned to look off-stage where Staff Sergeant Keogh was waiting. She nodded, and Jamie started forward. She was wearing her BDUs, and everyone in the crowd knew exactly what was happening as she entered the spotlight. Lana turned her face away to look at Codie, wanting to hide her tears, but she knew she couldn't miss the actual surprise.

Jamie was a few steps away from the stool when Alyssa realized something had changed and looked over her shoulder. She shrieked and knocked over her stool trying to stand up, but Jamie caught her in a tight embrace. Karen smiled and said, "Please welcome home Staff Sergeant Jamie Keogh, everybody! Alyssa, you can watch the rest of the concert backstage... if you even care at this point. Can I get a hug too, or is it strictly Mom time?"

Alyssa gave her a hug and thanked her, then latched onto her mother again. Jamie shook Lana's hand, mouthed 'thank you,' and guided her daughter off-stage.

"Okay, Karen. You want to try finishing that song?"

Karen laughed and wiped at her eyes. "I'll give it my best shot. No promises."

They finished the show, then met the Keogh family backstage. They signed autographs, posed for pictures, and again thanked Jamie for her service.

The next morning they woke to discover Mr. Keogh wasn't the only person who violated their no-camera policy. The video of the performance, starting with Lana speaking to Alyssa from the stage up to the tearful reunion, was streaming everywhere. Radiation Canary was trending on Twitter and, by the time they arrived in Washington, DC, it seemed like everyone online had seen the video. Lana got a text from Avery and smiled as she passed the phone to Karen so she could read it out loud.

"My mother just sent me a link to watch my girlfriend on YouTube. The kicker: she didn't know it was you. Congratulations, beautiful, you've gone viral."

Codie said, "I think that's the only time you'd want the person you're sleeping with texting you about going viral."

Lana laughed and looked out the window as they passed the Washington Monument.

## CHAPTER TWENTY-EIGHT

THEY WENT from DC to Pittsburgh to Camden in the space of two weeks. Codie came down with a stomach bug after their show in Pittsburgh, but a quick trip to the ER got her some "beautiful, beautiful drugs" to knock it out. She pointed out that they had to be the most vanilla band in music because the only drugs on their bus were prescribed antibiotics. Lana didn't have a problem with that. "If it means we don't have to waste time high or in rehab, I'm all for vanilla."

After Camden, they were supposed to take the bus to New York for ten days and two shows. Karen, Codie, and Vanessa were on the bus as scheduled, but Lana made a last-minute change. She called Naomi to let her know what she was doing, then bought a ticket so she could fly back to Seattle.

The flight was almost six hours. She flew coach to save a bit of money but she knew that she was spending over a thousand dollars just to spend a few extra hours in Avery's company. The shocking thing was how little she cared. She had joked about being rich but she still tried to be frugal. Dropping so much money on two plane tickets was something she ordinarily would never have even considered. But she was desperately missing Avery, and she felt the money was being well-spent.

People on the flight were courteous, but they did recognize her. She signed autographs and let them take pictures, but she asked them to wait a day or two before posting. "I'm trying to surprise someone. I don't want her to know I'm on a plane."

The second half of the flight was filled with horror story scenarios. What if she arrived and found Avery in bed with someone? That thought hurt so badly that she couldn't even entertain it as a hypothetical situation. What if Avery left early and Lana's entire trip was wasted? She was so distracted by her wilding mind that she almost didn't notice when the flight attendant put a folded piece of paper on her tray table. The woman rested her hand on Lana's wrist to get her attention, and Lana startled.

"I'm sorry," the woman said. "I just wanted to make sure you got this."

"Thanks."

The flight attendant walked off and Lana unfolded the paper. "Mile High Club? - Steph."

Lana stared at it for a moment, then twisted to look at the flight attendant. She looked back over her shoulder, smiled, and arched an eyebrow. She was incredibly gorgeous, with uncanny good looks. Brunette, mid-forties, high cheekbones, wide lips, a body that cartoon women would have killed for, and she was wearing a flight attendant uniform. It wasn't quite the 1960s stewardess fantasy get-up, but it definitely did the trick.

Though every prurient nerve in her body screamed at her to grab opportunity and then beg forgiveness, she knew that she would hate herself forever afterward. The indiscretion would be the end of her relationship with Avery, and there was no way she was willing to sacrifice what they had for a fling. So she smiled, shrugged, and mouthed 'Sorry.'

Steph pouted her bottom lip and mimed a tear running down her cheek, then smiled and winked again. Lana faced forward and slipped the note into her pocket. A few minutes later Steph came by again and put a full can of soda on Lana's tray.

"I apologize," she whispered, "but I would have hated myself if I didn't at least try."

"If I wasn't madly in love, you would have had a better than good shot."

Steph smiled. "Enjoy the rest of your flight, Miss Kent."

"Thanks." She cracked the top of her soda and sipped it as they flew across the Rocky Mountains.

They had been chasing the sun across the country, but as they sank through the clouds darkness descended around the plane as if someone had kicked time into overdrive. She rushed out of the airport, fighting the instinct to wait for at baggage claim even though she hadn't packed anything. She hailed a cab and gave the driver Avery's address, trying not to be nervous. She was doing a Bold Gesture, that was to be sure, but what if Avery thought it was presumptuous? What if she came off as clingy? Lana didn't even know what Avery's work schedule was. What if she was on-duty and left directly from the precinct to the airport? Her romantic gesture suddenly seemed more and more catastrophic with every passing minute. She put her fears out of her mind and focused on the city outside the cab.

For the first time in what felt like ever, it was *her* city out there. All the cities on the tour paled in comparison to her home. Weeks on the road, plus the time spent at the cabin, and the years living in London, being back in Seattle was a reunion. There was rainwater on the sidewalks and it caught the streetlights in a beautiful sparkling display.

"Sorry," the cab driver said. "You look familiar. You famous or something?"

She smiled. "I hang out with three famous ladies a lot."

"Oh," he said, obviously not understanding but unwilling to pursue it.

They arrived at Avery's building and Lana took pity on him as she handed over the cash. "I'm the lead singer of Radiation Canary."

"Oh-h," he said. "That's not really my kind of music."

Lana laughed. "Can't fault you for that. Have a nice night."

As she walked toward the building, she accidentally fell into step with a man who was also coming in from the parking lot. He glanced at her and then did an actual double-take. "Wow. You're Lana Kent."

She smiled politely, and then had an idea. "Do you live in the building?" He nodded. "Do you know Avery Hollenbeck?"

He grinned. "Aha! See, there was gossip that someone in the building was dating a celebrity, but no one was sure on the details."

"Would you mind helping me out?"

She explained what she wanted and then followed him to the apartment. He knocked, and Lana stood against the wall so she couldn't be seen from the peephole. She muttered, "Please be home" under her breath as the neighbor knocked. Silence for twenty agonizing seconds, and then finally a response from within.

"Yes?"

"Avery? It's Elliot Jordan. From 3A? I think the mailman put a package of yours in my box. Did you order something from New York?"

"New York? I don't think so." Lana heard the sound of the locks being opened. "My girlfriend is supposed to be in New York... soon..." She froze when she saw Lana. "Oh. Right. I think I did order this. Thanks, Elliot."

He smiled and backed away. "Any time."

Lana pulled Avery into an embrace. "Good thing you accepted delivery. The return policy on this particular item is a bitch."

Avery cupped the back of her head and kissed her hard. When she came up for air she checked to make sure Elliot had left. She chuckled and rested her forehead against Lana's.

"I'm kind of worried about how much I missed you."

Lana smiled. "Hey, I just spent a ton of money to fly across the country just so I could sit beside you on the flight back. You may be worried, but I'm a stalker."

Avery laughed. "I'm almost packed. Want to help me?"

"You're not *packed* yet?"

"Hey. I'm a procrastinator. Sue me."

"I thought I was bad. Holy crap." She let Avery pull her inside and shut the door behind her.

"I was thinking. I've been miserable in this apartment, wishing I was with you, and that's when you were in freaking Georgia. It was absurd, but I know that if you were just across town there was no way I could have stayed put. So when you get back from the tour, if the invitation is still open~"

"I never officially invited you."

"Oh..."

"So let me do it now. Please, Ave. Move in with me."

Avery smiled. "Okay."

"Tell me if you think we're moving too fast."

"No one's ever flown across a country just to kiss me before," Avery said as they kissed again. "I think we're moving at just the right speed."

Lana smiled. "C'mon. Let's get you packed."


They were on time for their red-eye flight, and the airport was so quiet that they managed to get through security in record time. Avery put her head on Lana's shoulder while they waited to board, then sat up and rubbed her eyes. "I need coffee. You came all this way and I'm going to ruin it by falling asleep on your shoulder."

Lana guided Avery's head back down. "Maybe I flew all this way just so you would have a shoulder to sleep on."

Avery said, "God, I love you."

Lana chuckled and let Avery doze for a bit. They were finally able to board and, as they sat on the tarmac waiting to take off, Lana noticed Avery was staring at her.

"What?"

"Nothing." She shifted in her seat and faced forward. "I just feel like I'm going to be telling this story a lot so I want to remember everything about it. You flew across America for me. That's awesome. That's... Hallmark Nicholas Sparks shit. I didn't think I wanted something so sappy, but you managed to make it good. Thank you, Lana."

Lana took Avery's hand and kissed the fingers. "I get a few extra hours with you. That's more than worth the effort."

"What if you're not back in time for the concert?"

"I have two days. If I can't make it to New York by then when I'm sitting on the plane right now, there are bigger problems than a concert. Besides, if the worst does happen, Karen can take over for me. People like her better anyway."

"That's not true."

"You're biased. I let you see me naked."

Avery laughed. "You're still my favorite."

Once they took off, Avery opened a book and Lana tried to figure out what was happening in the in-flight movie without the benefit of sound. They were somewhere over the middle of the country when Lana remembered the slip of paper in her pocket. "Oh. You need to know this so you'll understand just what I sacrificed by being smitten with you." She handed the paper to Avery. "I could have crossed that off my bucket list."

Avery unfolded it and laughed. "Where'd you get this?"

"A flight attendant on the way here from New York. Uniform and everything."

"Uniform," Avery said with a derisive snort. "Cop uniforms are way hotter."

Lana nodded. "Preaching to the choir, sweetheart. But I want points for being a good girl. She was incredibly sexy."

"How sexy?"

Lana thought for a moment. "Cindy Crawford."

"In her prime or now? You know what, either way, that's a two-syllable damn. If I'd been here I might have told you to go for it. As long as I got to watch."

Lana laughed and checked to make sure their conversation wasn't being overheard. The flight was only about half-full, and the people around them were either asleep or focusing glazed-eyes on one screen or another.

"So what was the bucket list part? Flight attendant or mile high?"

Lana said, "I've been with stewardesses. The mile-high thing would have been good."

Avery smiled. "Get out the blanket."

"What?"

"Get out the blanket and use it to cover your lap. And unbutton your pants."

Lana laughed nervously. "You're not serious."

Avery nodded her head at the blanket, and Lana again swept the area to make sure no one was paying attention to them. She retrieved the blanket and spread it out across her lap. Avery leaned heavily against her as Lana unfastened her pants. Her ears felt as if they were going to start steaming as she dragged down the zipper, positive someone had heard the quiet hiss and knew exactly what was going on. She tried to control her breathing.

"Put your head on my shoulder," she whispered. Lana complied, and Avery wet two fingers before putting her hand under the blanket. She wormed her fingers into Lana's pants, past the waistband of her underwear, and Lana gasped as she made contact. "Just relax," Avery whispered. "Just two tired women leaning against each other."

Lana wet her lips and shifted in her seat. She dropped her head to Avery's shoulder and nibbled on her neck in a spot that had proven very popular in the past as Avery extended her middle two fingers and began to stroke.

"I'm going to fuck you over four states," Avery predicted.

Lana dug the fingers of one hand into the arm rest, while her other slid up the inside of Avery's thigh. It was a monumental effort to be quiet, and Avery noticed the strain she was under.

"The singer has to restrain herself. Poor baby..."

Lana grunted and moved her lips up to Avery's ear. "I'm going to make you pay for this..."

"I can't wait. But right now, we're focusing on you."

Under the blanket Lana rubbed between Avery's legs as Avery touched her, two fingers inside before moving up to her clit. Lana's underwear twisted and got in the way, and Lana wished there was a way to strip down to make things easier for her. She settled for angling her hips so Avery's wrist wasn't stuck in such a dramatically awkward position.

"Everything all right, ladies?"

Lana's heart seized at the whispered question, and she buried her face against Avery's shoulder so she wouldn't be recognized.

"Everything's fine," Avery said. "Thanks."

"Okay. Let me know if you need anything."

The flight attendant continued on, and Lana lifted her head to peek over the top of the seat. She knew it couldn't have been the same woman as before, but she wanted to be absolutely sure. The invite had come from a brunette, and their accidental voyeur was blonde. When confirmation had been made she dropped her head back to Avery's shoulder.

"Do you think she knew?"

"I don't know," Avery said, "but you are so wet now... I think you liked almost getting caught. I'll have to keep that information handy."

Lana said, "Shut up and make me come."

"Yes, ma'am..."

Lana burrowed against the curve of Avery's neck to muffle her moans. When she sagged back into her seat, Avery sat up and kissed her.

"Bucket list item achieved, I think?"

"And then some." She pulled the blanket up higher so she could get her pants situated without drawing attention to what she was doing. "But I think to truly get the experience, we need to go up in a private plane. I happen to know a pilot who would be willing to keep her eyes front while we take care of business in the backseat."

"Good to know. And, ah, just for my own information, are there any other places on that list I might be able to help you with?"

Lana thought for a moment. "Well, a fairly recent addition is the backseat of a police cruiser."

Avery nodded. "Huh. I wonder what prompted that addition."

Lana smiled and winked. She found Avery's hand under the blanket and linked their fingers, and they leaned against each other to sleep for the rest of the way to New York.

When they arrived and began to disembark, a blonde flight attendant standing by the door caught Lana's eye and smiled. "I thought I saw you before we took off. I'm a big fan."

"Oh, thanks. Always nice to meet a fan."

"I'm sure. I hope you ladies had an... enjoyable flight."

Lana blushed and smiled as she hurried off the plane. "It was pretty good." She linked arms with Avery and led her out into the terminal. "Well, that was humiliating."

"Then why are you smiling?"

"Because it's a turn-on, too. Shut up. I'm kinky, it's better you find out now."

Avery laughed and spotted movement out of the corner of her eye. "Uh-oh. Fans, seven o'clock. They saw you come off the plane."

"We can ignore them. If we keep walking they'll get the idea and back off."

"Why?"

"You don't want to deal with all of that."

Avery slowed down. "Lana, I was a little antsy about dating a public figure when we first started going out. But I love to see you with the fans. Seeing how much they love you and how much you appreciate them... it makes me love you more. Do I want my face plastered all over the internet? No. But if I'm going to be with you for the long run, it's something I'll have to get used to."

Lana smiled at her, then looked at the girls who had been staring at them since they left the gate. She smiled and lifted her hand in greeting, then waved the girls over.

"You are her, right?" the brunette said. "You're Lana Kent."

"I am." She looked at Avery, who had faded off to one side. The girls were already digging in their bags for something to sign. "Do you have a pen?"

One girl produced a Sharpie. Prompted by the first group, other fans were converging on Lana. After signing a few items she looked up to see Avery leaning against a support beam, arms crossed over her chest, smiling as she watched Lana wrangle the crowd. Lana winked and handed back the magazine she'd just written her name on. Someone offered their iPod and Lana questioned if she really wanted it to have her graffiti on the case before she began writing.

The group finally dispersed, returning to their groups or hurrying away because their flight had been called. Lana looked at the Sharpie in her hand and looked for the person who had provided it for her.

"Shit. I think I stole someone's pen."

Avery said, "I doubt she'll mind."

Lana put the Sharpie down on a table in case the owner came looking for it, then she took Avery's hand to escort her to baggage claim.

"Sorry about that."

"It was fine," Avery said. "You were swarmed by a dozen young women who would do anything you asked of them, and you came back to me. That's the best ego boost I can think of."

Lana bumped her hip against Avery's and squeezed her closer, hoping there wouldn't be any further delays between them and the hotel. She had some very specific ideas about how to repay Avery for the flight, and they were all better behind closed doors.

## Chapter Twenty-Nine

**Fourteenth Show**
**Everything and a Hat, Studio 17B, New York City**

THEY WERE scheduled to do two shows in New York, but the first was an unusual creature. *Everything and a Hat* was a new breed of talk show. There were three hosts, one of whom wore the titular fedora. Instead of the standard format, each host spent ten minutes tackling a single topic in monologue format. The entire second half-hour was dedicated to a single guest. In Radiation Canary's case, they would perform a song, then sit down with one of the hosts for an interview, and then perform again to close the show. They would also show the video for "Face Value" after the first performance.

Though it was nowhere near as large or taxing as an actual live show, Lana tried to treat it with the same respect in terms of energy and audience engagement. She couldn't interact with them the way she usually did during a real concert but she tried her best to make sure they had a good time. Cartography requested their two songs cover both *Coal Mine Sessions* and *Westward Sky*. The first was "The Princess" to promote the free album, followed by "Learning How to Sleep" from the forthcoming collection. Lana had no problem with the arrangement. They hadn't played either song very much on the tour, and it would be fun to play something a little different.

Laura and Mason arrived the day after Lana brought Avery to the east coast, and the band had a family dinner at a restaurant near their hotel.

Scott and Nathaniel were the only ones missing but Vanessa made sure no one felt guilty. Her boys weren't being excluded; they were just needed back home for work. Karen's mother also arrived with her stepfather, and Karen introduced them to Avery.

Avery smiled as she shook Mrs. Everett's hand. "This is strange. I'm meeting my girlfriend's ex's parents before I meet hers."

Lana's smile wavered. "Well. You're not going to meet mine, sweetie."

"Shit. Right. Sorry."

"It's okay." She rubbed Avery's arm. The awkward moment was quickly brushed off and the dinner continued without further incident. The next day they arrived early at the studio to rehearse and do the pre-show interview. The network sent a car to pick them up and Vanessa exhaled sharply as she settled into the backseat between Karen and Codie.

"You okay?" Karen asked.

"Yeah, I'm fine. Did anyone else feel like the food was a little off last night?"

Lana twisted around in her seat. "It seemed fine to me. Are you okay? We can make arrangements for you to sit this out if you're under the weather."

Vanessa smiled. "Stop trying to replace me, Kent. I'll be fine. I just need some Pepto or something and I'll be fine."

They arrived at the studio and met with the hosts - two men and a woman - and rehearsed their songs on the empty stage. Vanessa got medicine for her upset stomach and the band met with a producer to discuss what was fair game for conversation during the interview portion. She warned that with seven people seated at the table it was bound to get a little free-for-all, but the hosts did their best to keep the chaos minimized.

The audience started to arrive ninety minutes before show time. Avery pointed out that she'd been exposed to more pop culture in the past few weeks than in the entire decade leading up to them. "I blame you for the things I know now," she said. "Horrible things about horrible people I can never un-know." Still she seemed more than willing to sit in the audience of a show she'd never watched before just because Lana was a guest.

When the three hosts were finished with their segments, a producer retrieved the band from the green room and escorted them to the stage. The set was designed to look as if one wall of a fancy hotel lobby had been sheared away and replaced with stadium seating. Despite the cameras and the fact she was standing in front of over a hundred people, Lana felt oddly like she was performing in someone's living room. She had anticipated the anxiety and had taken off her shoes prior to going out. She was famous enough for her barefoot quirk that the produce didn't even bat an eye.

The director cued the host - the man without the hat - and the audience erupted in cued applause. "Welcome back, everyone. Tonight's guests are a wonderful band from the Pacific Northwest. They took a little break, but now they are back and better than ever. Their recent album was released free via their website, so be sure to go check that out. Ladies and gentlemen, please welcome Radiation Canary!"

Karen opened the song with a wild violin that Lana beefed up with a guitar riff, leading into Codie's enthusiastic drumming and an almost rhythm-free crash of noise from Vanessa. The cacophony had a semblance of order but it was just a wall of sound until everyone dropped back so Lana and Codie could streamline it into a single cohesive sound, a throbbing beat accented by Vanessa. Lana stepped up to the microphone, her feet planted shoulder-width apart with her knees turned in.

*"Strong, beautiful, smart, baby, she's fearless*
*She's free with her kisses, soft lips, she's delicious*
*But when she strikes out, words are vicious, she never misses*
*She'll leave you alone, no witness, still she's your princess*

*She stole the addresses from your little black book*
*And she's aching to use her deft left hook*
*Though she could lay you flat with just one dirty look*
*You saw the warning signs everyone else dismisses*
*She cuts right through, what can you do, she's the princess*

*The angel on my shoulder is doing such devilish things to me*
*And I know that no one else can see so no one will believe*
*Oh, she's a terror, breaks your heart without a care, her*
*You wonder how she can even look at herself in a mirror."*

Lana stepped back for the bridge, which was another raucous miasma of sound. She'd written the song about Catherine, obviously, and the pain she had felt when their relationship fell apart. She took Codie's sarcastic nickname for her and applied it to Catherine, since it fit the glorified version of the Glamorous Actress she had lost. Once Codie heard the lyrics she'd offered to drop the nickname, but Lana refused. She liked being Codie's princess; the song was a different thing entirely.

Working on it at the Coal Mine and recording it in the safety of the studio had felt just as raw and painful as when the breakup was fresh. She remembered fighting back tears as she remembered the words that had inspired the song in the first place. Now, though, she was fighting to access the anger and hurt necessary to sell the lyrics. She knew exactly why she was struggling, and she scanned the crowd until she saw the familiar face smiling down at her.

She moved back to the microphone for the last verse.

*"And oh, I don't know how she got to be so cold*
*How she could let go when I tried so hard to keep hold*
*Did she see a disaster foretold and did it make her want to lie low?*
*But she'll never show, and though she let me go, the sad thing is this*
*I wish it weren't so, but even as I go, I know she's still my princess.*
*You'll always be my princess."*

The crowd applauded and Lana stepped back from the microphone a little breathless, smiling and bright-eyed as she lifted a hand to wave to the crowd. One of the hosts - the man with the hat - came over and shook Lana's hand. "Fantastic work," he said before turning to acknowledge the rest of the band. "Great stuff! The album is *Coal Mine Sessions* and it's available right now for download, so go get your copy today. When we come back, we'll show their latest video and have a little sit-down chat with the ladies of Radiation Canary. Don't go away!"

The cameras were turned off and they put up their instruments before crossing the stage to a teardrop-shaped Lucite table. The hosts sat on one rounded side, while their guests sat on the other. The band took a moment trying to logistically figure out where they would sit before Codie and Karen sat in front with Vanessa and Lana seated on a riser behind and just to their left. The director noted their set-up and tried to be as casual as possible. "Lana, you don't want to sit down in front with Karen?"

"Nah, I'm up front enough as it is. We have to dispel the rumors that Codie doesn't have legs."

"Okay," he said. "We're coming back in three minutes and going straight to the video, then we'll come back here for the chitchat. Sound good to everyone?"

The hosts agreed and the director scurried off to start spinning more plates on sticks. Some people wearing headsets hooked them up with microphones and then scurried off behind the cameras once more. The hosts made idle chitchat until someone gave the signal and the cameras moved in for a more intimate angle. The woman smiled into the camera.

"That was the music video for 'Face Value' by today's guests, Radiation Canary. You just saw them perform here, and you can see them live later this week at the Bowery Ballroom." She turned to face them. "Thank you for being here ladies."

Karen said, "Thanks for having us."

When she sensed the show was beginning to wind down, Avery left her seat and snuck backstage to wait in the green room. Lana had adjusted her rider so it would include a jug of apple juice for her. She still found it strange that her girlfriend could send a list to whoever was in charge of the theater, request whatever insane thing she wanted, and a flock of unseen interns or stage managers would scramble to make sure it was in place. The Canaries were pretty modest in their demands; they wanted flowers and scented candles, bottles of vitamin water, soda, beer, "local delicacies," and local postcards they could send home.

After the show, the rest of the band hurried off to other engagements - Karen and Laura were going to spend the day with Mrs. Everett, while Codie and Vanessa were going to see the sights - and Lana invited Avery to walk with her until they found someplace that served pizza by the slice. When they left the studio they turned right and quickly discovered a street with a phalanx of buses lined up outside a massive port structure.

"Cruise departures?" Avery guessed.

"Seems like a good possibility." She smiled. "Maybe when Radiation Canary is old and washed up we can be headliners on a cruise ship. You could come along and get a free cruise out of the deal."

Avery said, "Judging by what I just saw, it'll be a while before you're that washed up."

"Eh. I think you'll still be around."

"Yeah?" Lana looked at her and nodded. Avery bumped her elbow against Lana's. "That song. 'The Princess.' Was that about your ex?"

Lana wrinkled her nose. "Yeah."

"It's harsh."

"She broke my heart. I was hurting when I wrote it. Not so much now, thanks to you."

"You're welcome. I just wish you hadn't had to go through it."

Lana almost agreed but stopped herself. "I don't." She stopped and turned Avery to face her. "I don't regret it. If Catherine hadn't broken my heart, I probably would have been less depressed. I would have stayed to party with the band instead of wandering down the street in the middle of the night all by myself." Avery was wearing her hair down, so Lana gathered it and pushed it off her shoulders so the wind wouldn't push it into her face. "I've never made a mistake in my life. If everything was building up to put me on that street at that moment so I would meet you, then nothing was a mistake and I'm willing to own all the scars it left on me. The breakup, the band, everything was just fate conspiring to put me on that spot so I would meet you."

Avery's eyes were wet. "Marry me."

Lana laughed. "What?"

"That's... not what I planned to say. But that was the most beautiful thing anyone's ever said to me. And flying across the country to bring me here... and just looking at you I know how much you care about me. And it's thrilling because it means we're on the same page. I'm not good with the big speeches or the romantic gestures, but I love you so much. I'm not taking it back. You don't have to answer right now, but when you're ready, the question stands."

Lana squeezed Avery's hands. "I'll give it due consideration."

"Excellent. Have your people call my people."

Lana laughed and kissed her.

Karen's stepfather had to be up early for work, so they headed home not long after dinner. They'd spent the day after the show sightseeing and Mrs. Everett pulled Karen aside to show her a picture on her phone. It was a shot of Karen and Laura standing on a street corner. Laura had one arm around Karen's waist with her hand in Karen's coat pocket. Her other arm was around Mason, who was hanging on her other hip. Karen's head was turned to check traffic while Laura was looking at Mason.

"Fine looking family there," Mrs. Everett said. "Looks like you got it right the first time, unlike some members of your family. I'm proud of you, little girl."

Karen smiled and hugged her mother. "Thanks, Mom."

"Thank you for not following my example. That girl is perfect for you."

"I think so." She kissed her mother's cheek and asked her to email her a copy of the photo. When they left, Karen and Laura teamed up to get Mason ready for bed. Karen played him a lullaby while Laura sang and nursed him. Once he was down they alternated showering and got into bed before ten-thirty with the late news on TV.

Laura looked at the clock and groaned. "Are we boring? We're so young to be boring already."

Karen laughed. "Not boring in the least. Not to me."

They watched 'Everything and a Hat,' before they turned off the TV. They had only been asleep for an hour or so when Karen was startled awake by someone knocking on the door.

"Karen... Karen, please..."

She recognized Vanessa's voice, but the panic in it was so foreign that it made her sound like a different person. Laura reached over to wake her up, but Karen was already reaching for the lamp. She checked the time as she went to the door, shrugging into her robe as she peered out. She had a spiel prepared about how late it was, about how it could have waited until morning, but it all went out the window when she saw how ashen Vanessa's face was. A moment later she saw there was blood on Vanessa's pajamas. She opened the door wider and took Vanessa's hand.

"What happened?"

"I already called a cab. I just need someone to go with me..."

"Of course." She turned and saw Laura had arrived behind her. Laura covered her mouth when she saw the state Vanessa was in, vanished, and came back with Karen's shoes and phone. "Thank you."

"Go. I'll explain to the others."

Karen put her arm around Vanessa and guided her toward the stairs. "What happened?"

Vanessa's features twisted and she clutched her stomach. "I think I had a miscarriage."

"Oh, shit. Just hang in there, sweetheart." She held her shoes and phone in her free hand, knowing when they got to the elevator she would have time to put them on.

"This is going to fuck things up with the band," Vanessa said, her voice breaking.

Karen said, "Not a word about the goddamn band. I'll break the band up right now if you keep talking like that." She squeezed Vanessa's hip. "Let's get you help and then we'll worry about the little things, okay?"

"Okay. Thank you, Karen."

"Sure, Nessa. Sure. Just lean on me."

Lana was the first one at the hospital, her shirt inside-out and wearing Avery's shoes. Karen was in the middle of explaining to her what had happened when Codie arrived with Laura. Karen already called Scott to let him know the situation and promised they would be there for her since he couldn't. After the call was made and everyone had been informed, there was nothing to do but wait. Karen and Laura retreated to a corner of the waiting room to hold and cuddle Mason as he tried to sleep in his carrier. Codie paced the length of the hall, making laps with the waiting room as her home base.

Lana stared out the window as the sun began to rise, holding Avery's hand tightly as Avery dozed on her shoulder. When she lifted her head she looked at Lana.

"Hey." Lana seemed to snap out of a trance. "How are you?"

"My feet hurt."

"You're wearing my shoes."

She looked down. "Oh. Sorry."

"You were in a hurry when you left. I didn't want to say anything."

They traded shoes, and then Lana put her head down in Avery's lap. Finally a nurse came out. "Lana...?"

"That's me."

"She's asking to see you."

Lana stood up. "Just me?"

"For right now, yes."

"Okay." She glanced at the others and followed the nurse to Vanessa's room. Vanessa was sitting up, her face scrubbed clean of makeup and her hair tied back. The nurse left them alone, and Lana closed the door softly behind her. "Hey, Nessa."

Vanessa smiled. "Hi."

Lana pulled the chair closer to the bed. "I am so sorry." She took

Vanessa's hand. "If there's anything you need, just say the word and we'll get it. We're going to cancel tomorrow night—"

"That's exactly why I asked for you. Don't cancel anything, Lana. You guys have been threatening me this whole tour with my understudy. Just call her up and put her in. There's no reason everyone who already has tickets should suffer because of me. I'd feel horrible if that happened. The show must go on, right?"

Lana had no idea how she could possibly perform with her friend suffering, but she nodded. "If that's what you want, we'll give it our best shot."

Vanessa nodded.

"How long had you known you were pregnant?"

"Chicago," Vanessa said. "I took the test when Scott came in. We didn't want to tell people because we'd had a few problems with Nathaniel, and there was another miscarriage about a year ago. So if you even think about blaming the tour for this, I'll slap you silly."

Lana smiled despite herself. "I wish you had told us."

"There was nothing you could have done. And when it happened in a strange city, with my husband three thousand miles away, my sisters were here for me. You all did exactly what I needed you to do. Thank you."

"Anything you need, Vanessa. Honestly, anything at all, and we're here."

"I know. You can send in the others now. I just wanted to make sure you weren't going to blame yourself or do something stupid like cancel the show. I'll be discharged in the morning, and then after a few days I should be ready to perform again."

"Take every second you need," Lana said. "Our next concert is in three days, then ten days until we're due in Boston. That's almost two full weeks when you'll have me, Karen, and Codie waiting on you hand and foot."

"Thank you."

"I'll go get the others." She stood up and kissed Vanessa's forehead. "I love you, Nessa."

"I love you, too."

She stroked Vanessa's arm and went to get the rest of the band.


**Seventeenth Show**
**The Bowery Ballroom, New York City**
Lana stood backstage, just beyond the curtains, with Karen and Codie lined up behind her. They called Naomi to fill her in on the situation and she'd made a few calls to find a last-minute replacement. Mickey Fraser was a session musician who sometimes worked with Sarah Wiley, and she was willing to fill in as long as they needed her. They doubled up on rehearsals to give her a chance to catch up so they would be confident

when show time came, and she'd proven herself more than worthy. She even took the time to visit Vanessa at the hotel to get her blessing.

Lana couldn't quantify how bizarre it felt preparing to go on stage without Vanessa there. For all their talk about substituting anyone who didn't want to come back, the reality felt horrible and wrong. She couldn't wait until the band was truly back together, but she held out her fist and bumped it against Mickey's to let her know she was welcome.

When the time came, she led the others out onto stage. She was never prepared for the sound that went up when she walked out in front of an audience; sometimes she felt as if everything else in her life was just an excuse to hear that sound as often as possible. She lifted her hand in greeting and walked directly to her microphone as Karen and Codie took their positions.

"We wanted to start by dedicating this show to Vanessa Wayland. Vanessa's..." Her voice cracked and she tucked her bottom lip into her mouth. She lowered her head to compose herself. Vanessa had told her what to say, so she didn't have to come up with the story on her own, but it was still hard to make her grief sound so inconsequential. "Vanessa's been feeling a little under the weather the past few days. She's recovering, but she's not able to join us up here tonight. She asked Mickey Fraser to sit in for her tonight, so please welcome her up here. Mick?"

Mickey came out and took her position at Vanessa's keyboard.

"Vanessa is going to try to make it to the autograph session after the show, but no promises. We swear, she's not contagious, so no one has to worry about that. She just wants to make sure everyone gets the most for their money. So, without further delay..." She turned her back on the crowd to face Codie. They'd adjusted their set list with heavier guitar or cello songs, giving Mickey a little relief while downplaying Vanessa's absence. Their opening number was "Wheels Up," and Lana counted them in before she turned to face the audience once more.

As it turned out Mickey was more than capable. Naomi called her an aural chameleon, capable of mimicking someone's sound but not as adept at creating her own. It made her an ideal placeholder in an already-established act, and the songs came out sounding as identical to the recording as possible. The audience seemed hesitant at first but by the halfway mark they had accepted the temporary lineup.

When they finished they went backstage to find Vanessa watching from the wings. She grabbed Codie's hand and accepted a crushing hug from her sweaty, breathless friends.

"That was the first time I really got to enjoy a Radiation Canary concert. You guys are actually pretty good."

Lana waved her off. "Eh, we were operating at seventy-five percent. You should see us when we're going at full power."

Vanessa smiled and looked at Karen. "Thank you for loaning me your wife. She's been an amazing caretaker."

"Happy to share the love."

Vanessa nodded and reached for Mickey's hand. "You did me proud. You were amazing out there. Thank you for filling in."

"You're welcome. But I was just following your lead. I'm glad you're feeling better."

"I am. Now, Lana... you said I could sit in on the autograph session, right?"

"I think the crowd would like that," Lana said.

"Then lead the way, fearless leader," Vanessa said. "Let's go sign some shit."

something she would never say out loud in an interview for fear of being labeled a typical wacky celebrity, but she liked the idea of summoning the power of their fans to bring the band back to life.

Lana fogged up the glass with her breath and drew a very crude icon of their logo on the glass. They had seven shows left before the "ritual" was finished and they were once again a living, thriving band. She could hardly wait.

As soon as they arrived in Boston, they were escorted to a building owned by CrawlSpace Videos. They were a relatively new hybrid of streaming video that operated more like Netflix than YouTube. They described themselves as "a unique collection of creative individuals sharing their content in an organized and businesslike manner." As far as Lana could see it was just public-access television for the digital age, with the added bonus of a subscription price. Still, people seemed to like it.

They were scheduled to do three different interviews and they didn't have to leave the room. The hosts would come to them, and the space around them would be changed to give the appearance of being somewhere completely different. And since the shows were run by people who were all but amateurs, the format allowed for a lot of fun improvisation.

The first show, for instance, involved Lana and Codie competing against Vanessa and Karen in "The Band-lywed Game." Over the course of ten questions, they were able to impart information about their band, their lives, the new album, and the tour without sounding as if they were just reading a press release. Lana also got surprisingly competitive, dancing on her chair when she and Codie were announced as the winners. The other interviews involved impromptu recitals - "Play one of your songs using one of the toy instruments in the box and we'll see if Lana can guess what it is." - and a truth-or-dare game that quickly had all members of the band red-faced and laughing.

Scott arrived that night with Nathaniel, and the band let him take over with Vanessa. After dinner Lana was in her room playing around on the internet, and she thought back to her comparison of the tour as a ritual. If that was accurate, then there was one more thing she needed to do in order to be completely and fully reborn. She knew the time difference meant that it was insanely early in London, but she also knew Catherine was frequently up at four-thirty so she could work out before going to the studio. She sent a request for a video chat and waited.

Catherine responded twenty minutes later. Lana took a deep breath, let it out through pursed lips, and made the connection. Catherine's face popped up, devoid of makeup and looking freshly-washed. Her hair was pushed back with a hairband. Lana had seen her "in disrepair" hundreds of times, and it always warmed her heart. She was surprised at how little it affected her now even knowing why Catherine's power over her would be diminished.

"Well, this is a surprise," Catherine said. "Hello, Lana."

"Hi, Catherine. Sorry to call so early."

"It's fine. I was up." She crossed her arms on the table in front of her laptop. "Where are you?"

"Boston. We have a show in a couple of days."

Catherine nodded. "I've been reading about your tour. It would seem you're a big hit again. Congratulations."

"Thanks." Lana pulled her feet up into the chair, knees jutting out to either side as she gripped her ankles. "How is everything going for you?"

"Good. Great." She nodded and looked past the computer. "I've got a few auditions I'm excited about. Can't really talk about them, but they're fairly big deals. Exciting things if I manage to get them."

"You will," Lana said. "You're insanely talented."

Catherine smiled. "Thank you, Lana. But I can't believe that's why you called..."

"No." She looked down at her feet. "I wanted to say how sorry I was. When you ended our relationship, I said a lot of horrible things. But the thing I feel the worst about is when I called you a coward. What you did wasn't cowardly. You were brave. Braver than I think I've ever been. You saw that we weren't happy together, and our relationship wasn't working, and you were brave enough to set us both free. You didn't do it to be selfish, you did it because you knew we both had a chance to be happy. We both deserved a chance to be happy. I couldn't see that because I was confusing safe and content with real happiness. I was the coward. I'm sorry."

Catherine said, "Wow. I wasn't expecting that."

"Are you okay?"

"Yeah. Thank you, Lana. Uh, apology accepted, I suppose. Although it's not necessary. I've looked at things from your point of view as well. I could have been so much kinder than I was. I could have made it a discussion instead of a declaration. It's no wonder you felt attacked. I attacked you."

Lana said, "I guess hindsight is twenty-twenty."

"I suppose it is." She bit her bottom lip. "I know you've met someone because I've seen her in the papers. That lovely little dark-haired woman. If being with her prompted this call, then it must be quite serious indeed."

Lana smiled wider. "I think I'm going to marry her."

"Ahh, well done," Catherine said. "What's her name?"

"Avery Hollenbeck."

"Hollenbeck-Kent. Oh, God." She laughed and waved her hands as if to erase the sound.

Lana put a hand over her face and laughed as well. "Yeah. Not good."

"Avery Kent, though. Sounds a bit medieval. Middle English."

Lana nodded. "That, I do like. But we'll have to talk about that later on down the line."

Catherine said, "Yes. But unfortunately, I have a call-time to make. I confess, I answered you call because I knew I would have work as an escape hatch. Now I wish we had more time."

"We can always talk again later. I think we would have been a lot better as friends. It worked for me and Karen, so why not try it again?"

"I'm willing. I do still love you, Lana."

"I love you, too."

"Break a leg at your concert."

"Thank you. Talk to you soon."

Catherine kissed her fingers and waved goodbye before she shut off the camera. Lana did the same, shutting the laptop and bringing her knees up so she could wrap her arms around them. She felt lighter and freer. She thought about the lovely things Avery had said to her on a New York street in the shadow of looming cruise ships, and she knew her answer was going to be yes. She spent six years with Catherine and she could tell the difference between wanting something to work and *knowing* something was working. What she and Avery had was a perfect fit.

She would have to fight if Avery didn't want to take her name, though. She loved Avery with all her being, but there was no way she would change her name to Lana Hollenbeck-Kent. She would never again be able to introduce herself with a straight face.

Their second morning in Boston started early. Lana was woken by her phone, and she cursed under her breath as she fumbled with it. She initially thought it was the alarm and poked at the screen until the shrieking stopped, then noticed she had answered a call. She muttered again and put the phone to her ear as she dropped her head back to the pillow. "Hello?"

"Do you have a dress?"

Lana grunted. "Naomi, do you have any idea... no, wait, it's earlier there. Call me when it's light out, okay?"

"No, wait, Lana, this is important. Do you have a dress?"

She sighed. "No. Yes. Probably. You mean here with me? I packed some skirts..."

"Well, okay. You'll have a couple of months to plan."

She flopped her free hand over her face, becoming increasingly afraid that she wouldn't be able to get back to sleep. "What the hell are you talking about?"

"The Grammys."

"Mm-hmm?" She opened her eyes. "Wait."

Naomi laughed. "I'm not saying you have to wear a dress. But the nominees for Album of the Year should probably dress nice."

Lana was already out of bed. She was wearing panties and a T-shirt but she didn't particularly care. She kept the phone to her ear as she moved down the hall to Karen's room and knocked until the door opened. Karen glared at her, but there was real concern in her eyes. Lana remembered that the last time Karen got such a rude awakening they ended up taking Vanessa to the hospital and winced.

"Sorry. Good news this time, I swear." She handed the phone to Karen and said, "It's Naomi."

Karen frowned. "Hello?"

Lana stepped past Karen into the dark hotel room. Karen and Codie's rooms were connected and she passed through the connecting bathroom. Codie was lying on her back in the bed, and Lana pounced on her. Codie howled and lashed out, quickly identifying her attacker and protected herself accordingly. "What the shit, Kent?! Get off of me!"

"We're nominated for a Grammy!"

"What?"

Lana laughed. "Get up! They announced the nominees this morning. Album of the Year, baby!"

Codie whooped, then grabbed Lana's face with both hands and kissed her hard on the lips. Lana laughed when Codie let her go.

"Did that awaken anything in you?"

"I thought I told you to keep it in your pants," Codie said. "You're not wearing pants. I just kissed you and you're in your underwear."

Lana kissed Codie between the eyebrows. "There were extenuating circumstances. Don't make it weird. Come on." She got up and led Codie into Karen's room. Karen had retrieved a groggy but excited Vanessa, and the Lana pulled her into a hug. Karen was still on the phone with Naomi getting details, but she was flush and grinning from ear to ear. She held the phone up so everyone could say goodbye to Naomi before she hung up.

"So, uh," she said, "is anyone interested in details?"

"Not particularly," Lana said. "But go ahead."

Karen took a breath. "Okay. Album of the Year for *The Coal Mine Sessions*. Song of the Year for 'The Sailmaker's Daughter.' And Best Music Video for 'Face Value.'"

Lana laughed. "Three nominations?"

"Actually four. Sidra got nominated for Producer."

"Did Naomi call her yet?"

Karen held out the phone. "She thought you would want to do the honors."

Lana giggled and took the phone, dialing Sidra. "God, what time is it there? What time is it he– hey! Sidra. Listen, I have a bone to pick with you."

"Huh?" She heard blankets and sheets shifting. "Lana? God, what time is it? The sun isn't even up. What's wrong?"

"What's wrong?" Lana said. "What's wrong is that if we win all the Grammys we're nominated for, you have to take one of them home for yourself."

"Grammys?"

"Producer of the Year, Sid," she said, no longer able to maintain her angry tone. "You got nominated. We got nominated for Album, Song, and Music Video, but the producing award is all you. That's just selfish."

Sidra screamed, and then almost immediately said, "Sorry... sorry. I'll tell you in a minute."

Lana made a face. "Uh-oh. You're not alone? Sorry."

"Don't be sorry. This isn't something I'd want to read on Facebook. It's really real? Official and everything?"

Vanessa had used Karen's laptop to get online and Lana looked at the screen. She had opened an article with a large photo of Lana standing on stage with Karen out-of-focus behind her. She thought the stage was Phoenix, judging by the amount of sweat on her forehead, but she couldn't be entirely sure.

"I'm reading the announcement right now. 'Radiation Canary snags four nominations with their comeback album.' I think that's as official as it gets."

"That is amazing. That is..." She growled. "I have to hang up. I'm crying. I don't want to cry. I want you to think I'm a tough chick."

Lana said, "You're a badass. I'll call you again later." She hung up and faced the others, all of their pajamas in disarray, bleary-eyed and without makeup. She laughed and said, "So, who wants to go downstairs and get breakfast for the rest of us?"

CHAPTER THIRTY-ONE

**Nineteenth Show**
**Brighton Music Hall, Boston, MA**

THE HALL was packed, with a row of people lined up close enough to rest their arms on the stage. Any other time Lana would have felt crowded by their proximity but tonight she welcomed it. Vanessa was back on stage with them, they had the Grammy nomination to serve as an ego booster, and now they were standing in front of four hundred people who had paid their hard-earned money to hear ninety minutes of their music, people whose dedication to the band meant more than any award.

Lana ran her idea past the rest of the band backstage and they'd agreed that it would be fun flying by the seat of their pants. When Lana got onstage she stepped up to the microphone and smiled out at the sea of faces.

"Hello, Boston. Damn, but you're a good-looking crowd. I don't know if it was on the internet, but our last show was a unique experience. It was the first time we performed without Vanessa Wayland. She was feeling a little, uh, a little off, so we let her sit it out. But she's doing better now, and she wanted to be here for the fine people of Bean Town." She looked over at Vanessa and winked. "We're really glad you're back. It's just not as fun without you."

Vanessa said, "Nowhere near as bad as sitting backstage while you three have all the fun."

"True, true, true. Okay, in honor of that - and in honor of that little announcement that happened this morning some of you may be aware of...”

The crowd cheered.

“Oh, that did make the news? Okay. Just making sure. We’re going to do things a little differently tonight. We’re going to throw out the set list and we’re going to play whatever you guys want to hear. So whatever song you want... with the exception of ‘Say a Prayer.’ I think we want to save that one for the big finish, don’t you?”

The audience cheered and Lana stepped back to shade her eyes with one hand. She used her other hand to indicate the right side of the room.

“Okay, over here... shout out what you want to hear first.”

Suggestions ran from “Clap if You Believe”, to “Don’t Let Me Sleep Too Long”, and a few requests for “Something from the new album!” Lana snapped her fingers.

“You know what, I feel like playing something new.” She turned to look at Karen. “Let’s go with ‘Learning How to Sleep.’”

Karen nodded and swapped out her cello for the violin. “We might have to do a lot of back and forth depending on what songs we end up with.”

“Sounds like someone’s being a lazy whiner.”

Karen made a face at her and sliced her bow through the air as if she was slicing Lana’s throat.

Lana snickered and faced forward again. “This is a song from our upcoming album... it’s probably going to be out sometime next year, so keep an eye on the website for announcements. It’s called ‘Learning How to Sleep.’” She found the proper chord and began to play. She’d written the song while they were at the Coal Mine, before she started sleeping with Sidra, and she was still getting used to the idea of sleeping alone. She remembered that lonely feeling well, as she was feeling it again on tour, but now the loneliness wasn’t as bleak. She smiled as she stepped forward to begin singing.

*“I can hear whispered conversations, like ghosts visiting my room*
*I lie in the middle of my bed, arms folded on my chest, a mummy in the tomb*
*My body is weary and my eyes close against the gloom but my mind is muddled misery*
*Replaying everything that happened, looking for some new theory*
*I keep trying to change the end but it’s always the same sad story*

*So I’m learning to sleep again, after you showed me how to rest*
*Being in bed doesn’t mean as much without your head on my breast*
*You showed me how it could heal my hurts and make my soul refreshed*
*But without you I’m just in the dark, trying to find a way out of this mess*

*All I can do is put myself to bed and ignore my sadness and pain*
*And hope that someday I'll be able to learn how to sleep again."*

She finished the song and stepped back, biting her bottom lip as the crowd applauded. She held up her hand and rubbed her fingertips against her thumb as she scanned the audience. "There's a section of people over there wearing wings. We haven't seen that all tour, so thank you so much for keeping it alive. You guys want to hear 'Icarus' or something else?"

"Icarus!"

"Well, we've got to give the people what they want! I know space is kind of at a premium here, but I want to see those wings flying! Try not to hit your neighbors in the head."

Karen and Vanessa played the intro as the girls wearing the wings began shuffling around in their seats. At the moment Lana parted her lips to begin singing, the girls rose above the crowd by sitting on the shoulders of their dates. The sight was so unexpected that Lana laughed instead of singing and had to step away from the microphone. She turned to Karen and made a looping motion with her hand to bring the cue back around.

"Clever, ladies. Very clever... I love it."

The second time around she managed to hit her cue and began singing. The song felt ancient in a great way, like slipping into a comfortable pair of shoes. She didn't have to think about the words or the music so she could just enjoy watching the crowd. And as soon as she began singing, the audience joined in. Their voices joined into a chorus and Lana's grin widened as she ran her eyes over the people in the front row. She would never get used to that sound; hundreds of people echoing her words as she was singing them. After a decade of standing in front of huge crowds and having them sing along, she still got chills when their voices joined hers. It was a room full of strangers and yet they were harmonizing with each other, and Lana thought that was as close to religion as she would ever get.

After "Icarus" Lana decided to take advantage of the intimate setting. She sat on the edge of the stage between a woman in a red blouse and a man wearing a flannel shirt. She wanted to bring the microphone down with her, but it would have been too close to the speakers. So instead she lifted her voice to be heard throughout the space as she talked to the couple. They requested "Kelly Green," and Lana stood up again to perform it.

Eventually they had run out the clock, and Lana thanked them for being such a great audience. "Even though none of you requested 'My Walla Walla Sweetheart.' Codie is, I assure you, completely heartbroken that such a tender ballad was overlooked. But you have been so fabulous, and so well-behaved, and so utterly good-looking, that I think it's time to play 'Say a Prayer.'"

The crowd erupted and Lana faced the rest of the band. She stepped far enough away from her mic that it wouldn't pick her up, but she assumed the audience lining the stage could hear her. "Will you back me up if I go completely vocal on this? No instruments?" They all agreed, and Codie came down to share Karen's microphone.

Lana took off her guitar and placed it in the stand. "I think this needs to be just us. What do you say?" The crowd applauded. "Fantastic. Vanessa, I need you up here."

Vanessa joined Lana at the main microphone, while Codie and Karen vocalized behind her. Lana put an arm around Vanessa's waist, squeezed, and began to sing.

*"I need your help tonight*
*Alone, I can't win this fight*
*I tried to call*
*But I couldn't find the right words*
*I'm going to fall*
*And I'm so sick of being tired.*

*So say a prayer if you've got one*
*I'm starting to come undone*
*I've got demons I can't outrun*
*Please say a prayer if you have one.*

*I won't count the eight times I get knocked down*
*Just the nine times I get off the ground*
*I'm only so strong when I'm alone*
*I've done as much as I can on my own*
*If anyone's out there, if anyone cares*
*If you have one, please say a prayer."*

Again the audience joined in, and the sound was even more powerful without instruments getting in the way. The crowd was moving as one, swaying to and fro to the rhythm of the song, and Lana couldn't help but smile as she saw phones being lifted with images of flickering lighters. When she finished the song the room fell completely silent for a moment, the silence settling over the crowd like a fog before it was shattered by cheers and applause.

"You guys are wicked pissah," Lana said. "Thank you so much, Boston. Thank you! This is Vanessa Wayland. That is Karen Everett, and standing beside her is Codie Renton. You all have been so much better than any lousy trophy. Thank you so much, have a great night, and have an even better tomorrow!" She blew a kiss to the audience as she retrieved her guitar and carried it off-stage with her. As they went down the dark hallway to the dressing rooms, she could still hear the echo of everyone cheering for them. She put her free hand on Codie's shoulder and laughed.

"Never let me get used to it or take it for granted."

"I don't think we could. But I'll keep an eye out."

Lana patted her shoulder as thanks and laughed again as the crowd began chanting "Ca-nar-y!"

Naomi woke when it was still dark out, kissed her wife, and did her exercises in the dark. Afterward she showered, checked her hair for any new grayness and her face for new wrinkles, then dressed and went down to make breakfast. By that point the sun had illuminated the world outside enough for her to see heavy clouds building on the horizon. If Susan could get away for lunch, she might suggest going down to the harbor so they could watch the waves crash against the rocks. It was so chaotic that it was somehow soothing to her. There was nothing quite as soothing as sitting in a toasty-warm car while the weather turned nasty outside.

Susan came down after her shower, and Naomi presented her with oatmeal and a large mug of coffee. Susan kissed her again, and they sat in their breakfast nook to eat and read their respective devices. Naomi sipped her orange juice as she dragged her finger down the screen to scroll.

"I used to be cool, you know," Naomi said without looking up. "I hung out with rock stars."

"I know, dear. I've seen the pictures."

Naomi said, "I once had a girl I didn't know put her fingers in me just because I knew Dash Warren."

"It's very exciting."

Naomi said, "Now I'm old and boring."

Susan lazily stirred her spoon through the oatmeal. "Would you like to go back to the way things were before?"

She shook her head. "No. I just thought you should know what I was sacrificing for you."

"Sex, drugs, and rock-and-roll. Heard, understood, and acknowledged."

"Do you know what Dash Warren would do if she saw me right now? In my pajamas, at the crack of dawn, having a lovely breakfast with my wife?"

"What would she do?"

Naomi said, "She'd break down and cry and beg to trade places with me. I think she would have traded everything she had for... this. I know I would, in her shoes."

Susan smiled, and Naomi reached across the table and put her hand on top of her wife's. They stayed like that for a long moment before Naomi went back to reading.

"Why does Radiation Canary still matter?"

Naomi looked up at the apparent non sequitur. The band had just played the first of two shows in Boston, and they were set to make the jump into Canada after a break for Christmas. By all accounts the tour was a massive success. Album sales were up, reviews for the live shows were through the roof, and now they had the bump from being nominated for the Grammys. Susan seemed calm, not irritated or confrontational, so she couldn't make sense of the statement. She waited for her to continue, but she simply looked up from her tablet as if she expected an answer.

"I'm sorry?" Naomi finally said.

"I just found this article. That was the headline." She turned her tablet around so Naomi could read it. WHY DOES RADIATION CANARY STILL MATTER?

"Huh. Is it positive?"

Susan skimmed the article. "Yes."

"Read it to me."

"You can't read it yourself?"

"You have such a melodic voice. It soothes me."

Susan sighed. "You mean it makes you wet."

Naomi chuckled and brushed her thumb over the back of Susan's hand. "Come on."

"Okay." She cleared her throat and began to read.

"'Earlier this year, Radiation Canary surprised the music world by not only ending their self-imposed exile, but returning in grand fashion. On live television, the band literally emerged from the shadows and resumed their status as an actively recording and touring band. They also took the opportunity to reveal their new album was complete and would be given away as a free download (although the physical album will cost you, of course). Their fans welcomed them back without hesitation, as can be expected, but yesterday the music world rewarded their gutsy reemergence by nominating the band for four Grammy Awards.'

'One might wonder, and rightly so, why a band who publicly stepped out of the spotlight would choose to come back so quickly. In their own words it was because they simply realized they belonged together. Though Lana Kent found moderate success providing music for television shows, and Karen Everett premiered a thoughtful and mature solo album, there are few who would say this band is stronger apart than they are together.

'So what makes them special? In a world where a celebrity's actual work and/or talent is often just a footnote to their personal antics, Radiation Canary provides substance and power with every new release. From the very beginning these four ladies knew exactly who they were and what they wanted to say. There were no petty arguments about who would be the leader or who would write the most songs. It's a true partnership between four talented women who found their groove and have spent the last decade-plus building their home within it.

'Radiation Canary is special simply because they are standing against the flow. The hit songs of today are empty calories with an eye toward 'what's next.' The singers and songwriters - or rather, the personalities and lyric machines - who provide content knows that they're operating in a small window. Within five or ten years people will get tired of the formula being churned out now and the recipe will have to be changed to something else just as hollow and self-absorbed. Because the personalities are just figureheads, they will change and evolve and become whatever they have to be in order to maintain a fan base.

'Radiation Canary still matters because they stand against the tide of toothless and self-referential pop. They sing from their hearts and truly appreciate each and every fan who comes to their shows and buys one of their albums. Their reasoning behind the no-charge release of the very fantastic *Coal Mine Sessions* was simply that they wanted to thank their fans for all their support. And it truly felt like a gift, unlike certain other ham-handed attempts to give away albums in the past.

'Why does Radiation Canary matter? Why should we care that they've come back? Because they cared enough to go away in the first place. They stepped out of the limelight when their fame was just reaching a peak and it would have been the height of simplicity to just ride it out. But the Canaries chose to retreat, just a few steps, and make sure they were on the right path rather than simply forging ahead to an inevitable crash.

'Radiation Canary matters because they believe music matters. And this day and age, that sort of faith in the industry deserves to be reward.'"

Naomi smiled when Susan finished reading. "What magazine was that from?"

"VOCE."

"I'll have to get a hard copy of that so I can frame it."

"I can pick one up for you when I'm in town. I think Safeway carries it."

Naomi said, "Oh, if you're going to Safeway, can you pick up some buns? I want to have Oz and his wife over for a barbeque next weekend."

Susan looked out the window. "Weather permitting."

"Mm-hmm." They went back to their tablets and Naomi smiled. "Shopping list. Barbeques on the weekend. How boring."

"It's all I can do to keep my eyes open, dear."

Naomi moved her foot to brush it against Susan's under the table, chuckling as she started to read a new article.

## CHAPTER THIRTY-TWO

THE SECOND Boston show was their last American concert of the tour, and also their last performance for almost a month. At the end of the show, Lana said, "The American Revolution started here, and now our American tour is going to end here. Thank you so much for coming out, for being a part of this comeback, for absolutely everything you've done. It's supposed to snow tonight, so be careful going home. Drive safe and get home in one piece."

Someone to the left shouted, "We'll say a prayer!"

Lana grinned and pointed at them. "So will we! Goodnight, everyone. Thank you!" She took off her guitar and lifted it in the air, then followed the rest of the band backstage.

They finished signing autographs at two in the morning and went directly back to the hotel so they would be rested for their flight. Lana woke up first, showered, checked for any emails or texts from Avery, and texted Karen to see if she wanted to go get breakfast. She went to the window and looked out at the city to discover everything was covered with a fine layer of snow. It was the perfect amount; just thick enough to frost everything, but not enough to delay their departure. She fogged the glass with her breath and wrote Avery's name, drew a heart around it, and smiled at her own sentimentality.

Karen hadn't texted back so she assumed she was still asleep. She was hungry enough to get food by herself, so she left the hotel room and saw a lump of winter clothes huddled against the wall across from her room.

Avery looked up, her face ringed by the fur of her hood, and she smiled sleepily as she pushed it off and stretched.

"Flight got in an hour ago. Two can play this romantic gesture game, you know."

Lana helped her up and pulled her into a hug. "Looks like Santa heard me. Best present ever."

They kissed as Lana pulled Avery into her hotel room and kicked the door shut behind her.

Codie woke up to the sounds of sex from next door. It took her a moment to remember who was in that room, and another second to decide that Lana had a surprise visitor from Seattle. There was a time when that wouldn't have been a given. She loved Lana to pieces, but the woman was a cheater. She'd cheated in every relationship she'd ever had. Or, that wasn't true... as far as she knew, Lana had been faithful to Catherine right up to the end. But Avery was different. They'd been on the road for three months and Lana's attention had never strayed once.

When it became clear it wasn't going to be a quick welcome-to-Boston event, Codie got out of bed and dressed so she could go downstairs and get breakfast. She made herself a plate of eggs and a cup of coffee, then took it into the quiet seating area to watch the snow blowing around in the hotel parking lot. She was halfway through her eggs when she noticed a curious little boy kept looking over at her. She smiled, waved two fingers at him, and went back to her food.

A few minutes later he appeared next to her chair. "You were on TV."

She smiled without looking away from the window. "A couple of times, in fact."

He leaned closer and lowered his voice. "Are you famous?"

She matched his whisper. "No. But I have famous friends."

"I'm so sorry if he's bothering you," a woman said as she put her hands on the boy's shoulders to guide him away. "His father was supposed to be watching... him... oh!" She covered her reaction as best she could. "I-I'm sorry."

"It's no trouble."

The mother started to turn away, but she stopped herself. "I'm sorry. Are you Codie Renton?"

"Yeah."

"My daughter wants to be a pilot because of you."

Codie's polite smile faded and was replaced with genuine emotion. "Really?"

"Yeah. I mean, it's expensive, but no more than dance classes or learning an instrument. And she really seems to love flying. She would be sorry she missed you."

"Is she here?"

"She's upstairs getting ready."

Codie said, "I'll be here for a while. When she comes down, send her over. I'd like to meet her."

"Really? That would make her entire trip. She wanted to see your concert last night, but we couldn't make it work. I'll let her know to hurry."

"No rush," Codie said.

When the mother and her son retreated, Codie chuckled to herself. Lana might have Avery, and Karen and Vanessa might each have their broods, but she wasn't going to feel bad about herself. She was alone but not lonely. She didn't sit in her hotel room and pine for someone who was far away. She thought about what she'd almost had, what she could have had, or what she might have had with Nick, but she knew that was never going to be a long-term relationship. Maybe she would never be in one, either. She decided she was fine with that. She could be happy without a husband and kids and a house in the suburbs. She made her own kind of happy ending, and she wasn't going to let Hallmark and Hollywood tell her what constituted a successful life.

She was finished with her breakfast when she saw someone approaching out of her periphery. The girl was about fourteen, wearing a thick sweater and black leggings, and her hair was tucked up under a pink knit cap. She was leaning to one side so she could peek around the side of Codie's chair and, when Codie looked toward her, the girl backed up and clapped her hands over her mouth.

"Oh, my God. It's really you."

Codie smiled. "Hi. Your mother didn't tell me your name."

"Uh... it's Jessica." She looked toward her family and then snapped her attention back. "You're really Codie Renton. From Radiation Canary."

"I am. Sit down." She hooked her foot around the leg of a nearby chair and pulled it closer. "Your mother said you were interested in flying."

"Because of you. I read an article where you talked about flying, and it sounded like the best thing in the world."

Codie smiled. "Then I described it right."

Jessica hesitated by the chair. "I don't want to bug you."

"Hey, you want to talk about flying. You're going to have to stop *me* from bugging *you*. I have the time if you do."

Jessica sat down and folded her hands between her knees. She was barely settled before she started talking about her plan to get a plane one day, how she was desperate to get in the air and fly somewhere by herself. Codie listened and nodded when appropriate. During their talk it became clear to her that she was exactly where she needed to be in her life.

If she happened to fall in love with someone down the road, great, but for the time being she was just fine taking care of herself.

They arrived in home Seattle ten days before Christmas. The Canadian leg of their tour started on the eighth of January in Toronto. They had nearly a full month at home to relax and recuperate after spending three months on the road. The first thing they did was say goodbye at baggage claim and declare they would not be seeing one another for at least a week. They had spent far too long crammed into tour buses and living in connected rooms, so it was time to get a little space before they had to have another paintball shooting spree.

Karen lugged her bags home and let herself in to the apartment. Laura knew she was due back that night, but they agreed over the phone that Karen would get herself home while Laura entertained Karen's Dads and decorated the apartment for the holidays. As soon as she came in she could hear Laura and her father arguing about the placement of some ornament or another and she smiled as she quietly put down her bags and snuck into the living room. Ted was sitting on the couch with Mason in his lap, watching as the boy played with a stuffed cat. Ted and Mason both looked up at her, but Karen put a finger against her lips so she could sneak up on Laura.

She only made it one step before Mason said, "Mama!"

Laura turned to pick him up, stopping when she spotted Karen in the doorway. "Oh. *That* mama." She picked up their son and went to embrace her wife. Karen buried her face in Laura's hair, eyes squeezed shut as Laura and Mason both hugged her. Brief reunions in hotel rooms around the country couldn't compare to a true homecoming. She was in her own space, with her family. Tears pricked at her eyes as she squeezed Laura tightly, then turned and kissed Mason's forehead.

"Hello there, little man. Your mama is home."

Laura nuzzled Karen's cheek. "You okay?"

"Yeah. Hi."

"Hi. Welcome home, baby. I'm glad you're here."

"You are?"

"Yes. You can break the tie between me and your father. Although I hope you have a better eye than he does. The interior decorating gene might not run in the Everett family."

Karen sighed and hefted Mason against her hip as she went to settle the debate. The ornament in question was a silver-and-red bauble. Laura thought it belonged on the side facing the room while Karen's father wanted it on the side facing the window. Karen suggested hanging it on the window-side in such a way that it would reflect off the glass and still be seen in the room.

Her father smiled. "Always the diplomat."

"I do what I can."

Laura agreed that the compromise worked. Once peace had been restored, Karen handed the baby back to Ted and asked Laura to help take her bags into the bedroom. As soon as they were alone Karen wrapped Laura up in her arms and kissed her. Laura moaned and slipped her hands under Karen's shirt to stroke the small of her back.

"Welcome home."

"I have to leave again in a month."

"Just for a few weeks. It'll be nothing compared to this." She took a deep breath and kissed Karen's chin. "The house has seemed really empty without you in it."

Karen swayed with her. They stood just outside the reach of the hallway light's glow, holding each other in the shadows of their bedroom. "Oh. I have something for you. I found it when I was going through the closet for the Christmas stuff." She stepped out of Karen's embrace and retrieved something from the top drawer of her nightstand. It was a small wire figurine of a person playing the cello. "Remember this?"

Karen's eyes filled with tears as she took it. "The gift you gave me the first time we spent Christmas together. Best present I've ever gotten."

"Yeah?"

"Yeah. You gave it to me, and I... I thought... wow. A pretty girl likes me. Sometimes it still surprises me." She looked at Laura. "The Olivia Childress thing..."

Laura shook her head. "It's forgotten."

"No." She kept the figurine in her hand as she embraced Laura again. "I was never interested in her. I would never risk what we have for... for anything or anyone. This family the most precious thing in my life, and I'll protect it at all costs. I just got a little star struck, I guess. Part of me is still the meek girl who can't believe a pretty girl likes her, and gushes over the least bit of attention from the attractive, popular people. I got swept up in her attention without thinking what it would do to you. I'll do better. Because it doesn't matter if a pretty girl likes me... a beautiful woman loves me. That's all I need."

Laura swallowed a lump in her throat and touched Karen's cheek. She stepped closer and brushed her lips against Karen's before resting her head on Karen's shoulder. After a few seconds she sighed. "Should we actually unpack anything?"

Karen shook her head. "No."

"Just checking."

Karen smiled and tried to calculate how much time they had before her Dads came looking for them. She'd gone too long without Laura in arm's reach, and she wasn't going to let go a second before she had to.

Scott's car was still at the airport, left there when he'd flown to Boston to be with her. Vanessa was completely worn out, but she knew she would be back in fighting shape by the time they resumed their tour. Scott had been a champion throughout the whole ordeal, just as he had the last time. She reached across the console and touched his hand. She'd thanked him for being her support but nothing she said would come close to conveying how grateful she was for him.

When they got home she put Nathaniel down for a nap. Two cross-country flights in less than two weeks was almost more than an adult could take, let alone a toddler. He didn't give her any trouble as she tucked him in and kissed his forehead. He was always and would always be precious to her, but every time she was reminded of just how easily he could have been lost... She smoothed her hand over the top of his head and went back out into the living room.

Scott stopped her before she could even pick up the bag. "You need to rest. Lie down on the couch and I'll take care of this."

She brushed her hands over his arms. "You've done so much."

"I'm just putting cash in the bank, baby. Super Bowl is coming up."

Vanessa laughed. "I suppose you'll be leaving me alone with Nathaniel while you go get drunk and eat Buffalo wings with Lincoln?"

"Well, he's brought it up. So you see, I'm being totally selfish."

"Okay. As long as you're not taking care of me out of love."

"Eh, sixty-forty."

She let him take the suitcases and went to stretch out on the couch. She had just sat down when the doorbell rang, and she chuckled at the irony before pushing herself back up. She put on her glasses to hide the bags under her eyes before she peeked out the window and opened the door for Cheryl Perez, one of the women from their church. She was bundled against the cold, only her face visible amid the scarves and knit cap. Her eyes widened when she saw Vanessa.

"It's you!" Cheryl said.

"And it's you! Come in. God, you look half-frozen."

"Oh, more than half, I'd say. I'm glad you're home! It feels like weeks since we've seen you around here. Where have you been hiding yourself?"

Vanessa said, "I... w-was out of town. Business trip, I guess you could call it."

"Oh!" she smiled and unwound her scarf. "Well, I was just stopping by to give Scott a message, but now I can deliver it directly. The church is doing a Christmas play and we're short a wise man. Every role is being played by kids, and we were wondering if Nathaniel is old enough to do the part."

Vanessa thought about it for a moment. "I think he could manage it. I'll have to make sure before we commit to anything."

"Of course, of course. It would just involve walking out on stage and standing there while one of the older kids read the Nativity story. You could be up there with him, just in case he gets frightened. Would you be comfortable onstage?"

Vanessa almost laughed out loud. She stopped herself by pressing two fingers against her lips. "Yeah, I think I can handle being onstage."

"Excellent. I'll put you down as a 'maybe.'" She tapped her phone screen and then secured it in a deep pocket of her jacket. "So, welcome home! You were on a business trip?"

"That's right."

"You know, we've known each other for over a year and I'm not sure I even know what you do for a living."

Vanessa thought about all the times she had bent the truth, avoided the question, or outright lied in the past. It was easier when Radiation Canary was on hiatus. But now that she was going to be on television and magazine covers, now that they were recording and touring, she didn't want to hide in suburbia. She didn't want to be a Clark Kent who hid behind glasses and pretended to be something she wasn't. She had earned her place in Radiation Canary, damn it, and she was going to own that honor.

"I'm actually the keyboard player for Radiation Canary," she said. "We've been on tour for the past couple of months, but now we're home for Christmas."

Cheryl blinked. "You're... a rock star?"

"That's right."

"Well, that's fantastic!" Cheryl said, digging for her phone again. "We were just going to have prerecorded music, but if you don't mind using the church's organ, we could have live music. It's always better to have live music." She gripped Vanessa's wrist. "Oh, you should have told us about this sooner!"

## CHAPTER THIRTY-THREE

WHEN AVERY got to work for her last shift before Christmas, there was a flat gift taped to the front of her locker. It was too thin to be anything other than a single sheet of paper, although when she felt it she decided it was a photograph. A few years ago another officer had been outed by a homophobic fellow officer who papered the locker room with pictures of him and his boyfriend. But she was out, she was open with her sexuality, so she wasn't afraid of seeing what was inside. She sat on the bench and undid the tape, sliding out an eight-by-ten glossy.

It was a frame from her dash cam. She was standing a few yards ahead of the car, the color washed out by the spotlight. Standing in front of her was Lana, one hand up to shade her eyes as she handed over her ID. She put her fingers over her mouth as she looked at a frozen image of a night that seemed so long ago. She lowered her hand and traced a finger around the shape of Lana's body.

When she composed herself she looked inside the giftwrap and saw there was a note as well. She withdrew it and recognized her partner Victor's handwriting instantly.

"Think I'll make it as a photographer? I call this one 'First Sight.' Merry Christmas, Hollenbeck."

When she thought she had her emotions under control, she put the picture in her locker and changed for duty. She found Victor outside waiting in their squad car, and she got behind the wheel.

"You're no Ansel Adams, but you'll do in a pinch. But you couldn't frame it? It's a damn Christmas present, Vic. Make an effort."

He chuckled. "I'll go all out for the wedding gift."

Her heart skittered a bit; they hadn't revealed to anyone their conversations about marriage, but apparently it was obvious enough to everyone. Still, she shook her head. "Cart before the horse."

Victor raised an eyebrow at her. "You flew across the country for each other. If you don't end up married, that's just a waste of a romantic gesture."

Avery laughed and started the engine. When same-sex marriage was legalized in Washington she'd celebrated with everyone else but she never saw it affecting her personally. She'd lived so much of her life assuming marriage was off the table that she hadn't let herself dream. Now, though, it was legal everywhere in the country. Now she had a woman she could actually see herself loving forever. Now... now...

Now she had more important things to focus on. She had a patrol to get through, and thoughts of Lana Kent could wait until she clocked out.

It was decided that the only place large enough to have a Christmas party was Codie's loft. Karen stopped just inside the door, cradling her son with one arm while her other hand was tightly gripped in her wife's, and she remembered when the apartment was the site of their first release party. It seemed like a thousand years ago in another life. Laura seemed to sense Karen's nostalgia and kissed her shoulder before urging her inside.

"We've come a long way, huh?" Karen said.

"You still have a long way to go," Laura said.

Karen smiled and went to put Mason in the playpen Codie had put up for him. The apartment was absolutely gorgeous; fairy lights circled every window and combined with the tree, they cast a bright enough glow for the overhead lights to be left off. Ribbons had been strung in a crosshatch pattern over the living room and clear ornaments were hanging down like icicles. Laura reached up to touch one as she delivered the presents to the tree. Karen's dad was going to make an appearance as Santa in about an hour, and he would bring the rest of the presents with him.

Through the window, on the thin strip of concrete Karen still didn't believe was an actual balcony, she could see Lana silhouetted against the city. She kissed Mason's head and slipped out to join her. "Don't do it," Karen said, "you have your whole life ahead of you."

Lana smiled and looked over her shoulder. "You said the exact same thing ten years ago when you found me out here."

"Did I?" She stepped out and pressed her back to the wall. "Well, I was right. Just imagine what's still ahead now." She glanced down. "Please come away from the edge. I'm being serious."

Lana backed up and put her shoulders against the brick. "It's no different than standing on the edge of a stage. I've never fallen off a stage."

"It's completely different. Gravity is stronger up here."

Lana grinned.

"Is Avery here?"

"She was coming off duty, so she wanted to go home and change first."

Karen said, "Home to her place, or...?"

"She's moving in after the tour is over. She didn't want to move her stuff in and then stay there alone for a month."

"Makes sense." Karen reached out and took Lana's hand. "I want to say something profound right now. We're here, the same place we were standing before anyone knew our names, and now we're... we filled concert halls all over the country. We heard thousands of people singing our words back to us. It just seems like the moment calls for something epic. Something memorable we can quote later."

Lana said, "I'm all ears."

Karen smiled. "I'm completely at a loss."

Lana laughed. "Oh, no. If our lyricist can't come up with any words, we're done for."

"Okay, how about this?" She squeezed Lana's hand. "See you here in ten more years?"

"It's a date."

"Maybe by then we'll have jetpacks and I won't have to worry about you falling off."

Lana smirked at her and nudged her arm. "Okay, okay. We'll go back inside. I want to get some more punch anyway."

They crawled back inside to see that Sidra and her new boyfriend had arrived, and Lana went to greet her. Karen went to where Laura was playing with Mason and sat down on the floor behind her, letting Laura recline against her side. When the "Santa" arrived they would open presents, watch movies, and maybe go caroling... Naomi showed up with her wife and came over to see the baby, and Karen took the opportunity to scan the room.

For a moment she was fifteen again. Her mother bought her a cello and a violin as a way to soothe her. The house had been a battleground for years, and indulging Karen's requests for the instruments had been a way to prove she was loved. She received private lessons on both instruments but she never believed they would be anything other than a hobby. She planned to work in her father's hardware store.

But on those nights when even her music couldn't drown out the fighting, she'd crawled onto her bed and covered her head with a pillow. She'd burrowed into the blankets and tried to make herself so small that the fighting couldn't reach her. And on those nights she had prayed, begged, pleaded with whoever might be listening that she could just have a happy family.

She watched Lana hug Naomi, and she saw Codie escort Nathaniel over to the tree so he could look at all the decorations. Ted was lugging a huge bag of presents in, while her Dad was bringing the others in a few minutes. It was an eclectic family to be sure, but it was hers, and she loved it more than she could have thought possible.

Karen looked at Mason. "Let's have a second one."

"Right now?"

"No. It doesn't even have to be soon. But I think a second one would be fine."

Laura stroked Karen's hands. "Yeah. I could handle two."

Karen smiled and rocked Laura back and forth to the Christmas music coming from the stereo. Maybe she would carry the second baby. It would be a nice balance to the family if both she and Laura had given birth. But for the moment it was all still hypothetical. A very nice hypothetical. She tightened her embrace and rested her chin on Laura's shoulder.

The Canadian leg of the tour was bound to be different from traveling across America if just for the weather, but Naomi had also planned something special for them. Instead of traveling from town to town on a bus, they would travel between their first three concerts by train. Toronto to Winnipeg and from there to Saskatoon. They would get a bus in Saskatoon for the show in Calgary, and then a second train would take them over the Rockies to Vancouver. Lana was practically giddy with excitement about riding a train across Canada.

"I get that we still have to do shows," she said, "but now I'm all about the train. The shows are a secondary consideration for me."

The night before they left, the latest release by the Femme Reapers had gone gold. They celebrated with chocolate milk so Mason could celebrate as well. He enjoyed his little cup of it, but didn't seem overly thrilled with the new taste. Karen rubbed his chin with her knuckle.

"That's okay, little guy. Probably good that you're not keen on sweets."

Laura said, "I'll keep that in mind when I get his birthday cake."

Karen leaned back with a sigh. "I can't believe he's so old. I can't believe I've missed out so much of his life." She was startled when she realized she was on the verge of crying. "I'm a terrible mother. How can I even think of having a second child when I'm barely here to take care of the one we have?"

Laura reached over and rubbed Karen's shoulders. "Hey. You're no such thing." She pulled Karen to her. "You've been working your ass off to provide for this family. You put together two albums in the time it took me and Ella to make one. And you're outselling us by, what, five to one? You're providing for us. Don't for one second think that makes you a bad mother."

Karen lifted her head and kissed the corner of Laura's mouth. Her lips tasted like the chocolate milk she had just toasted with.

"Besides, it's almost over. You'll come home, we'll have a party for Mason, and then we'll have so much time together you'll be begging for me to go on tour."

Karen smiled and ran Laura's hair through her fingers. "When Mason goes to bed, I'm going to love you so good."

"You'd better. I'll need something to get me through the long nights you're away. Video chats can only get me so far."

Karen moved her lips next to Laura's ear. "But I love watching you touch yourself for me."

Laura shivered in her arms. "Yeah?"

"Mm-hmm." She nipped the lobe. "But that's not to say the interactive version isn't light years more entertaining."

Laura smiled and tickled Karen's stomach before she pulled back. "As soon as we get Mason to sleep, I'm going to give you the interactive performance of the century."

Karen turned toward the baby. "Rock-a-bye baby, in the treetop..."

Their first show in Canada revealed one of the major differences between the two legs of the tour: the crowds were much smaller, which led to much more intimate shows. In Toronto, someone in the front row got up to use the restroom. "If you're going to the bathroom," Lana said, "Mention my name. They'll give you a great seat." Codie played a rimshot as the embarrassed woman laughed and shook her head. Once she was gone, Lana climbed down off the stage and took the woman's seat to make conversation with the people on either side as they waited. "We wouldn't want her to miss anything, right? I mean, she got front-row seats..."

They left Toronto on the train the day after the show. Lana reverted to childhood as soon as they boarded, grinning broadly and looking out the windows as they made their way to their seat. Karen thought the train was noisy, cramped, slow, and a rough ride. She thought the views out the window were decent but nothing worth writing home about. She fully accepted the possibility she might have just been grumpy about leaving just as she had gotten used to being home again.

Some of her grumpiness faded once they were out of the city and she was able to enjoy the gorgeous Canadian countryside. When everyone else went to the dining car, Karen remained in her berth and pulled her feet up onto the seat so she could hug her knees. After a few minutes of solitude Vanessa came and sat across from her.

"Missing the baby?"

Karen chuckled. "I would ask how you know, but I guess you and I have a similar addiction." She put her feet down on the floor and stretched. "It's going to be his birthday soon. After we get back but before the Grammys.”

“One year!” Vanessa said. “Those parties are more for the mommies than the babies. Do you know what you’re doing for it?”

“I’m going to treat Laura to a spa day. She’s been amazing this whole tour, and she’s been working on her own album, so she deserves it.”

Vanessa smiled. “She’ll be forever grateful, believe me.”

“How is Scott doing with Nathaniel?”

“They’re fantastic. Nathaniel thinks Mason is his brother, by the way.”

Karen laughed. “Well, he is.”

“He is.” She looked outside. “This is our job, baby. It’s crazy, right?”

“It’s insane.”

“Sometimes I just think... what if I hadn’t gone to the effort of finding that rehearsal space? Or what if I’d had a friend who let me use their garage? What if I hadn’t been in exactly the right spot when Codie and Lana came looking? What if Codie hadn’t taken up smoking for, like, literally a month so you would offer her a lighter? A lighter you were only carrying because you hadn’t bothered throwing it out yet. Where would we all have ended up?”

Karen looked outside. “I’d probably be working at my Dad’s hardware store. Ten years... I’d be manager by now. I would probably have met someone and gotten married.”

“Would you have been happy?”

“I’d have been content,” Karen said. “Lana was content with Catherine. But she’s over the moon with Avery. I never knew there was such a gap between the two, but it’s a continental shift when you find where you’re supposed to be. If I married someone else, I’m sure it would be a good marriage. We would have fun. But unless it was Laura, it wouldn’t be right. How about you?”

“I think I would still be with Scott, since I didn’t meet him through the band. I’d probably have some boring desk job. I would read a lot. Just for escapism. Wondering if there was some other reality where I was a famous rock star trundling across Canada to a sold-out show. I...” Her voice caught. “I wouldn’t have had Nathaniel. I mentioned we had our problems conceiving. But the doctors we went to... I don’t know if I could have afforded them without Radiation Canary. We might have just given up.”

Karen said, “Hm. Wow.” The train took a turn and they both swayed to the right. “What about Lana?”

“Oh, Lana would be a star. That voice, those looks, the guitar. There is no reality where Lana Kent isn’t on this train.”

Karen snickered and nodded. “I concur. Codie?”

“President of the United States of America.”

Karen threw her head back. “Hell, I’d vote for her.”

Vanessa got up and sat next to Karen. “We’d all have a few pieces of the puzzle, but it wouldn't be anywhere near whole. When we took the break, we said Radiation Canary was the four of us. But that's not right. Radiation Canary is just a thing we do. Just something to pass the time when we're together. The thing that keeps us together. We were meant to know each other, and making music gives us the excuse we need."

Karen put her head on Vanessa's shoulder. "So we're going to stick together after *Westward Sky* comes out? Because I know Lana and Codie... when they decided to reunite, they were worried the two of us would be the holdouts. For good reason. We have spouses and babies to consider. But I don't want to stop again. I already have ideas for the next album."

Vanessa said, "Good. And yes, we're definitely sticking together. I tried really hard to be the boring housewife, but I don't want to go through life pretending I'm someone I'm not."

"Me neither."

Codie was laughing when she and Lana entered the berth. She slapped a hand on Lana's back and playfully pushed her into the seat across from Karen.

"You'd think this one had never been on a train before," Codie said.

Lana slid closer to the window and looked out. "I love trains. I've always loved trains, but it was always more practical to drive or fly. But taking a train across the Canadian Shield? Oh-ho-ho." She bounced in her seat and rubbed her hands together as she looked at Karen and Vanessa. "You guys should've come with us. We had train food."

"She even likes the *food*," Codie moaned. "Good God, y'all."

Lana kicked Codie's foot. "You're just upset because we're not flying."

"It's the twenty-first century," Codie grumbled. "If man were meant to inch along the ground on iron tracks, we wouldn't have created airplanes."

"Yeah, yeah." Lana said, "So what were you two talking about? You looked all nice and cozy when we came in."

"We were talking about what happens after *Westward Sky* comes out," Karen said. "It's going to be our tenth album."

Codie nodded. "Ten is a nice, even number."

"It is. But we were thinking about what we would have on our eleventh album."

Lana smiled. "I've been thinking about that, too. I even have a few ideas."

"Oh, you do, do you?" Vanessa said.

Codie sat forward and put her elbows on her knees. "We've got a couple of days stuck on this iron death trap. We might as well see what we've got so far."

Karen reached into her jacket and retrieved her phone. Her Notepad app had a whole section dedicated to new album ideas, and she swept her finger across the screen to access it. "I was thinking about the sign language interpreters we had at our shows on this tour. Have you ever watched them when we play? It's gorgeous. I was thinking we should do a song that really utilizes the movement of Sign and combines it with Lana's dancing. I think it could make a really beautiful video."

Lana nodded. "I like it. We'd have to find a consultant for the writing so we'd be sure we came up with something that translated right."

"Of course."

"What else do you have, K?"

Outside the window, the frozen Canadian prairie rolled by as the four women in their cozy train car huddled together to go through Karen's ideas for their next album.

THE COAL MINE SESSIONS</u>
1. Wheels Up
2. Soothing Sea Sounds
3. Echoing Mirrors
4. Best Laid Plans
5. The Sailmaker's Daughter
6. Enough for You
7. There Was I
8. Face Value
9. Words of Wisdom and Woe (from a Self-Proclaimed Madman)
10. I'm Breakable
11. The Princess
12. In the Wind Between Two Oceans
13. Twist Ending

WESTWARD SKY
1. Cold Shoulder
2. Only Tears
3. A Landfill of Beautiful Strangers
4. Breaking of Day
5. The Tragedy of Time Wasted
6. Learning How to Sleep
7. Ferry Country
8. Cathedrals
9. Where You End the Story
10. Imaginary Cities
11. No One's Someone
12. Fair Men & Gentleladies
13. Sea Level

**The Coal Mine Sessions**
* The Sailmaker's Daughter
"I thank my lucky stars every day that this car still starts
When I turn the key to warm the engine as the dawn fades
And I shudder and I'm reminded of the promises we made
When we fogged up the windows to cover the glass with hearts

The coffee is only there to thaw my fingers
And I hate how much that pot smell lingers
Now I hope it doesn't stick to my clothes
How I got to this point only God knows

Even in the summer the sun doesn't shine on this city
And I'd turn my face away even if he appeared

These heavy grey rainclouds suit me perfectly
They rolled over my head the day you disappeared

I watched my mother make sails when I was a girl
She'd take me down to watch the ships in the harbor
Her sails carried ships and their people to the seven wonders
Snaring the wind to pull them all over the world

Someday I'm going to build a boat from plywood and glue
I'm going to steal my mother's sail, head off into the storms
I'll bear any rough seas I find and I'm going to break through
I swear I'm not going to stop until I'm back in your arms

And I won't take my eyes off you
To the edge of the world I'd follow you
Where the lighthouse can't reach
On some dark and foreign beach
Or an undiscovered place
I will run to you, I will fall to you
My reward will be one glimpse of your face."

* Enough for You
"I never thought I'd have to get over you
I never thought you'd be anything but forever mine
Maybe if I sit here long enough I'll make it true
Maybe if I see your empty side of the bed one more time
Then maybe I'll know why I wasn't enough for you.

I never thought this was anything less than forever
I thought we could see our way through any stormy weather
When the rough seas rose up I promised I'd anchor you
We always said we could stand against the winds together
But I don't know when I became less than enough for you.

Do I let you go or do I stand to fight? (I don't know how I get up each day)
Will it make a difference if we yell all night? (And it gets harder the longer I stay)
I don't know how I'm going to get out of this mess (Tell me how to fix it, what to do)
The moon's gone dark, I'm stuck in the wilderness (When did I stop being enough for you?)
Did you become more or did I become less? (How much more until I'm enough for you?)

Do I let you go or do I stand to fight?
Will it make a difference if we yell all night?
I don't know how I'm going to get out of this mess
The moon's gone dark, I'm stuck in the wilderness
Did you become more or did I become less?
When did I stop being enough for you?
How much more until I'm enough for you?"

* Face Value
"You think you know me
But you've never seen me before
You've seen me on TV
On the magazines or at the store
These cameras always follow me around,
Cover my face and keep my head down
But you've only ever seen the mask
You call me beautiful, you never asked if
This illusion is real or merely plastic

Paint up my face, I'm your work of art
Spend an hour on my hair before we're ready to start
If I take off my mask and show myself true,
Would you still appreciate my face value?

You've always got to be on,
Dress up just to grab the mail
Never have a bad day, don't frown
Wave, grin, please stay out of jail
If you want a private moment you're just out of luck
Keep the curtains drawn if you're getting... intimate
You've got your own life, so be careful of mine
Walking down the street with me in the sunshine
And you'll end up on every website online

Paint up my face, I'm your work of art
Spend an hour on my hair before we're ready to start
If I take off my mask and show myself true,
Would you still appreciate my face value?

Everyone's comparing themselves to the prom queen
I'm bright and shiny and always squeaky clean
But I wake up half-dead just like everyone
Shave my legs and pluck off all my hair

The spotlight shines and I look just like heaven
You wouldn't even recognize me if I was laid bare.

Look at me and see just an ordinary pretty face
The same you'll see every day in a dozen places
We're tall and short and fat and thin
Makeup, heels, Spanx, just to fit in
We spend thousands of dollars trying to look better
One day we'll learn we're more beautiful without the armor

Paint up my face, I'm your work of art
Spend an hour on my hair before we're ready to start
If I take off my mask and show myself true,
Would you still appreciate my face value?
Will you ever even know my face value?"

* Words of Wisdom and Woe (From a Self-Proclaimed Mad Man)
"Can you ever have too much of a good thing?
Is it madness if you only see what's worth seeing?
It gets so bad you'll split your sides from laughing
The old man said familiarity will breed contempt
But I have a feeling you haven't seen anything yet.

Forewarned is forearmed, you better look before you leap
You live and learn and turn over a new leaf
Forgive and forget all your old injuries
Make sure the armies you're facing aren't just flocks of sheep
You'll find you have the devil to pay, without a wink of sleep

The old man said it's needs must when the devil drives
Thanks for nothing; I have other fish to fry
A bird in the hand is worth the two you let fly
So I'll have my cake, I'll make hay in the shining of the sun
I may have lived my life like a madman but I'll die like a wise one."

* I'm Breakable
"I never thought I could feel so fragile
Didn't know I'd be played for such a fool
Shattered me into pieces and all I can think is,
I never knew I was this breakable."

* The Princess
"Strong, beautiful, smart, baby, she's fearless
She's free with her kisses, soft lips, she's delicious

But when she strikes out, words are vicious, she never misses
She'll leave you alone, no witness, still she's your princess

She stole the addresses from your little black book
And she's aching to use her deft left hook
Though she could lay you flat with just one dirty look
You saw the warning signs everyone else dismisses
She cuts right through, what can you do, she's the princess

The angel on my shoulder is doing such devilish things to me
And I know that no one else can see so no one will believe
Oh, she's a terror, breaks your heart without a care, her
You wonder how she can even look at herself in a mirror.

And oh, I don't know how she got to be so cold
How she could let go when I tried so hard to keep hold
Did she see a disaster foretold and did it make her want to lie low?
But she'll never show, and though she let me go, the sad thing is this
I wish it weren't so, but even as I go, I know she's still my princess.
You'll always be my princess."

* In the Wind Between Two Oceans
"It's been hours since I last saw dry land
But I know these waters like the back of my hand
The stars are blinded by clouds rolling down like curtains
They're cast aside with a magician's sleight of hand
And I feel myself closed in the hand of Poseidon

Overcome with emotion
I can't explain the sensation
All these other words my friends have sung
And I'm at a loss for words for the sensation
Of being caught in the wind between two oceans."

**<u>WESTWARD SKY</u>**
* Breaking of Day
"Your elbow in my softest places
The pillows left creases on our faces
Your breath was bad, but mine was worse
We thought we found a steady course
Buried together in the sheets
Blankets covering all but our feet
That was the place we'd have killed to stay
But we had to rise and face the breaking of the day.

"The dawn breaks so hard you cut yourself on the pieces."

* Learning How to Sleep
"I can hear whispered conversations, like ghosts visiting my room
I lie in the middle of my bed, arms folded on my chest, a mummy in the tomb
My body is weary and my eyes close against the gloom but my mind is muddled misery
Replaying everything that happened, looking for some new theory
I keep trying to change the end but it's always the same sad story

So I'm learning to sleep again, after you showed me how to rest
Being in bed doesn't mean as much without your head on my breast
You showed me how it could heal my hurts and make my soul refreshed
But without you I'm just in the dark, trying to find a way out of this mess
All I can do is put myself to bed and ignore my sadness and pain
And hope that someday I'll be able to learn how to sleep again."

* Cathedrals
"Earth's tallest cathedral is five hundred feet high
A monument of faith casts its shadow on those who worship
Throwing around echoes of the sermon
Ever-present in the corner of your eye
Elegant Gothic spires stretch their arms into the sky.

Another church shines red when the neon brightens
Standing all but empty on a corner by the liquor store
The preacher raises his voice above sirens
His congregation would rather listen to the barman
But he's there every Sunday and he won't be beaten

Everyone has their own private religion
Everyone prays to some kind of god
And there's some sort of heaven we hope to get in
So I've got next Sunday's confessions all written
And I'll have to hurry if I want to get everything in.

My faith is written by drunks and preached by a junkie
Our hymns come through the static on late-night radio
And our holy books gather dust in dark libraries
Let's read from Scripture, just you and me
The Book of Cervantes and the Gospel of Bowie."

## About the Author

Geonn Cannon lives in Oklahoma. He is the author of several novels, including the Riley Parra series which is currently being produced as a webseries for Tello Films, and an official Stargate SG-1 tie-in novel. Information about his other novels and an archive of free stories can be found online at geonncannon.com.

9 781944 591076